The Family Game

BALLANTINE BOOKS

NEW YORK

The Family Game

A NOVEL

Catherine Steadman

Published in the United States by Ballantine Books,
an imprint of Random House, a division of
Penguin Random House LLC, New York.

BALLANTINE is a registered trademark
and the colophon is a trademark of
Penguin Random House LLC.

LIBRARY OF CONGRESS CATALOGING-IN-PUBLICATION DATA
Names: Steadman, Catherine, author.
Title: The family game: a novel / Catherine Steadman.
Description: First edition. | New York: Ballantine Books, [2022]
Identifiers: LCCN 2022012427 (print) | LCCN 2022012428 (ebook) |
ISBN 9780593158067 (hardcover; acid-free paper) |
ISBN 9780593158074 (ebook)
Subjects: LCGFT: Thrillers (Fiction)
Classification: LCC PR6119.T436 F36 2022 (print) |
LCC PR6119.T436 (ebook) | DDC 823/.92—dc23/eng/20220422
LC record available at https://lccn.loc.gov/2022012427
LC ebook record available at https://lccn.loc.gov/2022012428

Printed in the United States of America on acid-free paper

randomhousebooks.com

1st Printing

First Edition

Title page photograph by Ysbrandcosjin/Adobe Stock

Book design by Elizabeth A. D. Eno

I dedicate this book to my readers,
with thanks and huge gratitude.

The Family Game

Damaged people are dangerous. They know they can survive.

—Josephine Hart, *Damage*

Our most basic instinct is not for survival, but for family.

—Paul Pearsall, neuropsychologist

Prologue

I come to on the parquet floor of the entrance hall, my face pressed hard against its antique wood, with the clear knowledge that this is not how Christmases should go.

Around me the Gothic grandeur of The Hydes slides back into focus. The Holbecks' family seat, everything multiple generations of wealth and power can buy you; this imposing Hungarian castle ripped brick by brick from the Mecsek Mountains, packed, shipped, and grafted into upstate New York soil. Their ancestral home a literal castle in the sky dragged to ground and anchored into the American landscape and its psyche. A testament to sheer bloody-mindedness and cold hard cash.

In the 1800s a Holbeck bride wanted her beau to "lasso the moon," and here's the solid proof he did. He made a dream real. Some might say: more money than sense, maybe, but from down here, bleeding on their floor, even I have to admit this place is beautiful. And who, in love, doesn't hope for a lassoed moon? After all, that's what love is, isn't it?

Across from me the front door stands ajar, so close and yet so, so far. A crisp winter breeze tickling my face as I watch snowflakes float peaceably through the air outside, freedom just beyond my reach. Past that doorway the grounds roll out in all their splendor, snow-blanketed ornamental gardens, an ice-crusted boating lake, crystalline lawns that finally give way to miles of thickly packed Holbeck woodland. And at the limits of that moonlit forest a fifteen-foot-high perimeter wall, encircling us, separating the Holbeck family from the rest of the world. A sovereign state, an enclave, a compound with its own rules and self-regulating systems.

I have been found lacking, by one, or all. And steps are in motion. I might not survive the night.

If I could stand right now, if I could run, and scale the perimeter wall, the nearest town would still be over an hour on foot. If I had my phone, I could call the police. But given who I am, who they are, I can't be sure the way things would go when they got here. There is a way to read any story and I might have found myself with a slight credibility problem.

A girl with a past tries to marry into money and all hell breaks loose. We all know how that story ends.

It's funny: in-laws are supposed to be problematic, aren't they? That old cultural stereotype. I guess it's funny because it's often true. In-laws can be difficult. Families can be difficult. And I can't argue with the facts, here, bleeding on their floor.

I carefully ease up onto my forearms, the dark stone of my engagement ring shifting moodily in the light. A sleeping creature woken.

If I could go back now, to the day he proposed, would I do things differently? That is the billion-dollar question.

My temple throbs as I carefully wipe blood from my eyelashes.

They say head wounds seem more serious than they are, because they bleed so much. They say the human body can do incredible things in a crisis. People walked for miles to hospitals on broken legs after 9/11, women give birth in war zones, new mothers lift cars to save their children. I hope that's true.

Twenty years ago, I almost died. I hung in silence, death all around me, but somehow, I survived. And if I could survive that, I can survive this, because since you showed up, I have so much more to lose, and so, so much more to gain.

We're going to survive this, you and I. They say you can't choose your family but they're wrong. You can. It just takes way more effort than most people are willing to put in.

And with that thought in mind, I slowly push up and stumble to my feet.

1

Fairytale of New York

MONDAY, NOVEMBER 21

Christmas lights twinkle in the rain as I duck down Fifth Avenue—reds, greens, and golds glimmering in reflection on puddles and glass as I dodge along the busy sidewalk, my phone pressed tight to my ear.

"And the good news is, it's looking like we're going to hit the million-copy sales mark by the end of this week! We did it, Harry!" my literary agent, Louisa, cheers on the phone. Her voice is as warm and close as if she were bundled up against the cold beside me in the sharp New York City chill. I try not to think of the three and a half thousand miles of distance between New York and London—between me and my old home and its soft, damp grayness—but every now and then the pangs of homesickness wake and stretch just beneath the surface of my new life. It's been four months since I left England, and the pull of home is somehow stronger now that winter is setting in. New York can be cold in so many ways.

"For all intents and purposes," she continues with glee, "here's me saying you are now *officially* 'a million-copy bestselling author.'" I can't help but yelp with joy—a surreptitious half skip in the street. The news is incredible. My first novel, a runaway bestseller, has been on the charts since publication, but this new milestone isn't something I could ever have dreamed of until now. New York swallows my ebullient energy greedily. I could probably lie down on the sidewalk and start screaming and the festive shoppers would just weave unfazed around me. It's an oddly terrifying and yet reassuring thought.

"We'll be getting another royalty payout from the publisher at the end of the quarter," Louisa continues. "So Merry Christmas, everyone!"

It's funny, it's only November and yet it feels like Christmas is here already. I look up to the halos of light hanging above me, holiday decorations, sparkling from shop windows, strung in great swaths high over the main drag of Fifth. Everything seems to be moving so fast this year, a whirlwind, a whirlpool.

"How's it going over there?" Louisa asks, snapping me back to reality. "Settled? Happy? Are you living love's young dream?"

I let out a laugh of surprise because *yes,* as smug and as self-satisfied as it may sound, I really am. After so many years alone, after pushing relationships away, perhaps I've paid in full for my mistakes and I can put them to bed. Maybe I'm finally allowed a little happiness.

I shake off the dark thought and grasp back onto my new life with both hands. "Well, we've got furniture now at least. Not sure I've quite worked out the subway yet but I guess I'll get there in the end. Or I guess I won't," I add jokingly.

The truth is, while I know I am beginning to get a feeling for New York City, I realize I am trying to settle into a city that does not settle itself. The crowds, noises, faces, people, that frenetic fight-or-flight energy. I suppose it's only been four months—

I know it can take a lifetime to become part of a city, to find your place. And the world I've landed into here, with Edward, the new circles I find myself moving in, his rarefied life, that is something else again.

"And how is your dreamboat, how is Ed?" she asks, as if reading my thoughts. I slip past a gaggle of tourists in front of St. Patrick's Cathedral, its bells tolling anachronistically alongside towering glass and steel.

Louisa was with me the night I met Edward; I shiver at the memory of the look she gave me when I first brought him over to meet her. That silent swell of pride I felt to have my arm hooked through his, the pride anglers must feel cradling their outsized shimmering catches. Though I can only credit chance and timing with my iridescent prize. In fact, it would probably be more accurate to say Edward plucked *me* from the stream than the other way around.

I would be lying if I said Edward's background, his habits, his rituals—so alien to me—hadn't lent him a strange additional attraction. His world is different from mine, everything he does invested with the subtle shimmer of something gilded. Not that I knew who he was when he first spoke to me.

We met at my publisher's annual Summer Gala in London, a lavish, star-studded party packed with bestselling authors, high-flying editors, and superagents. That year it was being held at the Natural History Museum, the vaulting Victorian architecture festooned with bright bursts of tropical flowers: orchids and heady-scented lilies. Waiters in white tie, ferrying champagne high above the heads of the mingling household names, debut authors, and reviewers. It was my first big author event, my book having only just come out the week before and exploding directly onto the Top Ten. I'd bought a ridiculously expensive emerald dress in celebration and then spent half the night trying not to spill booze and canapés down it. Nervous, and completely out of my depth, I let Louisa usher me from important contact to important contact until I finally managed to escape the madness for the relative calm of the loos. I am no shrinking violet but too much noise, too many faces, trigger old wounds and set my senses to a different frequency.

It was on the way back from the toilets, empty champagne glass in hand, that it happened. At first I thought it was nothing, just my heel snagging on something, causing a little stutter in my step. But the snag turned into a halt, a tug, and a hot blush rising as a glance back confirmed that my high heel was firmly wedged in one of the museum's tiny, ornate floor vents. Victorian central heating.

I gave another tug and the heel seemed to loosen, but a few passing eyes found their way to me and I panicked. I tugged again, harder. And with a retrospectively impressive show of strength and an extremely loud metallic clatter I somehow managed to completely dislodge the 150-year-old wrought-iron grate from the stone floor, still attached to my Dior heel. The noise and spectacle now attracting the gaze of everyone in the vicinity.

With a deep desire not to prolong the experience but totally unsure what else to do, I hitched my dress and—drained white with shame—half lifted, half dragged the entire wrought-iron grate back toward its gaping floor hole. The grate clanked and banged as I tried to get it back in, all the time with my heel firmly attached. And that's when he saved me, a firm hand on my back, that warm American accent, his voice low, reassuring, like home.

"Okay, okay. I see the problem." His first words to me. And though, of course, he meant the problem with my shoe, and the grate—and that he could fix it—to this day I like to think he meant he saw the larger problem, with everything, with my past, with the holes in my life, and that he could fix those too. Listen, I'm no damsel in distress, trust me, I've survived a lot more than most, but you can't underestimate the overwhelming power of someone swooping in to save you after a lifetime of having to save yourself.

Those eyes looking up at me, filled with such a disarming calm, with an inborn certainty that everything would all work out just great. The warmth of his skin against my bare shoulder blades. I did not have time to put up my usual barriers, to insulate myself or pull away from intimacy, because there I was, stuck.

He dropped down on one knee, like a proposal, like the prince in Cinderella, this impossibly handsome man, and as he gently wriggled my mangled shoe loose from the grate with my hands on his strong shoulders, I felt something inside me shift. A hope, long tamped down, flickered back to life in the darkness. And the rest is history.

Here I am a year-and-change later, having moved a continent and my entire life to be with him.

"Ed is doing great," I answer, though we both know it's an understatement. Ed's start-up company turns over more money in a month than the literary agency Louisa works for does in a year. Edward is doing immeasurably well, but we're British and we don't talk about stuff like that. Besides, Louisa is well aware of who Edward is, the family he comes from. He's a Holbeck and with a surname like that, even without family investment, success was almost inevitable. "I'm actually on my way to meet him now. He's taking me skating."

"Skating?" I hear the interest pique in her tone. She's desperate to hear about him. About the Holbecks. Somehow I managed to bag one of America's wealthiest bachelors without even trying and everyone wants to know how I did it, why I did it. But more important, they want to know: what are they like?

For that, of course, there is Google. And God knows I did a deep dive or ten in the weeks after meeting Edward. Generations of wealth, woven into the fabric of America since the Gilded Age, shipping, communications, and of course that ever-present shadow of questionable ethics. There is no end to the op-ed pieces on them, the gossip column space, the business section dealings with the Holbeck name, and yet the air of mystery they maintain around themselves means one can never quite be satisfied. They remain elusive, mercurial. That, with their presumably ruthless brand of magic, is a heady and alluring mix.

"He's taking you skating? Like roller-skating?" Louisa asks, incredulous, though I doubt anything I told her about Edward would really surprise her.

"No," I say. "No, he's taking me ice-skating. It's a family tradition, The Rink at Rockefeller Center, start of the season. He wants us to go together this year."

"Oh my God, will his whole family be there?" Louisa erupts. She's dying to hear more about them but I haven't been able to furnish her with any more information than I've gleaned from the internet so far.

"No. Still haven't met them. No family yet. Edward's terrified they'll scare me off." I cringe as I say it; I know how it sounds. Millionaire playboy won't introduce girlfriend to family. I'm aware I've moved my life for Edward and I haven't even met his parents yet. But it isn't like that. I see the look in his eyes when we talk about them. He has his reasons and the time will come. Besides, I didn't just move over here for him. I've needed a fresh start for a long time now, and the success of the book and meeting Edward made that a very real possibility.

Funny, I always thought I'd end up over here. My mother was an American. Sometimes, if I close my eyes, in coffee shops and restaurants I can almost imagine her voice among the crowd, her round open vowel sounds all around me, the warmth of it, like the past.

It's funny I don't recall my dad's voice at all, but I was only eleven when it happened. Twenty years of new experiences having scribbled over what was once so clear. Though I miss him just as much. It's only natural to forget when remembering hurts so much.

Louisa chuckles. "I'm not surprised he's wary. They sound terrifying. Well, you know what I mean, fascinating but . . . hive inducing." Her tone becomes playful, confidential. "Although between you and me, bloody hell, I would definitely be willing to put in some awkward in-law hours if Simon had looked half as good in a suit as Edward does." Louisa and Simon split up last year. He was pretty useless by all accounts, but her compliment stands.

And she's right. I would be willing to put up with an awful lot to be with Edward.

"Oh, and how's the new book coming?" she asks with a studied nonchalance that almost has me fooled. I'm three weeks past the deadline for my second book.

I shiver in the winter breeze, waiting for the crosswalk light to change. The truth is I haven't been able to focus for about a month now. Even the thought of sitting down to finish drains me. The crosswalk *pip-pip*s and I join the swarm of commuters flowing across Fifth.

"Harry?" Louisa's voice drags me back to reality. "The book?"

"Sorry, yes. The book is coming," I say, which is true. "I'm almost there," I say, which is not true at all. "I just need—"

"—another month?" she interjects. She knows me too well.

"Um. Yes. That would . . . that would be great."

"Okay. I'll hold the publishers off one more month. Listen, the first book is still flying off the shelves so we're in a good place. People will wait for the next. But you need to be honest with me about where we are, Harry. You're definitely nearly there?"

The seriousness of her tone hits me hard. "Yes. Four weeks, probably less. I swear. First draft done." As I say it, I realize it will be hard, but I can do it. I just need to break my funk.

My eyes catch the time blinking high on the side of an office building. I need to finish this call. Rockefeller Center is right ahead and Edward will be there waiting.

"Oh, and I forgot to say: the publishers want to have a meeting about the paperback edition this Wednesday afternoon. At their main office, does that work?"

Ahead the glittering frontage of Saks comes into view opposite the entrance to The Rink and I realize the rain has stopped.

After I agree to the time and hang up, I pop my phone on silent, pull off my winter hat, and shake out my hair, checking my reflection in a shop window. Edward and I have already been together just over a year, but I can't imagine a time when I won't still get those date-night nerves.

Tonight will be special, I feel it. I'm being introduced to a family tradition and God knows I could do with some of those. Orphans don't tend to have many.

As I round the corner of Rockefeller Plaza, my breath catches, the scale of the Christmas decorations bringing me to a stuttering halt.

In front of me is a tunnel of pure light created by the forms of angels heralding, golden trumpets raised. Color, light, and warmth. And beyond them, the famous tree, rising up into the New York skyline. I'd read in the paper this morning that it's over eighty feet tall, but standing beneath it now that number finally sinks in. It's the largest Christmas tree I've ever seen. I stand slack-jawed as I stare up. Around me a few other kindred spirits look up transfixed as the rest of New York jostles past us. Eighteen thousand lights twinkle golden into the night air, thick with the scent of Nordic pine and the delicious aroma of Christmas treats wafting from the vendors dotted about the plaza.

A hand grasps my shoulder and I whip around to a familiar touch. Edward. Wrapped up warm against the chill in a cashmere scarf and coat, his hair tousled, his eyes smiling.

"You scared the shit out of me," I lie, too embarrassed to say I would know the feel of him anywhere.

"Sorry," he says with a smile. "I called your name but I guess you didn't hear." He nods up to the tree, slipping his arms around my waist as I lean back into him, his warmth against mine. "It's really something, isn't it?"

Beneath the lights of the tree, on the sunken ice-skating rink, we watch as people glide effortlessly across its pristine surface, bobble hats on, bundled in scarves. Amid the young, old New York is still present, an elderly man in a full suit and hat, two women of equally advanced years wrapped in thick furs, their hair set hard as rocks.

"I'm a terrible skater," I warn Edward later as we fasten our skates and hobble out of the enclosure toward the ice.

"Lucky I'm here then." He grins, pulling me tight. He backs out onto the ice first and offers me both his hands for stability. I take them, my breath held in concentration as he glides us out into the middle of the rink. It's not that busy. A handful of new skaters slip and weave around us, and after a moment my muscles loosen into his rhythm, his movements reassuring and fluid. He was an athlete—I suppose he still is.

Christmas music blares merrily over the ice rink's loudspeaker, and as a new song begins Edward loosens one of his hands from mine. "May I have this dance?" he intones, grinning as he slowly spins me. I realize the song they're playing is "Fairytale of New York" by the Pogues—its craggy lilt kicking in as we slip and slide across the ice, grinning like idiots. One verse in and everyone on the ice is gliding in time with the jaunty tune as above us one of the more vocal market vendors starts to sing along with the lyrics, his accent an appropriate lilting Irish brogue. Other skaters instinctively join in, merrily blasting out the odd phrase, tongue firmly in cheek, but we're all singing. And just for a microsecond New York is made of magic. I find myself thinking: *God, I love Americans.* British people just aren't like this, our toes curl at the slightest inkling of real sentiment, and yet here *I* am, singing, dancing, on ice. Everyone's caught in the moment as the song crescendos and we belt out the chorus. Edward releases my hand again and I wobble slightly as he swoops down in front of me, one wet knee on the rink. He's got something in his hand and suddenly my stomach tightens with soul-capsizing embarrassment as I realize what it is.

Oh, please, no.

This is too much. He can't be doing what I think he's doing. I swallow hard. People are looking at us now, smiling at us, clapping for us, and I keep smiling because what the hell else can I do.

God knows I want him to ask, but this, here, is too much, too public. I feel my panic rise as he opens the box and starts to speak and suddenly the world around us fades away. I feel tears come and my voice catch and he's taking off my glove and sliding a ring onto my finger. A small crowd has formed on the walkway above the rink and they're cheering and whooping as the song ends and "Chapel of Love" blasts out into the chilly air around us. The lights twinkle in time as I struggle to take everything in.

Edward pulls me close. "I love you, Harry," he whispers. And for a second nothing else matters, because when I look into his eyes, I know it's true. This is him trying to give me new memories, strong, bold, undeniable memories. This is him sharing his life, his past, and his future with me. I touch his face, so handsome I often marvel at being allowed to. His lips are warm on mine and the city around us disappears. The sound of cheering muffled by his hands over my ears.

Later in the rink's Christmas café, I inspect the ring on my cold-numbed finger while he fetches us hot toddies. The stone glimmers in the light, the color caught between a rich claret and a warm brown. I've never seen anything like it. A ruby, I imagine. Large, deep, expensive. The setting, and cut, old. It must be an heirloom, yet the fit is perfect.

Edward heads back over, balancing our drinks and two mince pies in his hands.

"Did you plan that?" I ask, taking a tentative swig of the sweet heady drink. "The music, the singing?" It fleetingly occurs to me that, with the means at his disposal, Edward could have rented out the entire rink and peopled it with ensemble actors twice over if he had so desired. It's a terrifying thought but thankfully a million miles from anything Edward might actually do.

He splutters a laugh and shakes his head, wiping mince pie dust from his upper lip. "No," he says. "I mean, I knew I was going to ask you tonight. I had the ring on me, but I wasn't planning for it to turn into a Broadway number out there. Guess that's New York for you; everyone's got something to say." He looks suddenly concerned. "Ah God. It was too much, wasn't it? Damn it, sometimes I forget you're British."

He's genuinely mortified.

"No, stop. It was perfect. I mean, I'm not likely to forget it," I quip. "And for the record, I'm not British anymore, am I? My US passport is as real as yours."

"Good, well then, consider what just happened out there on the ice your swearing-in ceremony. It's all going to get pretty un-British from here on in. But seriously, if anything gets too much, you have to tell me. No harm no foul. I don't want to scare you off. At least . . . not yet anyway."

He means his family. They must know he was planning on asking me; I'm guessing he had to ask them for the ring. And now that we're engaged meeting them must be in the cards. I raise my hand and consider the deep-red jewel in the light. "What stone is this?"

"Garnet. It was my great-grandmother's. Mitzi's." He studies my reaction. "You like it, right? No? We can change it. Get something new?"

"No, no," I blurt. He's so worried about the effect his family will have on me he can't read me at all. "Edward, *I love it,*" I tell him, taking in its gleaming facets. "I mean, God, I think I might love it more than I love you," I joke. "Seriously, though, I love that it means something. To you, to your family. That it's important. What was she like? Mitzi?"

I would be lying if I said I didn't already know as much as the internet can tell me about Edward's family.

John Livingston Holbeck, Edward's great-great-great-grandfather, was one of the original Gilded Age tycoons who made their fortune in the 1800s during a period of massive expansion across America. J. L. Holbeck created monopolies and reaped the rewards of a captive market by controlling a large percentage of all shipping, railways, and communications at the time. One of the handful of men who built America in an era predating taxation, J. L. Holbeck amassed a mind-boggling fortune and innumerable holdings; he was a contemporary of Cornelius Vanderbilt, Andrew Carnegie, and the father of the man who built the building we're now sitting beneath. Which makes me wonder if this skating-on-the-first-day-of-the-season tradition dates a lot further back than I had previously considered.

"What was Mitzi like?"

Edward ponders my question. "She was beautiful. And talented. She was an artist, she trained as a ballerina. German, but she left between the wars, then she met my great-grandfather. They had this great love affair, so the story goes, this intense love affair. Famously, theirs was the first marriage for love in the Holbeck family."

I choose not to open that can of worms. Though I have no experience of wealth I can understand the instinct to protect it, to fortify what you have. Love is an unknown quantity after all. It's a gamble at the end of the day. I'm more than happy to gamble with the few chips I have, but give me the GDP of a medium-sized country and I might at least consider a prenup. I'm sure the Holbecks have learned the hard way to question that first flush of passion.

"And your family's okay with this. With me? They let you have Mitzi's ring?"

I wonder what they'll make of me now that I know for certain they're aware of my existence. What Edward has or hasn't told them about me. Perhaps they've looked into me themselves? I shudder at the thought, then quickly reassure myself that while they might be able to research me, they can never know my thoughts, my memories. I am just a British novelist with no real credentials—except one bestseller to her name—no real history, no Ivy League anything, no Oxbridge. I can't imagine I'm what they had in mind for their firstborn son. I don't even have a family, let alone a notable one.

Maybe they just want Edward to be happy. Edward has promised me time and time again that not meeting them has nothing to do with me. He's had problems with them in the past, they like to exert control, he tries to keep his life at a distance from the madness of theirs. Things tend to get dragged into their orbit. Which makes the sudden appearance of this family ring now on my finger all the more interesting.

"Yes, they know about you," he says with a grin. "A worrying amount actually. Mother was over the moon when I asked for the ring. Insisted I use it actually."

"Really?" I ask, trying to mediate the surprise in my voice. It's not that I have a self-esteem issue, but it's slightly puzzling that a woman like Eleanor Holbeck would be insisting her firstborn child jump at the chance to marry an orphan from England.

"Really," he echoes and takes my cold hand in his across the table. "Listen, I know it's weird you've never met them. But I wanted to be sure we were in a good place before"—he pauses, trying to find the words—"before I let them loose on you. They are a lot to handle. But if you want to meet them, they *really* want to meet you. Especially now." He thumbs the ring on my finger gently. "We haven't had anyone like you in our family before," he says lightly, and the words imprint themselves in my mind. What does that mean? *Someone like me.* "And God knows we could do with fresh blood."

I feel my throat tighten at the thought of the type of person I actually am. But they can't know that. They cannot know what happened to me on the edge of that road twenty years ago; I was alone.

I shudder, and Edward lifts my hands to his lips to blow warmth back into them. "If you're worried about what they think about us, don't be. My great-grandfather had all the money in the world, and he married a woman without a penny. Granted, he was the only one ever to do it—point is, there's precedent." He laughs at my reaction. "I know, I know, you're hardly on the breadline! Plenty of pennies in bestselling author Harry Reed's coffers. But you know what I mean," he adds seriously. And I do, because whatever I have is only ever going to be a drop in the Holbeck ocean.

"Why did your great-grandfather choose a garnet? For Mitzi's ring?" I ask.

"She loved pomegranates."

I look down at the ring and smile. It looks just like the top of a ripe pomegranate seed.

"He knew he could make her happy and that she would do anything for him. They just fit. Two peas in a pod. And together no one could stop them," Edward says, studying my expression.

I take him in, this fiancé of mine, in all his glory. Tall, athletic, in cashmere and tailored Italian wool, and I can't hold back the grin. God knows how I found him. God knows how it got this far, this serious.

"When am I going to meet them?" I ask.

A smirk forms. "Apparently, my sister has been chosen to *ease* the transition. The powers that be have deemed her the most accessible family member to make an introduction," he says jokingly. "After me, obviously."

I can imagine Edward is the most normal—if that's the right word—of the Holbecks. He's clearly spent his life trying to be. After graduating from MIT, he actively moved away from the family business, handing his control of that side of things over to his brothers. He's a *self-made* man—as much as a Holbeck descendant can ever be, that is. He established his own tech start-up and grew the company into what it is today. Although I'm sure the glamour of his surname can't have hurt his success, alongside his intelligence and easy, affable charm.

"So I'm going to meet your sister first. Matilda?" He nods before I continue. "And she has my phone number?"

"Oh yes. That she does." Edward grins. "She's got your number, email address, *actual* address, dress *size,* blood type, donor consent status . . . kidding."

I narrow my eyes. "I thought you said I shouldn't be scared of her?"

"Oh no. You should *definitely* be scared of her. She's absolutely terrifying, they all are; you'd be mad not to be. But I think you want this, don't you? To be included, part of the family? A family?" He finds the answer in my eyes. "Just don't change your mind about me after all this, that's all I ask," he says, then kisses the ring on my finger lightly and grins.

2

An Invitation

TUESDAY, NOVEMBER 22

"His family could literally be insane. You've never even met them and you've already agreed to marry into it. You have no idea what you've signed up for. As your agent and friend, I've got to say it's dicey territory."

I can't help but bark out a laugh in spite of my throbbing head. Edward and I stayed out celebrating last night, and my champagne hangover is showing no sign of diminishing even after a pint of water and two paracetamols. I only rang Louisa for more details about my publisher meeting on Wednesday, but here we are. I wedge my mobile into a more comfortable position between my ear and shoulder and continue to tap away at my computer as I talk.

"Every family is crazy, though, right? In their own way. Money just highlights what's already there." I chuckle. "Plus,

I've only agreed to be his fiancée. It's hardly a legally binding contract."

"Oh, okay? So, you'll cut and run if they're all mad as hatters then, will you?" she challenges.

I take a moment to genuinely consider how bad the Holbecks would have to be in order to put me off Edward. "No. You're right," I concede. "They could basically be the Fritzls and I'd still try to make it work with Ed."

Louisa bursts out laughing. "I'm glad you're in a place where you can admit that, at least. My God, that proposal though. Singing, dancing, Christmas. Wowzer. I'm surprised your head didn't explode. No half measures there. You remember when Simon proposed to me? In our old back garden after breakfast? You and Ed make me sick."

"Hey, it *was* snowing in your back garden. Give Si some credit. Though probably best you turned him down in the end, all things considered."

"Yeah, I have quite the instinct for these things," she jokes. "Which brings me back round to Ed's family. Random Holbecks are just going to descend on you at some point, are they?" She must hear the sound of my keyboard, as she doesn't wait for an answer. "Hey. Are you writing now? While I'm talking to you?" she asks, mock-incredulous, then cheers loudly.

I pull back from the noise, my hungover brain reeling. "Please, Lou, I am very tender today. No loud noises."

"I'm just glad you're getting sucked into the draft. I knew you'd rally," she adds proudly.

I look at my screen. I have not rallied.

"I'm not writing, Lou. I'm googling Mitzi Holbeck."

An image of Edward's great-grandmother stares back at me on Google Images. A grainy black-and-white wedding shot from *The New York Times* in 1923.

"Oh. Hang on . . . there was a Mitzi? My God. *Fabulous* name."

I stare at Mitzi, and Alfred Holbeck beside her, a paparazzi shot from their wedding day for some old society column. They were celebrities back then. Alfred holds open a town car door for Mitzi as she beams out at the camera in her wedding dress, a knowing twinkle in her eyes. God, she was beautiful. Alfred too, gallant, handsome, a rough-hewn old-world prototype of Edward.

"I know, right, and she was really something too. An artist. She fled Germany between the wars—her family was originally from Bohemia."

"Bohemia? Is that even a place? Who are these people?"

"Bohemia is just a fancy name for Czechoslovakia, pre-1918, basically before—" A loud knock on the front door interrupts me.

I push my study chair back and stare down our long apartment hallway to the front door. Odd, I'm not expecting anyone this morning, and Edward left for a tech conference in San Diego earlier. "Sorry, Lou, one second."

"Everything okay?" Louisa asks.

"Yeah, just the front door." A second knock comes, more insistent this time.

"Probably a package or something."

As I make my excuses and hang up, another knock comes hard. I head out into the hall, scraping back my hair quickly as I pass the hall mirror. A brief glance at my reflection reminds me I haven't yet showered this morning. But then I'm supposed to be in full deadline mode. Perhaps with Edward away for the next few days I'll actually get time to write, to finally finish my book.

As I reach for the front-door latch, I freeze. Edward said I'd meet Matilda soon. My heart skips a beat as I realize she could be on the other side of this door.

My fingers hover over the latch; I am in no fit state to meet someone like Matilda Holbeck. I look down at my comfy writing clothes, my bobbly wool socks and cardigan, and groan internally. This is not the first impression I should be making. I've seen photographs of Matilda Holbeck and I'm pretty sure a wool sock has never even made it into her *Architectural Digest* apartment, let alone onto her feet. I squint through the peephole but our new Christmas wreath blocks my view.

Another loud knock comes, this time incredibly close to my face.

I could pretend to be out but I've hardly been stealthy this side of the door. If she knows I'm here and hiding that would be an even worse first impression than my appearance.

I take a deep breath, remind myself I am good enough as I am, and open the door.

Instead of Matilda's pale angular features, I'm met with the brisk outdoor energy of a bearded city courier. Disinterested, he hands me a crisp white envelope, gesturing for me to sign. I quickly scribble my name, half relieved, half spooked by my own paranoia, then watch as he wordlessly disappears around the corridor toward the elevators.

Back in the apartment I turn the thick card of the envelope over in my hands. On the front, my name and address are carefully inked onto the paper. I don't need to open it to know who it is from: no one I know owns stationery this nice; no one I know couriers mail. Matilda has sent me a letter. She could have called, sent a text message, emailed, but she didn't; she sent a hand-couriered letter. Hardly as accessible as advertised, but I can't deny there is a certain thrill to the feel of the watermarked correspondence in my hands.

In the kitchen I flick on the kettle and perch on a kitchen island stool, slipping a finger under the envelope's gum seal and carefully tugging out the note card from within. The thick white card is embossed at the top with the silver swirling initials MBH.

Matilda Beatrice Holbeck. Edward's sister. The next in line to the throne. Unmarried, five years my senior, the Holbecks' only daughter. Beneath her initials an elegant handwritten request to join her, tomorrow, at a fashionable Upper East Side members club for afternoon tea. Four P.M.

My stomach flips as I read; my publisher meeting is at four P.M. tomorrow. I am already in tricky territory with my deadline, so meeting the publisher is definitely not the kind of appointment I can push. It would send all the wrong signals. Which means I need to rearrange with Matilda.

At the bottom of the card in silver leaf is an RVSP email, her assistant. My shoulders relax slightly at the idea I won't have to turn her down directly. Her assistant can just reschedule—I'm free pretty much any other day.

I shoot off my RSVP and head back to my desk with purpose, to address my word count.

Four minutes later a reply pings into my inbox. Matilda's assistant, Max, writes: *That is unfortunate timing-wise. I will pass on your deepest regrets to Ms. Holbeck.*

My stomach tightens. He'll pass on *my deepest regrets*? Well, that sounds incredibly dramatic. Almost like I'm refusing to meet her at all rather than asking for a raincheck. Mild panic begins to brew but I tell myself I do not have time for this right now. I can only hope Max passes on my actual reasons. I force myself to stop rereading my email, and his, and I dive back into the novel.

An hour later I almost jump out of my skin when an extremely loud phone starts ringing in our hallway. I didn't even know we had a landline, and it's certainly the first time anyone has ever called it in the four months since we moved in. Edward must have had it installed at some point.

The shrill ring continues, impossible to ignore. I head out to answer it.

"Hello?"

"Hi, Harry, it's Amy at Grenville Sinclair."

My publisher. That's odd.

"Oh, hi, Amy?"

"Hi. So, I'm calling about the meeting scheduled here at the office tomorrow. Just to let you know we're rescheduling our end."

"Rescheduling?"

"Yes. We're happy to. So, that's fine," she says curtly. There's something odd in her tone. "Can you do next week, perhaps? Or if not, there's really no rush for this meeting at all. We could just postpone until the New Year if that's easier . . . for you? Timing-wise."

And suddenly I realize exactly what's going on here and I am genuinely speechless. It takes me a second to give voice to my thoughts, so bizarre is the conclusion they seem to come to.

"Amy? Did someone else just call you? Is this something to do with—wait, Grenville Sinclair is part of the Laurence Group, isn't it?"

She gives a nervous laugh. "It is, yeah."

"Right. And . . . the Laurence Group is a subsidiary of . . . ?"

"ThruComm Holbeck."

"Yep. Okay. Yep," I manage. "I think I see what's happened here."

While I of course knew that my publisher was in some way connected to the business interests of my future in-laws, the idea that they might ever use this fact as some kind of leverage had not even crossed my mind until now.

Matilda has canceled my meeting so that I can eat cake with her.

"Um, Amy, I am so, so sorry about this, I . . . if any—"

"No, no, no. Harriet, *please*. Really, it is absolutely fine. I mean, whatever we can do to accommodate our authors. That's always our primary concern here. So let us know, about next week or next month. Whenever you're ready. We're here."

"Okay. Okay, thank you, Amy."

The line is silent for a moment. "Yes, thank you, Harriet." And she's gone.

I stand in silence in the hallway for a moment to let what just happened sink in. And the realization hits me that however weird this situation is, this is only the start of my dealings with the Holbecks. Matilda is supposed to be the most restrained member of Edward's family, and if this is restrained then God help me.

Dazed, I head back to the study and grab my mobile, bringing up Edward's number, my thumb poised over the DIAL button. This is exactly what he was worried about. His family being too much for me. I take a breath and close the app.

I can do this. I knew his family would be tricky but this is what I want. I want to be with Edward, to start a family with him, to be part of something bigger than myself. I'm going to have to buckle in if I'm going on this ride. I can't balk this early. After moving continents for this, after leaving my old life and friends behind, I won't let this knock us off course. And I don't want Edward to be forever pulling me out of sticky situations. I can deal with this on my own.

I place my mobile back down on the desk beside me and type out a short email to Matilda's assistant, Max.

Am now available for 4 P.M. tomorrow.

My email swooshes out into the ether.

I sit motionless for a moment wondering if I have made the right decision or if I have allowed things to start off on slightly the wrong foot. I feel the mild panic of earlier rise again inside me and my hangover pound back to life. I try to breathe through it but suddenly I realize it's too late. I shoot up from my chair, an unstoppable urge to vomit surging through me. I burst from the room and hurtle toward the bathroom, hand clamped firmly over mouth as behind me I hear the ping of a new email landing in my inbox.

3

Two for Tea

The nausea hasn't abated when I arrive at Matilda's private members club the following day. The website listed the dress code as *smart casual* so I'm wearing heels even though I feel like death warmed up and have an irrationally strong desire to take them off and hurl them as hard as I can at the ten-foot ecru marble sculpture in the club lobby.

Pre-meeting nerves and illness have twisted my previously hopeful attitude into one of full-blown irritation at being forced into this situation. I should be working; I should be meeting my publisher, not here at the beck and call of a woman I've never even met.

And I have no idea why my hangover decided to stick around but it seems to have somehow morphed into some kind of stomach flu. Either way it's safe to say that—after a day and a half of nausea, vomiting, and lack of sleep, in spite of being absolutely exhausted—there is nowhere on earth I would rather be less than waiting to be seated for a formal afternoon tea.

But here I am, because I have to be. The truth is I want Edward's sister to like me way more than I care to admit, and postponing again, this time due to illness, might look a little too deliberate.

As I'm led into the club's lounge my eyes find her almost immediately, that vibrant pop of auburn hair, a shot of red in a sea of New York neutrals. She's even more beautiful in real life than in the photographs I've seen. Perhaps they all are, the Holbecks.

I glide past tables of elegantly dressed, artsy, Museum Mile hipsters. At her table she is turned away from me as she points to something in a menu, an attentive waiter leaning in to catch her order. I imagine she knows exactly what she wants. She must feel eyes on her because she looks up and meets my gaze with alarming precision, almost as if I'd called her name. A fresh wave of nausea hits me and I pray that Matilda's first memory of me won't involve me being sick.

I hazard a smile, but immediately realize that given her statuesque demeanor, she might not be a big smiler. A suspicion quickly confirmed when she raises a pale hand in acknowledgment of my arrival, her face remaining perfectly still.

My already queasy stomach tightens. This could be a long tea. Or a very short one. I'm suddenly reminded of Matilda's *helpful* phone call to my publisher yesterday and how easy it is for a Holbeck to make things happen or stop them dead.

Matilda's waiter unobtrusively pulls out a chair for me as I arrive, before smoothly exiting.

Matilda's eyes play over me as I settle and take her in: her crisp white shirt, that immaculate tailoring, those pillowy red lips and the two perfect emerald earrings twinkling through her flame hair. From her unwavering expression, I cannot help but wonder, for the first time, if Edward might have outright lied to me when he said his family couldn't wait to meet me.

She stretches out an alabaster hand across the table and then, to my unending relief, cracks a giddy smile. "Harriet. It's *so* wonderful to meet you," she says, her voice a bubbling brook of warmth and friendliness. I take her cool hand in mine and shake. "*Argh*," she continues, animatedly. "I'm *supposed* to be on my best behavior but—wait, do I call you Harriet? Harry? What do you like? Harry, right?" I nod and she barrels on. "Great. So, *Harry,* I'm *supposed* to be on my best behavior, representing the family, yada yada, but can I just get out of the way how excited I am about all of this? You and Edward. Edward settling down. With you. This is so good. Your move, the engagement, all of it. He's a tough little nut to crack but looks like you cracked him. He's had us in the dark completely. But then he barrels in asking for Gran-Gran Mitzi's ring. And here we all are." She takes a heady breath in through her nose before letting out a sigh. "It is so great that we are finally doing this. Meeting. Edward is such a grouch for keeping you to himself this whole time." She pauses, her beautiful features resetting into their statuesque stillness.

She's not the person I expected at all. She's easy and affable, with a girlish ebullience that instantly dissolves my preconceptions. It's hard to believe she'd make a power move like cancel my publisher meeting through anything other than presumed helpfulness. Unless this is all part of some elaborate act. But right now, with Matilda sitting in front of me, I honestly can't imagine us not becoming fast friends.

"Matilda, it is so wonderful to finally meet you too. I've heard so much about you from Edward—"

"All good I hope?" She smirks.

"Mm-hmm," I answer, my pitch a little higher than rings true. "Yeah, yes, all good. Well, you know . . ."

"Don't worry. I know Edward *very well.* He can be sensitive about his relationships. And about the family." She sobers slightly, her tone serious. "But rightly so, I understand why completely. He's had problems in the past with relationships and with Dad." Yes, Robert Davison Holbeck. Edward's father. Now, there is a terrifying man if ever there was one. Terrifying in the way rich, attractive men always tend to be. There are rumors of the type of man he might have been in his youth, the type of man he still might be. Allegations, payoffs, blackmail, business dealings in countries where there shouldn't be, and insider trading. But never anything more than allegations. His ability to ride anything out seemingly unstoppable.

"But you know it's hard, for any of us, to find a partner who's okay with all this," she adds conspiratorially, gesturing to the air around her. "At least that's my excuse for being perpetually single." She smiles, lightening the mood. "Hey, shall we order? I could eat a horse, hooves and all."

Tea poured, and Jenga-stacked truffle-infused finger sandwiches and French confections towering beside us, I force down my nausea and steer the conversation back to me and Edward. I need to get a feel for the lay of the land in the Holbeck camp.

"You said the ring was the first you'd heard about us, is that really true?" I ask tentatively. "Edward didn't mention me at all?"

"Oh gosh no. Of course, we all *knew* about you. It's impossible to keep things quiet in this family. We just weren't allowed to ask him about it. We were told in no uncertain terms to back off. That you might be the one."

"By Edward?"

She nods and I can't help the flush of happiness that comes from the thought of Edward saying those words.

"We knew he had a new girlfriend. You," she continues. "And that you met in London. That you're an author, which by the way is beyond fascinating to me—but we'll put a pin in that and circle back; I have a million questions. But regarding Edward, we gave him space, because we've made mistakes in the past. Forced issues that perhaps we shouldn't have. Anyway, this time things seem very different. You seem *very* different from his previous girlfriends."

I feel my hackles rise. I dread to think what it could be that makes me so different. But she's moved on before a sentient question can even form in my mind.

"He's never talked about anyone the way he talks about you. He has this certainty—that you're the one."

"The one?" I ask.

"Uh-huh." She nods, then leans forward, her elbows on the linen of the tablecloth. "And he's so much happier now. He came by the house a couple of weeks back to talk to us about everything, to get the ring. We hadn't seen him, God, not since last Christmas. It was a tough one between him and Dad. They're cut from the same cloth, you see. Before you, Edward was *work, work, work.* For years now. But since you he's mellowed. We thought he'd stopped trying to find someone, that he'd end up an old bachelor. Then you." Her voice lowers conspiratorially once more. "I'm going to be honest with you, Harry, because I like you. I'm not sure how much you know but things have not been great between Dad and Edward for a long while now. Dad pushes him, sometimes too far. It's a lot of pressure and in the past, with Ed's romantic choices, things haven't worked out at all."

I'm leaning in now too. "What do you mean? What went wrong?"

"Well, not to put too fine a point on it, Harry, but we-gotta-lotta-money." She lets out a little girlie snort at her own words.

"And that's caused problems? His exes had the wrong intentions?"

"Well, we'll never know now, will we? They never lasted. I'm not gonna lie, we can all be a little much, but we've got a nose for bad intentions, it kind of comes with the territory. Sometimes Ed lets his emotions get in the way of self-preservation. I know how the world views us: cutthroat, dog-eat-dog, sociopaths, or whatever. But we're only reacting to what we face every day. It is brutal out here. And you should know, coming into all this, everything we have, everything we are, other people want it. We developed tough skins because by God, we've needed them just to survive. But we love Ed, we want him to be happy. Here's the thing. Since the last girlfriend—he's kept his distance from the family. He got it in his head Daddy scared her off. That he'll scare you off." She shrugs lightly. "And maybe he did scare the last one, but maybe it was for the best. Some people aren't built for this, some people aren't strong enough to run with the pack." Her eyes flick across my features before she adds, "I see you, though. You're a strong one. I see it in your eyes. To get this far, to leave a life behind, to get that ring on your finger, you're a strong one, a survivor. Like us." She gives my hand a rallying squeeze across the table and I realize that even though she doesn't know me, she kind of knows me. "Listen," she continues, "don't worry about meeting Daddy, he's mellowed. The upshot is Dad wants Edward back in the fold, and you make him happy. Edward wants you and if any of us stand in the way I'm under no illusions that we'll lose him completely. I think I understand your intentions toward him. He's always been a good brother to me. So my question to you is: will you help us out?"

"Help you out?"

"Yeah, honey. Will you help the family out? We want him back; we want to keep him where we can see him. We think this engagement is just wonderful."

A strange warmth permeates me as I begin to understand what is going on here. They *have* to have me; they *have* to like me; they have *no* choice. As I said, I don't have a self-esteem problem but the idea of their immediate acceptance of a nobody from England as their new daughter-in-law was completely baffling, until now. Why would one of the wealthiest families in America endorse the engagement of their oldest son to a woman they'd never met? Here is the answer. It's reassuring in its simplicity. They pushed him away and vetoed his choices too many times and they've run out of *no*s. They either accept me or they lose him.

Edward's already chosen me over them, so they need me on their side if they want him back. I'm the missing piece that can bring them together again.

I'm no business tycoon but I do know that you can't sell anything without first creating a need. However uneven our power differential might be I have something that the Holbecks want: their son.

My blue eyes find Matilda's green ones. "I understand. And I'll see what I can do," I say with a smile.

"Fabulous." She grins. Then a thought seems to occur to her, almost in passing, almost as if she's only just thought of it. Almost.

"Oh, and listen, what are you both doing tomorrow?"

"Tomorrow? I'm not sure. Not much, I don't think. Why?"

She pauses, confused in some way by my response. Then she smiles. "Oh, of course, right. Well, we're having a little family dinner. It might be a nice occasion for you to meet everyone. There'll be a big crowd, but everyone's girlfriends/partners will be there too so there'll be lots to take the pressure off you. Just a quiet family dinner. I just think everyone's going to love you. I wouldn't suggest it otherwise, trust me."

"Tomorrow? Yeah, okay, I don't see why not. I'll tell Edward we're coming over."

Matilda squeezes my arm in solidarity. "That would be perfect. This is perfect. I can't wait."

Out on the street Matilda hails me a cab and slips the driver a wad of bills as I slide in.

"Oh, and honey," she barks through my open window. "Forgot to say. I am so sorry for that situation with your publisher. I thought I was helping but Mother tells me, 'All totally inappropriate.' So, lesson learned. Don't worry. It won't happen again, Sis." And with that she blows me a kiss and slaps the roof of the taxi, sending us off into the busy traffic.

Edward's still in San Diego so I tap out a text to let him know I've agreed to the family dinner. He'll be back tomorrow morning and there will be more than enough time for us to make it across town for the evening. Although the idea of meeting everyone tomorrow is incredibly daunting, I can't think of a better way to acclimate myself to them than in a large group where the focus will be spread out.

Edward's reply comes back almost instantly.

Tomorrow night?!

Yeah. Why?

And you told them we were free?!

Um, yes . . . we are free, aren't we? Is everything ok? Xx

You know what tomorrow is, right?

What do you mean?

Tomorrow is Thanksgiving!

I stare at my phone screen unblinking. *No. Oh my God, no.* I did not know that. I feel my face throb with heat, my nausea resurfacing, until colors speckle my vision of the city through the cab window.

She tricked me. Matilda straight up tricked me into a Thanksgiving dinner.

I may be British but I know Thanksgiving is a big deal and definitely not something to be wandered into lightly, the day before it happens, having never met another soul at the table. My stomach flips as I picture the scene in my mind's eye.

I open my cab window, letting the cold air cool my flaming cheeks. New York rushes past, and life goes on, the world keeps turning even though I am heading directly into the heart of the Holbeck clan, tomorrow evening, like a lamb to the slaughter.

Matilda tricked me and I didn't even notice it happening. If she's the presentable face of that family, then I will need to be on my toes tomorrow night. A shudder runs through me as I close the window and it hits me that I will finally be meeting Robert Holbeck.

I stare down at Edward's replies. He's worried. He's annoyed with them already. He thinks they're up to their old tricks. But if there's one thing Matilda said this afternoon that I can be sure is true it's that, her Thanksgiving trick aside, this time things will be different.

Edward's family needs me. They can't afford to push me away, because if they do, they'll lose him forever.

I carefully tap out a reply to Edward.

> Of course, I knew it was Thanksgiving.
> Matilda and I thought it might be a good
> way to kick things off x

4

The More the Merrier

THURSDAY, NOVEMBER 24

Edward gets back from San Diego earlier than expected the next morning.

When I hear the front-door latch lift I rush to quickly shut down the open tab on my screen, fumbling to delete the recent search history. I've been googling Edward's ex-girlfriends, the ones that didn't make the Holbeck cut. As if, somehow, I might uncover the secret reasons they failed.

Of course Edward has told me about them, and God knows I've looked them all up before now, but back in the early days I was only concerned with torturing myself through comparison; now I have my business brain on. I want to know the details.

I want to know what exactly made them sub-Holbeck in Edward's family's eyes. I have less than twelve hours till I meet them and I want to be armed, at least, with knowledge of how my predecessors failed.

Evidence of my deep dive erased, I head out to meet Edward as he lugs his suitcase into the hallway.

He looks up at me as he unlatches his case and smiles, impossibly fresh for this time of the morning—especially considering the flight he's just taken. I on the other hand look exhausted. I've been ill now for three days straight, the nausea and lethargy unabated. "You look awful," he says with a grin. "Did you miss me that much?"

It's just a joke and I know he loves me, regardless of my pallor, but to my utter horror tears burst from me unbidden. It must be the emotional buildup and low-key stress of the last few days breaking to the surface, though I hadn't really been aware of its presence until now.

I throw my arms around him, burying my face in his sweater to inhale the warm, fresh scent of his cologne. Cedar and citrus. This is very unlike me; I never cry. And I dare not look up at him now, crippled with the sheer weight of my own awkward need. I feel his hand in my hair, his mouth close to my ear as he speaks.

"I missed you a ridiculous amount too," he whispers, then kisses the top of my head. "How did it go with Sis? I'm guessing good given our Thanksgiving plans tonight."

I look up to check his expression, to see if Thanksgiving is a problem that we need to address, but his face shows nothing more than mild surprise at my sudden clinginess.

"So you're okay with tonight?" I check.

"I am if you are. But—and don't take this the wrong way— you don't seem like you're in quite the right frame of mind for tonight?"

He takes in my pasty, tearstained face. "It's food poisoning or something," I tell him, quickly wiping the tears away and pulling myself together. I am not going to be the reason tonight fails. "I'm fine. I'll be fine. I've had it a few days now. But it's manageable."

I untangle myself from him and head to the kitchen, hoping to locate something that might perk me up. "Tea? Coffee?" I ask him.

"Err, yeah, coffee, thanks," he calls after me.

From my research into Edward's exes this morning, being from a wealthy, notable family doesn't seem to be enough for the Holbecks. Edward's first girlfriend out of university was the daughter of a Fortune 500 founder and that didn't work out. I found a few society-page magazine photos of them on Reddit. Girlfriends of the super-rich. I know, I'm a terrible person. In the shots they both look so young, squinting in the harsh pop of a paparazzi flash. Rosy-cheeked, clammy hands held tight, like two wholesome Ralph Lauren models. Lily was beautiful, a good match for him in looks and height and breeding. She's married to a senator now, with three freckle-faced angel kids and a chocolate Labrador. So the Holbecks must require something else from their potential daughters-in-law, something more than money and looks and prestige. God knows what the Holbecks had against Lily, or—if Matilda is to be believed—what Robert Holbeck in particular had against her; I couldn't imagine a more perfect match for Edward.

Edward's second internet-documented ex was more recent, a relatively well-known French actress with an impossibly cool air. I stare at my own distorted reflection in the metal of the toaster and feel a kick of inadequacy. A lifetime without a family, constantly adapting to fit into new groups and situations, stripped me of any kind of default insouciance long ago—I might be able to look relaxed but I rarely actually feel it. Especially today. Now, apparently, I cry for no reason. I try to remind myself that I have been sick for three days, I'm just tired.

The kettle rattles to a boil and clicks off triumphantly. But as I fill the cafetière the rich scent of the coffee grounds hits me with overwhelming force. Do they usually smell this strong? My hand flies to my mouth and I run, full tilt, sprinting past a puzzled Edward as I race for the apartment's bathroom. I reach it just in time, retching into the porcelain of the toilet bowl until there is nothing left in my stomach. After a moment of hiatus, I catch my breath, my shaking body sinking down onto the cool tile floor.

A concerned tap comes from the door: Edward.

"You okay?" he asks, poking his head around.

"Yeah, fine," I lie, quickly wiping my mouth and pulling myself up to sit, with a modicum of dignity, on the rim of the tub. "It's just this virus thing."

"Virus? Okay. 'Cause it kind of seems a lot like you're—" he says, leaving the words hanging as if we're both in on a secret. Except I have no idea what he's talking about.

And now he's grinning at me. "You're not, are you?" he asks.

"Not what?" I croak.

"Pregnant?"

I stare at him, dumbstruck. Of course I'm not pregnant.

I'd know if I was pregnant. Wouldn't I? My mind races back over the last few weeks, my inability to focus on my writing, my bizarre fatigue, my complete loss of appetite, my intense sense of smell, nausea, vomiting, crying?

Oh shit.

Ten minutes later we're in the bodega beneath our building purchasing three boxes of pregnancy tests, Edward a ball of contained excitement by my side.

The cashier eyes us both with suspicion as I pay, a bleary-eyed, bedraggled woman and an immaculate, beaming man in a suit.

Back in my bathroom I rip open the tests and go to town. Three minutes later it's official: we're having a baby.

Edward scoops me up into his arms and spins me around the sun-filled sitting room, the trees of Central Park visible through our terrace windows, and I can't help but cry, happy tears this time, because I realize with sudden unearthly clarity what this means. After a lifetime alone, I am going to make my own family. *We* are going to be a family.

And with that surge of happiness comes, too, the relief of knowing that the writer's block, the unproductivity, of the last month or so isn't me losing my creative spark. I have been making a person. Growing the beginnings of a human brain and body deep inside my own.

I check my calendar and a quick calculation tells me that I must be close to eight weeks; what with settling into my new life here and everything associated with that, I must have missed my last period completely.

Edward looks up how long morning sickness lasts and I'm horrified to learn I have at least another month of this never-ending hangover feeling. Though right now, in this moment, I have never felt happier.

Edward makes a call to his family doctor and by lunchtime we are holding hands in Dr. Leyman's wood-paneled office as he looks at my hormone levels and blood test results.

My dates and maths seem to add up so Dr. Leyman books us in for a scan the following week, where we'll be able to see the fetus for the first time.

I'm prescribed pregnancy-safe anti-nausea tablets for the constant vomiting and Dr. Leyman talks me through all the things I should and shouldn't be doing from now on, but all I can think of is the future. The life beginning to take form inside me and what it means for us.

It's late afternoon when Edward and I get back to the apartment and we remember our almost forgotten Thanksgiving dinner plans.

"We can cancel," he says, a sliver of hope in his voice. And he's right in a sense, because just the idea of meeting *everyone* in a few hours sends adrenaline coursing through my already depleted body. But I know that now that we are becoming a family in our own right, there is even more reason to meet his.

"I have to meet them at some point, Ed. If we do introductions now it won't be such a bombshell when we tell them about the pregnancy. I'll be in the second trimester soon and we can tell them then. That gives them three weeks from now to get their heads around the idea of me before we land a baby on them too. It's probably best to get the ball rolling as soon as possible, right?"

Edward weighs my words. "Put like that, yeah. But I don't want you feeling pressured by any of this. Dr. Leyman said you should avoid anything too stressful until we get through the first trimester. We'll go tonight but if it gets too much you need to tell me straightaway. If anything concerns you, you tell me. Right?"

His tone has a seriousness that makes my stomach flip. He's not messing around; all joking aside, his family is going to be hard work. I think of Matilda, her smile, her ebullient warmth, and then the fact that she completely screwed me into a nonconsensual Thanksgiving. I'll be walking into a whole nest of Matildas tonight. A building full of people I might not even realize are manipulating me until well after the fact.

"Who's going to be there, again?" I ask.

His eyebrows lift. "The usual crowd, I'm guessing. Mom. Dad. Matilda. My brothers and their partners." His younger brothers, Oliver and Stuart, and their partners. "Then there's Nancy, my dad's general counsel—"

"Wait, wait, wait. Your dad's general what?"

Edward smirks. "General counsel. Nancy, she's head of legal at ThruComm Holbeck." He takes in my incredulous face. "She's been around awhile. He trusts her."

"I see. And his legal counsel comes to family functions. Okay, good to know. I hadn't realized we were living in Wolf Hall. Please continue. Anyone else?"

"Nunu will be there too, I'm guessing, with the kids."

"Don't understand any part of that sentence."

He laughs. "The family nanny, Nunu. She'll be there but at the kids' table."

"Family nanny, *Nunu,* right," I say, making a mental note to remember these names. "Wait, the kids have a separate table?"

"Trust me, you'll want to be at the children's table too once you've experienced the adult one."

"Okay," I say with a smirk. "There's a lot to unpack there. I'm going to want to hear a lot more about this whole family nanny/Nunu situation later—you never said you had one growing up. But put a pin in that . . . who else might be there tonight?"

"Marty Fullman's usually there. COO of ThruComm. And his dog, Grog."

"Oh for God's sake."

"So twelve adults, four kids, and a dog. Plus the staff, but I'm not counting them." I feel my eyebrows shoot up before he adds, "You know what I mean, it's house staff, maids, kitchen staff, a chef . . ."

"Right, so basically, I'm meeting everyone. But your brothers' partners will be there, right? How did their first dinners go?"

Edward takes a moment before answering. "Varies, but it was sort of different for them."

"Different how?"

"Well, because I'm the eldest. The firstborn."

I can't repress a laugh. "Oh, I'm sorry, Mr. Bingley."

"Ha, ha. Yes, very good. But technically, and legally, lineage is still very much relevant. Certainly, in my family. Primogeniture is part of the family trust. It's like entailment but it doesn't matter what gender the firstborn is—whoever they are they get the lion's share. You can refuse to be part of the family business but you can't get away from genetics—or the law. Unfortunately."

"So it matters more who *you* marry than who they marry?"

"Yeah. It does. To my family . . . and to the outside world."

"To the outside world?"

"Who I marry has repercussions. I'll control it all one day and they'll be part of that. It affects shareholder confidence, market valuation, future projections—our reliability, sustainability," he says with unvarnished simplicity.

"Oh," I answer, and though I try to stop myself from asking I can't. "What will marrying me indicate?"

"To the world: that times are changing. To my family: that I love them but they will not hold me back from doing what I want with my life. I waited a long time to find you. And now I have. You can read any story in a million different ways but I think my family and the world in general will understand the story of us. Don't you think?"

"Um, yeah. If I'm honest, I'm really glad I bought a new outfit for this now," I say, half joking, then I catch his expression. "You are worried about what they'll think of me too, aren't you? Honestly?"

"Honestly? Of course I am. They're my folks. I want them to like you. I want you to like them. Mom likes what she hears about you. There's no way she'd have handed over Great-Grandma's ring otherwise. And what Mom thinks trickles down to the rest of them eventually. Dad's trickier. But it's going to be fine. Matilda didn't say anything weird about it all, did she? When you met?"

Aside from flexing her undeniable power in a single phone call to my publisher and then tricking me into meeting every single person in her family, no, she didn't say anything weird.

But clearly *weird* is a relative term, excuse the pun.

I wonder if he suspects that Matilda asked me to help bring him back into the family.

That thought sparks another: After all, Matilda is second in line to everything directly after Edward. There could be more going on here for her, in particular, than I had ever previously considered.

I realize Edward is waiting for my answer. "She didn't say anything that strange, no. It was nice . . . meeting her, she wasn't anything like I expected her to be. She seemed to be happy, about us, the idea of us. And I'm guessing she isn't someone who'd shy away from brutal honesty if she had real issues." I give him a reassuring smile, even though now I'm not so sure at all. "I think it's all going to be fine, Ed," I tell him.

And it will be, I just need to stay on my toes. Which is never a bad thing, especially now that I have a growing family to protect.

And with that warm thought in mind I lean in and whisper softly into his ear, "Hey. We're going to have a baby."

5

Introductions

THURSDAY, NOVEMBER 24

The immense façade of 7 East 88th Street towers above us. At its red-brick summit, a golden weather vane flashes and fades as it wavers in the evening light, guarded at every corner by stone gargoyles. I watch as its arrow swivels high above the city rooftops like an omen of what is to come—an instrument to divine which way the wind is blowing.

I slam the car door and the Holbecks' town car pulls away, leaving Edward and me on the curb. Of course they sent a driver. I stare up at the grandeur of their Manhattan townhouse, one of the many Holbeck homes dotted across the globe. A six-bedroom, three-floor city pied-à-terre just behind the Guggenheim. They possess such incredible wealth that I find it hard to comprehend what it all really means.

Edward takes my hand in his, and I drag my eyes from the

glowing windows high above us in time to catch his expression. He's grinning at me. He's clearly enjoying the effect that fifty-seven million dollars' worth of real estate is having on me. I give his hand a firm squeeze; I'm going to need a little help tonight. Help is something that I'm slowly learning to ask for, and thankfully he responds on cue.

"It's just a house," he tells me, pulling me close. "Everyone gets nervous meeting their in-laws."

"But this isn't quite the same, is it?" I reply.

"No," he says with a smirk, following my gaze back to the warmly lit penthouse windows. Then he looks back down to me, pushing a strand of loose hair behind my ear and kissing me lightly on the lips. It's a promise. A reminder of why we're here.

I close my eyes and let the feel of him, so close, so real, clear my head. We are here tonight because he gave me a ring; because I will become a part of this family.

Beginnings are always hard, almost as hard as endings, I remind myself.

From behind the gold and glass of the building's entrance a doorman appears, in off-black livery. He holds open the door with a silent professionalism that does nothing to put me at ease.

Inside: a marble lobby and a buttonless elevator activated by the doorman's magnetic card.

As we travel up to the Holbecks' penthouse triplex I try to imagine what it must have been like to grow up with all this, the Guggenheim next door. "Did you spend much time here, as a kid?" I ask Edward over the gentle hum of the elevator. I can't really imagine a tiny flush-faced Edward dashing around this place in the 1990s Tommy Hilfiger sweatshirt I've seen in his childhood photos.

"No, not really. Dad stayed here, during the week, for work. Mother went between here and home. We were always either at school or at The Hydes."

The Hydes. The Holbeck family home in upstate New York. I can only speculate, along with the rest of the world, on what Edward's family house looks like inside. There are no pictures

online, only paparazzi shots of the gates bordered by dense woodland and a high perimeter security fence. Its interiors have never
been photographed for a magazine or an architectural supple-
ment and it hasn't been on the market since J. L. Holbeck built it
in the late 1800s. Edward has mentioned it and clammed up
when pressed on it. The place has remained a mystery, and while
I try not to press him on it, each new crumb of knowledge slowly
builds a picture of something more than I dare to think about
right now.

He squeezes my hand as the lift slows. "You doing okay?"

I nod and attempt a smile, then watch as he straightens his
collar in infinite reflections in the elevator mirrors. He's nervous
too, I can tell, though he's hiding it well. That tightness around
his strong jaw I've noticed during work calls, the same tightness
the evening of our first official date. An almost imperceptible tell
that I've picked up on over time; an oddly comforting glimpse of
his human vulnerability beneath. This matters to him, a lot.

I tuck my errant strand of hair back into my loose chignon.
Under my coat a dark-red jumpsuit, to match Great-Grandma
Mitzi's ring. I wonder if Edward's mother will notice the gesture.

The lift pings and glides open to reveal a Carrera marble
atrium, a sculptural glass chandelier glistening high above us.
There isn't a Thanksgiving pumpkin or turkey decoration in
sight.

Edward leads me from the elevator, our shoes tapping on marble, the quiet murmur of voices and music drifting to us from
somewhere deep within the apartment. I try to quell the sudden
surge of fear and nausea rising up inside me; I need to stay calm.
But when a man in gray suddenly appears from a doorway to our
left, I literally jump.

"Mr. Holbeck, Ms. Reed," he murmurs, sotto voce, giving a
muted apologetic smile. He's British. A British butler, of course
they have a British butler. I'm going to sound like the help, aren't
I? I squeeze Edward's hand as our guide gestures for us to continue on down the corridor. "The family's just taking drinks in
the drawing room."

"Who was that?" I whisper as we round the corner away from him.

"No idea, never seen him before in my life." Edward shrugs. "There's a pretty heavy turnover around here."

"Oh."

The voices coming from the door ahead of us become clearer as we approach, then I catch the jovial tinkle of Matilda's laugh. They sound friendly at least.

At the closed door Edward holds my gaze for a second; he's waiting until I'm ready. I take one last fortifying breath before giving him the nod, and he opens the door.

Three oversized white sofas face one another around a low glass coffee table, over which the entire Holbeck family and friends have arranged themselves.

All eyes in the room find us as we enter, and for a heart-stopping second Edward and I come to a halt, hands held, smiling like idiots. A silence, punctuated only by the gentle spit and crackle of the log fire in its marble fireplace and the dull clink of ice cubes in glasses, fills the room. I feel Edward bristle beside me.

My eyes flick across the group hungrily as I take in as much as I can. Visible, beyond the drawing room's far door, a lofty dining room opens out, its table set and glimmering in soft candlelight. This is where our evening will play out.

After an eternity that almost certainly stretches only a few seconds in real-world time, Edward's mother speaks, breaking the tension. "Harriet," she says with genuine warmth as she rises to welcome us. "Edward, darling."

The rest of the family seems to relax, life coming back to the room around us. In a microsecond they have, no doubt, made their judgments on me and on our relationship—if they hadn't already.

Glasses are raised in acknowledgment; smiles beam and positions shift as Eleanor glides over to us. I take her in, tanned and immaculately made-up, her gray hair cut into a razor-sharp bob. She modeled in the 1980s; I know this from Ed, but mostly from the internet. Her wide eyes and thick brows are hallmarks of a bygone age. I recall an image of her in profile, balanced on tiptoe in a ballerina costume, aged eighteen, for American *Vogue*. No wonder Edward looks the way he does. No wonder all his siblings do, with parents like Eleanor and Robert.

I scan my periphery for him, for Edward's father, but I know he's not here. I do not sense him and judging by the family's now easy demeanor, I know I must be right.

Eleanor takes my hand in hers in greeting, her skin warm and soft to the touch, the scent of her perfume fresh and powdered as she leans in to air-kiss my cheeks.

"I cannot tell you how pleased I am, Harriet," she tells me with a twinkle in her eye, "that you could both make it tonight. And at such short notice." There's something in her tone that tells me that she knows the favor Matilda asked of me and she appreciates my help.

She holds me back at arm's length and playfully makes a show of inspecting me, genuine joy lurking just beneath her surface. "Radiant. Absolutely radiant." I let out an evasive chuckle. I certainly don't feel radiant.

"I know. I don't know why she said yes either, but she did," Edward quips, making his way over to plant a kiss on Matilda's cheek. Beside her sits a kind-faced woman that I do not know, who pats Edward on the arm supportively as he shifts past her. In fact, there are five people in this room whom I don't recognize. Actually, that's not strictly true. I recognize some of them.

Eleanor gently slips my arm over hers. "Now, yes. I need to introduce you to everyone. Don't I?" she says, with a conspiratorial glint in her eye. "You know Matilda, of course." Matilda raises her gaze to us and flashes a ruby-red smile.

"Of course." I smile back.

"And you've met Edward," Eleanor jokes, to a couple of chuckles. "And that poor woman he's trying to squeeze to death over there," she says, indicating the woman with the kind face, "is Fiona, my son Oliver's wife."

Fiona is about my age, with soft features and a maternal glow. I try to remember what Edward told me about her and Oliver.

Fiona is a stay-at-home mom; she and Oliver have three sons and a Portuguese water dog. Oliver took over Edward's responsibilities in the family business alongside Matilda when Edward decided not to take them up.

Fiona rises and offers me an outstretched hand across the huge coffee table, and I shake it thankfully. She gives me an encouraging look; she's clearly run the gauntlet of meeting this family for the first time herself. She feels my pain.

"Marty and Nancy are old family friends," Eleanor continues, pointing over to a cheerful-looking older couple seated near the window, a black dog asleep at their feet.

Nancy gives me a wry smile and raises her glass, with Marty quickly following suit.

"We're not married," Nancy quips with a wink. "Just old. And the dog's his."

"Then there's Stuart there," Eleanor says, directing my gaze to the other side of the room, "my youngest son, and his partner, Lila." My gaze follows Eleanor's and I flat-out stare. Beside Stuart—who appears to be a shorter, thinner, and more irascible version of Edward—sits an incredibly familiar face. I recognize Stuart's girlfriend from glossy magazine adverts, gossip columns, paparazzi pictures, and a notable role in a new action franchise. Stuart's girlfriend is Scandinavian model-turned-actress Lila Erikson.

She looks up from her phone at the mention of her name, her perfect mouth pulling into a friendly albeit slightly tight smile. "Hey-hey, Harry. So nice to meet you," she says with a Nordic accent heavier and deeper than expected. In her lap her phone screen begins flashing up a call. She groans. "I'm so sorry, everyone, it's them again, I really have to take this. So embarrassing." She sighs in apology, shaking her loose blond hair. "Sorry, Harry, it's very rude. It's so great to meet you. I just need to sort out this total *fucking shitshow* of a double booking. My *asshole* agent."

"Li, it's fine," Stuart interjects, jumping on her expletives, "just take the call." I watch as his nervous eyes flit quickly back between his girlfriend and his mother and then he catches me staring, surprised to have pulled my focus. He studies me quickly as beside him Lila slips from the room, then turns back to chug from his glass bottle of Coke as Lila's voice wafts back to us in Swedish from the hallway.

Mrs. Holbeck gives me a contained smile. "Poor Lila, such long hours. What with work and little Milo and her charities it's a wonder she's still standing." It's unclear if this is a compliment or a sugarcoated criticism. "Well, it's just nice to have the whole family together for once," she continues. "We all have such busy lives these days."

As if on cue another member of the Holbeck family ambles in through the dining room doorway, the family resemblance unmistakable. I'd put him in his mid-forties, so I'm momentarily thrown as to who he could be. Too old for a younger brother, too young for a father. Edward is meant to be the eldest at only thirty-eight. The new arrival is a bear of a man, bigger and stockier than Edward, with an imposing footballer's physique.

"There he is. Oliver," Mrs. Holbeck coos. "Oliver, this is Edward's Harriet."

Edward's Harriet. The words are loaded, but again it's hard to tell with what exactly.

Oliver raises an eyebrow in mild surprise as his eyes find mine. I'm not what he expected, clearly, but then neither is he. Oliver Holbeck, the third child, is supposed to be four years younger than Edward but looks half a decade older. Gray peppers his stubble and temples. And then as if in answer to my unspoken question I hear the crescendoing shrieks of children as Oliver and Fiona's three young boys hurtle into the room, drawing up short at the sight of me. Three little sets of eyes join those already on me.

Having three young sons certainly might explain the apparent age differential between Oliver and the rest of the Holbeck siblings, although looking back at Fiona, the same can't really be said of her. Perhaps it's that the Holbeck family business has taken its toll.

"Wonderful to finally meet you, Harriet," Oliver says, his voice deeper than Edward's, with an almost transatlantic, New

Hampshire lilt to it, like Eleanor's. Edward doesn't have that. Perhaps New York beat it out of him. Oliver's greeting sounds genuine, heartfelt. I see something in Edward shift. Oliver must be important to him, his support valued but not taken for granted.

Edward moves to pull his younger brother into a tight bear hug, and Oliver reciprocates, his arms fully enveloping Edward's taller frame. "There he is," Oliver chuckles, the two slapping each other's backs. "Big bro's back."

Watching them it's clear that tonight is as much a reunion for the family as it is an introduction to me. I find myself wondering if Oliver ever begrudged having to take on Edward's mantle, if he wanted a different life or if he cannot believe his luck from one day to the next.

When the brothers pull apart Edward greets the young boys, ruffling his eldest nephew's hair, the boy dodging away and causing the whole group to dart off in different directions.

"Stay close, boys," Oliver booms after them. "No running, no shouting. Stay away from Granddad's study. Dinner in twenty."

"And where is Dad?" Edward asks, turning back to the room in general. Odd to think that anyone could refer to a man like Robert Davison Holbeck as Dad, or Granddad for that matter, but I suppose they have to call him something.

"Call," Matilda responds, absentmindedly twisting her braceleted wrist into a telephone gesture.

"And he shall appear," a resonant voice intones from the doorway. I catch Edward tensing at the sound of it before turning to take in the tall, brooding frame of his father standing, scotch in hand, in the doorway.

I feel my expression freeze in place as I take him in for the first time, a strange sensation fizzling through me. It's undeniable—his questionable past and ethics aside—and as much as I would never admit this to another living soul, there is something overpoweringly attractive about him. I hate myself for thinking it, but there it is. If it looks like a duck and quacks like a duck . . .

Of course I've seen him before in magazines and on newspaper stands, but in the flesh, the resemblance between him and Edward knocks the breath from me. Though clearly older, Robert Holbeck looks almost exactly like the man I've agreed to marry. Edward's looks, his rakish smile, the knowing behind his eyes, are as present in the father as in the son but somehow, unsettlingly, more so. More present, more dangerous, more elusive.

Robert Holbeck's eyes find mine, the deep brown of them eerily similar to eyes I have stared into for over a year, but these eyes are filled with a different history, an unknown past I will almost certainly not be given access to.

I feel the heat rise in my face.

Of all of the reactions I thought I might have on meeting my father-in-law, sexual attraction is not one I would have ever considered being a problem. I suppose I could blame my hormones: I am pregnant after all. If ever there was an excuse. Perhaps R. D. Holbeck is my own personal version of craving a jar of pickles in the middle of the night. If pickles were incredibly powerful billionaires.

Robert releases me from the hold of his gaze, his eyes gliding back to Edward.

"Edward," he says. There's a careful humility to it, an offering not of peace so much as acceptance that some things must be taken as they are in life.

"Dad." Edward nods and I feel an infinitesimal tightening of his hand around mine, the fully grown man beside me thrust unwittingly back into the role of son.

Eleanor deftly breaks the weight of the moment. "R.D., this is Edward's Harriet," she coos.

Edward's Harriet. There it is again.

I watch this new information pass across Robert Holbeck's features as his eyes find mine once more.

He takes me in fully now and I realize I've stopped breathing. I couldn't break his gaze if I wanted to, and for some reason it suddenly seems deeply important that I'm not the one to look away first. Half challenge, half invitation—though to what I do not know.

After a moment the skin around his eyes creases, something amusing. For not backing down I am rewarded with a smile.

One thing is for sure now: I have Robert Holbeck's attention. For better or for worse: he sees me. And I see him.

6

Dinner

The table is laid, twelve crystal glasses gleaming in the candle-light.

On the walls above us hang oil paintings that seem to date back as far as the first Dutch American colonies. The Holbecks' ancestry. No doubt the paintings are priceless, but I wonder how the living Holbecks can stand to have the dead ones staring down at them. Family members long gone, their milky eyes watching while the living make merry, oblivious, or long inured, to their persistent gazes.

At the head of the table Robert is flanked to his right by Nancy and a glistening-eyed Matilda. He clearly appreciates the company of women.

As my eyes play over the other guests, I understand that the family's ranking system is in evidence in tonight's seating plan:

the heart of the Holbeck machine, and its inner workings, made visible. I'm placed as far from the seat of power as it is possible to be, slotted neatly between two other minor plus-ones: Oliver's wife, Fiona, and Stuart's girlfriend of two years, Lila Erikson.

Lila leans in conspiratorially as she unfurls her napkin. "They're creepy, right?" For a second, I'm certain she means our hosts, but then her eyes travel up to the faces hanging silently above us, the gaunt white visages looming from the walls. "I hate them," she chuckles and grabs for her drink. "Bunch of creepy-assed colonists. Oh yeah, and lest we forget, Happy Thanksgiving." I let out a snort of laughter and she clinks her glass of wine with my glass of water. "Cheers."

Across the table Edward throws me a rallying smile. I smile back, grateful to have been placed beside someone I can actually talk to.

"No wine, Ms. Reed?" a voice behind me inquires loudly. The gray-clad butler proffers a decanter that I had seamlessly managed to swerve on its first round of the table. But this guy isn't going to back down quite as easily as the previous server. I weigh my next move.

What would draw less attention: outright turning alcohol down or pouring it and not drinking it?

Lila's interest is piqued by my hesitancy, so I bite the bullet.

"No, no wine, thanks." I give a grateful smile, but the butler doesn't flinch.

"Perhaps you'd care for a white instead? Or a *cocktail*, maybe," he asks, managing to imbue the word *cocktail* with a whole spectrum of negative connotations. I notice a few eyes around the table flit to us with interest.

"No, no thank you. I'll just stick with the water for now. No need to—"

Eleanor chips in now too. "It really is no trouble, Harriet, if you'd like a different drink. Whatever you'd prefer we can get for you. I should have checked beforehand, your drink, of course," she admonishes herself. Now that our hostess is involved conversation drops off around the table, and as Edward goes to speak, I start to babble.

"No, no. I love red wine. Love alcohol in general but I'm just not . . . tonight. Honestly, water is fine. I'm . . . basically . . . I'm not drinking at the moment."

God, now I just sound like an alcoholic.

Stuart must agree because it's his turn to dive in. "Yeah, I'm *not drinking* at the moment either. We unhappy few, we band of brothers." He toasts me with his glass Coke bottle. Great, they all think I'm in AA now.

Matilda leans forward in my defense. "Not quite, Stu. Harry's recovering from a bout of food poisoning. Right, Harry? She was an angel to come to tea with me this week and she's a positive saint to take on a Holbeck Thanksgiving, all things considered. So let's give her a break, shall we?" I watch her words work on the group, their interest in me waning, except for R.D.'s. His eyes fix on me and I catch the ghost of his curious smile again before he breaks the connection.

Heads dip in concentration as the food is served, and intermittent conversation bubbles along. My eyes catch Matilda's and she winks.

After the first course I take the opportunity to swivel in my seat to gently insert myself into Lila and Oliver's conversation about their respective children.

"I don't know how Fiona does it though, Ollie," Lila croons. "Your boys are so independent. Milo is—" She breaks off, throwing a look across to the children's table where her son, Milo, sits with his halo of soft curls. Her child from a previous relationship. "He's sensitive, you know," she continues. "He needs to know I'm around or he goes crazy." She grimaces. "I mean, like, crazy crazy, *all* the time."

"You should talk to Nunu," Oliver says. "She spent some time with Billy before he started preschool. He wouldn't leave Fi's side but now he's fine. Some boys are just that way."

I look over at Billy, the youngest of Oliver and Fiona's boys.

He sits happily playing beside Milo, the Holbeck profile already taking hold of his tiny features.

My gaze flits to the much-feted Nunu, a jolly-looking woman in her fifties. She must have been so young when she nannied Edward and his siblings back in the 1990s. She looks across, feeling all of our eyes on her, and gives a warm smile before signaling for Oliver to come over.

Oliver leaves me with Lila, and I take the opportunity to try to fill in some gaps in my family knowledge.

"Nunu's quite young, right?" I ask, and when Lila raises an amused eyebrow, I can't suppress a giggle. "No, I mean she's much younger than I expected her to be. She was their nanny too, right? Edward, Matilda, Oliver, and Stuart's?"

"No, they had someone else back then," she says with a smile. "But that one left after the whole thing with Bobby," she adds casually.

"The whole thing with Bobby," I echo, trying to remember if Edward ever mentioned a "Bobby" to me.

"Yeah," she says, her tone suddenly sobering. "Can't say I blame her for leaving. You couldn't have paid me enough to stay after that. The whole thing was just—"

Oliver's hand firmly lands on Lila's shoulder, interrupting her. He smiles down at us both. "You're up next, Lila, Nunu will see you now. I put in a good word for Milo. And *apparently*," he says with raised brows, "Milo is already asking if he can stay over tonight with the rest of the boys. Without Mumma."

"No. Oh my God." Lila rises and turns to me with a yelp of excitement. "Hey-hey. Nunu certainly doesn't mess around, does she?"

As Lila glides away, two questions drift in her wake. Who the hell is Bobby? And why have I never heard of him?

7

Billy, Bobby, Strudel, and Port

THURSDAY, NOVEMBER 24

As the second course is taken away, a wave of nausea resurfaces and I calmly make my excuses to head off in search of the nearest bathroom.

Safely installed in a large cream marble bathroom I let my shoulders relax, releasing a tension I had forgotten I was even holding. Nausea temporarily abated, I lean on the basin and inspect myself in the mirror. My makeup is still in place despite my strong expectation of it having completely melted from my face through a combination of hot flashes and social anxiety. My hormones are all over the shop.

I place a hand on my abdomen. *What are you up to in there?* I ask my tiny raspberry-sized passenger. *Whatever it is I need you to stop, just for the next few hours, just till we're in the car home.*

A knock on the door sends my pack of mint gum flying out of my hand and skittering across the immaculate bathroom floor.

"Shit." I sigh, hunkering down to fish it out from behind an oversized potted fig tree. "Just one second."

After dusting myself down I crack the door but there's no one there. Until I look down. Little Billy stares up at me, his expression blank save for two tellingly tearstained eyes.

"Oh, hey Billy," I say, and hearing the uncertainty in my own voice I suddenly remember for the first time in a long time how terrible I am with kids. I never had the benefit of siblings, or babysitting jobs, or friends with kids—absolutely no day-to-day experience to draw from. Which obviously doesn't bode well at all for the future.

Billy must have been looking for his mum and found me instead but decides I'll do for now. He grasps both my legs in a surprisingly robust hug.

"Oh, okay," I say, a hand patting him gently on the head as I check the corridor for literally anyone else. Not a soul in sight. I guess this is up to me. I bend to meet him on his level, his grasp loosening to let me. "Hey, honey. Billy? Look at me, sweetheart."

He looks up, his little angel face tear-blotched and puckered. His tawny hair so like Edward's. God, what a beautiful family. Billy stares at me, his eyes expectant.

"What is it, honey?" I ask him. "Did you hurt yourself?"

Billy shakes his head, suddenly shy, suddenly doubting whether he should have come to me with this. He turns to look back down the hall.

"Did one of the boys do something? Did they upset you?"

Billy pauses and then nods firmly.

"I see," I say, and some unknown reflex makes me gently push the hair from his eyes. "Do you want to tell me what happened?"

He looks back down the hallway again, the sound of adult laughter reaching us from the dining room. Then after a moment, satisfied no one else is coming to help, he nods.

"Uh-huh," he mumbles, feet shuffling.

"What is it, sweetie?"

"The boys. They said I had to sleep in Bobby's room on my own tonight, or I can't play w'them," he manages before the tears slowly return and he buries his face from me once more.

Bobby's room. Again with Bobby.

Billy continues, muffled now into the dampened cotton of his sweater. "I don't like it. I don't want Bobby's room."

This is my chance to find out who Bobby is, I suppose. Decisively I take his tiny hand in mine and squat down beside him. Then face-to-face I calmly say, "Okay. Why don't you show me Bobby's room?"

I flick on the lights and the room bounces into view: An anonymous-looking guest room. The same well-appointed furnishings as the rest of the apartment, nothing that would look out of place in an interior magazine's spread, but there is nothing personal here. Whoever's room this is, or was, it certainly isn't occupied anymore.

So the question is: why does this innocuous room scare Billy?

"It looks nice, don't you think?" I ask the little man in my arms.

Billy surveys the empty room discerningly then turns to me with mild concern. "Yeah, nice. But closet?"

"Oh right, yeah." I forgot kids get scared of wardrobes. "Okay. Let's see," I say and head over to the cupboard to crack the door open. The internal lights click on. It's empty save for six cedarwood hangers, a stack of freshly laundered towels, and a bathrobe.

"Looks like the coast is clear in there, right."

Billy leans into the closet to inspect it further before confirming solemnly, "Yeah, coast all clear, Auntie Harry-ept."

I feel a warmth spread through my chest. *Auntie Harry-ept.*

"Right, then," I say in all seriousness, matching his business-like tone, "I think a sleepover in this room might just be okay after all, mightn't it?"

"But . . . *Bobby*?"

I pause, unsure where to go next before landing on, "Well—I don't see Bobby? Do you?"

Billy looks around worried for a second, then lets out an embarrassed giggle. "Nope."

"Nope is right. So . . ." I say carefully, letting him get down onto his feet, "why don't you go tell the other boys that you don't care where you sleep tonight and if they *do*, then they are just big babies, right?"

Billy finds my joke hilarious. "Big *babies*," he echoes, gratified. "Okay. Okay thanks Auntie Harry-ept," he adds, quickly bolting from the room and disappearing down the hall.

I flick off the lights of Bobby's room, pulling the door closed, and bump directly into a man standing right behind me.

"Jesus Christ!" I gasp, jumping back.

Edward stands bemused and amused in front of me. "Er, sorry? I guess." He grins. "Just wondering where you'd gotten to. Thought you might have made a break for it between courses."

"Who the hell is Bobby?" I demand. Edward's eyebrows rise at the question, then, distracted, his eyes catch someone coming toward us along the corridor. Eleanor.

"There you both are," she calls, her voice merry and alcohol-infused. "Come on, you two lovebirds. Dessert's ready. Marcia made your favorite, Eddie, she'll be heartbroken if you don't have some." She turns on her heels expecting us to follow. "Shall we?"

It's funny she makes no reference to where we are standing, or why. Perhaps this Bobby thing isn't quite the secret I think it is.

I look back up at Edward inquiringly, then whisper, "Bobby. Later, okay?"

He gives me a firm nod. "Okay."

Back in the dining room the warm, flaky pastry of a fourteen-person apple strudel is ceremoniously sliced, the scent of cinnamon and sugar hanging in the air.

"This was Great-Grandma Mitzi's strudel recipe, Harry," Matilda calls down the table. "Marcia, in the kitchen, makes it for us every year. It's Ed's favorite." She grins at him, delicately forking a morsel into her mouth, her eyes oddly locked with his. I watch Edward stare back at her, and though his expression is patient it's obvious there is some family stuff going on here that I do not understand.

"Has Edward told you much about her?" Matilda continues. "Mitzi?" My eyes flash to Edward. I suppose I know an above-average amount about his great-grandmother. Edward smiles back at me encouragingly. "I know Alfred and Mitzi married for love," I hazard. I notice, in my peripheral vision, R. D. Holbeck pulling back from his conversation with Nancy, his focus now on me. "And Edward told me she loved pomegranates!" I add lightly, hoping to God someone will step in.

The corners of R.D.'s mouth curl, and he looks down. "Well, it sounds like you've covered all the key points there, Edward. Well done."

Edward's eyes fly to his father but R.D. has already moved on, reaching now for his wine.

Matilda's voice drags my gaze back to her. "Show us," she demands, waggling her own ring finger. I raise my left hand obligingly into the candlelight and watch Mitzi's garnet glimmer.

"Beautiful," Nancy sighs as Fiona, beside me, takes my hand gently in hers, turning it and sucking in a breath.

"They don't make them like they used to, do they?" She chuckles softly. I realize I've hardly said two words to her since we sat down, so engrossed in conversation has she been with Eleanor. I make a mental note to try harder with Fiona going forward. She seems nice.

"No. They do not," R. D. Holbeck intones. It's clear his meaning extends beyond jewelry. "I think it's time for a port, what do we all think?"

And I can't help but feel that this is code for dinner being over.

"I'm game," Marty concedes.

"Port for anyone who's having it. We're celebrating after all." The butler in gray steps forward as his employer rises from the head of the table. "I'll take mine in the study."

Before turning from the table, Robert lifts his wineglass and waits for the rest of the table to follow suit. "To the happy couple," he booms. "Welcome to our family, Harriet Reed." Eyes flit from family member to family member, giving the distinct impression that Robert doesn't do things like this very often. Stutteringly the assembled diners echo his sentiment before sipping liberally from their glasses.

Edward is first to lower his glass. "Thank you, Dad. We appreciate it, and dinner, so, thank you." He gives a diplomatic smile.

Robert studies him for a moment before replying, "Very good." He smiles. "Very good."

Then Robert turns to me. "Harriet," he says lightly, "would you mind joining me for a port in the study. Ah, no, on second thought, for you a tea perhaps? James?" He gestures to the butler in gray.

All eyes in the room flash to me, and my heart flutters with panic in my chest. If a sinkhole opened up beneath me and took me from this world forever right now, I'd be glad of the quick death.

"The night is young and we have much to discuss, Harriet. Indulge an old man."

I look to Edward for help; I was not warned about this, I had not planned for this. But Edward looks as pale as I feel. No help there.

"Um, sure," I answer, rising from my seat and somehow managing to sound halfway human. "Yes. That would be lovely. Thank you." I throw Edward a bewildered smile.

"Wonderful." Robert grins. "Shall we?"

I gulp back the last of my water, avoiding Edward's no doubt very concerned and concerning expression, and follow one of the most powerful men in America out of the room.

8

The Game Begins

THURSDAY, NOVEMBER 24

"I hope I didn't put you on the spot back there," Robert says as we enter the vast green cavern of his study.

I give a shake of the head though fully aware it's a rhetorical question. He barely acknowledges my presence as I follow him and hungrily absorb as much as I can from this new environment, and this unexpected access to his inner sanctum.

I know I should be nervous; this man, so much more powerful and self-possessed than me, has me on his own ground. And yet I'm not. Well, I am, but not to the extent I should be. Because here's the thing: I have a secret; a warm cozy secret that I hold close to me, like a comforter in situations just like this. No matter what happens here, I know I can handle myself—better than most. I have been through too much to doubt that fact. I know I can do what I need to do when my back is to the wall.

My eyes fly up as the room opens out above us: a mezzanine library. Books line the room, breaking up the obsidian walls, a cursory glance at the shelves revealing everything from thick reference tomes to cutting-edge releases and thin poetry periodicals. Ahead a jewel-toned Persian rug proffers two low club chairs facing each other in front of a crackling fire. The lighting in the room gives a warm glow, and a wooden staircase, spiraling up to the mezzanine, slips into shadows, the covers of the books beyond it indiscernible.

But the thing that stands out the most is the subdued but persistent flashing and flickering coming from above the bookcases where wall-hung plasma screens display a constant rolling stream of live news channel feeds. Each screen a different network, on mute. Newscasters stare down at us, not dissimilar to the oil paintings in the dining room, except these move.

Text scrolls. An oil spill off the coast of Brazil, a Hong Kong billionaire under house arrest, another police shooting, the GDP growth of the Indian economy.

"Take a seat," Robert says, gesturing to one of the club chairs, and I head over to the fire to sit as instructed.

I watch him, this older, more storied Edward, move across the room and push the heavy door of the study closed, eclipsing the sounds of the apartment beyond.

He notices my eyes flit to the screens above. "I like to keep my finger on the pulse," he says, wafting a hand up at them dismissively. "Let's call them the pulse."

I smile at the remark and he turns from me, seemingly at ease with me in his space. Wordlessly he heads across the room to a cabinet beside the spiral staircase and, lifting the lid of a brightly colored box, he pulls something out from within. "Does it bother you?" he asks, without looking over, and I can't tell if he means the silence or the situation. But when he turns, I see that he actually means neither.

He lifts his hand, showing me an unlit cigar.

"It doesn't bother me, no," I answer after a moment. "I've always quite liked the smell if I'm honest."

That smile again. "Well, it is always important to be honest, isn't it? Especially with one's self." There's something in his eyes a little too knowing for comfort. He cuts the cigar end and sets about lighting it. It's only then that I stop to consider the impact his cigar smoke might have on the raspberry-sized fetus growing inside me. But it's too late to turn back now. Embers flare red as the dark tobacco leaves transmute to wavering white ash when he takes a puff and sinks into the armchair opposite mine.

Beyond the flickering screens, in the deep darkness, I make out his desk, a wide monstrous thing lurking in the half-light, its wires, cables, hard drives like tentacles reaching into the shadows.

R.D. leans back in his chair, his eyes cast up to the rich smoke pooling above us. There is a painting above the fireplace. J. L. Holbeck, Edward's great-great-great-grandfather, the man who started it all.

It must be hard to look at him every day, to know that everything in your life is due to the hard work of another man. And no matter how hard you strive, no matter how much you achieve, in your heart you'll always question how much of it was due to you. Hard to be faced with that kind of legacy every day.

But here I am feeling sorry for a billionaire.

I study Robert's features again as he looks up at the screens and feel the strangely familiar ache of excitement I felt the first night I met Edward.

That dangerous fizzle of possibility. A desire to possess, to be possessed. To smell him, feel him, close. I feel a blush rising up my neck and try to shake off the thought. I know it's deeply inappropriate; a sharp twang of guilt pelts me from within for my thoughts. I love Edward, I am here because of Edward, and I know the only reason I am feeling this right now is because the man sitting in front of me reminds me so much of the man I love. But with a thrill of something else.

After a moment he looks back at me. I wonder if he can read my thoughts, if he can feel this strange pull between us too.

Shut up, Harriet.

God, I want him to like me. I've seen pictures of Robert as a young man; I've seen the magazine interview photos of him in the 1980s, lithe and dangerous in Wall Street double-breasted suits. But at sixty-five, his hair silvered, it's clear that right now is his real peak.

There's a gentle knock on the study door.

"Come in, James," Robert calls, breaking the silence. I look away as the butler glides in with our drinks, certain he can read every one of my inappropriate thoughts.

"The Fonseca '84, sir," James says placing the bottle down on the table. "The family has withdrawn to the drawing room, sir."

"Wonderful. Thank you, James," Robert answers absentmindedly, thumbing his cigar.

"Not a problem, sir. Is there anything else I can get you?" James asks, eyeing me as I pour my tea.

"No. That will be all, thank you, James," Robert says, looking up now and noticing James's gaze. "And close the door on your way out," he adds curtly.

As the study door closes, Robert's focus returns to me. "I'll be honest with you, Harriet—having determined, as we have, that we both value honesty, I'll share the truth about my son." He pauses for a moment, taking a swig of his port. "I am sure he's told you; we've had our problems. But I want to be clear about things with you. To be clear *for* you."

"Of course. I appreciate that," I say. "He's told me a little. About previous relationships—I know things have been difficult between you and him."

"Do you?" he asks. "I wonder." That wolfish smile again.

I feel that dark tug of desire again. *Oh, for fuck's sake.* Is it normal to fancy your father-in-law?

No.

But then look at him. That little tell behind his eyes, that world-weary calm, the feeling that at any moment he could switch on me, the tone could change, and a man like him would have the power, the ability, to do almost anything and get away with it. I don't see how that couldn't be both terrifying and intoxicating. Edward has it too, that deep undertow of power, that sense that I may not be good enough, smart enough, quick enough to live in his world.

He studies me, in my silence. "You love him? My son?" I feel a knife twist of guilt at my thoughts, their direction.

"Yes," I answer honestly. "More than anything."

Robert's expression softens. "Be careful of that: 'more than anything,'" he warns. "Never quantify."

"Why?" I ask.

"As the saying goes: If you can measure it, you can manage it. People can rarely be managed." He lets the words settle before continuing with a boyish grin. "Oh, I read your book by the way."

I feel suddenly exposed. The fact that he has read my book puts me firmly on the back foot. Which I imagine was the idea. I'm learning very quickly that Robert likes to play linguistic games. He's testing my boundaries, mapping my character.

"I enjoy a thriller every now and then," he continues with a wry smile. "Fictional horror as a balm for the everyday sort." He takes a long puff on his cigar. "You're good at it. Telling stories. Untangling them." He dips his head at me in congratulations. "It's hard to surprise me . . . but you did," he adds lightly.

I sink into the warmth of the compliment.

"Thank you." I hear my tone veering toward the edge of flirtation. I need to work on my poker face—then again, judging by the reemergence of his grin, perhaps I don't. He's enjoying whatever strange game we're playing as much as I am.

"You liked it, then?" I ask, every nerve in my body alive to his response. "The twist?"

The curl of his lip, the tap of ash into an ashtray, the slow release of rich tobacco smoke.

His eyes level with mine. "I did. Very much. You're clever, very clever, young Harriet, but I suspect you already know that, don't you?" He pauses before adding, "We could certainly use another clever girl in the family."

Girl. I know my feminist hackles should rise but they don't.

There's something in his tone as he says it, something incredibly self-aware, the noun carrying a respect I haven't often heard it imbued with. I think of the women who work for him, with him—perhaps he's come to recognize the no-frills, relentless efficiency of female energy.

He liked my book. I absorb his very particular brand of acceptance, aware that there is a kind of understanding growing between us.

"Thank you," I tell him with genuine gratitude, "that means a lot."

"Coming from *me*?" he asks, amused. Another test. Am I playing the game of elder statesman and grateful young woman? And if I am, am I doing it deliberately?

That smile again. If this isn't flirting it's definitely in the ballpark. So I guess the question is, will I play ball?

"Yes," I say, my eyes on him. "It means a lot—*coming from you.*"

And just like that we both know where we stand. I am game and so is he. Anything could happen.

He nods to himself and raises his port to me in acknowledgment.

It makes sense that he would be this charming in person; people don't tend to get, or stay, in his position without knowing how others tick. But I know how people tick too. After a lifetime of trying to fit in, working people out has proven essential.

I watch him refill his port glass. "We have something in common, you and I," he tells me.

"Aside from Edward. And our love of thrillers?" I quip.

He takes a slow puff of his cigar, watching me. "Indeed, our cups runneth over already. No. We are orphans. You and I both suffered loss at a young age. Your parents died. My parents died."

He's gone straight for my weakest spot, my soft underbelly. He knows. Edward must have mentioned it to his mother, and I know how these things spread. Like wildfire.

And just like that my brain lights up like a Christmas tree with memories I do not want. An upturned car, bodies hanging in the air. Fire and pain. Images press in on me fast and hard. Before and after. Driving down that early-morning road, the chill in the air, the startling, the bracing, my mother's face turning to me, the look in her eyes, the words I never quite heard. Then sound, pain, and darkness. Even here in the Holbecks' penthouse I smell that mix of country air and petrol. After all these years, no matter how far I go, it follows.

"I'm sorry," Robert says, after a moment. "That was unnecessary. I should know better than that. Especially at my age. The past can catch us if we don't see it coming, can't it? I apologize, Harriet."

He really can read me. But then perhaps he speaks from his own experience.

I recall his words. "How did you lose your parents?"

"My mother went first. When I was seven." He breaks off, looking back into the darkness of the room. "She was a good woman. Full of love. Maybe too good. She left a hole when she died; my father lost his way. As I said, one must be careful not to love any one person 'more than anything.' Life is fragile. We both know that. My father was a case in point."

"He killed himself?"

"In a sense, but no. Illness. He put up little fight. It was quick."

"And what happened to you? Afterward?" I ask.

"Alfred and Mitzi Holbeck happened to me. My grandparents took me in. The woman who wore the ring on your finger raised me."

I look down at it, the garnet's arterial red glimmering in the firelight, and I wonder for the first time exactly whose idea it was to give me this ring. Either way Edward must know its significance to his father.

"Was it hard after they died?" I ask, more to hear him speak than to hear the answer I already know.

"It was. And for you? You miss them."

"Yes. I try not to think about them," I say simply. "But they come back. Every day. A tune, a laugh, a memory. Every day."

"Every day," he says almost to himself. "But do you still look for them in crowds?"

My eyes snap to his in surprise. A laugh of recognition. "I do. Do you?"

He nods warmly, leaning in to top up my tea. "Always. Even now, when time has meant that they would be long gone regardless."

I watch him as he pours. To have all this and no one to see it.

"I'm glad Edward found you, Harriet. You're not his usual. But then the woman you ask to marry you never is, is she?" I don't know why, but something about the way he says this unsettles me.

I'm reminded of Edward's exes, and the power Robert has had in the past to decide who is or is not right for him. I remind myself that it is only a quirk of fate that Robert has decided to approve of me. And that approval is conditional.

"I don't know how much he's told you?" he continues. "About our history? About the family."

"Not much, to be honest," I say carefully.

He studies my face for the truth of that and seems to find an answer there. "That's interesting," he says, "very interesting."

He seems to come to a conclusion, leaning forward on an elbow. "He left ThruComm. He wanted to make a go of things on his own. His own way in the world." He leans back now with a nod. "A noble idea, of course, to build a life from scratch. But a family business is a group endeavor. We take from the past and give to the future. We add more and pass it on. Edward is my eldest, the company should be his. But he chose another way." He gives me a wry look. "Now, Harriet, don't misunderstand me. I've made peace with that part of the story. My concern now is for my family. I want him back here. Eleanor wants him back with the family. Matilda spoke with you, I understand. We all want him back, and we think this engagement is a good thing. You're good for him. I see that."

Robert stops speaking and the crackle of the fire fills the space.

I look down at my tea, and I can't help but feel a little disappointed. All of this just to get to Edward.

"You're willing to put up with me because you need *him*," I say, addressing the elephant in the room directly. "That's what this is about?" I ask, gesturing between us.

A chuckle of surprise. "No, no, Harriet," he says, his tone precise, "I did this to see if I was right about you. You are going to be a part of this family so it's very important we understand each other, it's important we both know the facts about who we are. Because you'll have to believe me when I say, I know the facts about you. I'm sure you won't be surprised to hear that you were vetted. Due diligence. All possible concerns noted, flagged."

A slow blossoming of dread at the possibility of what a man like Robert Davison Holbeck could dig up on me. Ghosted boyfriends, broken promises, weakness. But I know he can't know the worst—no one can—because I was alone the day my parents died. Only I know the things that happened that day.

He knows the shifts and ebbs of my life, the everyday missteps and the mistakes of youth. Things that do not touch the sides of what it is possible to truly regret.

"You're everything I hoped you would be, Harriet," he says, then gestures between us. "*This* is not about Edward. This is about us. If I lose a son in all this, I hope at least that I might gain a daughter."

9

A Novel Idea

THURSDAY, NOVEMBER 24

As we rise to rejoin the family, he gestures for me to wait, heading back past the flickering television screens into the darkness where his desk lies. He flicks on a green desk lamp and slides open a drawer.

The rattle of brittle plastic on plastic, the very particular sound of a cassette tape in its case. The lamplight clicks off and Robert wanders back to me.

"Now, as we know, we have several things in common, Harriet." He smirks, leaning against the arm of the nearest club chair. "I wasn't sure about sharing this. But I have a good feeling about you, and from what I've seen I'm almost certain you can handle a challenge." He looks suddenly younger, enlivened by whatever is about to happen.

He reveals what rests in his hands. It's a relic from before my

time: a tiny little cassette in a miniature case. He lets out an invol-
untary laugh as he catches my puzzled expression, his face more
handsome than ever.

"It's a Dictaphone tape, Harriet, not a carrier pigeon. Don't
look so baffled or I'll start to feel my age."

His ease with me is almost as intoxicating as whatever the hell
he's up to right now.

"What's on it?" I ask.

He holds my gaze, danger crackling in the space between us.

"I'd like your advice, Harriet. Your expertise—shall we
say—on it," he says, tapping the tiny tape, his expression hard to
read for a moment before he cracks an uncharacteristically sheepish smile. "Let's call it an idea for a novel, maybe. It's not a book,
yet, but perhaps it's the bones of one." He rattles the case, the
bones of Robert Holbeck's story. "It's a start, to something," he
continues. "Perhaps we'll find out the story I have to tell together." He looks at me, and I catch the heady glimpse of an offer.

Robert Holbeck has written a story. Or at least recorded one.
His voice, his words, on tape. I shiver with excitement at the
thought of all that potential.

I watch him turn the tiny tape in his hands absentmindedly
and wonder if it's fiction or not. Because whatever is on that tape
could be of interest to a lot of people. I can only imagine what a
publisher would pay for it, given the author. Given its possible
content.

"You wrote a book?" I ask carefully, then quickly correct myself. "You recorded one?"

He nods, amused by my clear interest.

"What's it about?" I ask.

"Well, now, that would give the game away wouldn't it," he
replies breezily. "Let's call it a thriller, shall we?" Then after a
pause, "It's definitely in your wheelhouse."

This isn't the first time I've been asked to look at someone's
idea for a thriller. Friends, acquaintances, taxi drivers, baristas,
plumbers, you name it—as soon as people know you write, they
want to tell you their story. Everyone's got a book in them, as the

saying goes. Though sometimes that's probably where it should stay.

Though something tells me Robert Holbeck's story might be worth a read.

"Why a thriller?"

He casts his eyes up at the flickering screens, stories upon stories feeding through to us in silence. "I like their mechanics, their intricacy. But in the end, all is explained." He shakes his head, lost in thought, and finally looks back at me. "That kind of clarity, it's so rare we find it in life."

"I see," I say, then echo his words from earlier. " 'Fictional horror as a balm for the everyday sort'?"

He raises an eyebrow, amused. "Quite. One must be careful of what one says around writers, mustn't one? Or risk being remembered a little too accurately."

"You have nothing to worry about, Robert," I reassure him, my tone soft. "I could never fully do you justice if I tried."

He rises then, closing the space between us, a panic instantly flexing within me. And before I know it, he's close enough to touch. The warmth of him is tangible, and then I feel his warm hand take mine, pick up the scent of expensive soap and cigars. He folds his tape into my palm, nothing more, then steps away. "I would appreciate it if you kept this between us. At least until I know what you think?"

I nod almost reflexively.

Adam offering Eve an apple, a small, brittle plastic apple. And there's nothing I can do but accept it.

10

Nobody Puts Bobby in the Corner

11:43 P.M.

THURSDAY, NOVEMBER 24

In the back of the car, Edward's silent presence beside me, I watch New York glide past the window as I replay the events of the evening in my mind.

"What did you talk about?" he asks, finally, with a commendable lightness. The question must have been burning a hole in his thoughts since I followed Robert out of that dining room. I pause before replying because, the truth is, I've been trying to figure that out myself since I left Robert Holbeck's study.

"Well, we spoke about writing, how he lost his parents—and he spoke about you." I say this in a very particular order.

"Wait, he told you about his parents?" Edward repeats, surprised.

I nod and he raises an eyebrow, incredulous. "Right. Okay.

Why? He never talks about them. In what context did he talk about *them*?"

There's an edge in his tone that I don't quite like, a glimmer of derision, and it's my turn to look incredulous. "In the context of what he and I have in common, Ed. His parents died young; my parents died young. Remember? He was trying to find common ground with me."

Edward considers this for a moment before responding, "I see. Common ground. And he managed to find some." It's the first time I've seen Edward be genuinely skeptical of someone's motives. "He didn't mention anything else—about his parents, or our family?"

It's an odd thing to say.

Suddenly I remember Bobby, the intensity of the rest of the evening having overshadowed him until now.

"Talking of family, who the hell is Bobby, Ed? Because I get the distinct feeling I could have used that information tonight or, I'm guessing, at some point over the last year! Am I supposed to know who he is? Everyone else there tonight seemed to."

"My father mentioned Bobby?" Edward asks, suddenly direct.

"No? Lila did. And then your nephew Billy seemed to know all about him too, and he's a child."

"Billy talked about Bobby?" he echoes, and there's an odd timbre to his voice.

"Yeah, the older boys were scaring him with stories."

"Jesus," Edward breathes, rubbing his eyes. A weariness seems to overtake him, but looking at me he senses he really needs to start talking.

"This is not how I would have done this . . ." he continues, his voice trailing off to such an extent that I can suddenly see where this story is going. Bobby is dead.

In the silence that follows I give Edward's hand a squeeze to let him know I am here for him, no matter what. After a moment he squeezes back, straightening in his seat.

"I should have told you this before. Someone was bound to mention him eventually but I've always found remembering so much more unhelpful than forgetting." He looks away from me, eyes glistening in the passing streetlights.

"I think I really need you to remember for me at this point, honey," I nudge gently, my tone sensitive but clear.

"Yeah. So." His features scrunch with discomfort. "I find it hard to talk about growing up. The tough bits, whatever," he says, finding the words as he speaks them. "I mean, people like us, we've hardly had it hard. What goes wrong is easy to box up and store. There's an expectation we won't dwell."

"Who was Bobby, Ed?" I repeat.

"My brother. Our brother."

I study Edward's face for the truth of these words. "You had another brother?"

"Older. Oldest," he clarifies, and the significance of this doesn't pass me by.

"He was next in line, before you," I say piecing things together. "How the hell do I not know this, Ed?" I ask as gently as I can, because this is definitely the kind of information fiancés should be sharing with each other.

Edward grimaces, but my thoughts are gathering speed. "Wait, Ed, *seriously,* how do I not know about this? I mean, there's not even anything about this online. Nothing anywhere about another Holbeck son. I would have seen it. There's no mention of a *Bobby* at all."

"I know," he says, almost to himself, trying to wrap his head around the fact that he will have to explain a lot more than he would like to. "That's deliberate. Not my choice. It was kept out of the papers, the press. For the family, insurance, or investors, I don't know. I was eighteen when it happened, I did what I was told. We all did. The investigation went through all the proper channels, then disappeared. Press embargo. Favors called in; deals made. Things were easier to control back then, pre-internet craze, before everyone filmed everything, before everyone had a platform; it was easier to make things fade away."

I shiver and pull my cashmere coat tighter around me. I know how easy it was for things to disappear back when we were kids.

I doubt I would be sitting beside Edward now if that weren't the case. The details of what happened the day my parents died were only a byline in the local papers, columns long pulped, facts forgotten by all except those involved.

"Bobby was twenty, a junior, at Columbia," he continues, trying to keep his voice in check. "He got into Yale too," he says with an unexpected chuckle, "but Columbia was closer to the New York apartment, and he wanted to stay close for Marcia's dinners. That's the kind of guy he was. He used to drive back to see us too, at The Hydes on weekends. Always family first." He breaks off.

"You were eighteen when it happened?" I ask.

"Yeah. Matilda was sixteen, Ollie fourteen, and Stuart must have been, what, twelve? It messed with him the most, I think. Bobby loved Stu. He was a cute kid." He looks at me, his eyes full of regret. "We don't talk about it to each other, so it surprises me that Billy knew, that Lila was talking about it. After Bobby died, our parents sent us to see separate therapists. A therapist for each of us. I think they were scared we'd cross-contaminate, or something, if we all went together. Or maybe that's how therapy works for kids, I don't know. We just stopped speaking about him with one another after that. We had designated people to talk to and talking about it at home only made Mom cry so—it was easier to box it up and time just passed. The years passed and it became the way we did things."

"How did he die?" I ask as delicately as I can, still reeling from the knowledge that Edward could keep such a formative part of his life from me for so long. I push from my mind the thought that I am guilty of doing just the same, because that is, of course, different. "Did he get sick?"

"He was healthy, thriving, playing varsity, grades impeccable; they always were," he answers, eyes cast out at the city rolling by. "But little things started to change. He switched from economics to law. In retrospect there were signs. He became a little snappy, short-tempered—that wasn't like him. Things between him and Dad became difficult; the pressure Bobby had on him to be the best, to toe the line. An *A* student, popular, the guy who does it all and makes it look easy. Always cheerful, always thinking of others. We didn't know until it was too late. The autopsy found traces of meds—we knew about the pain medication, an old football injury; that wasn't the problem, but it had mixed with something else. He'd been cramming his work between football practices, on weekends, whenever he could fit in the time. It was just Adderall or something similar but the drugs interacted. That's what they call it when two drugs mix and poison you without you even realizing. *Interaction.* All those tiny shifts in personality, his sudden fear that it would all slip through his fingers, the anxiety, insomnia, and finally . . . a seizure. No one saw it coming. He wouldn't have realized himself, why he suddenly felt the way he did. Why everything was becoming so hard for him. He must have thought he'd just reached his limit. I can't imagine how scared he must have been in the days before it happened."

Edward's words sink in, Bobby's death infuriatingly preventable. Mixed meds. A simple mistake that could have so easily been avoided, and for the Holbecks to know *that,* how arbitrary and preventable the loss of their son and brother was. It's realizations like that that can change a person.

I should know; what happened to me at eleven changed who I am.

"Edward, I love you, but at any point over the last year could you not have told me this? We've discussed my family, their deaths, multiple times. Did you not even think to share this with me then?" I can't help but be unsettled by this fact.

"I'm sorry," he says, fully aware of the inadequacy of the apology. "I know. I should have. I'm an idiot and I took the coward's way out. I don't know what I thought would happen, that it would just disappear? I mean, it's not as if no one was ever going to mention Bobby."

Guilt seeps in through the tiny breach opened in our relationship and fills me. I have not told him everything about my childhood. In the same way he kept this from me, I still keep my biggest secret from him. But that is for the best.

"Your father didn't mention Bobby," I say, a question implicit in the statement. I can't help wondering if the family doesn't talk about Bobby because they feel culpable—for applying too much pressure, for not noticing until it was too late.

"We really don't talk about it, I promise you. It isn't just you. I should have told you. Please don't think that I price my own loss higher than yours. I just, I guess when he left, the burden passed on to me. I try not to think about the bad places things can go."

Edward studies me for a moment. "Did you like him? My father?" Edward asks.

"I did," I answer honestly. After a moment I add, "I think I passed whatever test that was."

Edward laughs, and his eyes catch mine in the pooling light of streetlamps as we weave on through the streets. "Of course you did," he says, his tone changing as he observes me.

They say sex and grief are inextricably linked; I feel the shift between us.

He takes my cheek in his hand, almost appraisingly, then softly brushes a thumb over my lip. "How could you not. You're a very unique individual," he whispers with an oddly familiar tone and suddenly I'm back in Robert's study, the air thick with cigar smoke and dangerous ambiguity. I try to block Edward's father from my thoughts but in my mind father and son have become mixed; they morph seamlessly.

I feel Edward's lips on mine, but Robert is there too. I let them happen, the thoughts, even though I know I shouldn't. I know the warm ache rising inside me is for both of them, and it is tinged with danger and a bitter twist of guilt. It feels wrong, but by God do I want it.

They say your sex drive can go wild during pregnancy. That must be it. A chemical reaction, nothing to do with me, or with my character.

As Edward pulls me close, I become aware of the scent of Robert's tobacco on me, in my hair, on my clothes. I open my eyes and there is Edward, Robert thirty years younger. I bury my hand in his still-dark hair, my body pressing into his, as I desperately try to separate the man I am thinking about from the man I am kissing. The hard ridges of Robert's tape cassette dig into the skin of my upper thigh through the velvet of my jumpsuit, less than an inch from my silk underwear. I wonder if I should pull away and stop this before it goes any further. But I do not.

As Edward's lips travel to my neck, my gaze flutters to the Holbecks' driver, a thick sheet of glass dividing us. His eyes are glued to the road, oblivious.

Back in the apartment, hours later, I sit on the edge of the bathtub, my feet cold against the tiles. I can't sleep but it's not morning sickness this time; it's everything else.

Bobby, Edward, and Robert Holbeck himself.

I tap Bobby's name into the search bar of my phone. The apartment is silent around me, Edward fast asleep back in our bed.

The search results load but to my surprise have autocorrected to *Robert Holbeck*. For a second I'm baffled, but then it clicks and I kick myself for being so stupid.

Bobby and Robert have the same name. Father and firstborn son. The weight of that tradition hits me afresh as I stare at the screen. Bobby never really even had his own name.

I scroll past the autocorrected business articles and op-ed pieces on Robert Davison Holbeck's empire, its reach, its impact. Google images of Robert's roguishly handsome face slip past and I try to squash the bizarre mixture of feelings they give me, shame, desire, and anger at myself.

I don't locate what I'm looking for until the third page of the search results. There is a straightforward, no-frills obituary in *The New York Times*.

Robert Alfred "Bobby" Holbeck, aged 20, died on October 18, 2002, at Mount Sinai Hospital, New York, after therapeutic complications. Born on January 3, 1982, to business magnate, investor and philanthropist R. D. Holbeck and his wife, Eleanor Belinda Holbeck, a former model and Goodwill ambassador. Robert was in his third year as an undergraduate at Columbia University in the city of New York, studying law. He was a bright student, a valued member of the undergraduate community, and a highly skilled young athlete. He will be greatly missed by all who knew him and his family kindly ask for privacy, and the space to grieve, during this difficult time.

A memorial service will take place on November 18 at St. Paul's Chapel on Columbia's Morningside Heights campus for those who wish to pay their respects.

I notice the date of Bobby's memorial service. The anniversary of it would have been last week, just three days before Edward proposed to me. I can't help but wonder if thoughts of Bobby somehow influenced Edward's decision to ask me. A sense of carpe diem perhaps.

I look down at the glimmering jewel on my finger. Did he give me this ring out of love or out of fear that he might end up like Bobby? That his family might slowly push him to the edge?

I skim the obituary again, shuddering at the strangely bureaucratic language used to describe his death. *Therapeutic complications.*

There is precious little else about Bobby online. Edward was right, the Holbecks really did manage to keep Bobby off the internet. A year after 9/11, I guess the city, the world, had bigger fish to fry. Easy to lose one accidental death in the abundance of human tragedy around that time.

I know from writing research how search results can be made to disappear; the EU has its own online right-to-be-forgotten law. Anyone can request that their personal information be removed from search results. You just have to prove it is more damaging to the people involved for it to remain in the public sphere than it is beneficial to the public for the information to be available.

The US doesn't have a similar law yet, but there is legal precedent. I'm sure the Holbecks could avail themselves of that fact.

Matilda rearranged my work life in under thirty minutes. Given a long enough time frame, I'm sure that for people like them, anything is possible.

Robert must have gone to extraordinary lengths to protect his family after what happened to Bobby. I feel that odd ache again and push the feeling away angrily. But it's not just for Robert, it's for all of them, the family, their strange history, and the aura surrounding them. They are utterly terrifying and bewitching.

The tape Robert gave me is safely nestled in my bedside drawer—a glow blossoms in my chest at the thought of it. I have been entrusted with something special. If I had something to play it on, I would play the whole thing now, but I don't.

In spite of the extremely early hour, I suddenly have a desperate urge to write, a desire I haven't felt in months. I pad swiftly through the apartment to my study, ease myself into my writing chair, and flip open my laptop. Through the window New York twinkles and I get the thrill that every early riser gets, of being the first to live the new day.

I open a fresh document and the words just come. A new story. The story of an intoxicating family with a secret.

11

The Man in the Carriage

FRIDAY, NOVEMBER 25

Dawn breaks across the city skyline, pinks and apricots giving way to crisp azure as I close my laptop. I have three new chapters. I am back. Robert and the Holbecks have reignited the fire inside me.

I let the sun warm my face as I remember with an illicit thrill that Robert's tape is waiting for me, like an early Christmas present demanding to be unwrapped. The sooner I can find something to play it on, the better.

In the kitchen I make a plump stack of silver-dollar pancakes with streaky bacon and wait for Edward to emerge from the bedroom. I know I should tell him about the tape, about the conversation with his father last night, but selfishly I want to hear what's on it first. That, and I promised Robert I would keep it between us, for now.

When Edward finally enters the kitchen, bleary-eyed and hungover, my desire for total honesty has thankfully passed.

Once I'm showered and dressed, I slip Robert's tape into my pocket. I need to do a little research. If I want something to play the miniature cassette, I'm going to need to find a specialty store.

As I head out the door, Edward kisses me goodbye, a portrait of hungover shame. "Thank you for breakfast. You're too good to me," he says with a shake of his head. "And listen, I'm sorry again about last night. I should have prepared you better. I should have told you about . . . I'm sorry if you felt thrown in at the deep end."

"It's okay. It's always weird meeting someone else's family. Probably good I didn't know about Bobby. It would have been another thing on my mind."

He takes my hand across the table. "How did I get so lucky with you?"

I feign remembrance of our first meeting. "I think you picked me off from the herd while I was trapped. That sound about right?" I ask with a grin, the hard plastic angles of R.D.'s cassette tape digging into my thigh with almost anthropomorphic insistence.

Out on the blustery streets of Manhattan I check my route again before heading down a set of subway steps. The temperature has dropped in the city in spite of the cobalt-blue sky, my fingers already red and numbed as I swipe my MetroCard. I was warned about New York winters; they sneak up on you.

After a little googling, I managed to find a secondhand electrical store down in the Financial District. The store specializes in used audio and recording equipment, so if I can get my hands on a Dictaphone, I could be listening to Robert Holbeck's story before the day is out. I would be lying if I said the idea of that alone wasn't enough to propel me across town.

The tiny tape Robert handed me last night is an Olympus XH15 microcassette, placing its time of manufacture firmly in the late 1990s. According to the internet, I need a similar micro-cassette recorder to listen to it.

Although the tape is old, it's impossible to know when he recorded it. I get a jolt of excitement at the thought of hearing a younger Robert's voice, his words coming to me directly from the past. I wonder what the tape will tell me about his life, his family, his children.

As every writer knows, even if a story is pure fiction, there are truths hidden in there—about the writer, about the time it was written—that are incontrovertible. I get a now familiar shiver of guilt as I hop through the doors of the subway carriage and slide into one of its glossy plastic seats. I shouldn't be this excited about hearing Edward's father's voice.

But thoughts are just that: thoughts. It's impossible to police them, and as long as they stay just thoughts, I have no reason to feel guilty—do I?

I put this odd little infatuation down to two very simple things: early-pregnancy hormones and novelty. I haven't had access to Edward's family until now and I'm getting carried away. This mild obsession with Robert is just an obsession with everything to do with that family, with Edward's life before me, as shrouded in mystery and exoticism as it is.

I'm no psychoanalyst, but I'd say there's definitely some orphan/daddy stuff thrown in there too for good measure. But fantasies are fantasies, and I haven't actually done anything wrong.

I relax back into my seat, my eyes flitting over the packed subway carriage. A sleeping girl with headphones on catches my attention, her face so peaceful as the subway rattles on around her. I used to be able to do that back in London, sleep on the Underground, but I don't think I ever could here. Then, breaking the tranquility of the moment, I notice a man beyond the sleeping girl staring at me.

He isn't looking at the girl; he's looking directly at me. As soon as I catch his eyes, he stands and calmly slips deeper into the busy train car, as if caught. As if I knew him or he knew me.

I repress a sudden urge to jump up and follow him, to confront him. Oddly, I can't help but feel this has something to do with the Holbecks. The knowledge of Robert's tape and what might be on it is burning in my mind.

The train doors slam open and a fresh batch of travelers bustle on, replacing those that disembark. I watch the crowded platform beyond, hoping to catch a glimpse of him disappearing, but he is nowhere to be seen.

I run his appearance back through my mind. White, mid-forties, short brown hair, dark trousers, dark sweater, nondescript jacket, and a dark baseball cap. All deliberately unassuming.

Before I can stop myself, I am up on my feet and making my way farther into the car, in the direction he went. I dodge through the packed carriage as it shudders on, my nerves tightening into a ball in my throat. I know how irrational I am being right now. I have no logical reason to be doing what I am doing. I'm just following an instinct.

Then, just as that instinct begins to wane, a woman ahead of me shifts position and I see through to him in the next car. The baseball cap, that same oddly calm energy. His eyes meet mine, and I see a flash of concern.

The carriage doors behind me clatter open at the next stop. Another passenger pushes roughly past me, my focus momentarily breaking as my bag is knocked from my shoulder onto the carriage floor, its contents scattering chaotically. Keys, wallet, phone, and everything else, suddenly tumbled between the legs of strangers.

I dip, frantic to gather what I can as more passengers surge on and off the train past me, jostling my loose possessions. But as I squat to gather them, Robert's tape slips from my pocket and ricochets away from me in the melee. I watch it skitter across the carriage floor, wedging itself precariously in the rubber gap between the closing doors and the carriage floor. I lunge toward it to stop it from slipping out onto the tracks below, but when I reach it it's thankfully stuck solid in the closed door, until I give it a good yank and free it still in one piece. I deposit it safely into the pocket of my coat, much to the interest of everyone watching.

When I rise and look back toward the next carriage, the man in the black baseball cap is gone.

12

MH Electricals

FRIDAY, NOVEMBER 25

"We got it, but you gotta wait—few hours, maybe," the short, animated electrical store worker tells me with a little more vehemence than my question really warranted.

"No, no, that's fine. I don't mind waiting," I lie politely. Because, of course, there is a rush. I need to listen to Robert's tape *now,* this very minute. I need to know what's on it.

I watch the short man tap through his computer system searching for what I need as my mind wanders back to the incident on the subway. The more I replay it, the less sure I am that the man in the other carriage was the same man after all. Had he been wearing the same black cap, or had his been a blue one? I get a twinge of concern at the direction of my thoughts; I've been on the lookout for this very feeling since I packed up my things and moved here from London four months ago.

Throughout my twenties I had recurrent bouts of PTSD, from the trauma I experienced the day my parents died. Major life overhauls always seem to trigger them: a job loss, a breakup, change. These periods are marked by hypervigilance, paranoia, familiar faces seen in crowds, with all the physical symptoms of panic though without the actual feeling of being panicked. But I haven't felt anything like that in years. The pregnancy could be to blame for what happened earlier, or this sudden and intense introduction to my new family.

I knew change would have consequences, and besides, a brief google on the walk here from the subway station told me that twenty percent of pregnant women experience anxiety and paranoia at some point during their pregnancy anyway.

"So you definitely have something I can use?" I ask, refocusing. I notice the store worker's name tag: SYLVESTER.

His brow creases, followed quickly by a pained expression at the computer screen. After a moment he calls out to the back room: "Marv? *Marv,* you got an Olympus? Ready now? Microcassette." Marv and Sylvester.

Marv's voice comes back throaty and loud. "What model?"

Sylvester looks back to me and—finding no help there—answers for me. "Er, Pearlcorder? Or whatever you got."

A pause before Marv's gruff voice rejoins, "Yep. Got a compact. Spruce it up in an hour."

Sylvester lifts an eyebrow in my direction. "Compact sound good? You happy with that?"

I pause, with absolutely no idea. "Will it play the tape?"

"Sure," he says, shrugging.

It suddenly occurs to me that Robert could have just loaned me one of these players, but chose not to. This is part of the test, no doubt—the thrill of the chase. And I can't say it isn't working. I need to listen to what's on that tape more than ever.

Sylvester pulls a calculator from his overall pocket and tots up some unknown figures. "Okay, for the wait I'll do you a deal. Fifteen percent sweetener. So . . . let's just call it . . ." He sucks his teeth. "How does a hundred and sixty dollars sound?"

"A hundred and sixty dollars?" I repeat with slight disbelief, though I had no idea how much an old Dictaphone would cost in the first place.

Sylvester, misreading my signals, comes back hard and fast with an amendment. "Okay, okay: one forty, final offer."

None the wiser, I agree. I hand over my credit card and settle into the idea that I will be hearing Robert's voice in just over an hour.

13

A Word to the Wise

Safely cocooned in an end-of-aisle subway seat, coat tight and scarf pulled high, I slip my new gadget from its MH Electricals bag. It's a relic from another time. I notice a few interested glances flit my way as I prize open its anachronistic wire band headphones and slide the red foam earpieces over the surface of my ears. It's crazy to think this is how people used to listen to music, the foam pieces barely balancing over my earholes let alone covering them, and yet I feel an ache of nostalgia for a simpler time. A time before me, before upgrades and updates and digitization. I tuck the plastic bag away and inspect the device.

Sylvester gave me a brief tutorial in the store but there's precious little that can go wrong with the player. *Unless*—and I have been resoundingly warned by both Marv and Sylvester—unless I accidentally hit RECORD/PLAY instead of PLAY; the buttons are tiny and right next to each other. If I do that, then I'll record over the tape, erasing its contents.

But that will not be happening, because unlike Marv and Sylvester, I do not have giant bear hands. And now that I've been forewarned, I am forearmed. Robert's tape is safe with me.

I fish the cassette from my pocket, open the player, and slide the tape in. It shuts with a satisfying click.

I press PLAY and the machine responds with another gratifying clunk, then a low fizz and an ambient crackle as sound bursts to life in my ears. I brace myself for Robert's voice.

Through the headphones, I pick up the distant muffle of speaking, then I distinguish the low rumble of fabric rubbing on the mic, as if this were recording in someone's pocket.

It could be the murmurs of a private conversation or something already badly recorded over. I spin the volume dial up in the hope of hearing more, but the words remain indistinct. And then I get the odd feeling that I am listening to something I shouldn't be.

There's a chance Robert might have given me the wrong tape. He retrieved it in the half-light, after all.

I consider turning it off but suddenly the quality of sound changes in my headphones; the muffling lifts. I strain to hear more, sliding the volume up to its highest, and then I hear it. The sound of breathing first, and then, in earsplitting volume, the unmistakable voice of Robert Holbeck.

Reflexively I yank the headphones from my ears with a yelp. In front of me an elderly woman is staring directly at me angrily, her face slack with age, her expression unambiguous. "What are you, deaf?" she shouts, her tone implying she knows I'm not. "You gonna answer it? Or we all gotta put up with it?" she spits, jutting a bony finger toward my bag, and I realize what the hell she is talking about. My phone is ringing, loud and persistent in the car.

"Oh, er, thank you," I manage, and she shrugs dismissively as I fumble the offending article from my bag and answer it.

"Sorry, yes, hello?"

"Oh hi, Harriet. Is this a bad time? It's Amy at Grenville Sinclair. Is everything okay?"

I straighten in my subway seat. It's my publisher. Again. I dread to think of what could be sparking this second call in a week.

"Amy, no, no, I'm free. What can I do for you?"

I look down at the Olympus microcassette player on my lap. Through its small window I watch the reels of the tape continuing to turn. It's still playing. *Shit.* I clunk down the STOP button and then the REWIND and watch the reels reverse their movement.

"Oh, fantastic. Wonderful," she says with relief. "I'm so glad I caught you. I tried you on your home phone but there was no answer. My mistake. I thought I recalled you once mentioning in an interview that you write from home. Where are you writing these days? It sounds busy there. Do you write out and about?" Her tone is friendly and conversational but the unspoken upshot of the call is that we both know I am not writing right now. And I should be. My deadline has passed and I am under contract.

"No, actually, I'm just out doing a little research," I lie. And yet considering the new direction my novel has taken, perhaps calling Robert's tape "research" isn't such a stretch.

"Oh, fascinating. Can you tell me more, or is it all still bubbling away?" she asks.

"Bubbling, yeah," I say, floundering. "Listen, Amy, I am so sorry about what happened the other day. I think wires got crossed and—"

"Not a problem at all, Harriet. I totally understand the situation. And your agent, Louisa, has emailed about your extension request, which is actually why I'm calling."

"Oh, great," I respond optimistically, though something in the change of her tone makes me realize this is not a good call.

"Yes, so Louisa mentioned you're almost there with this draft. More than two-thirds. Now, you know how much Grenville Sinclair loves you; we even looked at pushing publication dates. But the thing is, not much more can be done at this end. We're in a bind. I know this is a lot to throw at you, but we're really going to need that manuscript by the second week of December."

I swallow hard, my mouth suddenly arid. "The second week? As in . . . ?"

"Two weeks? Is that doable?" Her voice is a little crisper now, a little more businesslike. "It sounds like you're nearly there anyway, right?"

"Right," I lie. I have fifty thousand words of a ninety-thousand-word novel and last night I entirely reworked the plot.

Two weeks to write forty thousand words and pull the whole thing together. I feel my pulse skyrocket but force myself to remain calm. This isn't the moon landing. It's a curveball, for sure, but it's doable. It's a high daily word count, but I've managed it before. After all, I got seventy-five hundred done last night alone. I seem to be back in the game, which is the most important thing.

"Okay. Okay. I can do the eleventh. That is not a problem. Thank you for letting me know, Amy."

After I hang up, my eyes drop to the cassette player on my lap. I definitely do not have time for this now. I need to be working all day, every day, until December 11. No interruptions, no distractions. I click off the cassette player's power, carefully wrap the headphone cord around it, and open my iPhone Notes app.

Robert will have to wait. All the Holbecks will have to wait. Though judging by their previous track record, that doesn't seem like something they're used to doing.

14

Red Rag to a Bull

FRIDAY, NOVEMBER 25–TUESDAY, DECEMBER 6

It turns out, as predicted, the Holbecks don't take kindly to other people's commitments.

The first call comes that evening. As I hole up in my study with ten pages already under my belt and a half-eaten sandwich at my elbow, Edward pokes a tentative head around the door. He knows where things stand with the book and what I need to do in order to get over the line. He lifts the phone muffled in his hands apologetically.

"I know you're right in the middle of it. I told her. She knows. But *my mother* wants a word," he says, his face sheepish. Something about Edward plunged into the role of put-upon son makes me laugh—though I doubt I'd find any of this quite so amusing if my word count weren't as high as it already is this evening.

"Yeah, it's fine. I can speak to her. I might stop for the night now anyway," I say, taking the phone from him. "What's it about?" I ask before raising it to my ear.

He shrugs. "Won't tell me."

I twitch an eyebrow in interest, and he smirks, slipping out of the room, leaving me to find out.

"Hi, Eleanor, it's Harriet. Everything okay?"

"Oh, hello, darling. Now, listen, Edward has explained the situation. You're a Trojan; good for you. And I'll be out of your hair imminently. I just want to get your advice on something. Gauge your thoughts really. Robert and I, of course, want you *both* over for Christmas this year, but as you're aware it's a delicate topic with Edward. I don't want to cause a fuss, scare him off, so I thought I'd hold off asking him at all if you thought it was perhaps too soon . . . for him?"

This is not the conversation I was expecting. "Um, I—"

"You see, last Christmas was the first we all spent apart," she blusters on. "We tend to cluster together at The Hydes most holidays. But of course Edward was in London with you last Christmas and everything was a bit fraught between us, as you know. The whole family comes to us usually. It's very festive. We'd love to get back to the way things were, you understand."

I think she is inviting me over for Christmas. But it's hard to be sure.

The idea of it is terrifying and thrilling in equal measure. A chance to look inside The Hydes, a chance to study Edward's family in its natural habitat and absorb their strange magic free from constraint. But in order to do that, I would actually need to *spend* Christmas with them.

"Um, well, it sounds lovely, Eleanor. I really appreciate the offer, and I'd personally love to, but I really don't know how Edward would take to that idea at the moment. Or, to be honest, how he'd take to you asking me the question in the first place," I say gently, my voice lowered in spite of the fact I can hear Edward pottering around in the kitchen.

"I see," she says, circumspectly. "Noted. Well, in that case, perhaps we just need a little more time to ease him into the idea. Softly, softly, catchee monkey, as they say." She sighs, though a smile is evident in her voice. I can't help but relish her old-world familiarity with me given the fact we've only met once. "Well, thank you for your honesty, my dear. We'll give it a little more time perhaps." She pivots. "Now, listen, Edward told me about your situation with Grenville Sinclair. Is there anything the family can do to help—?"

"No!" I blurt, but quickly recover myself. "No, it's all good. Thank you, Eleanor. It's actually very motivating, a hard deadline. I've never been so prolific," I add lightly.

"Oh, that's so good to hear. But you must take care of yourself, Harry dear. You must be exhausted with the house, and your work."

The question blindsides me to the extent that I find I don't really understand it. "The house?"

"Running the house and working full-time," she clarifies.

"Oh, well, it's just an apartment really. And we don't make much mess, so—"

"Yes, Edward mentioned you hadn't managed to find a suitable housekeeper in town yet? You know, I'm not surprised. I know it can be a real nightmare when you first move to the city. People hoard the good ones."

I find myself once again lost for words. Edward thinks we need a housekeeper? "Er, well, we actually don't really need a housekeeper, I don't think." Yet even as I say it, I'm wondering if I'm wrong. Apparently, Edward needs to make excuses for the fact that we don't have one. Suddenly I wonder if he finds it weird that we don't have a cleaner, that I hoover and tidy myself, that he sometimes has to cook?

"Harriet, darling, you're not cooking and cleaning yourself, are you? Not on top of everything?" she asks, as diplomatically as it is possible to, given the inference. I look at the limp half-eaten sandwich beside me as she continues. "You will run yourself ragged trying to do it all. But who am I to tell you how to do things? I'm sure you know your own mind. Here's the thing: We're dyed-in-the-wool Democrats, my dear, to a man. We're all liberal, woke, pro-union, patrons of the arts, what-have-you, but let's be honest here: chapped hands help no one."

I stifle a giggle. This is the strangest conversation I've had with a partner's mother. And I'm pretty sure there's some blurred definitions in there.

"You certainly make a robust argument for it, that's for sure, Eleanor. I'll give it some serious thought," I tell her, and bizarrely I mean it. I don't want to fight any battles I don't have to, especially as I get further into pregnancy. I chose to enter Edward's world and it looks like this is what it is.

"Do, my dear. And thank you for the advice. I'll let you get on with your important work. All my love."

There's a knock at the front door early the next morning. Luckily I'm up and dressed this time and already two hours into my day. The view through the peephole is still blocked by the Christmas wreath, so I'm none the wiser when Edward quizzically pops his head out of the bathroom and asks who it is.

"No idea," I tell him.

"Right, if it's any of them, I'll deal with it. I promise, just give me a minute to put some clothes on," he calls, disappearing back into the steam of the bathroom.

I wonder if it's odd that I don't mind his family's attention half as much as he does. But then this is all new to me. I've never really had *relatives* before, and now there seem to be a lot of them.

I lift the latch and swing open the front door to reveal a beaming and incredibly tall Maori woman in her forties. She's dressed in a pristine gray uniform, and in her arms she is carrying cleaning supplies and a large brown bag of groceries.

"Ms. Reed? My name is Ataahua. Mrs. Holbeck asked me to come over, if it's okay? I'm so excited to be helping you with the house for the next few weeks. Is it okay if I come in?"

I stare completely dumbfounded at my newest employee. Eleanor sent us a housekeeper.

"Hi, Ataahua. This is, wow, *yes*, this is so exciting. Thank you so much," I say with a smile as I wonder how in God's name I am going to explain this to Ed when he gets out of the shower.

By the end of the month my phone is filled with missed calls from various Holbecks and I already can't imagine life without Ataahua—though I'm perfectly aware that once my deadline has passed, we'll both just be standing around in the empty apartment together. I can't deny, however, that the last few days with her have been a writer's dream: everything clean, ironed, and spotless when I emerge at the end of a working day after locking myself away.

I'll miss her gentle knock on the door and her maternal face peering around it offering me delicious home-cooked food. Eleanor almost certainly overstepped the mark, but I can't deny that part of me is so glad she did.

On this occasion the Holbecks' interference was much welcomed, though Edward has been quick to warn me that thinking that way could be a slippery slope. But then he doesn't know what I know, the reason they are on their best behavior: they need me or they lose him.

And boy, have they gone all-out to pull me in. During the past few days, I have been inundated with calls, texts, and offers to get to know me better. The strangest coming from Stuart, who suggested I join his tennis doubles group on Thursdays. I've never been so relieved to admit I don't play tennis.

And then there was a request from Fiona to join her for coffee and a *chat* that I grudgingly had to raincheck, desperate as I am to glean some insider gossip from another Holbeck partner. I think perhaps Fiona's world might intersect most comfortably with my own, and I'm curious to know how her start with them went when she got serious with Oliver.

Speaking of which, even Oliver managed to send a short but friendly email a couple of days after Thanksgiving, welcoming me to the family and saying how wonderful it was to finally meet me.

The only offer I have accepted is one from Lila, not because of who she is but due to the fact that she seemed to be the only one in the family who was willing to postpone until after my book is in—something that hasn't seemed to occur to a single Holbeck.

With one week to go until my deadline, I am slightly ahead of myself in terms of word count, my story coming together with pleasing clarity. The tale of an incredibly wealthy family and their secret history. Of course, I have concerns about the content, the idea that Robert might read my story, that any of them might—but this is what I do. I can only go where my mind will let me go, especially now that my focus is so split. And now that I finally seem to have my flow back, I can't let embarrassment or fear of what other people might think stop me from moving forward. Besides, I would assume that the Holbecks would appreciate the difference between fact and fiction, and I can only hope be a little flattered at the fleeting similarities. But perhaps that's too much of a stretch.

I think of Robert reading my first book and imagine him reading this one too, my mind naturally going to his tape, safely shut away, hidden in the suitcase under my bed, the only thing I own with a lock. I had to move the tape player there two days ago after Ataahua wandered into the kitchen holding it and, oblivious to its content, started asking where she should put it. I had thought it was safely buried under my side of the mattress until then. Clearly not.

Every fiber of my body wants to listen to what is on that tape. And every Holbeck text, call, and email I have received this week has reawakened that urge. But I know if I start listening, I will keep listening until the end. I'll lose a day, or two, and if what is on there is good, I might lose my focus altogether. I cannot risk missing my deadline. I am not a Holbeck, and to think I can get away with the things they get away with would be to delude myself.

I cannot risk being drawn into the Holbecks' orbit. At least not for five more days.

15

Lila

MONDAY, DECEMBER 12

It's just past midnight on the twelfth when I push send on the email to my publishers, ten minutes over my deadline. As the manuscript wings its way through the ether and out of my sphere of control, I slump back into my chair and let out a sigh of internal surrender.

My Herculean challenge finally complete, I contemplate a cold glass of wine before quickly remembering I can't do that for another seven months. Unless I take the Continental approach to pregnancy and start on a glass a night for good measure. At this stage the idea has a certain ring to it, but perhaps a hot bath and a bar of chocolate might do just as well.

I close down the sent document triumphantly. Two days ago, I set a password on my manuscript. Call it paranoia, call it cowardice, but Edward asked about the plot that morning and I got the jitters. I was so close to the finish line, and I didn't want to run the risk of him balking at the hook of my story before I sent it. Not that there's anything in it to balk at, and I can amend things in the edit, if anyone raises concerns. The point is: the family in my story isn't the Holbeck family, and the lost son isn't Bobby. In my story, the son doesn't really die. He comes back.

The fact remains I password-locked the document, to stop Edward from reading it, whatever that means in terms of trust. It's not that I don't trust him, and there's nothing wrong with curiosity and it's flattering to imagine he might want to sneak a peek, but I didn't want to feel encumbered at the first-draft stage by outside judgment. The truth is I am pleased with it, come what may. It might be the best thing I have written. We'll see.

The next morning, after a well-deserved lie-in, I take a short walk from the apartment to meet Lila at an open-air Christmas market at Columbus Circle. I've seen it in passing since it went up last week, on the few rare occasions I've left the apartment for writing breaks.

I considered making a start on Robert's tape this morning, but wanted to enjoy it without having to break it up. If Edward's not home before me tonight, I will begin.

The Christmas market is a small, festive shantytown of painted alpine huts, glowing warm and each stocked to the brim with crafts and imported delicacies from across Europe. There's something so nostalgic about it that as I approach, it almost feels like coming home. The market's walkways are swathed with thick pine garlands that twinkle with fairy lights, and the air is filled with the spiced scent of glühwein and roasted nuts.

I catch sight of Lila ahead of me in front of a large Christmas tree, totally at home in the anonymous crowd, though she stands a few inches taller than passersby. She looks amazing, every inch the Swedish Christmas dream: snow boots, leggings, and a shearling coat wrapped tight against the cold. She smiles as she catches sight of me.

"Harry," she cheers. "You did it! You finished." She pulls me into a hug and claps my back harder than I expect her to, making me cough slightly. "You're finished. Yes? Deadline over?"

I crack my own smile now. "Yep, all done."

"In that case, let's celebrate," she says, looping an arm through mine and guiding me purposefully into the tightly packed market.

As we go, she tells me about herself, how she moved to New York as a young model, her childhood in Sweden, her disastrous first marriage to a well-known Boston Irish basketball player that led to the birth of her gorgeous son, Milo, and finally how she met Stuart.

"Zermatt. Skiing with friends. We were thrown together. I'm sure you know, Stuart doesn't drink. No alcohol, no substances. Our friend groups, well, they can all get a bit cokey, you know. A bit much. I grew up modeling. I've seen some things, too young, you know. I don't touch any of that stuff, never have. It scares the bejesus out of me. My ex always got messy drunk. I don't like it." She studies my expression for a second, then continues. "I know what you're thinking. She's going from one guy with a drink problem to another, right?" I go to protest but she smiles. "It's fine. Stuart isn't like that. He's ten years sober, still goes to meetings; he's a lifer. Trust me, I've met a lot of addicts in my life, a lot of liars, and you get a sense for people, of who's kidding themselves . . . Stuart is a good man; he might seem like a black sheep, but that's just another way of saying how rare he is. He's a good stepdad to Milo."

We stop at a hut selling glühwein, glögg, and hot chocolate. The vendor clearly recognizes Lila and becomes mildly awkward. In the short time we've been together I have already noticed a few roving eyes and open mouths.

"You ever had glögg?" she asks me.

"I don't think so. What is it?"

"It's like glühwein but much better. It's Swedish." She grins. "It'll warm you up from the insides."

That's exactly what I'm afraid of, and I politely decline and settle instead for a fully loaded hot chocolate with marshmallows and a crumbly chocolate stick valiantly wedged into its creamy summit.

We wander on, sipping our hot drinks, and I steel myself to ask a question I've been longing to ask since Thanksgiving. "Did you know about Bobby?"

Lila's focus turns to me, an eyebrow raised. "Of course. I know they are very sensitive about it. The whole family. You didn't know?" she asks, interested by this new information.

I shake my head, and after a moment's thought she pats my arm in sympathy.

"Well, Stuart talks a lot. I blame AA. He's an open book. But Edward, he's different. More like Robert, I think. A tougher nut to crack. I think you're a good match, though. Me, on the other hand," she adds with an impish smile, "my nutcracking days are over. I like to keep it simple."

The market complete, Lila flags us a taxi downtown. In the sheltered warmth of the cab, she turns to me excitedly with a question. "Are you scared of heights?"

I only fully understand the question when we're deposited outside One Vanderbilt and I look up at the jutting steel and glass towering skyward above us. I've read about it. It's been closed most of this year while they changed the internal exhibits.

Lila pulls two lanyards from her bag and they jostle in the wind. "It officially reopens on Friday night; social posts are embargoed till then, but we can get content anytime. VIP passes." She slips one over my head and for the second time today I remember she's a celebrity. It's odd to think how one can forget that so quickly in the context of the Holbecks. Even fame like Lila's seems to fade in significance beside the reach of that family.

We're fast-tracked up to the ninety-first floor, our ears popping at the speed of the elevator's ascent as a guide straps an electrical bracelet to our wrists.

When the doors open, I see the relevance of Lila's question. The entire cavernous ninety-first floor of Summit Vanderbilt is made of glass and mirrors suspended a thousand feet over Madison Avenue, reflecting everything in it back ad infinitum. Lila steps out of the elevator first, her wristband light blinking as the sounds of birds and the ocean fill the space.

"The bracelets map each wearer's vital signs," the guide tells me, gesturing for me to step out of the elevator too. "The space responds to the people that fill it. Think of the building as a massive mood ring. Different types of stimuli, reflecting you back to you."

A sensory hall of mirrors. The idea is a terrifying one for a person like me, who fears truly being seen, but I have little choice but to follow Lila as our guide disappears.

I feel my wrist vibrate gently, and the sound of fire crackles to life around us. Lila spins to face me, a Cheshire-cat grin blossoming. The sounds I am unwittingly producing are so unexpectedly telling that it sends a hot flush of fear up my throat and into my cheeks.

"Harry, that's you. The sound of you. It's beautiful," she says, beaming. I feel my pulse beat faster at the intensity of her focus but force myself to stay calm, to center. I cannot let the sound, or the memories associated with it, overwhelm me.

As the fire's roar settles into the low crackle of a campfire, I follow Lila across the building's glass floor to the full-height windows and the panoramic view of the city beyond.

I watch, strangely disconnected, as Lila takes the shots she needs for her social content before finally returning to my side.

"Look down," she says. And when I do I see that where we are standing a thick sheet of glass is all that holds us both suspended a thousand feet above Madison Avenue. I feel my heart rise an inch higher in my chest at the realization. Lila holds my gaze playfully and starts to crack her high heel against the glass beneath us, grinning the whole time.

I am not scared of heights, but my limbic system, millions of years old and incapable of understanding the modern world, causes my blood pressure to drop ever so slightly. I feel the woozy vertiginous rush I am supposed to.

Lila must feel it too, because the reactive sounds around us seamlessly mellow, soften, to the slow, pulsing beat of rain drumming on a roof. Through the glass, New York City is laid out in lines and blocks. So tidy and easy to understand from up here.

The Empire State Building, Top of the Rock, and the Chrysler Building. Model skyscrapers made by men like Robert Holbeck—the building we're standing in now just the same.

"This is a good test," Lila says with a chuckle.

"Of what?"

"All sorts of things. But it's good to know," she answers simply. "You don't scare easily."

16

Krampus Is Coming

MONDAY, DECEMBER 12

On my way back to the apartment, my phone rings in my bag. It's an unknown number. It's too early to be hearing back from my publisher about the book; I only sent it last night. Curiosity piqued, I answer.

It's a female voice I don't immediately recognize. "Oh, hi, Harriet. Is this a bad time? Are you still working? I wasn't sure if you would be. Sorry, it's Fiona here. Fiona Holbeck."

"Fiona? Oh, hi." Weird that Fiona is calling me, I think, given I have just left Lila. For a second I wonder if they're all in constant contact on some kind of family WhatsApp group, but then realize the thought of Robert Holbeck on WhatsApp is ridiculous. Plus Fiona has been trying to get hold of me for a few days now. "No, I'm free, now is fine," I tell her, slipping into a shop doorway to better hear her. "What's up?"

"Wonderful. I'll cut to the chase," she says conspiratorially. "It's a madhouse here," she adds. "The boys are taking part in the end-of-term show at their school and it's like wrangling cats trying to get them to practice."

I can't help but smile at the idea of little Billy in a tiny costume, singing, and the logistics involved in that. "It sounds very cute, though," I say in what I hope is a supportive way.

"Ha. *Never* have kids, Harry," she chuckles wryly, in the way that only mothers can. "Now, listen, I'm calling because every year we have a thing at the house, a party, and I was wondering if you'd like to come along to this one? Billy has been especially insistent about me asking you," she adds.

"Really?" I ask, a sliver of pride in my voice.

"Oh yes. He's been asking if you can come since the Thanksgiving dinner. To be honest I don't think he's going to stop asking until I give him a definitive answer. And of course we all want you there too." She breaks off for a second, her attention elsewhere, her tone of voice changing as she talks to someone beside her. "I'm asking her now, honey. Yes: Auntie Harry. I'm asking her now. Okay, then. No, let Mama talk to her first, okay?"

It's Billy. I get a fuzzy aunty feeling followed by an odd ache, which I guess must be broodiness. Thank God that just kicks in at some stage; I had thought it might not for me.

"Okay, Harriet," Fiona singsongs. "Are you free on the sixteenth of December? You and Edward, of course?"

"Um?" I answer hesitantly, suddenly wary of being tricked into another unwitting Thanksgiving situation. It occurs to me that this invitation might be a slow preamble toward Eleanor's Christmas. But perhaps that's not so bad. "Sorry to ask, Fiona, but the sixteenth isn't some big American holiday I don't know about, is it? Nothing like that?"

Fiona chuckles. "Definitely not. It's just a regular American Friday evening. Though it is something we do every year. It's this Friday," she adds helpfully.

"Then I guess we're free," I tell her. It works out perfectly, as

Fiona is next on my list to get to know better. I'm dying to hear more about the family from her perspective.

"Oh, that's just great. Billy is going to be over the moon. All right then, so just to tell you a little bit about it. It's family tradition, every year, for Krampusnacht." She says it breezily, as if I will know what that means. Her German pronunciation is perfect and immediately intimidating. "I mean," she continues, "technically Krampusnacht is supposed to be on the fifth, but we always push it to the last weekend before the Christmas break. It's just easier for everyone." Sensing my lack of comprehension, she chuckles. "I've lost you, haven't I? It's a silly German thing— a Holbeck Christmas tradition. I took over organizing from Eleanor when we had kids. It's ostensibly for the children but there's fun to be had for the grown-ups too." There's a smile in her voice that tells me food and booze will be involved and, while I can't drink, I can almost certainly eat.

"That sounds fun. I'd love that. Krampusnacht," I say, testing the word in my mouth. "Do I need to bring anything? Wine?"

"Oh no. No need to bring anything at all. Well, unless . . ." She pauses a second. "Do you own a flashlight?"

"A flashlight?"

"Yes, a battery-operated flashlight? A big one."

I frown at the glass beside me in the shop doorway and catch my own bewildered expression in it.

"No. But I can get one, I guess, if I need one?"

"Great. Well, that's settled," she says brightly. "Yes, I know Edward has one. He used it last year, but, anyway, we'll get a car over to you on the evening too, so don't worry about all that. Does seven P.M. work?"

Edward was at their house last year while we were still doing long distance from England. It must have been one of the last family events he took part in before he came over to spend Christmas with me.

"Seven P.M. Yeah, great," I say, remembering the question. "Wait, will Billy be up if it starts then?" Though as soon as I've said it, I recall how late the boys were up for the Thanksgiving dinner.

She chuckles. "Oh yes. The kids don't tend to sleep on Krampusnacht. They'll be exhausted the next day, of course, but they always stay up for Krampus."

After we hang up, I google Krampusnacht on my phone and stop dead in my tracks, an immovable object on a bustling sidewalk, pedestrians forced to flow past me, an island in a cursing, jostling stream. I stare at my phone's screen absolutely dumbfounded as the results for *Krampusnacht,* or *Krampus Night,* load.

I gawk at the main Google image. A towering monstrosity of fur and teeth with barely recognizable human features, its body twisted in pain and rage. Jesus Christ, what the absolute hell is a Krampus? And why in God's name are Fiona and Oliver having a night for it? I must have typed the word in wrong, or perhaps this is Fiona's idea of making a joke—a very strange, very worrying joke? Again, I remember what Lila said earlier about me not scaring easily. Perhaps that's a good thing if this is the Holbecks' idea of humor. But then, thinking of Fiona, with her friendly, open face, I doubt she would make a joke like this. I must have just misheard the German word she used. There has to be a rational explanation for this, I tell myself, yet at the same time I read on.

Krampusnacht is celebrated as an accompaniment to the feast of St. Nicholas. The feast of St. Nicholas? Father Christmas has a feast? It occurs to me possibly for the first time in my life that while I've celebrated Christmas every year since I was born, I have absolutely no understanding of most of the traditions surrounding it.

The Krampus, I read on, *in Central European folklore, is a horned anthropomorphic creature; a mythical half-goat, half-demon monster who must punish misbehaving children at Christmastime. Krampus is the evil brother or "shadow self" of St. Nicholas. Traditionally the pair appear as a team, working together, with St. Nicholas (the patron saint of children) rewarding*

the good once a year while Krampus punishes the bad. The leg-
end of the Krampus is believed to have originated in Germany
and Eastern Europe, the name deriving from the Germanic word
Krampen, *meaning "claw." The Krampus is often depicted as a*
Christmas devil carrying chains and birch sticks, which he uses to
whip bad children, and a sack on his back in which he can drag
them to hell.

Drag them to hell. Jesus, actual, Christ.

Krampusnacht celebrations often include an appearance of the
two characters and usually end in children receiving presents, in
shoes they have left out—something nice if they have been good
and birch sticks or coal if they have been bad.

Okay, so they don't get dragged to hell, at least. That's a relief.
I suppose, in a way, it kind of sounds like trick-or-treating. Perhaps Krampusnacht is a sort of Christmassy Halloween for Eastern Europeans. It could be a fun night, I reason tentatively,
though it does potentially sound like low-level child abuse. But
then I guess even the tooth fairy could take on a sinister edge
viewed through other cultures. Why would a fairy need to collect
so many human teeth? What does she do with them?

Krampusnacht games: races are popular in some European
countries such as Austria, Germany, and the Czech Republic,
where a costumed Krampus will terrorize excited children into
behaving themselves throughout the year.

Outdoor games. I suppose that explains why I might need a
torch. Fiona said Edward had brought one last year. How did I
not know he attended this event last year? You'd think he might
have mentioned it at least in passing on one of our long-distance
Zooms. I guess he'd have worried it would sound weird, but as
weird as it does sound, I am interested. Still, it would seem I'm
interested in everything to do with Edward and his bizarre family.

I round the corner of our building, stride into the lobby, and
head straight for the lift up to the apartment. I have a lot of questions for Edward, and I presume he has answers.

17

Forewarned Is Forearmed

MONDAY, DECEMBER 12

Edward face-palms when I tell him that I've signed us up for Krampusnacht. "You've done it again, haven't you?" he asks, half amused, half incredulous. "Accepted an offer with absolutely no idea of what you're getting yourself into. Why the hell didn't you just say we were busy?"

"Because we're not busy, and your family is making a lot of offers and I can't turn them all down. Besides, I thought it might be fun. Festive."

He snorts a laugh. "Yeah, it'll be festive. You've basically signed us up for a night of babysitting, you know that, right?" he says with a light shake of the head.

"We're hardly babysitting, Ed. It's a party? Or a dinner, isn't it? I don't know," I admit. "But I think it's sweet that Billy wants me to come. He likes me; it's cute."

"Of course he likes you. You are the most caring person I know. It's crazy that you don't see that. Even Billy sees it." He pulls me close to him, his arms round my shoulders. "It's the first thing I noticed about you. Beautiful *and* kind. It's rarer than you'd think."

I give him side-eye. "Thanks for the flattery, but it's not going to get you out of explaining to me what the hell a Krampus is."

He laughs, releasing me. Perching on a kitchen stool, he splays his hands out on the countertop. "Okay, where to start? A potted history of Holbeck Krampusnacht. I guess it started with Mitzi; her family did it and she brought it over from Germany with her. Alfred and Mitzi did it for their kids when they had them—that was my father's father and his uncles. Then when my dad was a kid, his parents did it until they, you know—"

"Died?" I offer.

"Yeah, and after that Dad moved in with Alfred and Mitzi at The Hydes and they did Krampus Night there for him and his friends. Then we came along, and Mom and Dad did it for us at The Hydes. Then Oliver had kids and now it happens at their place. It's just kept going. It's fun, I promise you. Weird, but—"

"How weird?" I chip in again.

He laughs. "Pretty. But . . . mostly just harmless fun. Hide-and-seek, parlor games, scary masks and costumes. Kids love it. Well, it terrifies them, but you know what I mean. It's character building. That's why Dad kept it going for us and why Ollie does it for his kids. Maybe one day we'll do it for our—"

"Whoa there!" I interject quickly. "Let's just get through *one* Krampusnacht before we start making sweeping statements, okay?"

"Okay," he says with a shrug of acceptance.

"Great. Now, why exactly do I need a torch?"

As I lie in bed that night, not for the first time, I try to imagine the bizarre childhood Edward and his siblings must have had. I picture Robert as their father, how he must have been with them, how he must have wanted to share a piece of his own childhood with them. And then my thoughts move to Eleanor, the woman holding the whole family together, her old-world connections and diplomacy capable of anything but discussing death with her own children. The Holbeck siblings sent off to their respective psychiatrists and the gap Bobby left filled with other things. The day Bobby died, all of the expectations and responsibilities heaped on him fell to Edward. No wonder things have been hard between Edward and his family; this was never his birthright. All of this duty should never have been his to bear; I can't blame him for running scared from a family that ostensibly killed the last guy who had the job before him.

I wonder if Robert mentions any of this on his tape. If his story is a memoir or a thriller, or if that was just a joke. I didn't have a chance to listen to it as I had hoped when I got home earlier, but I could listen now with Edward sleeping beside me. I feel a jolt of that illicit thrill at the idea of hearing Robert's voice, but I'm not sure I could stand the shame if Edward found out what I was doing next to him. No, best to wait until he's out tomorrow. Edward stirs in the sheets as if my thoughts had seeped into his dreams and I can't help wondering if I am a bad person.

But I know the answer to that: I *am* a bad person. Good people don't do the things I have done. There are no mitigating circumstances. What I did was not in self-defense, or in the heat of the moment, or by accident. I did what I did in cold blood. My pulse was steady and I was thinking straight, and *that* is how I know I am a bad person.

Edward loves me, but he wouldn't if he knew what I was capable of, what I did on the side of a road on a cold morning twenty years ago. We all have something inside us that we fear would repel the world if it ever came out. But for most people that thing is something that the light of day would only render harmless. My secret would put me in jail for the rest of my natural life.

I shake off the thought and tell myself I am not that person anymore. We change, we grow; I will never be her again. Though

I know that's not true. I feel her inside me down dark alleys; late at night when things get scary I know she is there in the shadows with me. I know she has my back; our back.

I try to imagine what Robert Holbeck would think if he really knew who his son was marrying. If he knew he'd chased away so many perfect partners and ended up letting me slip through the net.

Unless of course he does know.

That thought hits me hard. I look at the digital clock on the bedside table beside me. It's three A.M. This is insomnia, this is anxiety, this is PTSD. Robert Holbeck does *not* know. He might have a sense for people, he might have a feeling about me, but he cannot read minds. No one was there that day. You could call it a perfect crime except it wasn't perfect; it was horrific.

I turn in my fresh Egyptian cotton sheets and try to clear my mind. The past is gone, my family is gone, and right now, I need to think of the future.

The next morning after Edward leaves for work I slide my suit-case out from underneath the bed and spin its combination lock until the numbers align and retrieve the microcassette player.

It's finally time to listen to Robert's story. I want to hear it—him, his voice, his words.

I make sure the front door is locked as I pass by it and set my-self up in the sitting room, the chunky Olympus player nestled in my lap. I slip the red foam headphones over my ears, carefully adjust the volume, and press PLAY.

18

The Tape

PART 1

Things I remember from that morning. The warmth of sun on skin, dust hanging in light, her hair in the street breeze.

There would be a tent, eventually, to cover him. His college sweatshirt, with all but the A of COLUMBIA obscured. I often recall her face looking up at me as she explained what happened, her expression serious, her words lost in the traffic and the wind. It did not need explaining, what happened. Although it would be explained. Thoroughly.

His head hit the sidewalk at thirty miles an hour. He did not brace himself; he did not break his fall from six floors up, which initially mystified at autopsy. My boy, my good, kind boy, lying broken on the sidewalk like leaking left-out garbage.

Her face again as she spoke words I could not hear, her eyes filling with tears as the wind played with that soft blond hair. The weather vane glinting high above us.

I would hear the story again. Many times. And then later the police would, in turn, ask me. Lawyers. I would search for you in each detail she told me. Knowing the truth was hiding somewhere in there. Knowing she knew *why* you did it but was unable to articulate it, and I could not hook it out of her.

Things had gone wrong between me and you, my son, that much everyone knew. He was good, a good boy, better than me, and there is a particular pain to knowing that the one you want the world *for* does not want your world. That your way is the wrong way. You wanted change, and though I feared it, deep down, I wanted you to prove me wrong. To show me this great change. To prove me wrong about the way the world works, and show me that good triumphs and kindness wins the day. But you did not show me that, unfortunately. You showed me this. And the world kept turning.

The blood was so dark it looked black on the sidewalk.

He jumped, so the story goes, but why?

After lunch, he went back to his room to study, she would tell me. He was tired. He had bitten off more than his still-adolescent mind could chew, more responsibility than he could shoulder unaided. And the poison inside him. But she did not know this then. It would be weeks until we knew what he had taken. The medication, a slow daily drip of meds on top of meds, the results unnoticed at first. And what could be more like him than choosing a drug that pushed him to *be* more, to *do* more. So clever, so undetectable to everyone who knew him, it's no wonder it passed for so long.

If I think on it long enough the blame always lands on me.

I pushed you too far.

What you did. What I did after.

A hasty word to you, a lack of malleability in myself, my poor show of example. But it was done, and it cannot be undone: my work, your work. The solution to it all writ large.

After the funeral she would not come back to the house. I started to suspect she knew. I am not a bad man. But my family is sacred to me.

What you did that day, the mess you made, what you forced me to do to protect those you left behind did not end then. That was the beginning of something. A loosening of something. The boundaries loosened.

I found her.

Her elegant neck, its pale skin delicate, leading down to an alabaster carved clavicle. Beautiful, and all that soft-spun hair, the velvety scent of peony. She made noises as she struggled. She fought. But it did not help. As close as lovers in those last moments. Her breath warm against skin. Her eyes inexplicably calm, as if she knew something the rest of the world did not. Perhaps how little fighting might help in the long run.

She slipped away, and was dealt with. She knew too much about those final hours.

Then a two-hour drive. A two-hour hike, with only the sky and the wind and the rain as companions. There I left her. In the shadow of a green mountain past the calm of a lake. To the wolves. To the wolves because that is where she would have thrown us. And I will never let that happen to us. To my family. Let it not ever be said I let others do my dirty work. I dealt with the mess. That is what we must do.

That was the first.

This is not a threat, *Harriet Reed*. Take this as you find it: a work of fiction, a parable? But take from it that my meaning holds. My family will protect itself. Know that.

19

The Name of the Game

TUESDAY, DECEMBER 13

I gasp and whip off the headphones at the mention of my name, flinging the machine and Robert as far away from me as I can. Across the room the machine spools on undeterred beneath the coffee table, the slow murmur of Robert's gravelly voice still audible.

He recorded that tape for me. To give to me. It's about Bobby's death—and a girl. And it sounds a lot like a confession.

No, I think again. It sounds like a warning.

He must know what I am. What I am capable of. And he's warning me to be very careful.

He wants me to know he won't let me hurt his family. That he will do what is necessary to protect them. It occurs to me with razor-sharp clarity that I have to see this man again in three days.

I leap to my feet and grab the whirring tape player, shutting it off, then perch on the sofa and catch my racing breath.

The recording is so personal. His thoughts about Bobby, his guilt, his culpability. And to tell me about the girl, that he killed a girl. What is he hoping I do with this information? I think of the man on the subway yesterday and suddenly my behavior doesn't seem quite so paranoid.

I wonder if I should call someone. I should call the police, or Edward. But what would I say? I listened to a tape that may or may not be fictional? This could just be another Holbeck test—a game, a cruel joke even. It must be. I look down at my trembling hands, the sight of them shaking a clear indication that I need to calm down.

I remember Lila's words. I'm not supposed to scare easily. Is this what she meant? Does every Holbeck girlfriend get a bizarre tape? Surely someone would have said something, wouldn't they?

I blow out a few slow deep breaths. This is too much for me, so I'm guessing it's not great for the baby. I don't want to push my luck. The first trimester is the most fragile, according to Dr. Leyman; I don't want to miscarry. I need to calm down.

I stride into the hall, grab my coat and bag, and slam the front door behind me.

Out on the street, the cold air hits my flushed cheeks, cooling them as the sounds of the city drown out thoughts and my pulse begins to regulate.

I have found over the years that mindfulness works best for me when panic sets in: the wind on my skin, the sound of the city, the feeling of the cold sidewalk through my shoes.

As I walk, my thoughts reshuffle.

Robert Holbeck gave me that tape for a reason. It's either a warning, or a test. Another game. He clearly enjoys those. It's hard to know if the story is even real; it sounds like Bobby's story, and the building Robert mentions sounds like 7 East 88th Street—its weather vane glinting in the afternoon light—but Bobby didn't jump to his death, did he? His medications interacted.

I pull out my phone and rack my brain for the year Bobby died as I hit Central Park. Edward was eighteen, so it would have been 2002.

I type in: *suicide, East 88th Street, 2002.*

The first search result is a photo. I draw in a sharp breath as I catch the unmistakable shape of a white incident tent erected beneath the Holbecks' apartment building. It discreetly covers something. I blink away the thought of Bobby's black-stained Columbia sweatshirt.

Edward lied to me. Bobby jumped; he didn't die from a drug interaction. The story on Robert's tape is true. That dignified, quiet death Edward described is fiction.

I feel my knees weaken. I need to sit down. Edward kept the extent of this horrendous event from me—he must have known how much more seriously I'd take his reticence to spend time around his family.

And that's when I feel it; eyes on me. Surprised, I stop midstride and scan the park, not entirely certain what I'm looking for. I dodge a woman and stroller caught short by my sudden stop, looking back up just in time, and then catch sight of something. The man with the baseball cap, from the subway, across the park. His eyes lock with mine and I realize now with absolute certainty: Robert has had someone following me since he gave me the tape.

In a reflexive act of self-preservation, I let my eyes slide from his as if nothing had happened, and I continue on my way. If Robert is monitoring me, waiting for me to listen to his tape, then I need to make sure my next move is well thought out. I need to buy time.

Thinking fast, I calmly take the next left and exit the park, heading toward my favorite local diner. I must have spent almost as much time writing in there as in our apartment since I moved here. I'm pretty sure the man in the baseball cap won't follow me inside.

I slip into the warmth of the place, a waitress nodding me over to an empty booth. I slide in, my eyes locked on the door as I wait.

After twenty minutes, I let myself relax. My shadow didn't follow me, and I didn't catch him passing the large condensation-misted windows. I can't be sure he's not waiting out there, but that won't be a concern until I leave at least.

I order a coffee and a Danish, sipping the hot liquid gratefully as I pore over the internet for more on Bobby's suicide. The few articles that mention the East 88th Street suicide do not name the deceased, but the description on the tape appears to be true. I can't find anything about a blond girl, though, so she could be fictionalized. I suppose the question is whether or not a girl disappeared after Bobby died. I know from Lila that the Holbecks' old nanny left after Bobby, so this could be the person Robert is referring to.

I shiver at the thought of everyone at that Thanksgiving table knowing that Bobby jumped from that apartment. No wonder Billy was so terrified of sleeping in Bobby's room. For all I know, that's where he did it. I push the morbid thought from my mind and try to focus on the issue at hand: whether the Holbecks' nanny resigned after Bobby's death, or if she simply disappeared.

I cast my eyes across to the fogged diner windows and watch the huddled shapes of pedestrians glide by. Somewhere out there Robert is watching and waiting to see what I do next. If he *has* killed before, and if he has done so more than once, I am in serious trouble. And yet I was alone with him in his study, we sat opposite each other; it would be impossible to deny the strange connection we had with such seeming ease. The confusing thing is, Robert Holbeck likes me. And suddenly it dawns on me: *that* is why he is telling me this. He has chosen me because he likes games, because he likes thrillers, and because he has decided I am a worthy opponent.

I search on my phone for *Holbeck family nanny* and a couple of grainy paparazzi shots of Nunu standing beside the family celebrity, Lila, come up alongside gossip columns. No sign of the old nanny, though. All I have to go on is that she was blond.

I realize the best way to find a photo of her is to search for ones of Edward and his siblings as children. I head to Getty Images and search Edward's name.

Photos of the Holbeck brood at various ages fill the screen. Then I catch one. A young Eleanor carrying a swaddled Edward in her arms, beside her a youthful Robert holding her hand, then, in the deep blurry background, out of focus, a figure pushing the two-year-old Bobby in a stroller, a baseball cap covering her hair. The nanny.

Halfway down the page, I find an in-focus shot. Her face is turned away, half in profile, but I can see she is a woman in her early twenties, beautiful and fresh-faced with her soft blond hair pulled back in a loose ponytail.

My breath catches. It's her. The woman described on the tape. He was talking about the Holbecks' nanny.

I squint at the photo credit caption beneath.

(L to R) Robert Holbeck, wife Eleanor Holbeck, with their two sons, Edward and Robert, and a family friend, as they attend the Children's Aid charity luncheon, July 31, 1985.

A family friend. No name. I scroll on, skipping ahead to the late 1990s, getting closer to Bobby's death date. And I see her again, at some kind of garden party. She gets her own photograph this time, beside Eleanor, Pimm's glass in hand, as they are caught mid-laugh. The nanny's soft blond hair is swept back up in a French twist, her pale neck and delicate collarbone bare. She is older here: but now that I consider it, there is an eerie similarity between us. I can't help but wonder if it's ever crossed Edward's mind how much his fiancée looks like this willowy figure from his childhood; I imagine it has crossed Robert's.

The photo credit reads: *(L to R) Eleanor Holbeck and Sa-*

mantha Belson at the Melfort annual Summer Gala, August 7, 2002.

Samantha Belson.

I have a name. Now I just need to find out if she's still alive.

My next move depends very much on the type of game we're playing here, and I've got exactly three days in which to find that out.

20

The Plot Thickens

THURSDAY, DECEMBER 15

"So, this is for the new book?"

Retired NYPD lieutenant Deonte Hughley sits across the table from me in a cozy booth at Tom's Diner in Prospect Heights. He gives me a wry smile as he takes off his pristine cowboy hat and places it gently down on the bench seat beside him.

My American publisher put me in touch with Deonte two years ago after I requested they connect me with someone in the NYC police force who could fact-check my first novel.

Lieutenant Hughley was keen to help, having recently retired, and was an invaluable resource on my first book, always sparking creative ideas and handling my layman's knowledge with diplomatic kid gloves. During the final edit, I spoke with him regularly, running legal and sometimes infuriatingly granular procedural questions by him. At what temperature is DNA evidence completely destroyed? Can a cause of death always be determined? Do cops really like donuts?

It always helped that he answered with a certain lightheartedness, given the sometimes unsettling nature of the content. We've kept in touch via email since, and spoke most recently last week, in the final frantic throes of my new novel's first-draft deadline.

We know each other fairly well by now, a shared language emerging from his honest disclosure and my unending interest in his answers. We've certainty duked out a lot of plot strands together, though this might only be the fourth time we've actually met in person.

"Uh-huh. Second book. Exactly. Just piecing it all together," I say with a smile. And in a way it's true. My questions are about a family, a family with the power to cover up anything. But it isn't my book I need Deonte's help with this time. It is my life.

He shakes his head, slow, and stirs his coffee. "I don't know where y'all come up with these ideas. So in this one, a girl finds a cassette tape with a confession right there on it. Ha. Now, that is a case I would have killed to be on."

"Why, because it's a sure thing? Convictable? Given the evidence?" I ask, perhaps a little too hopefully.

Deonte raises an eyebrow. "Nah, because it sounds like a fun one. I think you know by now, at least from our conversations, most crime, well, it ain't fun. It's a god-awful, draining, soul-destroying slog. But this tape, that sounds tasty—juicy, exciting, you know. Like a movie. I'm in. Hell, I wanna read it now."

"Well, that's a good sign." I give a reassured smile. "So my main character, the girl, is given this tape by the perpetrator of the crimes. But here's the thing: the crimes mentioned on it, it's not clear if they really happened or if this man is stringing her along, toying with her. She doesn't know if the events described are real," I add, then break off, unsure how to get to the nub of what I'm asking. "I guess I want to know what evidence she'd need in order to take this to the police? To be sure it wasn't a fake, or to ensure a conviction without leaving herself open to reprisal."

"Reprisal? Who's the tape maker? What type of guy? What type of killer? You know, background, motive?" he asks, his tone serious now, his old NYPD instincts kicking back in and lifting Deonte from friendly graying retiree back to a force to be reckoned with.

"He's rich, well connected . . . incredibly powerful," I say carefully.

He winces. "Trump-y?"

"Definitely not. Old, old money. Ingrained in everything. Establishment."

Deonte studies my face for a moment, and I suddenly wonder how much he knows about my private life. If he knows about Edward and the Holbeck family. If he does, he doesn't mention the glaring equivalence. But then why would he? Authors write close to home, and I am just an author with a few outlandish questions.

"Damn. So he's playing cat 'n' mouse, taunting her. Okay, now we're talking. She can't let on she knows, until she's sure it's real. Can't tell the police, can't be sure if this whole thing's a scare tactic. And she's got to be careful who she trusts, because if that tape's real, and this guy is that powerful—anyone could be feeding what she does back to him. Leaks in departments, hired hands—yeah, got it: one false step and she's toast."

A flicker of doubt blossoms inside me. Leaks in departments, hired hands, trust. I suddenly wonder if I should even be speaking to Deonte. My connection to him comes through my publisher, after all, and the Holbecks have proved their reach on that front already.

I push the paranoid thought away. If push comes to shove, I'm confident Deonte's got my back. "Exactly. She can't trust anyone until she has real evidence that the tape is an actual confession. Then she can decide whether to hand it over to someone."

"Sensible. She's got a job, reputation, I'm guessing? Doesn't want to make a fool of herself if the tape maker refutes the validity of the recording." I nod. "So, seems reasonable she'd need to be sure the people mentioned in the confession are real people, and they're dead people. Best not to go to the police until then, if she doesn't want a libel case or worse hanging over her. Even then, if she does find a death, she'd need to find something suspicious about it; she'd need to look at cause of death. If it's murky, though, or in keeping with that confession—well, then, she's cooking with gas." He looks momentarily pained. "Thing is, if these victims are just missing, you got problems. That's trickier. It'll be easier for your plot if she finds an actual body; then they can exhume, run a fresh autopsy if there wasn't one first time round. Things are much more accurate these days, if they got missed the first time—less cracks to slip down."

"And if the girl finds something? If the tape is real?"

Deonte lets out a puckish whistle. "If the confession is real. If she finds a body, and the circumstances of death are hazy, then it's go-time; she needs to lawyer up and hunker down. Then it'll be a legal battle there on out. Full O.J." He ends with a flourish before adding, "Oh, and before I forget—this girl, she damn well better copy that cassette tape. I don't wanna be screaming at this book: *Why didn't you copy the damn thing?*"

"Noted," I say gratefully. It hadn't occurred to me until now, but the import of this hits home.

"Why does he choose her? This cold-blooded killer?" Deonte asks, catching me off guard. It's a good question, but then that's Deonte's profession, asking the right questions. And the answer to it is just a little too close to home for me.

Whether or not Robert knows what I am capable of isn't clear, but what is clear is that he knows I am the kind of person with more to lose than appearances might suggest. He sees me.

"I can't tell you that. It'd spoil the ending," I say with a grin, thinking on my feet.

His eyes sparkle in recognition at my swerve.

"Okay. So, Deonte," I continue, "if this girl wanted to find someone and she only had a name to go on, how would she go about doing that, do you think?"

"This girl's just an ordinary person? Not a cop?"

"Just an ordinary person."

"And . . . this is for the book?" Deonte asks with a wry smile.

Back at the apartment I put the tape recorder back in the suitcase and lock it safely under the bed, its cassette not even a quarter played yet. If I'm honest, what's on it scares me, and until I know what exactly I'm dealing with here I need to be careful what I expose myself to. Besides, somehow, I will need to act normal tomorrow night when I see him again. The more I know about his crimes, the less successful I am going to be at pretending I haven't heard any of it yet. Given how busy I have been with my deadline, I can still safely hide behind the idea of my own ignorance.

I have thought about bowing out of the party tomorrow night, but I'm sure that kind of reaction would be a red flag for Robert, and I would have to explain my reasoning to Edward.

I open up Facebook and search for Samantha Belson. Within an hour I've emailed twenty in the right age bracket; she would be around sixty this year. If she's still alive. Unless Robert made up his story just to scare me.

That night, by the time I hear Edward's keys in the door, I've already received five replies. But none are from the Samantha I'm looking for; they never worked either in New York or as a nanny.

I head out to the hallway just as Edward walks in.

When he looks at me, his face is a pale mask of concern; for a second I am absolutely certain that he knows everything. That he knows about Robert's tape, about the confessions and my unintended complicity. About my own secret.

"Your cell is dead," he says, his tone panicked.

I pull it from my pocket. He's right; the screen is blank, the battery long dead. "I couldn't get hold of you most of the day," he continues. "I thought maybe something might have happened. How are you feeling?"

"How am I feeling?" I ask, confused by the question.

"The baby, Harry? You're pregnant, remember? I couldn't get

you; I've been trying all morning. I've been worried. But you're okay, right?"

I had completely forgotten about the pregnancy.

"Harry," he prompts me again, coming over and placing a cool hand on my forehead. "Are you hot?" he asks solicitously.

"No, no, I'm fine," I say apologetically, pulling away. "I'm sorry, honey. I didn't realize I'd run out of battery. Was everything okay today? Did you need me?"

"No, I just wanted to check in. Oh, and to tell you I'm out for dinner tonight. A Chinese company wants to press the flesh. That okay for you?"

It's not. I don't want to be in this apartment on my own tonight. I don't want to sit here thinking about that tape. Worrying if I'll get an unexpected call or visit from a Holbeck. I want Edward to stay home, but I realize from the look on his face the significance of this Chinese company. Edward has been wanting to expand his tech company into the Chinese market for a while now and this sounds like inroads.

"Yeah, of course. Go," I tell him, though for a microsecond I consider spilling everything. The tape, the confession being drip-fed to me, my rising concern.

"Thank you," he says, kissing me lightly on the lips and heading into the bedroom to change for dinner.

Down the hall in my office, I hear the unmistakable electronic ping of fresh email landing in my inbox. I swing a look back to the office. Another reply from a Samantha Belson. I left my laptop open.

Once Edward is dispatched, showered and suited, I dash back to my computer and read the new email.

This one is only three words long, but it's enough.

Who is this?

The concern implied in those three words is telling. I emailed her through an anonymous account, a brand-new Gmail address; I could be anyone. I gave a plausible reason for reaching out and signed off with my initials, but whoever wrote this reply needs more than that, which is interesting.

I type out a response, and attach the Getty Images photo of Samantha Belson laughing beside Eleanor Holbeck.

> Is this you? Did you work for this family between 1982 and 2002? I am not a journalist. It's an entirely personal, and confidential, matter. You are guaranteed complete discretion. Would you be happy to talk? Your help would be greatly appreciated as I believe you are the only person qualified to set the record straight around a certain matter.

Her reply comes back almost immediately.

> Are you a member of the family? Or do you work, in any capacity, for them?

I wonder how best to answer, fingers poised over the keys. I'm guessing it will not help my case in any way to explain I'm about to marry one of them.

> I am not involved yet. That really depends on you, and what you might be able to tell me.

I stare at my inbox and wait. After half an hour I consider giving up for the night and checking in again tomorrow. And then it comes.

> It is me, in the photo. I'll meet with you. I will pick the venue and time. Come alone.

> If I feel unsafe, I will leave.

I bark out a triumphant *whoop* at the empty apartment. The woman in Robert's confession is alive; he did not kill her. Whatever this tape *is,* it's a game, nothing more, and I've won the first round.

A new thought surfaces and my smile withers: I have no way of knowing if that was Samantha Belson messaging me, or if I've just made a plan to meet someone else entirely.

I open her Facebook profile and scroll through her photographs. The account looks real, and while she might not have quite the same soft blond hair she had as a young woman, I see the same curve in her smile, the same crinkle around her eyes. This is Samantha Belson, aged sixty. Whatever happened, she didn't die in 2002.

I type back a quick reply.

Thank you, Samantha. I have lots of questions.

21

Krampusnacht

FRIDAY, DECEMBER 16

And just like that, it's Krampusnacht.

We're standing on a Brooklyn curb in front of the glowing windows of Fiona and Oliver's five-floor brownstone as it looms over us, its door festooned with foreboding Christmas decorations.

I look at Edward beside me. "This is weird," I say. "Your family is weird." Somehow the weight of everything I can't tell him is in those words, as well as the weight of my fear at having to see Robert again. I will feign ignorance tonight, but I know he will be watching me carefully. The truth is I'm scared of what could happen next, of what Robert might do.

Edward nods in solemn acknowledgment. "Oh, I know they

are. Believe me." His expression softens as he looks down at me with a smile. "Remember, tonight is just an Austro-Hungarian version of Halloween. Nothing to worry about, right?"

"Got it," I agree, allowing only a sliver of the vulnerability I actually feel to surface.

He offers me his hand and I take it, letting him lead me briskly up the brownstone steps to the elaborately carved dark-wood-and-glass front door.

Edward pushes the doorbell and through the glass I just about make out its ghostly tinkling. In the hallway beyond I can make out rows of shoes already lined up against the thick eighteenth-century baseboard, shoes lined up for Krampus. It looks like there's quite a crowd in there already. I note that there are adult shoes mixed among the children's and my stomach tightens. We all have to take part in the Krampusnacht games it seems.

Edward looks at his watch, then back into the dim hallway, light and movement visible at the end of the corridor. "We're late," he mumbles. "They probably just can't hear us."

It's my fault we're late. I had no idea what to wear, and I don't mean in the usual sense. I mean I genuinely had no idea what to wear to a Krampusnacht.

After another minute, the front door flies open in front of us, revealing a beaming Fiona.

"Hello, hello, hello," she cheers merrily, and through another doorway along the hall Oliver appears, a bottle of red in hand and a smile on his face.

"Hello, strangers," Oliver bellows, clearly making an extra effort. It seems to settle Edward. In all of my own very particular terror about tonight, I had forgotten that Edward is the prodigal son. Oliver pulls him into a hug before bending to plant a quick peck on my cheek. "Shoes off, both of you," he orders us merrily. "You definitely know the rules by now, Ed. No excuses."

I look between the brothers, an easy familiarity beginning to settle in alongside both parties' hypervigilance. Fiona places a reassuring hand on my arm.

"You told Harry about the shoes, right, Ed?" Fiona asks, half teasing, half concerned.

"He did," I say, answering for him as I slip mine off, as instructed, and into the immaculate row. "Yeah, we have to leave them out for Krampus," I add with a smile, as if Krampus were the milkman and not a seven-foot-tall deformed goat-demon. "Right?"

"She's got it," Oliver replies, winking in such a mock-theatrical way I can't help but laugh.

"That's the spirit," Fiona tells me, and there's a hint of apology in her voice as she takes me conspiratorially by the arm and pulls me toward the kitchen.

"I know you're not drinking," Fiona whispers, with a level of knowing that slightly concerns me, "but I have something you might be interested in seeing in the kitchen." She raises an impish eyebrow that suggests to me there is food involved and I follow gladly, looking back just in time to see a relaxed Edward follow Oliver into the party.

My appetite has skyrocketed over the past week, but whether I'm eating for two or just making up for the nausea and loss of appetite of the preceding weeks, I do not know.

"How much has Edward told you about tonight?" Fiona asks.

"Not much—just hide-and-seek, costumes, masks, that kind of thing," I say lightly, my mind on the room Edward just walked into and the prospect of whether or not Robert Holbeck is in it.

"Okay. Well, listen," Fiona tells me, slowing us down to a halt. "I don't want you going in blind tonight. My first time, Oliver thought it would be hilarious not to tell me anything at all, so I almost had an aneurysm when it all kicked off. Not that it's that bad. It's fine," she adds quickly, catching my expression. "I'm probably just a scaredy-cat. And I wasn't expecting it. Anyway," she says brightly, pulling me along again.

The kitchen is a massive stone-floored affair with a large provincial farmhouse table and Le Creuset–lined shelves. Hired caterers and chefs bustle about the space transferring beautifully crafted savory creations onto small dishes and shucking fresh oysters over at the sink.

The air is filled with the fresh scent of salt and sea, and the aroma of something sweet baking. My hunger dips into a groaning ache just as I catch a face I recognize bent over by the range cooker.

Lila looks up from the tray of blood-red cookies with a broad smile, her cheeks rosy with the kitchen heat, her hands stained red by the dough. "Hey, Harry!" she calls, sliding her cookies into the oven. "You made it." She gives me a gooey-handed wave. "I'm making Krampus cookies," she continues with a grin. "Pretty weird, right?"

"Krampusnacht? Sure is," I agree. *As is the thought of having to see Robert Holbeck and pretend I'm normal and he's normal,* I think. "Is this your first Krampus too?" I ask Lila as Fiona busies herself with the kitchen staff.

Lila pulls an expression that I don't really understand, then says, "No way. We sometimes do it in Sweden. It's my third here, I think." She counts on blood-dough fingers. "Yeah, third one. Milo loves it." She shrugs as if to say she comes for Milo but stays for the weirdness.

I know if Lila is here everyone is here, and that anyone could walk into this kitchen at any moment.

I reorient myself against a kitchen counter in order to keep the kitchen door in my periphery. I want a little warning before I have to put my guard all the way up.

I am not meeting Samantha Belson until next week. I know Robert didn't kill her as he suggested, but I'm sure there's more to uncover there. I don't know yet how far this all goes—though there is a world in which Robert's tape is just a joke and I'm just a bad sport. I suppose I'll see.

Fiona joins us with an exasperated sigh. "I need to learn to delegate if it's the last thing I do. I'm a real pain in the ass," she groans, then hands me a tall glass of sparkling water with a wink. "So the plan is: drinks, canapés, and snacks until around nine P.M.

The kids play among themselves until then. But at nine o'clock you'll hear a bell—"

"Like a cowbell," Lila chips in helpfully, though it clarifies absolutely nothing for me.

"A cowbell, okay," I echo.

"The kids will flip out at that point," Fiona continues. "Then there'll be three loud knocks on the front door; that's Krampus arriving. And that's the beginning of the Krampus Race, which ends when the Evergreen is found, at which point Krampus *disappears,*" she says with a finality I'm not sure she's earned. "Oh, and after Krampus disappears, we unwrap the presents in our shoes."

I'm not sure Fiona knows how mad she sounds.

"Right. Krampus, Evergreen, presents in shoes. I think I've got it," I say regardless. Edward's explanation didn't mention anything called an Evergreen.

I take a sip of my icy water and wonder when Fiona will drag us out of the relative safety of the kitchen into the main party and closer to Robert. My stomach flips with dread.

"Now, Harriet, you're doing the Krampus Race with Billy this year. As a team. Is that okay?" Fiona asks.

I splutter a little of my water back into the glass.

"Don't worry. I'm doing the Krampus Race too, with Milo," Lila says.

"Oh, um, sure. If that's . . . Is everyone doing it?"

"No, just you and Lila and the kids. If you're happy to? Billy asked for you especially."

I gulp back the rest of my water and try to ignore the emotional blackmail, resigning myself to the fact that I have to play a weird game with a bunch of kids while the rest of the adults, including Robert Holbeck, stay in another room. Which actually works out perfectly.

I put down my empty glass with a triumphant smile. "Great," I say. "In the meantime, could I get some of those canapés we saw go past, Fiona? I'd better get my energy reserves up or the kids might not be able to tell the difference between me and the Krampus."

Lila gives a high giggle. "I don't think there's much danger of them getting confused about *that*." Something in the pitch of her laugh unsettles me, and a concerning question slowly begins to form in my mind.

"Hang on. Who plays the Krampus?" I ask with a grin.

The two exchange a look, then burst out laughing.

"No one *plays* Krampus, silly," Fiona giggles. "Krampus is Krampus." She gives me a stage wink that does nothing to settle me—if that was its intention. "Let's get you some food, though," she continues, making her way toward the kitchen door with a beckoning gesture. "We'll go through to the others."

I feel a pressure drop within me, my anxiety shifting into a higher gear, as I reluctantly follow in Fiona's wake, leaving Lila and the safety of the kitchen behind.

"Are Eleanor and Robert here yet?" I ask as we go.

Fiona nods with a smile, her eyes playing over me with interest. "They are," she says, then, seeming to sense something off, she stops, pulling me into a hallway recess beside the sitting room door.

"How many weeks along are you?" she whispers conspiratorially.

"You know?" I ask, my voice breathier than I expect it to be. "Did someone tell you?"

Her eyes hold mine. It's clear she's off the family script; she's the only one who knows. "No. I have three children, Harry. The signs kind of burn into your brain," she says quietly, her eyes checking the door beyond my shoulder. "How far?" she asks again.

"Early. Eight weeks," I answer simply. There seems like little reason to deny it.

"Still too early to tell anyone then," she says, before clarifying, "No one else in the family knows?"

"Just me and Edward."

She looks surprised. "Edward knows! And he was okay with you coming tonight?"

I frown. "Of course he knows. And why wouldn't he be okay with me coming to a party?"

Fiona pauses, then gently shakes her head. "Oh, no reason, I guess. If he's okay with it then it's fine. Just be careful tonight, please. I know it's just a children's game, but people can get carried away, you know, in the heat of the moment."

It's unclear if she is deliberately trying to scare me or annoy me. The idea that I might somehow get so caught up in a child's game that I would actually hurt myself is frankly insulting.

I bite back the desire to follow that line of response. She's just trying to be nice, I assure myself, to offer pregnancy advice, even though with three kids of her own she should know how badly that tends to come across.

"Noted," I say with a smile. "I'll take it easy. What gave me away?" I add. I should probably stop doing whatever that is if I want to keep this pregnancy quiet for now.

"Not drinking, of course. But mainly, when you took your shoes off earlier. Edward put his hand on your lower back, to steady you." She absentmindedly looks down at the ring on her finger. "Oliver does that—did that—during my pregnancies. He'd steady me. It's an unconscious thing, a protective instinct. Maybe it's a Holbeck thing or a man thing. But it's impossible to miss if you know what to look for." She shrugs off the thought. "Anyway, my lips are sealed. Your secret's safe with me." She gestures toward the sitting room. "Shall we?"

Fiona's sitting room is filled with people, warmth emanating from a large fireplace that laps and crackles beside two large sofas. Through the milling guests I make out an enormous Christmas tree positioned between the two large sash windows. At its tip a glittering golden star almost skims the paintwork of the brownstone's high ceiling; its thick branches are festooned with red and gold ribbons, twinkling baubles, and softly glowing lights.

The gentle babble of polite conversation and unseen music steadies my nerves as my eyes rove the faces for one in particular. It's mid-December but in this room, with its soft flickering candles and heady aroma of fresh spruce, one might imagine that it could be Christmas forever.

My eyes find Edward first, by the fire in conversation with Oliver. They seem intent on something—not a disagreement so much as a debriefing of sorts. I make a mental note to ask Edward about what later. He catches me watching, his serious expression lightening as he raises his glass in my direction.

"I can introduce you to everybody, if you like?" Fiona says. I had almost forgotten her beside me. "There's family here you haven't met yet. Robert's cousins, their children; the extended family." I still can't see him in the crowd but I can feel he is here. Fiona points out an elderly couple milling by the piano in conversation with the only biracial couple present. "That's my side of the family. My parents. And my brother and his wife. Their daughter, Olivia, my niece, is here too somewhere with the boys—" She breaks off suddenly as a waiter beckons her from across the room. "I'll be right back. Will you be okay alone for a moment?" I start to speak but she is already gone.

The room is filled with faces I do not recognize; waiters weave among them with food and drink. I pluck a few things when they glide by and as the crowd shifts, I spot him sitting beside Matilda on one of the low chintz sofas, my chest constricting slightly as I prepare for his gaze. I take him in before he notices me, his tall, powerful physicality at odds with the soft domestic setting. I watch Matilda talk to him, their expressions serious, and I can't help but wonder if there is a problem. If something I do not know about is happening in the Holbecks' world, if there is an issue with the company, or worse.

Robert must feel eyes on him. He looks up, his gaze magnetically finding mine.

A shiver runs through me as his words from the tape come

back to me. Visceral apprehension, and a desperate curiosity to know why he is doing what he is doing to me, fizzling through every fiber of my being.

He looks younger than I recall from Thanksgiving—stronger, smarter, even more of a credible threat. He tips his head in acknowledgment of my presence and taps Matilda deftly on the knee. She stops talking, her eyes following his to me, her energy changing seamlessly, like Edward's and Oliver's—a lightness seeming to click on inside her, her features blossoming into a smile. "Harry!" she calls across the room. "There you are."

Robert watches me carefully as I tentatively sink into the sofa beside Matilda. He's trying to figure out if I've listened to the tape yet. He can't ask with Matilda here but the quiet calm in his eyes tells he's not averse to waiting.

"How have you been?" Matilda inquires enthusiastically. "We've all been desperate to see you. How's the book?"

I realize with a wave of relief this might be the closest I get to talking to Robert tonight, so I can indirectly sell my excuse for not listening to his tape yet. "Great. I handed it in just the other day. I've barely come up for air since we last met; no time for anything."

Matilda's hand flies to my back in congratulations. "Oh my God, Harry. That is so exciting. You must be exhausted. When can we read it? Did you hear that, Dad? Harry's been at the grindstone with her book."

It suddenly occurs to me, in earnest, that the Holbecks might genuinely be concerned about what I write in my next book. I suppose if I become part of the family, I will ultimately fall under the same scrutiny that they are prey to—or I could be kidding myself about my own importance. That said, my last book was read by over a million people, and that's a sizable reach.

And then another thought emerges from the shadows of my mind. The idea that Robert gave me his tape for that very reason, to have me write his story. But that would bring the entire house of cards crashing down around him. That can't be his intention.

I snap back to the present at the sound of his voice. "The new book is complete. That's wonderful news, Harriet," he says lightly. "I look forward to reading it." He gives me a polite smile, his expression otherwise unreadable.

There's a scuffle by the door and I see that the children are beginning to flood into the room. It must be time for the race and for my time with Robert to end.

The party crashes into silence and after a moment I realize why. A cowbell is clunking somewhere beyond the room. I watch the children's features fizz with terror and excitement as adults exchange knowing glances.

I see eight children in total. Fiona's boys: Sam, Tristan, and Billy. Lila's Milo and three other boys around Sam's age. Olivia is the only girl present and clearly the eldest. She sticks close to Fiona's middle son, Tristan; I imagine she's been told to pair with him. He can't be more than two years older than Billy.

"You're taking part in the race, aren't you, Harry?" Matilda whispers, her voice low as the bell clunks again ominously.

"I am. Though I'm not entirely sure how it all works. I didn't realize Edward wouldn't be playing with me," I answer, suddenly realizing I might have left everything a bit late. "Any tips?" I ask, an entirely new clutch of nerves stirring inside me.

Matilda grins, her red lips parting to show a perfect set of white teeth. "Yeah," she says with a throaty chuckle. "Run for your life."

22

Run for Your Life

FRIDAY, DECEMBER 16

I join the rest of the players congregated in the hallway, the children, me, and Lila all sectioned off from the adults now, the sitting room doors closed behind us as we wait for whatever is about to happen.

Lila is busy hushing an anxious Milo as they wait by the staircase, my way to her blocked by jostling children who skitter about the entrance hall with pre-game excitement. There simply isn't enough time now to ask what the hell I'm supposed to do other than run. Besides, I too have more pressing matters to deal with. Billy tugs my trouser leg again and I crouch to meet him at eye level.

"What's our plan then, team captain?" I ask brightly, but his concerned little face makes it clear it's going to take a lot more than my casual optimism to quash his mounting fear.

"We gock to run away and hide, Auntie Harry-ept," he tells me with solemn decisiveness.

"No problem. We can do that, easy-peasy. I know loads about hiding spots. Is that all we need to do in the game, honey?"

I'm aware I should have dug deeper into the actual rules of the game before now, instead of trying to decipher them from a terrified toddler at the absolute last minute. But I had other things on my mind. And a game's a game; you only really pick it up as you play anyway.

"You good a' games, Auntie Harry-ept?" Billy asks, giving me a quizzical look I find oddly exposing.

"Um, yeah. I think so." He looks unimpressed, so I follow up with a perhaps overly confident, "No, yeah! Best hider ever! I've got you covered, little man."

Billy thinks for a minute, then puffs out his chest, buoyed by my certainty. "I guess then we could look for *stick*? If you fink you know hiding places."

"Look for a stick? Is that part of it?"

"Yep. Ebbergreen stick." He gives a firm nod as he tests the word in his mouth again.

I remember Fiona's sketchy explanation from earlier. "Yes, the *Evergreen*? If we find that the game stops, right?"

"Yeah, *Ebber*. You got to show the Krampus the Ebbergreen, then you win; he goes away."

Right, so we need to find a hidden stick and not get caught while we do it. It sounds like the game Capture the Flag. "We just show the stick to the monster—I mean the Krampus—and that's the end?"

"Yep. Das it." He stares up at me, wide eyes filled with a mix of fear and hope that I realize I am supposed to make good on.

I'd like to ask Billy: Why a stick? Why an evergreen? Why a Krampus? Why any of this? But he's three and it all seems a little above his pay grade.

Thankfully, Sam, Billy's older brother, must have overheard our conversation, as he leans in to elaborate.

"Basically, you need to find the Evergreen because Evergreen wood is the Krampus's weakness, so the only way to kill him is to run Evergreen through his heart."

I frown. "Oh, right. But we're just *showing* the stick to the Krampus, right? We're not running it through anything?"

Sam smirks as if I'm playing a trick on him. "No, of course not, that would be stupid. You just find the stick then you shout 'Evergreen' as loud as you can and stay exactly where you are and the Krampus stops chasing everyone. Then he'll come and find you and the stick." I feel myself frown and Sam continues, "He has to check you have it. If you do, you'll be safe from him, don't worry. As soon as he sees you have it, you win."

I turn back to Billy with a big smile. "Well, that sounds great, right?"

"Yep, great," Billy agrees, trying his best to be brave. "Up, up," he adds, his arms outstretched, and I scoop him up onto my hip, the flashlight looped around my wrist thumping heavy against my thigh.

"Oh, and one more question, Sam," I say turning back to him. "What do I do if I get caught by the—"

But I do not get to finish as the house plunges into darkness and the children begin to scream.

From outside the front door, the cowbell clunks mournfully and the shrieks stutter to a halt. The darkness is suddenly filled with nothing but the sound of muffled breathing and fear. Then three reverberating knocks hit the front door and echo through the house. All eyes turn to the grotesque and towering silhouette beyond the glass of the door. Then the sound of something barely human screams out into the night air, cutting through everything.

Jesus fucking Christ. I was expecting an uncle in a costume, and maybe a little growling, not whatever the hell that is.

The door handle turns and, at that point, the kids go absolutely berserk. Bloodcurdling screams filling the house as panicked feet pound up the staircase and away, down hallways, into the darkness of unseen rooms. Only Billy and I remain in the silence, Billy completely frozen on my hip as I gently try the handle back into the adults' room. I don't think I want to play anymore.

But the sitting room door is locked; beyond, only silence. They've locked me out. The front door slowly creaks open, the last barrier between us and the silhouetted creature. Billy wriggles with blind panic in my arms.

"Run! Harry-ept, run!" he screams, and I spin in time to see what he sees, the blood draining from me. I don't know what I was expecting, but it was not this. This is not a Holbeck brother in a furry suit; this is not something digestible, or child-friendly.

My breath comes in short, tight gasps. It stands seven feet tall even as it crouches under the frame of the front door, panting wet animal breaths, haloed in streetlight against the night sky. Its face, partly stripped of skin, is bleeding, its teeth jagged, yellowed, and slick with strung saliva. Its distorted face is part human, though its jaw is distending in pain. And around its neck a rusty dented cowbell *tunk*s with its every movement.

I reel back instinctively, the wall knocking the air clean from me as I hit it, and Billy's grip tightens. The creature's eyes watch us carefully, the slowest of the herd, left behind. It cocks its head, taking in the stairs to our right as it anticipates my next move, but I do not think twice; I bolt as fast as I can, because whatever this is does not feel like a game.

Behind me the creature lunges as I scramble up the stairs, Billy clinging tight to me. When we reach the top, I dart behind the landing wall where, pressed against the paintwork, breath coming high and fast, I try to listen. There is no sound from the stairs.

I cannot hear him. *It. Krampus.* Only the rasp of my own tight breaths.

The house is silent save for the muffled sounds of children's feet in the darkness. The cowbell must have been silenced, because I can no longer hear the creature coming.

Whatever that thing is downstairs, it won't be announcing its presence anymore; it'll come stealthily and slowly and God knows what will happen if it finds you.

Of course, I'm a rational person; I know the thing down there is someone in a suit. It has to be. I just wasn't expecting the suit to look quite so terrifying, to be quite so real. But I suppose with all the money in the world you can afford realism. And this Krampus is just that—a movie-grade prosthetic marvel. I know monsters are not real, my rational mind knows that, but like it or not my heart will not stop pounding. First Robert's tape and now this; games definitely don't feel like games in this family.

After a few more seconds of recovery, I carefully heave us both up to standing. In the half-light I make out Billy's terrified face. He watches me silently, the unfathomable trust in his eyes demanding clear action.

"Which way goes up?" I whisper to him calmly. I know from the outside of the building that it has five floors including a basement level. There should be another two more floors above us. The higher we are, the safer we'll be for now.

Billy holds my gaze for a second then raises a tiny hand in answer, pointing across the landing to a corridor that disappears into the darkness.

We'll need to pass the open stairwell again to get there. I look back at the blackened void between us and then, in the corridor beyond, a flashlight beam swings through the darkness and I see Olivia peek around the doorframe. Catching us in her beam, she quickly clicks the light off, but I am already blinded by its afterglow. Vision spangled, I need a moment to readjust, and when I do I see she has crawled to the edge of the landing wall on her side. Behind her, little Tristan shuffles into view, timid and silent.

I catch Olivia's attention and indicate we should both cross the landing at the same time. She thinks a moment and then nods. We double our chances of not getting caught that way. If there's something waiting in the stairwell, he can't catch us all.

I hitch Billy higher on my hip and signal Olivia to go on three. But we don't reach three when a shrill and bloodcurdlingly real scream rips through the house from downstairs. It sounds like Milo. I tell myself it's fine, Lila is with him, but for the first time since the game started I think of Robert's tape. Of the girl on Robert's tape.

Olivia breaks cover, yanking Tristan along behind her as she pelts past the stairs toward us. Reflexively we burst from our hiding spot, barreling forward across the landing too.

We pass Olivia and Tristan mid-landing and plow on in our respective directions, plunging back into the darkness of opposite sides. In the safety of the dark corridor, I look back in time to wonder what Olivia's plan is, but a gentle tug on my hair refocuses me.

"Up," Billy whispers, his mouth close to my ear, his breath warm on my skin.

"Up," I agree as I move us onward into the darkness.

We round a bend in the corridor and I clink on our flashlight for the first time. The beautifully restored interior wood paneling of Fiona and Oliver's house bursts into view as we creep around another bend and a thin staircase appears ahead. In spite of everything, as we stride toward it, I can't help but wonder how many staircases this place has and what something like this might be worth in the current climate.

But the hot warmth of urine spreading across my hip from Billy's trousers snaps me to reality.

"You okay?" I ask him, concerned. "You scared?"

My anger at the Holbecks, and in particular at Fiona, resurfaces. Why would she put her child through this? Why would any of them make me do this? And why on earth didn't Edward tell me what this was really like?

"Yeah, scared, but mainly soda," Billy replies with a judicious shake of the head. "Should have gone before." He looks circumspect, then adds, "Sorry, Harry-ept."

He's scared but dealing with it incredibly well. "That's okay, sweetie. We'll sort it out later. You're doing a great job." I smile for his benefit, in spite of the fact that his family has put me in a totally inappropriate position and my whole left side is soaked in hot piss.

I hoick Billy a little higher on my hip, try not to think of all the damage I could be doing to the growing fetus inside me, and shine my torch up into the dark stairwell above us.

It's just a game, Harry. An incredibly weird one, granted, but just a game. The baby will be fine. Billy will be fine. Whoever that was screaming downstairs will be fine. And Robert did not kill Samantha Belson because I am meeting her in three days.

When we reach the next landing, Billy nods up again, the staircase narrowing, closing in around us as we reach the top of the house.

A pink door comes into view above, cracked paint and a lift latch, something ominous about it making me slow as we approach.

The door swings open with a creak and I can feel the sheer size of the space beyond it; it's cavernous. The whole top floor of this house must be open-plan. I sweep my torch beam into the murk. Odd things catch in the light's path: the edges of a circus tent at one end of the room; a full-sized horse frozen mid-gallop, its body accurately rendered except for the bright red plastic of its saddle and reins. At one end of the room a small network of road markings covers the floor, littered with child-sized cars and bikes, a street in miniature, and beyond it in the far distance I make out the backs of eight teddy bears in a picnic circle of more. It's a playroom. The whole top floor of Fiona's brownstone is a massive, creepy playroom.

"Is there anyone up here?" I call carefully into the darkness. Billy presses a finger to my lips.

"Sshh," he whispers with a shake of his head.

Wind chimes jangle from somewhere in the darkness and, nerves frazzled, I jump, my shoulder bumping on a light switch in the stairwell that clicks on and bathes the penthouse playroom in bright light.

The lights work here. Without a second thought I dash into the playroom and shut the pink door firmly behind us, blocking the light's path down the stairwell.

I scan the brightly colored room, its proportions ludicrous, larger than our whole apartment put together. The sound of a scream from many floors below springs me into action. I plop Billy down onto the floor, head over to a large bookcase filled with crates of toys, and speedily remove them all. I then slowly drag the bookcase across the carpet to block the doorway, reinserting the toy crates one by one to reinforce our barrier.

Pink door blocked, I flop down onto the carpet completely exhausted. "Come 'ere," I huff to Billy, my arms outstretched, and he totters over, wet pants sagging. "We should be safe in here."

He collapses into my arms too. "Yep," he says simply, then looks up. "Where's Mumma?"

I consider.

"I really don't know. But I'm sure she's fine. You definitely don't need to worry about her." I look at Billy's little face, his soft blond curls, and I wonder what the hell Fiona was thinking letting him play this game. Then I conjure the image of a three-year-old Edward pissing himself, thirty-odd years ago, on some unknown nanny's hip. What was it Edward said? *Character building.*

I look around the playroom and can't deny it's cute. Fiona and Oliver clearly care about their kids, in spite of what tonight might make one think.

"Is this your place, then?" I ask my little friend.

He splays his hands, indicating both indifference and pride. "Yeah. My toys." He looks thoughtfully around before adding, "And Tristan and Sam's."

"It's nice up here."

"Yep."

I look down at my watch. Thirty minutes have passed already. "How long till the game is over, Billy?" I ask.

"Not till Ebbergreen."

I look up abruptly. That can't be right; it just keeps going indefinitely until then? "Are you sure, Billy? It doesn't stop until someone finds the stick?"

He nods.

"And how long does that usually take?"

He shrugs. "Sam said they stayed up past midnight last time. And only Uncle Edward could find it 'cause he was a grown-up."

Lila is, given Milo's scream earlier, probably already out of the game and I am the only adult left playing.

It's nine-thirty now; I cannot do this until midnight. I'm already exhausted and freaked-out, but all that aside, I need a wee now too and I don't want to have to piss my pants like Billy.

A thought occurs and I scan the room, hoping that Billy's accident might be less of an anomaly and more of a regular occurrence demanding contingency plans. I find what I'm looking for in a corner of the room near a large industrial-looking metal unit. A small wardrobe.

I rise and head over to the wardrobe, Billy following me wordlessly. If we're staying here until midnight, we're sure as hell not doing so covered in piss.

The wardrobe is full of costumes. Magician, unicorn, Marvel characters, frog, fireman, cowboy, and lederhosen.

"Okaaaay," I say, as Billy peeks into the wardrobe beside me and lets out a tiny, world-weary sigh.

He kneels down and pulls open a drawer revealing a fresh stack of clean underwear and socks.

"Great work, little man. That'll do for underneath. But what about on top?"

Five minutes later a urine-free lederhosen-clad three-year-old stands before me. I try to stifle a giggle but it's his anger at the outfit more than the outfit itself that gets me.

"Stop, Auntie Harry-ept. Not funny. Stupid."

"I'm not laughing at you, sweetheart, I prom—"

A knock sounds abruptly from the pink door and we both freeze.

The knock comes again. Billy's eyes are wide like saucers. But a Krampus wouldn't knock, would it? And just like that I'm up and across the room, my ear pressed to the pink door. "Who is it?" I whisper.

"Olivia," a soft voice answers.

After a couple of minutes huffing and shuffling, I open a gap big enough for Olivia and Tristan to slip through the doorway, and together we all reassemble the barricade.

Once it's back in place, Olivia turns to me. "Have you found it yet?" she demands.

"Found what?"

"The Evergreen."

"Um, no," I say with slightly more vehemence than anticipated. "Wouldn't this be over if I found it?"

Her face falls. "Yeah, but I thought maybe you'd found it and you didn't know what to do." She looks to Tristan, disappointed, then rallies. "Where have you looked, then?"

I pause, genuinely considering whether or not to lie to a child, but deciding it's probably not a great precedent to set. "Nowhere. We've just been hiding up here."

"Oh. Okay." She's disappointed, and I try not to let the shame drown me.

"To be honest," I say, leveling with her, "I have absolutely no idea what is going on here, Olivia, or what I'm supposed to be looking for. I'm just trying to keep him safe." I eye Billy in his lederhosen.

"Why is he wearing that?" Olivia begins, before thinking better of it. "Never mind. We've checked the second and third floor already but we haven't been up here yet or in the basement."

"What about the ground floor, where everyone started?"

"That's out-of-bounds; the only open doors there lead upstairs or downstairs."

"Okay, so if it's not here, it will be in the basement."

"Yeah."

"And how do you know where to look? Are there clues?"

She looks aghast. "Are we the first people you've talked to since the game started?"

"Yeah," I say, noting her derision.

"Oh, okay, I guess that makes sense. It's you. The clue is your name. It's always the name of the oldest player. If you'd asked anyone, after the game started, they would have told you the clue is hidden in the letters of your name."

"I was supposed to ask someone after—" I begin, but quickly lose the will to continue. "Okay, so . . . The clue to where the

Evergreen is hidden is in the letters of my name: Harriet Reed. An anagram?" I ask.

Olivia nods, pulling out her iPhone and tapping away furiously, her brow furrowed. "Maybe I'm spelling it wrong. Here, you try."

She hands me the phone, the screen open on a letter-reshuffling app. She has typed my name in correctly: H-A-R-R-I-E-T—R-E-E-D. The best suggestion comes up beneath it: *reheated.*

"Reheated," I mutter. "Could there be a microwave, or an oven, in the basement?"

Olivia shakes her head. "Kitchen's on the ground floor. And out-of-bounds."

I look at the letters again. "Oh my God," I say, my own slowness surprising me. I tap in the initial of my middle name, Yasmin, and I press RESHUFFLE once more.

The letters of my name rearrange into a new word and I shake my head at the nerve of the clue. *Hereditary.* Someone in the Holbeck family's got a real sense of humor all right. I spin the phone back to Olivia.

"I don't know what that word means; I'm thirteen," she says.

"It means inherited characteristics, or inherited property," I tell her. "Is there anything up here or in the basement that the word could refer to?" That said, I think, is there anything in this house that it wouldn't?

Olivia grins broadly, her eyes suddenly alive. "Oh my gosh. I know what it is. This was J. L. Holbeck's first home in New York. It's been in the family ever since. There's a placard in the basement. Like a foundation stone. Everyone who's ever lived in this house has inherited it."

"Great," I cheer, the prospect of the end almost in sight. "Now, how in hell do we get down to the basement from here?"

Billy raises his tiny hand once more, his finger pointing toward the large industrial-looking unit in the corner of the room. "Hatch," he says with authority.

23

Down the Hatch

FRIDAY, DECEMBER 16

Olivia slides the hatch doors shut on me and I flick on my torch in the darkness of the service lift.

I try not to think about the empty lift shaft beneath me and content myself with the fact that I am not above the maximum weight warning on the hatch door.

Olivia would have been lighter, but there was no way I was going to let a child travel down five flights in a service hatch lift on my watch.

Besides, if you want a job done right, do it yourself. I want this game over.

The lift clanks down and I think of the Holbecks and the bizarre drinks party they must still be having in a different part of the house, pure anger burning through me. I could laugh at the situation, sure, but cramped up in a service lift covered in toddler piss at eight weeks pregnant, it doesn't seem like that much of a joke.

I flick off my torch as the lift rattles to a stop and sit in silence for a moment. No sound from the basement beyond. No seven-foot monsters. Or men in seven-foot monster suits, I should say.

Gently I slide my fingers into the gap between the hatch doors and prize them open. The room beyond is dark.

I slip from the hatch then follow the right-hand wall along as per Olivia's meticulous instructions. I need to follow this corridor and pass two doorways before I reach up. Above the final door-frame is the placard, and the Evergreen should be there. I count the doors to my right as I pass them.

One.

I shuffle on in the blackness, noises of the party above just audible from down here: faint music, laughter. Then I hear another noise. I freeze. Ahead of me, the sound of breathing. My hand flies to my mouth to mask my own.

I stay still for a second listening, but the noise is gone as quickly as it came. I hold a moment longer then remind myself that if I don't end this, no one will. I force myself to continue, to creep on past the second door.

Two.

After three more steps I feel the lip of another doorway. This is it. With incredible care I raise my arms above the doorframe and sweep my hand along the lip. My baby finger makes contact first but I react too slowly and the stick rolls away from me, my stomach clenching with primal terror as I wait for it to clatter to the ground. There's a moment's hiatus in the thick blackness and then it does just that.

I drop immediately into a low crouch, scrambling to grab it before it rolls away. There's the sound of breathing again; deep, hoarse, animalistic breathing. I freeze. It's here; *he's* here. Who-ever it is in that suit is down here with me. The Krampus.

I wonder who could be inside that costume. And how odd it is that whoever's in there is still keeping up their monster act when it's only me and them down here.

I push the thought away. The Holbecks obviously take their traditions very seriously. As I reach in the dark, images of who it might be flash through my thoughts: Oliver, Stuart, Edward. Then my mind inevitably lands on Robert, and it will not budge. I think of the girl on his tape, of what he said he did to her, and the silliness of being down here in the dark melts away, leaving only dread. I push the thoughts away and try to locate where the sound of the creature is coming from.

It is to my right, about six feet from me. Two large strides away.

But the Evergreen stick is near, and the end of the game is tantalizingly close. I want to go home.

I tentatively let my fingers search for it. But I need to stretch farther, and I realize that if I want this game to end, I'll need to turn on my torch, come what may.

Every nerve in my body rebels at the idea, but the truth is that all I need to do is grab that stick on the floor right in front of me, and shout the magic word. It doesn't matter if he sees me. It'll all be over. I can grab it before he reaches me.

I clutch the torch tight and flick it on.

The space around me bursts into vision, the terra-cotta of floor tiles and, three feet ahead of me, the thick Evergreen stick, a rod about a foot long. I dive for it and as I do I hear the rush of movement behind me. I fumble the stick into my hand as I spin around and point my flashlight back at the massive form rushing toward me. I dodge and scramble desperately up to my feet, the Evergreen branch firmly in my grasp, but he does not stop. He plows into me, his dank fur pushing me back against the basement wall. The wind is knocked out of me and my torch clatters to the floor. I look up at the dim figure pinning me to the wall, its wet mouth inches from mine. It studies me, now that it has me pinned, its head tilting as if it were trying to work something out. I try to call out the word *Evergreen,* its wood held tight in my hand, but, like in a nightmare, the word does not come.

The creature, still so real, even at this proximity, forces a wet hand over my mouth. I think again of who is in that suit and the nature of what is happening suddenly changes.

Is it Robert pressing me hard against the wall? Is it Edward? Is he trying to scare me? Humiliate me? Paralyzed by anxiety and confusion and the sheer strength of him, I cannot do anything but let him continue. His breath is hot on my neck as his free hand traces lasciviously down the side of my body to where my hand hangs, gripping the Evergreen branch firmly. The nature of the situation changes again to something threateningly sexual, bordering on assault. It is only when his clawlike fingers reach my thigh, wet with toddler piss, that my paralysis is broken. My anger bursts its banks as I think of the night I have had. The night Billy has had. I am incandescently angry—at this family, at this game, at all of this bullshit.

I summon all my strength, then pull back and slam my elbow as hard as physically possible directly into the creature's face, not caring who is in the suit, and not caring about the consequences. The creature howls and reels back, releasing me. I choke in a lungful of air and I yell with every ounce of anger I possess, "EVERGREEN."

Instantly all the lights blast on. Throughout the house, around me and above, I hear the sound of doors electronically unlocking.

It's over. The game's over. I won. But my anger is not replaced by triumph. If anything, it hardens into something denser.

Around the corridor, I hear a door open and the gentle hubbub of the party, and laughter, carries along to me.

I hear Fiona before I see her. "We have a winner. Good job, Harriet!" She appears around the corner smiling with an excited round of applause. "That was fantastic."

A medic appears, moving past her to attend to the prone creature on the floor behind me. He hoists it up to sitting and gently helps to remove its mask.

The man inside it is finally revealed, but he is no one I have ever seen before. He takes a glug from the water bottle the medic offers him and wipes the moisture from his sweat-stung eyes. I try to make sense of who he is but can't. He's in his late twenties, hair slicked to his tanned skin with sweat from the heavy suit. His red eyes squint up into the light, his breathing still snagging from exertion and my blow to his head. I feel sick with guilt. And yet whoever he is ruined my night, felt me up, and scared me half to death.

"How are you, Mikhail?" Fiona asks him cheerfully. He looks up and flashes a handsome if exhausted smile punctuated by an athletic double thumbs-up. "Remarkable performance again, Mikhail," she continues. "Best yet." I get the impression from Fiona's tone and volume that Mikhail doesn't speak much English.

"We hire a motion capture performer every year," she tells me, taking my arm in hers and leading me away from him. "To be Krampus. Mikhail is a special effects CGI performer. He's done Krampus for us for two years running now. He's a phenomenal find; we're very lucky to have him."

I let her lead me, dazed, up the basement stairs into the bright light of the hall, my anger morphing into bald incredulity now. The house around us is alive once more with the sound of children, as if nothing out of the ordinary has happened. I stare at Fiona as she leads me to a ground-floor toilet and starts to dab a wet flannel onto my damp, piss-covered trousers. I stare at her, dumbfounded.

"I always tell Billy to go before things start but he never listens," she says ruefully.

I stop her hand mid-dab and she looks up at me.

"What the absolute hell was that game, Fiona? You think that was okay?"

Fiona looks at me, confused for a second, then touches my forehead. "Why? Do you not feel well? Was it too much?" she asks. "For the baby?"

"Are you fucking kidding me? It was too much for me. Why the hell didn't you explain it to me? Why didn't anyone?"

Her gaze flits to the bathroom door and then back to me, conflicted. "Because that's part of the game," she tells me, her tone low. "You're not supposed to tell new family members how to play; they have to find it out, like everyone else. It's a test. Of character. Of working together, as a team, one generation with the next. Teamwork." She smiles. "And you won. You should be happy." Her tone is tight now, slightly irritated, as if she'd laid on the whole evening for me and this was all the thanks she'd gotten.

"And what about Billy? Weren't you worried about him?" I ask, and a question falls into place. "Wait, how did you know he wet himself? Were you watching us?"

She nods. "Of course. I'm not going to let a stranger run around in the dark with my child, am I?" she says softly, and I can tell I've hit a nerve. "This house got broken into fifteen years ago. The whole building is rigged with cameras now. You'll see next year. We all watch the game." Her attention returns to my wet trouser leg. "I'm not sure how much I'm actually helping here," she says. "Let's leave it, shall we? I'll get you a fresh pair of mine instead. But right now, we need to get moving. It's time for presents," she says brightly, then, assessing my expression, she adds, "If you're ready, that is?"

I give her a look that I hope conveys exactly how ready I am.

"Right. I see," she says carefully. "Well, the children are waiting for their auntie Harriet. And I think they'd be very excited to see the winner, don't you think?"

I decide I hate Fiona and that feeling that way is okay. I grab the flannel from her hands, briskly rub my own wet hip, and toss it away.

"Yeah, let's get it done."

24

Diamonds Don't Come from Coal and Other Facts

SATURDAY, DECEMBER 17

The lights in Mount Sinai Hospital make the diamond bracelet around my wrist sparkle. My present, my prize, for beating the Krampus. I was a good girl; I protected the children and saved the day. I'm a regular hero.

It's a beautiful bracelet, I can't deny it, twinkling on my wrist in the strip lighting of the pregnancy ward.

The Krampus, or St. Nicholas, or whoever the hell, left it in my shoe. All the shoes along Fiona and Oliver's hallway were stuffed with gifts, good or bad.

My shoes alone were coated with black coal dust; a joke, apparently. Coal for the naughty. If only they knew how naughty I have actually been in my life. Though, given Robert's tape, perhaps they do.

In my left shoe there was a leather box. Inside was a note, and beneath that note, a gift.

As I watch other couples head in for their scans, I try not to think about last night. I try to let the anger dissolve. I would be lying if I said I am not concerned that being chased by the Krampus might have done more damage than any of us realize, that this morning's scan—instead of showing me a heartbeat—will show me only stillness. Life can be fragile sometimes.

I look down at the diamonds throwing light into colors, the only shimmer in this sterile ward.

Edward fastened it onto my still-trembling wrist in Oliver and Fiona's hallway last night, silent in the knowledge of the almighty shitstorm coming his way as soon as we got home. He saw on camera the hand sliding down my body, the look in my eyes.

Matilda sidled up beside us to inspect the winner's spoils. "You get coal and diamonds, ha. That's funny; Dad's sense of humor all over. It's a common misconception, that diamonds come from coal. Not true obviously. Coal is compacted rotten matter. Diamonds existed long before anything organic could even rot." She grins knowingly. "Coal comes from coal and diamonds come from diamonds."

I straighten at the sound of a nurse's sneakers squeaking down the corridor. Edward's hand slips into mine. I look him in the eyes, heavy from lack of sleep, and I do not pull away.

Last night was our biggest argument. Don't get me wrong: we're a normal couple; we argue. But last night was a big one. It didn't so much end as run out of words. In a nutshell, Edward didn't warn me about the game.

"You're supposed to go in blind; that's part of it. I thought you'd get a kick out of it. How could I know you'd take it that seriously? I warned you it was weird—*they* were weird—and you told me it was fine. That you wanted this," he'd argued, his pillow and bedding stacked in his arms, as baffled and upset by the extremity of my reaction to the evening as I seemed to be by his. "I didn't know you'd freak out, did I? How could I know that? You should have just stopped."

"I don't know, Ed, I was scared. Maybe if you'd told me about the seven-foot deformed goat-man I'd have been able to make an informed decision? Maybe me being pregnant should have twigged something for you? That, and having to run around all night carrying a toddler up and down a five-fucking-story house?"

"I didn't know you'd carry him. And not to undermine your, whatever, but Fiona's played it pregnant. I'm pretty sure Mom did too. I didn't know it would be an issue. I just thought you'd be good at it; that you'd find it good weird. Was I wrong? I mean you won it, didn't you? And in record time. You did that; I didn't make you do that." He stops, looking at the now stony aspect of my face before continuing: "It was a game, Harry. Part of it is you didn't know the rules. You could have stopped—you didn't need to run, or win. You know, the kids who get caught by the Krampus get taken to the kitchen and have ice cream!"

And that fact had put the nail in the coffin for me.

"Oh my God, Edward. How could I have possibly known that? Jesus fucking Christ! You didn't tell me anything. Anything at—"

"That's the point, Harry! To see how you do under pressure. Teamwork. And it turns out you do incredibly well. Okay. And you're fine."

"Do I look fine, Edward? Do I? Having been chased around and felt up by a motion capture guy? Do I look like I'm avoiding stress like Dr. Leyman said?"

And so on, and on, in circles, until sleep caught up with us.

Lying on the scanning table, warm goo spread liberally across my only slightly swollen belly, I try to calm my mind, to think positive thoughts.

"Today is just an initial look to see if everything is going according to plan with the pregnancy," the sonographer tells me.

"And hopefully we should be able to ascertain a due date." Her hand finds my shoulder. "Now, I need you to know, in case you have any concerns, that if we *don't* pick up a heartbeat today, that doesn't necessarily mean there is a problem. Okay? So bear with us. There's always a chance we have our dates slightly wrong; it happens every so often. We wouldn't expect to hear a heartbeat until at least six weeks, okay?"

It's like she can read my mind. Or, on second thought, maybe it's just my face she's reading.

Edward shifts beside me too. I can feel his concern, his expectation, as keenly as my own as I look up at the Styrofoam ceiling, like innumerable women before me, and wait for the sonographer to find life.

After a moment she turns her screen, wordlessly, around to show us. My eyes dance across the black and white trying to make sense of the undulating picture. And like an optical illusion, you appear.

A tiny butter bean, a sea creature, a little life wriggling and squirming inside me—of me, but independent from me.

I hear a gasp and I cannot tell if it's Edward's or my own. The sound kicks in now. The aortic *whoosh, whoosh, whoosh* like a deep-sea vent, pumping life in and out, hard and fast. And somehow, even though I've only just met you, I already love you.

An imagined future for you spools out ahead of us in my mind. Baby, toddler, child, teen, and adult. I see you, though you flick between genders, heights, looks, and ages, but I love every iteration of you. Birthdays, Christmases, fun and heartbreak. All of it. I want it all for you. Everything, all at once.

The sonographer smiles and turns the screen back deftly. "Congratulations, Mom and Pops," she says, carefully wiping the goo from my stomach. "We're at eight weeks today. You're welcome to get dressed and we can book you in for your next scan and a gender blood test as early as next week if you want to?"

———

On the subway journey home, we sit close, our argument now forgotten, our hands entwined. The game last night, so important before, has already slipped into memory, a funny story to tell our child one day. The bracelet on my wrist a Holbeck rite of passage. A talisman of how brave I can be when it is required.

Back at the apartment I help Edward pack for another work trip; his dinner with the Chinese investor last week went well, necessitating a trip to Hong Kong. We let name ideas flow between us. Our quiet contentedness morphing into full-blown excitement at the idea of knowing our child's sex a few days after Edward returns, the speed at which this is all happening thrilling and daunting.

I push the tape and Robert from my mind. I do not mention it to Edward. I won't until I have spoken to Samantha, until I know what this new game is.

"I'm serious when I say this," Edward tells me later as he lugs his bags into the building's elevator. "If you don't want to be so closely involved with them, if it's too much—which I think anyone might agree it could be—then we can step back from them. *You're* my family now. Both of you," he says, placing a warm hand on my slowly doming belly.

I think of the family—of Lila, Billy, Eleanor, and Matilda, their friendship, their glamour, and their approval—and I can't help but feel a pang at the thought of losing what we could become. "Can we play it by ear?" I ask him. "I don't want to throw the baby out with the bathwater, as they say. Once we pass the twelve-week mark and tell them about the pregnancy, they might settle down, right? Besides, I want our child to have a big family—grandparents, uncles, aunties. If they don't get yours, then they don't get any."

I watch from the building's lobby as Edward's cab pulls away and disappears into the flow of traffic.

I have three days on my own; three days to decide if I want to be part of this family, three days to work out exactly what Robert's game is and how I can beat him at it.

25

What the Nanny Saw

MONDAY, DECEMBER 19

Samantha Belson looks surprised as I catch her eye across the busy service station cafeteria. Perhaps she was expecting someone different, someone older or less whatever it is I am.

I recognized her as soon as I entered the food court, her once blond hair now dyed a natural brunette, her petite shoulders bundled up thick against the Pennsylvania weather. I don't know where she lives but I agreed to meet her here, at a busy freeway service station, just outside of Philadelphia, a two-hour drive from Manhattan.

Up close she looks younger than her sixty years. Good bone structure, I guess; a simple, stress-free life. After the Holbecks, I'm sure that's what she would have wanted.

She rises to shake my proffered hand.

"Harriet?"

I nod; her guard is still up.

"It's Harriet Reed," I say, introducing myself formally, and I note she bristles slightly at my British accent—another thing she wasn't expecting, another potential barrier rising between us. "Thank you so much for meeting me," I continue, trying to exude a trustworthiness that I have no idea whether I possess. "I really appreciate you coming here today. I know it's a pretty unusual request."

I pull out my chair and sit, hoping she will do the same, and after a cautionary scan of the cafeteria she does. We face each other, two strangers, across a bright-yellow table.

Something about me, or the situation, seems to have settled her enough to make her stay. She must sense I'm no direct threat, and it's glaringly obvious I'm here alone.

"How did you find me?" Samantha asks, leaning back into her seat appraisingly.

"Using a very blunt instrument," I answer honestly. "I messaged every single Samantha Belson in her sixties that I could find online."

Samantha chuckles in spite of herself. "Fair enough. I suppose it worked. Was I the only one who responded?"

"No. But you were the only one who responded in the right way. You seemed concerned about being contacted in relation to the family at all, concerned about the questions being asked. The questions wouldn't really have bothered anyone but you."

She tenses as she realizes the truth of my words. Her own caution gave her away.

She toys with her empty takeaway cup. "Yes, well, no one had mentioned their name to me for years. They were ghosts to me. Ghosts I didn't want to stir," she says, her voice gentle as a primary school teacher's. "So who exactly are *you* in all this, Harriet Reed?" She looks at me with fresh eyes, as interested in what I might have to tell her as I am in what she can tell me.

"Nobody. Just an observer. With concerns," I answer, deciding it's probably best not to tell her I'm marrying directly into the

Holbeck family just yet. "I'm not a reporter, or anything like that, if that's what you're worried about. I was just concerned about what happened to you after the accident. I thought perhaps something might have happened—after you left their employment."

"I see," she says, shifting forward in her seat.

"The Holbecks are an unusual family, we both know that, but it's hard to know exactly how unusual they are, if you catch my meaning. I needed to see to what extent they stray from the norm."

Samantha gives a terse laugh that confirms she knows exactly what I'm talking about.

"You want to know why I left the family?" she asks, her expression settling into something more serious.

"I do."

"I left because of what happened."

"With Bobby," I push.

"You know I can't talk about Bobby," she says curtly, her gaze flitting back on me, suddenly on edge. "You're a wife, aren't you?"

I flounder, caught out by the directness of the question.

"No, I'm not. Not yet," I say carefully, and as I say it the reality of that fact hits me for the first time in weeks. I have made no promises; there are things I might learn that might make marrying into Ed's family impossible. "Why can't you talk about Bobby?"

"The NDA."

I feel my eyebrows rise. "They made you sign a non-disclosure agreement—about Bobby?"

She looks irritated by the question. "No. Everyone who works for the Holbecks signs an NDA the day they start. It's not unusual in wealthy families. It gives them a sense of security. Families discuss their private lives, their businesses, their family relationships, we hear it all—" She breaks off, with a look to me. "I wish I could help; you seem like a nice girl, but I'm afraid I can't speak to specifics. Especially around something as delicate as Bobby. If they were to sue—I have nothing except my house, Harriet. I'm sure you understand. I bought it with the payout they gave me."

"Why would they give you a payout if you chose to leave yourself?"

She looks at me mutely. I've caught her out.

"Samantha, please. I just need to know what I'm getting into here," I beg, then quickly change tack. "Why agree to meet me, if you can't or won't say anything? Why come?"

"Because you dusted off the past and presented it back to me. I needed to know who you were; if this might become a problem for me."

And then, as much as I hate myself for doing it, I use my trump card. "It might become a problem for you. I'm pregnant and I'm concerned about my safety around these people. I need you to tell me about them. It will go no further, I promise you. I don't want to put you in a compromising position."

Her eyes drop to my stomach and I feel her take me in in an entirely different light.

"Oh, I see," she says. "Well, at least now I understand why you're here. That makes sense. One of the boys. Yes, yes, I suppose you had better ask me what you want to know and we'll see where we get."

"Bobby. Was there something strange about the way he died?" I ask immediately.

"Strange how?" she asks.

"Did he jump or—"

"Or was he pushed? He jumped," she says with a firmness that tells me this is not the area I should be looking into.

I throw my mind back to Robert's tape. He describes Samantha's death because she knew something incriminating about that day. If Bobby jumped, then what could she have had over Robert? "Did something make Bobby jump? Was the suicide triggered by a person or an event?"

Samantha holds my gaze, then her mouth pulls into a pinched

line and she gives me a tight nod. "Mm-hmm. Bobby was having trouble with his father at the time. Too much pressure on him for sure. But *he* jumped all by himself."

Something in me loosens slightly at the reiteration of that point. Bobby killed himself and Robert killed no one. He made up the murder and Samantha is alive. The tape is a trick.

"The Holbecks like playing games, don't they?" I ask.

She straightens in her seat. If I didn't have her full attention before, I have it now.

"Oh yes. Yes, they do. Some of them can be very cruel."

"Some of the Holbecks?" I clarify.

"No. Some of the games."

I let her words sink in. There are other games; I have only experienced the tip of the iceberg.

Another question springs to mind about her role as a nanny.

"You were there in New York that day, the day Bobby died; you ran down to him on the street, after he fell; you were the first responder. Robert Holbeck joined and you tried to explain what happened, but who was looking after the other children while you were—"

"Wait, what?" Samantha interrupts me, her face blanching. "What did you just say?"

I freeze, her tone raising the hairs on the back of my neck. I flash back through what I've just said but she beats me to it.

"I wasn't there the day Bobby died. I wasn't at the New York apartment; I was at The Hydes with the children. I was always with the children. Why would I be in the city? Bobby was a twenty-year-old man; he certainly didn't need a nanny."

Something crystallizes inside me. Samantha isn't the blonde on Robert's tape. It wasn't her hair blowing in the breeze that day; it was someone else's. Samantha Belson might be alive, but that has little to do with anything. I've found the wrong woman.

I think carefully before I speak next.

"Samantha, there was a woman with blond hair at the apartment that day. Do you know who that might have been?"

Samantha considers. "Um, I so rarely went there, I'm not sure who came and—" Suddenly her eyes flare. "Oh my God, wait, no. It can't have been her," she falters. "Are you sure there was someone there with *blond* hair? You're certain?"

"I'm not certain, but I am extremely concerned that something might have happened to a woman of that description, yes. I thought I'd found her in you and that she was safe. Who came to your mind just then?"

Without warning, Samantha rises to her feet and hastily buttons her coat. She's realizing now how serious this could be, how close she is to being dragged into the past and the consequences of it. Our interview is over.

"You know who it is, don't you? Please, Samantha, could something have happened to her?"

Samantha grabs her bag and slips it onto her shoulder. "I think that's enough," she says with finality. "I can't be involved in *this*. I can't get sucked into their world. Please don't contact me again. Don't mention my name. If I find out you have, I will pass on your information to the police." She goes to leave, then pauses, a tug of guilt pulling her back to me.

"Do yourself a favor: Don't mess with these people, do you understand me? Not in your condition," she says, her tone serious. "They aren't like you and me; they don't operate in the same way; they don't even operate in the same world. Just walk away. I don't know your situation but my advice is: Drop whatever it is you think you're gaining from this. Think about yourself. Think about your child." She stops abruptly, a thought occurring. Her face sharpens with focus. "Which one are you marrying?"

"Edward," I say after a second's hesitation.

"Oh," she says simply before continuing. "The blonde—the one who sprang to my mind just now—was Bobby's college girlfriend. They broke up a month or so before Bobby died. I don't know why she might have been at the apartment that day. But she was young and she was blond."

"Do you remember her name?" I ask.

"It didn't seem important at the time," she answers, looking outside at the parked cars, her eyes flitting from one shadowed windshield to the next. "Don't contact me again," she reaffirms, her voice low and vulnerable. "And if you want my advice, Harriet Reed? Be very careful what you do around the Holbecks."

26

Who Is She?

Be very careful what you do around the Holbecks.

Samantha's warning echoes in my mind as I drive home and it occurs to me, not for the first time, that given her advice, I probably should not have just written a thriller loosely based on a wealthy family who loses a son. What seemed like an interesting idea at the time now has the potential flavor of outright baiting. But I can fix that in the edit. Or not.

Though right now, I have more pressing matters. I need to find the name of Bobby's college girlfriend and check whether she's alive, for starters.

And if she's not, I need to go to the police. I try not to think of what will happen to me and Edward if I am the one to bring down his father, his family. Which raises the question of why on earth Robert gave me his tape in the first place. Does he have a death wish?

I can't help but wonder if Edward ever had his own suspicions about his father. He lived in the same house as the man for years. Perhaps I might have stumbled on the real reason they fell out.

Samantha's question about who I was planning on marrying sticks in my mind. She didn't seem that concerned about Edward, which makes me wonder who she *might* have been concerned about me marrying.

Oliver, Stuart, or even Robert himself.

Edward's car safely returned to the parking lot under our building, I head back up to the apartment, shedding my winter layers as I pull up a chair at my desk.

I type *girlfriend Bobby Holbeck* into my internet browser.

But once again, the results autocorrect to Robert Holbeck, filling the screen instead with a plethora of images of Robert Holbeck and various models and heiresses from the 1970s and '80s. In among them, I spot a young Eleanor, doe-eyed and mysterious— the woman he would eventually marry.

Without a name, I know I won't find Bobby's girlfriend.

In the kitchen I grab a consolatory snack to pep my energy and consider my options.

I could just ask someone. I could just call Edward, or Matilda, or Eleanor. Granted, it would be an odd question—what was your dead brother/son's ex-girlfriend called?—but it would save me a lot of time and anxiety. But then I recall Samantha's words and for some reason I am reminded of the conversation Matilda and Robert were having in Fiona's living room the other night and I'm suddenly not sure I can trust any of them with a question like this.

But Edward was his brother, and this is his house, so there're bound to be photos of Bobby somewhere in the apartment. All I need to find is one from Bobby's time at college, a party, a mixer, a ball game, anything. If they were a couple, she'll be in one of them. Bobby's stuff must have gone somewhere after he died, because it sure as hell wasn't in his old room.

Standing in front of Edward's closet, I suddenly balk at the idea of rooting through his personal belongings. Since the night of the proposal, I realize, I've unwittingly been chipping away at the bedrock of trust between us. Do I really want to rifle through Edward's things, his dead brother's life? Because I wouldn't want him to do the same thing to me, and I know exactly what he'd find if he did.

But if I can just find out who this ex-girlfriend is and whether she's okay, then I'll know Robert's tape is a trick and I can go to him and end this.

Buoyed by my resolution, I grab a chair so I can reach the high shelves above, where shoeboxes peek out over the edge. Up there I find exactly what I thought I might: an old school trunk, and a sun-bleached file box.

I pause, a dark thought blossoming. If I find a photo, and the girl is dead and Robert's tape is real, I will have to do something about all of this, and if I do there's a chance my own past might be dragged into things. I push the thought away. I'll have to cross that bridge when I come to it.

An hour into my search, legs numb from sitting on the floor, I come up for air, taking in the chaos fanned out around me. Photos from Edward's school days, university, weekends, and holidays. Friends, partners, family members I do not recognize and a precious few I do. Hugs, kisses, alcohol-rouged cheeks, and practical jokes. Wet hair, Bermuda shorts, and suntan-lotion-smeared books I didn't even know he'd read. Snapshots of Edward's life lie all around me. I try not to focus on the other girls. The fresh-faced women he has known and loved. I try not to judge myself against a poem written to him on the back of a postcard.

I try to have eyes only for Bobby. But I cannot find him among the old letters, gap-year trinkets, and report cards.

I stand to better take it all in, the relics of Edward's life so far. Bobby is not here.

It's only natural that he wouldn't be, I suppose. That he'd keep

Bobby in a separate place. I do not keep the soft-focus 1990s disposable-camera shots of my own long-dead parents with the other memories of my life. I lock them away; I can only see them if I make a conscious effort to see them. No surprises. It's easier that way.

If my own experience is anything to go by, then Edward's photos of Bobby will be somewhere else, somewhere safe, possibly somewhere locked.

I jiggle life back into my legs and head out to Edward's home office. His is larger than mine and rigged to the gills with cutting-edge computer tech, hard drives, and multiple screens. The similarities between the studies of father and son suddenly hit me.

I slip past the double-banked screens and head to the wooden filing cabinet next to Edward's desk, but fifteen tiny drawers later I am none the wiser. Invoices, statements, correspondence, but no personal items. I turn back to his desk and try the drawers. Nothing.

I let my eyes scan the room: bookshelves, hard drives, paperwork. On the bookshelves across the room, I find a row of dog-eared old coding books bookended by a small lockable steel storage box. My eye snags on the box. I remember noticing it before. Something so analog in a room so full of new tech.

I head over and gently lift the dark-gray metal box from its resting place. It's heavier than I expect. Full. There is no helpful key slotted in the lock, but looking at the rudimentary design I know I can open it. My aunt used to keep my maintenance allowance in a similar steel petty-cash box in the short time I lived with her after the accident. It took me a while to pluck up the courage, to get the knack, but back then days rolled into one another with nothing but reminders of what was gone. I had time.

These boxes can be opened with a paper clip, nothing more technical than that. It's a wonder the companies that make them are still in business given the—I'd imagine—widespread knowledge of this fact.

I slip a small metal paper clip off one of the documents on Edward's desk and take the box into the sitting room, placing it on the couch while I straighten out one side of the clip, leaving the other end still hooked. Then I crick my neck, lift the box onto my knees, and set about revisiting the magic touch I had at age eleven.

There is the satisfying slide of the simple wafer lock and, just like that, the small catch releases. The people who buy these things must know they offer no protection. I think of Edward and I can only assume he's aware of the box's flimsy nature. I suppose they offer more of an honesty system than anything else; the person who uses one is telling other people that they'd prefer you not to look inside.

I flip the lid. Inside is a thick stack of photographs. *Jackpot.*

The first is a shot of the Holbeck children, arm in arm, grinning broadly. Bobby and Edward in their teens; Matilda, Oliver, and Stuart younger. They look so happy, and it occurs to me that in spite of having an incredibly strange upbringing, at least they had one another. For a while, anyway.

The photo beneath is of a girl I do not know, her dark, wild curly hair as showstopping as her unselfconscious smile. I've never seen her before, but she's beautiful. One of Edward's undocumented ex-girlfriends no doubt, or a crush. I feel a sharp twang of jealousy at the idea of him keeping this photo under lock and key. But I know I have similar pictures hidden in my still-unpacked boxes.

I shuffle quickly through these special, chosen photos, trying not to dwell too long on each. I know what I'm looking for and halfway through the pack I find it, my hands stuttering to a halt as I catch sight of his Columbia sweatshirt.

Bobby beams out at me standing in front of a lush green football field. It must be after a game; smiling spectators and players mill and beside him, his arm encircling her, pulling her close, an equally happy blond girl. Her sweatshirt is a carbon copy of his, a cheerleader's skirt beneath it, her soft pale hair pulled back from her face in a shining ponytail.

My breath catches. I found her. She went to Columbia too. I turn the image and find, written on the back:

'01.
Bobby 'n' Lucy.

Lucy. Her name was Lucy. She looks the same age as Bobby, which means she would be forty this year. She could be alive somewhere out there right now—or she could be out there in the woods, two hours outside New York City, as Robert described on the tape.

I shiver looking at the blurry noughties photo, the happiness of it, the promise.

I have a first name; now all I need is a last.

27

Lucy

That night I dream I am on East 88th Street again.

It's 2002 and the sun is low in the sky, giving the evening a warm glow. On the other side of the road a small cluster of people mill. Something terrible has happened down there, and I realize it is the Holbeck building. And an understanding of what I am witnessing hits me like a punch to the gut.

With sickening dread, I head toward the crowd, drawn inexorably to what they are staring at. The noises of the street are muffled as if heard through a wall, or through water, everything caught in a kind of slow motion.

I cross the street in a daze, picking my way through stopped traffic as drivers, like sleepwalkers, slowly rise from their cars, having witnessed something fall. The weather vane high above us glints and swings in the evening breeze. There is an open window in the eaves, a net drape caught in the wind. And below, on the sidewalk, amid the legs of strangers, I make out a huddled shape on the ground, blackness all around it.

I feel Robert's presence before I see him, his strong, angular frame, from behind. Over his shoulder, a woman is just blocked from view, a wisp of her pale hair visible, fluttering in the wind.

Suddenly I am kneeling in front of Bobby, his sweatshirt thick with blood, his hair matted wet. I look down and I am wearing a Columbia sweatshirt too. I am Lucy. I am Bobby's girl.

I feel a gentle hand touching my shoulder and I turn as if drugged, as if trapped in resin, my movements heavy and slow. It is Robert Holbeck, but younger than I have ever known him.

He recognizes me for who I am and looks surprised to see me here. He knows I am not Bobby's girl; he knows I come from a different time and should not be here, in this scene, in this memory. He seems to understand the problem and slowly lifts a finger to his lips. Behind us a car horn blares and I gasp awake.

I bolt up in the darkness of the bedroom, my heart pounding, sweat-soaked. I wriggle free of the heavy duvet and lurch to the edge of the bed, my feet gratefully finding solid ground. I try to reorient myself. I am safe, I am here; it was a dream. I am not Lucy. My eyes adjust to the darkness of the bedroom and I look down at my chest. The Columbia sweatshirt is gone; instead my pajamas stick to my skin with perspiration.

As my mind focuses, a thought clarifies itself. I grab my bedside water, drain it, and head straight for my office.

I click on the desk light, drag my chair up to the computer, and open Google. I don't know why I didn't think of it before.

I type *Lucy, Columbia University, 2002, missing person* into the search box.

Lucy must have been a junior at Columbia too; if she went missing, people would have noticed.

I let out a yelp of triumph as thumbnail after thumbnail of Lucy fills my screen, the sound curdling in the silence of the room as I read the results.

Search for Missing Columbia Student Lucy Probus in Its Fourth Day

The parents of Columbia undergraduate Lucy Probus, 20, are "deeply concerned" for her welfare following her disappearance last Saturday night. The student was last seen returning to campus at around midnight on the night of October 27.

Lucy was reported missing after failing to attend scheduled activities the following day.

The third-year anthropology major, a dedicated member of the Columbia University cheerleading squad, formerly a resident of Pittsburgh, is described as petite and slim with blond hair and green eyes.

She was last seen wearing a burgundy jacket, jeans, and a gray hoodie bearing the distinctive blue C of the Columbia cheer squad. (photo insert above)

In a statement, NYPD chief Jim Westerly said: "We remain open-minded as to the circumstances behind Lucy's disappearance, but naturally, as the search enters its fourth day, our concern for her is growing. We are aware that Lucy had recently undergone significant trauma due to the loss of a close friend, and family and friends have described her recent actions as 'out of character.'

"I would like to appeal to Lucy directly. If she sees this, please make contact with the police or with your family."

Jesus. I close the tab and scroll down, opening up an article published earlier this year. Perhaps they found her?

Family of Columbia student Lucy Probus, who went missing 20 years ago, mark her milestone 40th birthday by appealing to those "haunted" by knowledge of what happened to come forward.

I stop reading abruptly. The girl with the soft blond hair was never found. The girl Robert described in his tape was never seen again.

The tape is real. It's a confession. He left Lucy's body in the woods two hours outside New York City.

Without missing a beat, I lunge back toward the bedroom and pull my suitcase out from under the rumpled bed to retrieve the tape player. I pull its red foam pads over my ears, fumble REWIND until it clicks off, and press PLAY.

Back in the office, in sweat-soaked pajamas, I listen to Lucy's story again, as New York glitters beyond my dark windows.

The thing is, there are a *lot* of woods two hours outside of New York. I bring up an online map of New York State, a search perimeter website I've used before for researching my novels.

Pen in hand, I scribble out the maths on a pad. The time it takes to get out of Manhattan, the average miles per hour a car is likely to maintain on the interstates and highways surrounding the city—the distance achievable in the space of two hours. I drop a boundary line down on the map and within its wide circle assess all the possible wooded areas where Robert could have left her in a 360-degree perimeter around Manhattan.

I then add another circle beyond that one. After his drive, Robert mentions hiking with her for another two hours. I do the maths once more: the average person can hike between two and three miles an hour, but he was carrying her, so let's say only two miles an hour. My second circle extends another four miles out past the original circle. It's a huge area. She could be anywhere out there.

But then Robert mentions other factors: a mountain and a lake. Still, the huge catchment area is peppered with mountains, lakes, and reservoirs. Two whole mountain ranges lie within my circles: the Catskills and the Adirondack Mountains.

I will never find her out there. But then, that is why he told me.

I need to tell Edward everything. We need to go to the police.

I shudder at the thought of Lucy out there in the cold. But

she's been there so long already. I can't do anything right now, and after two decades, one more night will change nothing.

The clock on the desk reads three forty-five A.M. I'm not going to get any sleep tonight, and Edward will be back from Hong Kong in just five hours.

I look down at the tape player in my hands. As much as I do not want to hear more, I know I have to; I need to see how deep this goes. I need to find out why he is telling me any of this and what he wants.

With grim determination, I sink back into my chair, slide the headphones back on, and pick up where I left off.

28

The Tape

PART 2

I have no doubt you will feel resistance to this recording. To this story. But I also know you will use your inquiring mind to sort through what lies before you. All I can ask is that you bear with me, dear Harriet, as I continue, because there is more for you to know.

I suspect you have already thought of telling my son about this recording. But the fact that you are still listening tells me you have not. I suspect you have weighed the pros and cons of such a decision. The knock-on effects of that choice. You are an intelligent, resourceful woman; that is why I have chosen to confide in you. But I advise you to tread with incredible care.

God knows, I love my son. I love all of my children, but I am not above taking action to protect the future of our family. Too many have given too much for us to let it all slip away, for it to be squandered by one unknown quantity. In his way Edward knows what I have done for this family, not in the details, but we know the men we are.

So I ask you for his sake, do not act rashly. This cassette recording is meant for you, and you alone. Listen carefully to what I tell you, weigh the content, use your faculties, and when you are ready to talk, talk to *me*.

I have faith in you, Harriet. We are alike, you and I. In what we have done for our families. As you will see.

The second girl was harder than the first. And Gianna fought. She screamed and clawed and left marks. She wanted to live but she saw too much.

A fashion party, 2004, a warehouse loft on New Year's Eve. There were red balloons, and a drive for the future as present and tangible as the glitter on young faces. Her eyes did not waver as she danced. That look of hers, intent, determined, a challenge. And she was beautiful, her lips stained dark, her thick curls tumbling around her. She had pushed and pushed for more but she could not have more. She was not suitable. Good fun, but not worth the investment she seemed to require, or demand. And so, to her place.

The boom and the pulse of the warehouse left behind. An argument, a scuffle, but, once words were spoken, she calmed enough to come willingly. Her rooms were dark and full of foreign objects. Low light, blue-black linen sheets, and the smell of jasmine. Mirrors everywhere so that she could watch what happened. Her lipstick imprinted on a crystal tumbler, the kiss of her wet lips as she drained the fluid, as her slender throat swallowed. She looked like she knew what she was drinking, but she did not know.

Do not worry, Harriet Reed. I did not touch her as I lay her in the fresh sheets, only softly arranged her for whoever would find her. Her breathing already too slow, already ebbing away.

In the drained glass: too much of what she had already had. A mixture of excess. That is what she was given, simply more of what she had already had, because that is what she wanted in a sense. It was what she wanted to give us. More of the same. More of her. So you see, she had to go.

Sitting in the corner of the room, I watched her slow to a stop. You could say watching is cause enough to give up on a person, and perhaps you would be right, my dear. After all, who would do such a thing? Who would watch another person die?

But we both know the answer to that, don't we? We know the kind of person who would watch another die and do nothing. We both know the kind of person that takes, don't we, Harriet Reed?

The question is: Is there a difference between you and me? Between what I have done and what you have done? And you must believe me when I say I *do* know what you have done. I imagine you reason that I cannot possibly know about that lonely morning on a country road, and my answer to you is simple: I do. I know enough.

Enough to fill in the gaps, enough to color the picture and present you with my findings. I am not the writer here, Harriet, but indulge me if you will.

I see you. Little girl in the back seat of a car, in a world of your own, safe. The babble of parents up front. Perhaps you felt the air change as the moment came, an unexpected intake of breath from the driver, a tensing, a sudden movement of the wheel, a jerk. Your gaze flashing forward too late. Did she turn to you, your mother? Did she catch your eye before it hit, her last instinct to protect you?

I cannot presume to know what happened in those last moments. The life you came from, the ones who loved you, taken from you.

The car impacted, flipped, skidded, and came to a stop in a gully beyond the road. In the silence that followed that deafening noise you slowly came to, your own cries inaudible beneath the buzz in your ears. Around you glass and twisted metal, the taste of blood and the thick fug of gasoline. Your left arm broken, torn muscles in your neck and both shoulders. Broken ribs. You hung suspended by nothing but your seatbelt.

You all hung; a silent family suspended as if stopped in time. Your mother's auburn hair swaying just out of reach, the car's windshield decimated, plant life inching deep into the car. Whether you said her name or not, I do not know. Whether you leaned forward to try to wake her I do not know; but she would not have stirred. She was an object jostled, nothing more. Your father beside her, equally silent.

I don't know how long you waited and hoped and tried to rouse those silent bodies. But after a time, an animal instinct moved you. Even at eleven years old you knew to cut your losses, to chew through a trap. Or perhaps you thought you could save them, get help, that someone else would come.

You disengaged your seatbelt and tumbled into the roof well, scrambling out on bleeding hands and knees. In my mind, Harriet, you did not look back as you passed them. You did not want to remember them that way.

The dead feel different, don't they? Once the light has gone, the people we love become strangers, don't they? We cannot reach them and something different is left in their place.

You clambered out of that broken windshield, snagged by branches and barbs of twisted metal. You did not pull a phone from their pockets; you did not think to do so in your rush.

I have no doubt that over the years you have stewed over why you did not think to do that in the moment. But rest assured, there was nothing you could have done for them; I have seen the medical reports. They left you before you even knew.

Back on the road, shaking and bruised, you saw what hit you. He was there. His car tipped, immobile, its windshield shattered milky by the impact. You saw him, pinned by his own steering wheel, shivering, crying, his body trapped in the twisted metal.

Did you speak to him? Did he scream for help, shriek his regret? I imagine, even at your age, you could tell he was drunk, that this was why you had lost everything. Judging by what you did next, I think there can be no doubt about that.

Crashed cars rarely explode in real life, but small fires are common. A spark at the front of his vehicle. A fuel leak at the back. The two so rarely connect.

There was a witness. A local woman, a farmer. She heard the sound of the crash and rushed across her fields toward a pillar of smoke. As she ran, she saw a girl standing by the wreckage. She saw flames lick along the ground, from one end of the car to the other. A rush of burning heat along the tarmac like a magnesium strip, there and then gone. She watched as the car's cabin exploded into flames, as you stood motionless beside it. The screams from inside it jolted her into a run. She ran to you but by the time she reached you the screaming had stopped.

A short sharp shock and your work was done.

Later, when questioned, she could not be sure what she had seen: if you had tried to put the flames out as they went past you or if you had been doing something else. When the police arrived, you did not speak.

We both know what happened that morning. And Harriet, my dear, let me tell you as an outside observer, what you did that day could never have been different.

I would have done the same. A man took your family, through his own stupidity, through his poor choices. You acted in everyone's best interests. A child forced to do an adult's work. Actions must have repercussions. They must.

I have seen the reports, the files. It is always important to know the type of person one is welcoming into one's home. After all, one's home is one's sanctuary. I wanted to know the type of person you were, Harriet, my future daughter-in-law. I had the logistics run, and that is why you are listening to my voice now. Because that road was level, and fluid—water, gasoline—can never travel unaided, Harriet. I do not know if they suspected then, if it crossed their minds, but the facts stand.

If it were to happen today, Harriet, with the technology we have, with the procedures now in place, you would not be marrying my son. You would not be who you are in the world.

I am in absolutely no doubt that you are fully acquainted with the law in your country. I am sure you have checked in on it many times since you were a child. The minimum age of criminal responsibility in the United Kingdom is ten years old. *Ten,* Harriet.

You were eleven when your parents died.

And again, I am certain you know this, but there is no statute of limitation for criminal offenses in the English courts.

It must plague you. Or perhaps you reasoned that after all this time you might be safe. Well, you are safe with me. Whatever succor that might bring.

So you see, we *do* have a lot in common, Harriet Reed. We both lost the ones we loved and found new ones. We would both do anything for our families.

For what it is worth, Harriet, I like you. I forgive you. We must remember, you were just a child; your parents killed and the man responsible there in front of you. It's at moments like these that our true nature is revealed. You did a terrible thing, but you did it for your family. And I have done the same for mine.

Now, I believe, we are singing from the same hymn sheet.

As I said earlier, I would prefer it if you did not share this tape with my son, or with anyone for that matter. And I will return the favor. We both have skin in the game.

You may be asking yourself now, why is he telling me any of this? On that front, I will ask you to bear with me, Harriet. I am telling you this because I know who you are; I know what you are capable of given the right circumstances. And I have chosen you for just that reason. I will ask something of you. I will ask something of you very soon.

29

Gagged and Bound

WEDNESDAY, DECEMBER 21

The tape crackles and clicks off. Side A complete.

I sit, stricken, in the silence of the apartment.

It's funny having your worst fear realized and the world still spinning. A sigh shudders from me, and with it something dislodges deep within me.

A wave of jumbled emotion erupts, overleaping itself, bursting up and out. Warm tears roll down my face, the taste of salt hitting my lips, because this is the first time anyone has articulated what happened that morning. What happened to me. What I did. And why. A tightness held for twenty years begins to loosen.

I know I should feel shame, dread, fear—and in part I do, though those feelings are old friends. The new feeling weaving and twisting among them is a surprise, something I never even considered: acknowledgment. Hearing his words—even given who he is and the terrible things he has done—I feel known. For the first time in my adult life, I have been seen by another person. And they did not shrink away in disgust. I know Robert Holbeck is no arbiter of moral character, no great judge of human worth, but someone knows and they have done worse, and they understand. Of course I fear what this means, that a man like Robert knows and can wield my darkest moment over me, and yet I cannot lie: it feels good to be known.

And however confusing it might be, I feel oddly grateful. Grateful to him.

We are not alike, he and I; I refuse to acknowledge that, but in a terrifying way I feel a tiny bit less alone in the world than before.

I slowly pull myself together, wiping my eyes and nose with my sleeve and carefully removing the Olympus headphones from my ears.

The tape is clear. Robert Holbeck kills women. He kills them when they know too much, or when they get too close and threaten his family. Both women knew enough about the family's dealings to pose a grave threat to their future. I recognize the description of the second woman, Gianna, from a photograph in Edward's locked box earlier. The girl with wild curly hair and fearless eyes. Gianna must have been seeing Edward in his first year at MIT. A distraction, who was asking for more attention than the family was willing to give. Robert must have feared that Edward, now next in line, might go the way of Bobby. Robert took her out of the equation.

Did Edward suspect foul play or did he think the overdose was fueled by her unhappiness at not being able to be with him? People around the Holbecks seem to find life harder to deal with than most.

Robert had already lost one son; he couldn't risk losing another. He drugged Gianna and made it look like an overdose while he sat back and watched.

I understand the predicament I am in now; I understand the

terms. I cannot expose Robert because he will expose me. But I know why he has chosen me and what he wants—a favor.

I roll-call the dead in my mind: Bobby, Lucy, Gianna. Bobby started it all; he could not handle the weight of the Holbeck name and jumped, but something else happened there that day. And Lucy Probus knew too much. She knew Robert was in the house, and rumors can build and take on a life of their own.

But both Gianna's and Lucy's perceived crimes against the Holbecks are not worse than mine. I am a murderer who is trying to marry their firstborn son. I set a man on fire and watched him burn. It's a wonder I'm still alive.

I suppose, as long as Robert needs something from me, I am safe.

Robert knew about me the night we met. He knew who I was, what I did. I recall the electricity between us, in his study that night, the intoxicating danger. The way he looked at me, the connection we had, instinctive; he knew who I was and he was comfortable with me. But perhaps only a man like Robert Holbeck could ever feel comfortable with me. Edward can never know; the thought alone makes me sick to my stomach.

Laurence Fletcher was his name—the man I killed. He begged, but I was not listening. I took my chance and I made him pay, because men like him don't change.

It would be a misreading to say I did what I did with the best of intentions. I did not. I wanted him to suffer; I wanted to *see* him suffer. I didn't do it to protect the world, or others, or because I could sense he was a *bad* person. I didn't know anything about him the day he died, except what he had just done to me, to us.

I got to know him over the years that followed, though. I'd find out all there was to know about the man who changed my life. His divorce, his addictions, lost visitation rights, harassment, and abuse. Somehow, through it all, he'd kept his job; I guess he saved his worst for those he loved. He wasn't a great person, it turned out, but that wasn't why I killed him.

I killed him because I wanted to and because I could. And because, for a second, it took the pain away.

In that sense, Robert and I are alike. We are not on the side of the angels. The only difference between us is that I only killed once.

Once was enough for me—enough to put me in prison, enough to ruin my life. Enough to end a career. Enough to make Edward hate me if he were ever to find out. Once was already one time too many.

I cannot go to the police about the tape and I cannot tell Edward. Not if I want him to love me. If I want him to love me, he can never know who I really am.

I scour the apartment for traces of my search for Lucy Probus. I erase my computer search history and put Edward's steel lockbox back on its shelf in his office, replacing the paper clip I took from his documents with a fresh one. When Edward returns it will be as if none of this had ever happened. And I will bide my time until I can work out what Robert wants.

Edward's "hello" from the hallway wakes me with a jolt. He's back.

I sit bolt-upright in the bedsheets, panic coursing through me as I try to remember my plan, or if I even had a plan, my thoughts ricocheting through my mind.

From the safety of the bed, I listen to him moving about the apartment, dropping his bags, removing his coat, and wonder how I am going to get through what is coming next without Edward, without anyone, to share this with.

I force myself out of the bedroom and into the kitchen, where I find him making breakfast. He looks up with a smile that I do not deserve and I head straight to him, squeezing him as tight as I can.

He leans down to kiss me, mistaking my silent embrace for a warm welcome home.

"Hey, sleepyhead. How have you been?" he asks. "Get up to anything exciting while I was away?" I do not answer and when I unbury my head from his chest he laughs.

"Let it be noted," he says, breaking away from me to flip whatever he is cooking in the pan, "that I am actually *cooking*."

He's happy; his trip must have gone well. "Listen, I love Chinese food," he says, by way of explanation, "but I have not been able to stop thinking about bacon and eggs for two days straight." He stops while pulling milk from the fridge, suddenly noticing I haven't said a word yet. "Are you okay?" he asks with concern. "You look a little pale, or something. Is the baby okay?"

I give him a halfhearted smile, the desire to tell him and not tell him almost unbearable. "No. I'm fine. Still half asleep."

He slips a hand around my waist, resting it on my abdomen. "How's it all going in there? When's the next scan again?"

"Day after tomorrow," I answer, as cheerfully as I can, the idea of bringing a baby into the current situation beyond terrifying. I tell myself it's going to be okay because somehow, I am going to fix all of this. I will make sure that we are safe and that Edward's father can't ever hurt us, that my past can't hurt us.

Edward looks at me with so much love in his eyes I want to burst.

"Okay, no laughing. I'll say a boy's name, you say a girl's. Ready?"

"Ready." I smile.

"Okay. Three, two, one. George."

"Iris."

"Iris and George," he repeats back, testing the sounds. "Love 'em. Hell, let's have two kids and use both."

He mistakes my sudden tears for joy, or hormones.

I pull back and quickly wipe them away.

"You okay, really?" he asks, unable to decipher my emotions but aware something is very wrong. "If there is something happening, if you need to tell me, I'm here," he says, his expression gentle but serious.

I hold his gaze a moment, taking in his handsome face, the look of concern in his eyes, and I realize I can do this. I can do this alone, for us, for him, because this man is worth fighting for.

"I'm fine," I tell him finally. "I'm just really glad you're back."

We gorge ourselves on Edward's breakfast while he updates me on his business trip to Hong Kong.

"They've made a preemptive offer on the company." His eyes glisten in the morning sun that streams through the apartment windows as he lets that fact land on me.

"Wait, what? The whole company? They want to *buy* the whole company? I thought the plan was expanding over there?" I ask, my surprise obvious enough to draw a snort of laughter from Edward.

"Yeah, I know. That was the plan, then Li-Chen wrote a number on the back of a business card, pushed it across the table, and suddenly the plan changed. It's a healthy number," he tells me, his smile broadening into a grin. "A really goddamn healthy number."

I feel my chest tighten; Edward doesn't use superlatives. I feel my head swim at the idea of a figure he'd be genuinely impressed by, a price he'd be willing to sell his entire company for.

"And what did you say to Li-Chen?" I say carefully, the unpredictability of our conversation destabilizing my already scrambled senses. "Is that something you'd want to do, sell the company? You've built it from the ground up—"

"There will be other companies. I can do all this again and the next time I'll have capital behind me." He loses the smile, becoming serious. "I have a few days to consider, to approach other investors, or buyers, if I want, but with an opening offer like this, not many players would be in the running."

"What about ThruComm? Couldn't your family buy it, subsume it?" Even as I say it, I realize what an unattractive prospect that is, even to me. Nobody wants to be subsumed, especially by their domineering family.

Edward's eyes crinkle into a smile. "ThruComm's already priced out. They're not capable of matching this."

"Holy shit!" I gasp, my hand flying to my mouth. "You're serious?"

"Yeah." He nods, pleased that I am finally getting the scope of what he is trying to tell me. "We've just got to play it right."

"Okay. How long do you have to decide?"

"Close of business tomorrow."

"And when will it—"

"As soon as I sign the documents."

The extent of what Edward is telling me slowly dawns on me. If I thought he was wealthy before, this deal could make what he has now a drop in the ocean. The sheer level of protection, and power, that money would give us hove into view. Whatever methods Robert Holbeck has used to avoid his own past will suddenly be available to me, to us. It won't solve the problem of Robert, but it could certainly even the playing field.

Edward rises from the table, his energy infectious. "Right, I'm going to get going. I've got meetings all day. I love you," he says, then, from the doorway, he adds, "You are okay, aren't you?"

"Yes, I am. Go, go," I order him.

He heads out of the kitchen with a grin then circles back.

"Oh yeah. Did Matilda get hold of you yesterday?" he asks.

"Yesterday?"

"Yeah, about Christmas?"

My blood freezes in my veins. I have no idea what he is talking about but I can tell I am not going to like it one bit. "What about Christmas?" I ask.

"Damn it. I thought they'd have called by now. I said if you were happy to do it, we'd do it."

"Do what, Ed?" I say, finding it hard to keep the snap out of my voice.

"Um, Christmas," he says, surprised by the bite in my tone. "They want us over for Christmas; three nights, at The Hydes.

It's family only. They've never invited anyone not married into the family. They want you and Lila there this year. Call it a stab at modernization. It's a step in the right direction. You said we'd play it by ear so I said maybe. I think it's sort of an apology for Krampusnacht. Though I know I'm as much to blame for what happened then as anyone else. Up to you, though?"

I struggle for how to respond to this appropriately because I absolutely cannot sleep under the same roof as Robert Holbeck.

"When would we go?" I ask, buying myself a few seconds to think.

"The twenty-third. Day after tomorrow. The deal should be all wrapped up by then so it works for me."

A palatable excuse drops into my mind and relief floods my body. "Ah, damn, we can't. That's the day of the scan. The twelve-week scan. We need to be in the city for it, remember?"

He tilts his head as if I'm joking. "Yeah, but the scan's only in the morning. We'll drive out of town after. It's not like we had big Christmas plans anyway. Or are you thinking we should maybe put a bit of distance between them and us? Because that's fine too. I can just call Mom and tell her we're doing our own thing?"

I have to physically stop myself from leaping up and kissing him in gratitude. But the relief is short-lived because I know there is no getting away from Robert. He knows what he knows and if Edward says we're not coming, his family will think I have stopped playing ball, and Robert will know I am scared of him. He will know I have listened to his tape.

My mind flies through my options and comes up blank. There is no excuse that won't sound like I'm running scared.

"Is there something you want to tell me?" Edward asks, after I fail to reply. "Did one of them do something, say something, while I was away? Was it Matty? Fiona? Dad?"

I search his eyes, careful not to react to any one name. "Why do you ask?" I answer, trying to gauge how much he knows of anything.

"I don't know. Has someone upset you?"

"No. I just, I'm sorry, I'm just not over our last visit yet, Edward. I don't want you to upset them, or tell them I don't want to go, but I just can't do anything like that game again," I say. It's risky but worth a shot; perhaps he can think up an excuse to give them for me.

"You don't need to worry about that. Christmas won't be anything like Krampusnacht. No one is going to make you join in any of our weird family stuff if you don't want to, okay? Besides, everyone will know you're pregnant by then. We'll tell them as soon as we get there. You won't have to lift a finger. This way, Christmas, everything, is done for us—zero effort; festivities covered. We don't have to decorate, cook, clean up. Sounds pretty good, right? We don't have to live in their pockets either. We usually only get together for meals and drinks. It's a big place. The rest of the time we'll do our own thing," he says, then lets out a surprised laugh. "And if you want to go at any point, we go."

I mean, what the hell am I supposed to say to that?

I find myself wondering if the fact I'm pregnant will change Robert's plans for me, because one thing is for sure: I will not be able to avoid him at The Hydes.

30

Bigger Fish to Fry

10:34 A.M.
WEDNESDAY, DECEMBER 21

While Edward showers and changes for work, I set about preparing for Christmas at The Hydes.

Carefully listening for sounds from the shower room along the hall, I roll the combination lock on my suitcase and relocate the tape player to its old hiding place under my side of the mattress.

I fill my now empty case with travel essentials, then turn toward my wardrobe to examine what clothes I own that might in some way be appropriate for a Holbeck family Christmas.

I pull out the ridiculously expensive emerald-green slip dress I wore the night I met Edward, its silk like liquid in my hands as I hold it up to myself. Perhaps too much, but who's to say. If the Holbecks don't dress up for Christmas, then who does? And who's to say I'll last that long anyway?

I carefully fold and pack it. Three nights of festivities; who knows what will happen?

I inspect the best of what I have as I play Robert's words back in my mind. His description of the day I lost my family is achingly redolent. He is so far ahead of me in this game, I wonder if it might ever be possible to catch up.

I take a black velvet Versace dress from the rail, one I bought for my last birthday, egged on by Edward, and pack it neatly.

I try to guess what the tone of their celebrations might be, and pack some more casual items too. It's impossible to know what the other Holbeck women might wear over this short but no doubt telling visit. This Christmas invitation feels like a kind of Balmoral test. A test to weed out those who do not fit in with the family from those who do. If I manage to match some unspoken codes, hell, if I manage to survive, then perhaps they will accept me as one of them.

Christmas seems to have become the final stage of a Holbeck test triptych that I didn't know I was signing up for: Thanksgiving, Krampusnacht, Christmas. Each one, I'm guessing, progressively harder than the last.

Finally, I pack the claret jumpsuit I wore for Thanksgiving and three dressy outfits, then I add shoes and call it a day. I have bigger fish to fry. I need to listen to the rest of Robert's tape, but I can't do that with Edward in the house.

I listen for Edward still busying himself along the hall. If I want to listen, I'll need to do it away from the apartment, even though leaving the safety of the building means potentially being followed again. The man with the baseball cap springs to mind. While I made sure I wasn't followed the day I went to meet Samantha, I was in the car and that made it somehow easier. I deliberately wound through the streets of Manhattan before I headed for the Lincoln Tunnel. I could take the car again but I would have to think of a reason to tell Edward now that he's back. No, I'd better go on foot—I just need to go somewhere the man with the baseball cap can't follow.

Somewhere men aren't allowed.

The first place that comes to mind is my gym, and the women-only changing rooms. Going to the gym isn't going to raise any alarms, and there are lockable stalls there. I could listen in safety.

I grab my gym bag and swim things from the closet and slip on my sneakers before retrieving the tape player from under the mattress.

Edward's head pokes out of the bathroom as I make my way to the front door and raise my gym bag in explanation. Tooth-brush in mouth, he gives me a cheerful thumbs-up as I head out the door.

The desire to slip on my headphones and start listening as soon as I leave the building is almost too much, but I hold off. I need my wits about me until I can get someplace where I can't be disturbed. Robert's confession isn't an interesting podcast to be listened to on the go—the future of my family entirely depends on the words on that cassette.

I swipe through the turnstiles at the gym, heading straight for the women's changing rooms, which I find, thankfully, empty. I slip into a cubicle, lock the door, and plop down onto the cubicle bench. After a moment of welcome silence, I pull my gym bag onto my lap, unzip it, and retrieve its precious cargo. I take a breath and shuffle into a more comfortable position, then flip the tiny cassette over onto the B side, slide the headphones on, and press PLAY.

31

The Tape

PART 3

Before we discuss the future—and what it holds for us—I want you to be in full possession of the facts. The body count, if you will.

Bobby started this story. He jumped.

Then Lucy had to go.

Then Alison. And Gianna.

Gianna was the easiest. Her family accepted the version of events presented to them. Their daughter was like that, you see: hard to manage. It was only a matter of time, they concluded, before something like that happened. And accidents do happen. Losing friends can be hard. But I digress.

The point is, if one does one's homework, people can disappear with surprising ease. It is possible to briefly come into contact with someone and make them slip out of the everyday flow of life. Subtly, ambiguously, conveniently. Gone.

Not *your* chosen technique for ending a life, I know, Harriet. And while I have never tried your fire-and-brimstone approach, I can see its warm allure. Forgive me if I am being facetious.

My point is, if ending a life is unavoidable, it is usually best to be ambiguous about it. Better *not* to burn out than to fade away.

I am getting old, Harriet, and the truth is I cannot continue to do things as I have in the past. I cannot contain all of this indefinitely; I alone cannot hold this family together. And that is where you come in. I must share what I know, pass on the baton. These are the names, the places, the dates.

It seems only fair, given I know the details of yours, that you should know these. Quid pro quo, as they say. Do as you wish with the information, but know the consequences.

I expect you'll want to get a pen.

Lucy Probus, 2002.

Alison Montgomery, 2003.

Gianna Scaccia, 2004.

Aliza Masri, 2020.

Melissa Brown, 2021.

I thought for a period of time that the urge had passed. That it was over and I would not need to intercede in matters again. But it came back—the need, the necessity to correct the errors of others.

These are the facts and this is your area, Harriet Reed. Do your best. Use that sharp mind of yours, but move with care, because I think you know how this all goes if you make the wrong move.

You are not the first person I have divulged these secrets to, but you could be the first person to survive the knowledge. I have faith in you, at least.

32

Cat 'n' Mouse

WEDNESDAY, DECEMBER 21

I jab the PAUSE button and scramble in my gym bag for a pen, settling instead for my iPhone Notes. I rewind the tape, then, phone resting on knee, I hit PLAY.

Once the final name is spoken, I click off the recording and look at my list.

Lucy Probus—2002
Alison Montgomery—2003
Gianna Scaccia—2004
Aliza Masri—2020
Melissa Brown—2021

Five names. Five women.
A gap of sixteen years between the two sprees. Two of the

deaths are recent. I shiver as I look at the final date. I met Edward around the time of Melissa Brown's death. I can't help but wonder if Robert gave her a tape too.

I notice a new name wedged between Lucy and Gianna, one I have not heard before. Alison Montgomery. Robert hasn't mentioned her until now.

There's a soft rap on the changing room door and I jerk up, sending my iPhone clattering across the floor.

"Sorry," an apologetic voice comes from beyond the cubicle. "Just wondering if you're nearly done in there?"

Shit.

I notice the bustle now coming from the changing room. I hadn't registered it till now, but the lunchtime rush has begun. "Um, yeah, yeah, sorry, one minute." I quickly shove everything back into my bag, iPhone slightly wet and stinking of chlorine. I'm just about to pull open the door when it dawns on me that I've come into a changing room and done nothing. I can't just leave the gym. If anyone was following me, it would almost certainly raise suspicions if I never even made it out of the changing area.

I dump my bag back on the seat, strip off, and slip on my bathing suit.

Outside the cubicle I find a woman in her late forties, patience waning, with a towel wrapped tight around her. Behind her a full changing room, bodies in various stages of undress. I find a free combination locker, store my bag securely, and head to the pool.

On the subway ride home, hair now suitably damp and redolent of swimming pool, I google Gianna Scaccia and find what I expected to, what Robert has already described. Death by accidental overdose. I stare at her beautiful face, her eyes alive with possibility, her caramel skin and tumbling curls.

But as I tap through the article, something unexpected jumps out at me, stopping me dead in my tracks. I reread the paragraph to be sure I haven't misunderstood.

"It's important to understand," Marion Scaccia, 58, Gianna's mother, tells us, "that while someone with an addiction might appear to have things under control, relapses can be triggered by anything. Gianna was going through a lot. The loss of a close friend is always hard, but in the case of suicide doubly so. I think she was having trouble processing it. The fact that Gianna hadn't seen Alison's suicide coming, at all, hadn't noticed her friend's troubles, plagued her. After all, there was no outward explanation for why Alison did what she did. My daughter blamed herself for not seeing the storm cloud coming. And she turned to substances to lighten her pain."

I sit bolt-upright in my subway seat. Alison Montgomery, the second girl on Robert's list, was Gianna's close friend.

Alison can't have committed suicide, though. She wouldn't be on Robert's list if she had. Gianna must have worked out what happened to Alison, that the Holbecks were involved, and she must have let them know.

I type Alison Montgomery's name into my search engine.

Death of MIT Undergraduate Alison Montgomery Highlights the Abnormally High Suicide Rates at the University

Legal questions are being asked about the extent to which educational institutions can be held responsible for the deaths of their students after Alison Montgomery, 21, was unexpectedly found dead in her dormitory last week. Alison becomes another student in a long list who have committed suicide at the institution since the 1990s. Alison, in her final year of study majoring in data, systems, and society at Massachusetts Institute of Technology, was described as "a warmhearted and brilliant young woman." Her death has come as a shock to many and has raised questions about why the warning signs were not picked up sooner by the university.

I look up from the article abruptly.

Edward was at MIT the years both girls died. My heart thunders in my chest as his proximity to Alison hits home. My mouth is suddenly dry. *Oh God.* Edward must have known both Alison and Gianna. Did he date them? Did Robert consider Alison a distraction and Gianna a complication?

I lean forward, head on hands to keep from fainting, as I try to push the thought away, but it will not go. Edward must have known. He must have suspected something strange was going on. Is that why the rift opened between him and his family? And if so, why in God's name are we cozying up to them now?

Edward told me he had a girlfriend at MIT, but that they broke up after the first year. I feel like I'm going to be sick as the subway car rattles into the next station and I bolt for the door, managing to reach the nearest platform bench before a wave of dizziness drains the blood from me and my vision blurs.

I try not to think of the fact that I'm almost twelve weeks' pregnant, and how totally trapped I am in my situation. I take a deep slug of water from my gym bottle and force myself to stay calm, to think. How could I get so far into all this without noticing what must have been right in front of me? Edward did not want me to meet his family, and since I have, he has been on guard to make sure no one oversteps a mark. I pushed to meet them. He could have, *should* have, told me if he knew any of this, but then could he really know? I push my cold hands into my burning cheeks and try to calm down.

First of all, Edward didn't really know Lucy Probus; Lucy was Bobby's girlfriend. Edward was living back at The Hydes when Bobby was attending Columbia; he was just a teenager. He wouldn't have had anything to do with Lucy. He might not even have been aware that she went missing.

The simple truth is, Edward must have been seeing Alison, and Robert didn't like it. He broke up with her at the family's behest and as her exams approached Alison took her own life. And as far as Edward knew, Gianna, her wild and guilt-ridden best friend, overdosed shortly after. It's not as if Edward would have had a tape to explain all of this. Alison's and Gianna's deaths were made to look innocent. And life can be hard for some people—tragedy, while awful, is rarely more than that.

As my faintness subsides, I rise, carefully, and board the next train as it pulls in.

Finding a seat, I turn my attention to the two most recent women on Robert's list: Aliza Masri and Melissa Brown. If I can work out their connection to the Holbecks, things might come fully into focus.

Wikipedia tells me Aliza Masri is a visual artist.

Born in Lebanon to an American mother and a Lebanese-Syrian father, Aliza attended international school in Beirut before moving back to the US with her mother. Aliza's work has appeared in notable galleries across Europe and the US.

Masri slipped into notoriety in late 2019 when it was alleged, after controversial comments made on social media, that she may have supported the contentious movement the FFI, who are known to have strong international links to Hezbollah.

As of January 2020, Masri's exact whereabouts are unknown, though it is thought the artist may now be residing in her native Lebanon.

I search for her name in conjunction with the Holbecks and my phone screen fills with pictures.

My breath catches at what I see.

Matilda looks back at me, from Instagram, beaming beside Aliza, her thick red curls and pale skin unmistakable. A photograph of the pair attending a gallery opening of Aliza's work. Matilda looks beautiful, and so happy, her free hand tenderly placed on the small of Masri's back in a gesture I recognize as entirely Holbeckian.

Aliza and Matilda were together. I look at the two of them, in love, caught in the amber of the moment. It's undeniable—the happiness, the hope, in their eyes. So much ahead of them, and yet somehow it—their relationship—went wrong.

I pull my phone closer and zoom in on Matilda's features, her intelligent green eyes, the soft curl of her lips. Could she have killed Aliza? Could she be capable of that? Did she kill them all? But there would be no reason for her to kill Lucy, Alison, or Gianna. Besides, she wasn't older than sixteen when Lucy disappeared; younger than Edward.

The tape is trying to tell me something, but it's not yet clear exactly what. I kick myself for not being able to piece it together. Unless, perhaps, the next name on the list might be connected to either Oliver or Stuart. Could each sibling have lost someone they cared about?

I google *Melissa Brown, 2021,* but the only online result is for a LinkedIn account. No social media, nothing. The account tells me she has been a personal assistant to the CEO of Lefroy Henshaw since 2014. A sliver of hope glimmers as I quickly bring up the Lefroy Henshaw website. There's always a chance she could still be alive.

Lefroy Henshaw is a hedge fund firm. I read the "About Us" section until my hope curdles in my veins. Lefroy Henshaw is part of the Laurence Group. It's owned by the Holbeck family; Stuart is listed as its CEO.

Melissa Brown was Stuart Holbeck's personal assistant, and I'm guessing, being on Robert's list, she isn't still alive.

I look at Melissa's photograph on their website—her soft, friendly features a far cry from Lila's ethereal beauty—and I wonder if she and Stuart might have been having an affair. All the other women on Robert's list got too close to his children. And while Melissa is clearly not a catwalk model like Lila, there is a soft, gentle beauty to her. She might have made Stuart happy, made him laugh, understood him. But then I think of the way Lila spoke about Stuart and I'm not so sure he didn't have someone to do that already. Perhaps Melissa simply saw too much, knew too much?

Robert said on the tape that she died in 2021, but she hasn't been removed from the Lefroy Henshaw website.

The train rattles into my station. I grab everything and disembark.

Up on street level, I decide to cut to the chase and call up Lefroy Henshaw and just ask if she still works there.

After eight minutes I am plucked off the automated system by a friendly voice.

"Hi there, sorry, you're calling about Mel, right?"

"Um, yes. Melissa Brown. I'm trying to track her down. Is she still working there?"

"Technically, yes. But she doesn't work from the office anymore. She's satellite. Can I ask who's calling?"

My mind scrambles for a story and bizarrely lands on, "Yeah, sure, I'm calling from her dentist's office. We can't seem to track her down. We have an unpaid invoice for . . . two hundred and seventy dollars that I need to get paid. She has Lefroy Henshaw down as her primary address for some reason."

The other end of the line is silent for a second. "That's weird. Really? I can email her?"

"Yeah, I've tried emailing, but nothing," I add quickly.

"How odd. She's usually super on it. Maybe you're going to junk. I'll email now from here. She should get that."

That's interesting, I think. She must still be answering emails. In which case I definitely don't need this call flagged to whoever is answering them.

"Okay," I reply, "that'd be fantastic. Actually, why don't I forward you her bill and you can pass that on to her directly too?"

The voice on the end of the line hesitates, clearly not keen on being dragged into a credit control situation. "Me? Um, actually, you know what, why don't I just give you her postal address. What's your office name again?"

"Morningside Dental," I answer, using the name of a dentist I used shortly after moving to New York.

I hear the tap-tap of a Google search and a grunt of acknowledgment.

"Oh yeah, I see you, perfect. I'll give you the address I have listed for her. That's the best I can do, I'm afraid."

"That'd be great, thanks," I affirm, with the appropriate level of enthusiasm that I assume a dental receptionist might have for this offer.

As I pass a bodega, I grab a chained-up pen and carefully scrawl Melissa's address and phone number onto the back of my cold hand.

33

Melissa

THURSDAY, DECEMBER 22

Edward has left for work before I'm up the next morning.

I lie in the warmth of the sheets a little longer, pushing my life and the facts of it away for another few more precious minutes before slipping a hand beneath my T-shirt and noticing the gathering swell of my tummy there. Twelve weeks tomorrow.

I force myself from the bed. I have one day left to find the connection among the women on Robert's list and to work out how I survive what's coming next.

The address and phone number written on my hand are long gone, safely stored on my phone. The phone number I tried before Edward returned last night was out of service, as I predicted it might be, but I still have the address.

I shove everything I need into my handbag, grab a baseball

cap, and call down to the doorman for a taxi. I figure I'll be harder to follow in a car.

As the taxi slips out of the underground pickup zone, I lower the peak of my cap and scan the sidewalk outside the building; the street is clear. I lower my gaze as we roll away and I don't look up or behind until we clear a full block.

Standing in front of Melissa Brown's apartment building in the winter sun, a knot of nerves forms as I realize the reality of following through with my plan to see if she's there, alive and well, or if she's not.

I stare up at the building, its windows glinting in the morning light, before I head along the landscaped garden path to the glazed front door and gingerly press her buzzer. I wait with the warmth of the sun on the back of my neck, the sound of birdsong reaching me from a small park across the street. I press again, almost resigned to the fact I won't get an answer, when the speaker crackles to life.

"Yep, hello. What's up?"

My heart leaps into my throat and my mind goes completely blank. "Um," I stumble. "Hi, is that Melissa?"

The voice hesitates. "What? Who?"

"Melissa?" I know I'm playing a dangerous game here, because (a) if this *is* Melissa, then who the hell am I supposed to be? And (b) if this *isn't* Melissa, then who the hell is it?

"No, I'm not Melissa. I'm Nina. Who's Melissa?" she asks with annoyance.

It's a curveball question. I definitely have the correct buzzer number so I leave the question hanging a second longer. I hear the sound of a muffled conversation, then:

"Oh shit. Sorry, sorry. Yeah, Mel's not here. Actually, you know what, I'm coming down. Wait there." The intercom cuts out and I wonder if I should run.

I rack my brains for an answer as to who I am when Nina inevitably asks again, but my musings are cut short by the arrival of a bouncy, pastel-crop-top-wearing twenty-year-old.

"Hey, man. Sorry, who are you again?" she asks with an easy affability.

"I'm, just, I'm a friend of Mel's." She raises an eyebrow at my accent. "From England," I add.

"Oh, okay. So you're not on the board, right?"

"The board?"

"The residents' board?"

"Er, no. Why—"

"Oh, okay. That's cool. Yeah, so," the girl continues, relaxing her weight against the doorframe, "Mel's been subletting to us, which we thought was fine but, well, she's been leasing to Karen actually, but we're all paying. Anyway, point is, Mel's not here. She doesn't *live* live here right now. Sorry, man. I think Karen might have her cell, though, if you want it? Did you come all the way from England to see her?" she asks.

"No. No, I didn't. Listen, odd question, but," I push on, "did Mel's place come fully furnished? Are all her things still in there?"

"Like her books and stuff? Yeah. Why? We moved them into the small room, though. Like, they're safe and everything, so—"

"No, it's fine. I just wasn't sure. Sorry to bother you. I didn't know she was away. I'll call her. I have her cell already. Thanks."

"Oh, okay. Cool. So, we're fine?" she asks, more concerned about how she will come out of this interaction than with who or what I might be.

"Yeah, you're fine," I tell her. She smiles and shrugs, then disappears back into the building.

I wander back toward the park, a sinking feeling dragging me down to the truth of what I just witnessed. This is what Robert meant by people "fading away." Melissa is gone, but the cogs of her life are still turning. Someone is keeping it all going, for now—subletting her apartment, paying her taxes, and responding to emails when necessary. Melissa has become a ghost.

I am now as sure as I can be that every woman on Robert's list is dead: Bobby's girlfriend, Edward's girlfriend, Matilda's girlfriend, Stuart's assistant, and a girl who got caught in the crossfire.

I feel anger fizz inside me at the fact I cannot untangle the knot Robert has presented me with. There is really nothing more I can do but go to The Hydes and face whatever he has laid in store for me.

I plonk myself down on a bench in the park opposite Melissa's old apartment and let my eyes play over the treetops as the breeze sways them. And then it hits me. Oliver is the only Holbeck not to have lost someone. Fiona is alive and well. They are happily married with kids and, now that I think about it, Oliver is the one who took over the company after both Bobby and Edward stepped aside. He seems to have come out of it all a lot better than the rest—could he be the key to this in some way?

Time is nearly up, and I'm almost out of avenues to explore. There is a reason Robert is telling me all this. He thinks I can piece it together, but I wonder if I can—if there is enough; if *I* am enough.

I place a hand on my abdomen as I wonder if the life growing inside me might be any kind of protection against Robert and his family. I can't assume being pregnant grants me immunity, although he has given me his word that I am safe for now because he needs me to do something.

If I'm really going to The Hydes tomorrow, and going in blind, then I'm going to need more protection than his word.

I pull my phone from my bag, scroll through my contacts, and press DIAL before I can talk myself out of it. I might be stretching my luck by bringing things this worryingly close to home. The phone rings four times before he answers.

"Hi, Deonte, it's Harriet. You free to talk?"

"Ah, it's Ms. Reed. Yes, you caught me at a good time. Out walking the dog. What can I do for you, ma'am?"

"Okay, plot holes. You remember the girl with the recording, the taped confession?"

"Sure do," he singsongs, happy to dive back in.

"So, it turns out she's got a secret of her own and the guy who gave her the tape knows it."

"Ooo, juicy. She killed someone too?"

"She did," I say.

"But hers was accidental, right?"

I hesitate. "No, no, she straight-up killed someone. She's occupying a . . . gray area."

He takes a moment to consider this twist, and I can't help but wonder if he senses something off with me. If he can read me like my own open book. "Ha. Okay, interesting. So, he's confessed his crimes but she can't report it 'cause he's got something over her. Blackmail kinda thing."

"Correct. And he wants her to meet him, to come to his home, to be with his family. He says he's chosen to confide in her because of what she did, and he needs her to do him a favor," I explain.

"Oh, okay. He's gonna ask her to kill someone for him?"

I pull up short, my eyes immediately focusing on the park around me again.

Robert wants me to kill for him.

My mind hadn't gone there, but now that Deonte has articulated it, that seems entirely probable. I suppose my only USP, in his eyes, could be the fact that I've killed a person. I recall Robert saying he wanted to pass on the family baton. Is that what he meant?

I realize I've left Deonte hanging. "Um, yeah, it could be that. I haven't entirely decoded what the favor is yet, but possibly," I manage with what I hope sounds like creative reticence.

"Um," he muses, "but we're still rooting for her? She's still the hero, right?"

"I think so," I answer, tentatively, unsure anymore if we're speaking about a plot or my actual life.

"Well, if she goes to meet him, to hear out this request, she needs to leave a trail. And she needs this guy to know she's left one, too. He's got to know it won't be easy to get rid of her without drawing a lot of focus. She's copied that confession tape, right?"

I grimace into the receiver. "No. But I'm not sure she would. The tape has her crime on it too."

Deonte laughs. "That a joke? This some kind of historical drama? She can just edit her crime out. She's only gotta cut out that one bit, and then carry on, right? Easy. Done. Confession gone."

"Sure, but she can't erase the fact that the guy who gave her the tape knows. If his crimes come to light, he'll drag her down with him."

"Well, then, I guess she's got two choices. She does what he asks her to do and hopes it ends at that, or—"

"Or?" I nudge.

"Or she kills the tape maker and hands in the edited tape to the cops. If she's killed someone before, she should be okay, right? In a way it's a kind of self-defense."

"Is it?" I ask, incredulous. "What, legally?"

"Legally? Hell no! That's first-degree murder right there. I meant in the book; in the story it seems like self-defense. We'd buy it as necessary, right—poetic justice? But, ha, no, *legally* it's premeditated murder. We'd be talking life without parole."

I swallow hard, my mouth so dry again. "Yeah, no, I thought so, just the way you said it was . . . weird."

"But here's the thing with your stories, Harriet. Morally, it's different. I don't know, your characters are likable, we side with them; that's gold dust. People can get away with almost anything if they're likable."

"Thanks, Deonte. God, I hope you're right."

After I hang up, I sit in silence and wonder to what degree Deonte was aware of the levels of that phone conversation. And to what degree I may have legally screwed myself if anything was to happen over Christmas. That said, I am certainly starting to leave a trail.

34

Leaving a Trail

THURSDAY, DECEMBER 22

Back at the apartment I pull some stationery from a drawer, grab a pen, and begin to hand-write, for the first time in God knows how many years, an actual letter.

The clock on my desk reads four fifty-six when I lay them out before me: three thick card envelopes inlaid with my initials, my cursive clearly spelling out the names and addresses. Former NYPD officer Deonte Hughley; Dermot Jones, my solicitor back in London; and my agent, Louisa.

I keep my letter to Louisa fun and incidental, and it would only be on a second reading, in a certain set of circum-stances, that anything might pop out to her. I tell her about my pregnancy, my excitement about the future and our child. And then, buried deep within the text, I fleetingly mention the tragedy of Bobby, and of Alison Montgomery, Edward's first girlfriend. And I am confident that if anything was to happen to me, she would be perfectly capable of putting two and two together.

If Robert wants to kill me, he had better make sure it doesn't look like a suicide.

Inside the envelope to my solicitor, I place another carefully sealed envelope. On the front is an instruction to only open it in the event of my death. In the cover note I apologize for the dramatics but respectfully ask that they carry out my request.

Inside is a written account of the events of the day my parents died—my own confession. And in a separate letter inside the sealed envelope, I put a written account of Robert's confession, his list of names, adding my own to the end.

My letter to Deonte is simpler and fits on a small note card.

Thank you for your wise words and help, Deonte. You are a lifesaver. I don't know where I'd be without you.

Also, I forgot to mention when we last spoke that I am getting married next year. Into a rich and powerful family. Guess I'd better watch out! I don't think you ever got a chance to meet Edward Holbeck, my fiancé, but I would love it if you and your wife Regan would be able to make it to our wedding when that happens. It would be great to have some friendly faces on my side of the congregation— I've never been over-subscribed in the family department.

I'm sure the similarities between my life and the new book won't have passed you by—life imitating art. But let's hope not too much so, given everything we discussed.

As a wise man once told me: always leave a trail.

Speak soon,
Harriet x

I drop them in the mailbox across the street. They won't make the Christmas post, but the letters will arrive eventually, and the threat of that is all I need.

Back in the apartment, step one complete, I open a new email and address it to my publisher, Grenville Sinclair. In a flurry of keyboard taps, I outline the changes I intend to make to my manuscript in my next round of edits.

It will be the same story I have told Deonte and the story I am living through now. A story where an author finds herself trapped when her father-in-law gives her a tape, the contents of which force her into a terrifying and complicated position. I fire off my email and delete my SENT folder. The trail Deonte told me to lay is laid. Robert will not find it easy to make me disappear.

I retrieve the tape player from my gym bag, set up my iPhone beside it, and when it's rewound, press PLAY and start to record it on my iPhone. I leave the recording to do its thing while I head to the bedroom to arrange one last thing.

I don't have a gun, and a knife is too premeditated a weapon to take. I need something that isn't a weapon but can be used as one. On a shelf in the bedroom, I find what I'm looking for: the palm-sized glass paperweight I won as a secondary school prize for writing. A good-luck charm, a talisman. Inside its translucent heft is a smoky swirl of lilac, a ghost of a color caught in tiny bubbles. This will do.

I know from hours of research that the weakest point of the skull is the pterion, the area just behind the temple. The bone is the thinnest here, where three sections of skull meet, and a solid blow can easily rupture the meningeal artery hidden just beneath. I remember, after I unearthed that horrifying little fact, I went straight out and bought myself a cycle helmet.

Back in the bedroom, I tuck the glass ball neatly inside a rolled-up pair of socks and bury it deep in my suitcase. It might not be a loaded gun, but it's all I've got. I can explain away my paperweight as an old Christmas gift with sentimental value if ever questioned on it.

The rattle of keys in the apartment door snaps my eyes to the bedside clock. It's six o'clock and Edward's home.

"Harry?"

I close the lid on my case, flick the clasps, and spin the combination lock, heaving it up to standing. Packed. Ready. "Just coming," I holler back. "One second."

He's in the kitchen with a smile on his face when I find him. He raises both hands, a bottle of Bollinger champagne in one, a gift bag in the other. His grin broadens and I know what it means.

"It's done. Signed," he cheers, pulling me into a tight bear hug.

"Oh my God, Ed."

"Two point eight," Edward says meaningfully.

I stare at him for a moment, the number too abstract to grasp. "Two point eight?" I ask.

His eyes have an almost electric charge. Billion; he means billion. My stomach clenches at a number that doesn't sound quite right, quite healthy.

"Two point eight billion." I mumble the words, their meaning gone. I set down the two glasses in my hands carefully. If there was ever a time to make an exception to my no drinking rule, this might be the time.

Edward laughs but I do not. He carefully removes the foil on the bottle, twists the wires, and pops the cork. Foam rises.

The numbers terrify me. Like a sudden timer set on my life. Like a price on my head. The numbers are too high. Fate, karma—whatever—will not allow it.

I swallow hard and try to think of the right thing to say as he pours for us.

I try to focus on Edward, how happy he is. I try to remember who we are, who I am, why we are doing any of this. I close my eyes and bury my face in his chest. There he is—his smell, his touch, the sound of his heart. I breathe in the scent of the man I met at the Natural History Museum a year-and-change ago, the man I have laughed and cried with, who has been beside me ever since. I let my body relax into him.

He's still here; I just need to focus on him.

He pulls back with a smile, a thought occurring. He lifts the thin rope handles of the gift bag and hands it to me.

"It's a lot to take in, I know. Give it a minute. But, in the meantime, I wanted to get you a thing," he says with a grin. I feel my cheeks flush hot as I take the gift and carefully unwrap its delicate tissue paper. The bag is discreet but the tissue sticker reads BALMAIN, and when I unfurl the folded article within and hold it up against myself, I see it is a dress. But nicer than any dress I have ever worn. The weight of its fabric is heavy in my hands. It's beautiful, something from another world, another life—black bouclé, thick gold embossed buttons, shoulder pads, the tailoring immaculate. A Balmain blazer dress. I have never owned anything like it. It's a work of art. I catch my reflection in the kitchen window, the dress pressed to me.

"It should fit perfectly. I wanted to get you something to wear for Christmas. Holbeck Christmases can be dressy," he adds with a smirk, downing his glass.

"I'll go try—" I nod toward the bedroom, grateful for the excuse to take a moment to process.

In the bedroom I sit in silence and try to calm myself. Everything is moving too fast, the world around me changing at breakneck speed. I try to order my thoughts, to keep my mind on why I am doing any of this. To be with Edward. To have a family. I let my hand linger on my swelling bump and pull myself together.

In the large bedroom mirror, I step carefully into the dress, its lining cool against my skin. I need to get back to Edward; I've taken way too long. I untie my hair and shake it out, and when I take in the full picture I have to stifle a giggle. I look like someone else; I look amazing. Like a 1990s CEO, or a coffee-commercial singleton, an Italian *Vogue* editorial. A late-twentieth-century idea of what "having it all" might look like. Who'd have thought? Shoulder pads really do make you look thinner and feel more powerful . . .

I pull on a pair of heels and stand back.

"I'm ready," I call out to Edward, but the apartment is silent. I wait a moment before calling again. "Ed?"

Nothing.

Something is not right; I feel it instantly. "Ed, is everything okay?" I call again, moving to the doorway.

I strain my ears but there's nothing but the rumble of New York beyond our walls. The bathroom door remains ajar, as do all the others along the hallway. I swallow, softly, a lump having formed in my throat. Something has changed in the air.

I duck back into the bedroom instinctively, certain there is someone else in the apartment. I dash to my discarded pile of clothes to find my phone. And it's then that the crashing realization hits me. My phone isn't here; it's recording Robert's tape out loud in my office. But why would Edward be in my office?

"Ed?" I yell through the apartment. I hear the sound of movement from my office and I bolt from the bedroom, barreling down the hallway, my heels snagging on the carpet as I fly into the room using the doorframe for leverage. Edward looks up at me, the bright-red headphones now on his ears, the tape cassette out of the player and in his hand. He gives me a confused smile before sliding off the headphones.

"What is this?" he asks simply.

"Um," I flounder, my breath snagging in my throat. Before I can speak, he gives a low whistle and looks me up and down.

"Wow. You look insanely hot," he says plainly, his eyes surveying my body.

"Er, thanks, yeah, it's a good fit." I fumble for an understanding of the situation. "You okay? You good?" I ask with a little too much vigor.

I don't know how else to find out how much he's listened to. If he's heard his father's voice, why is he acting like this? Why is he acting so normal?

I point to the tape player in his lap. "Did you . . . ?"

"Listen? Yeah," he says happily. "Well, I tried to, but this side is blank, right? Was there supposed to be something on it?"

"What?" I say, the blood draining from me. "Blank?"

Then it hits me. Oh my God, I must have accidentally nudged

the RECORD button when I pressed PLAY. A flood of relief bursts through me; Edward heard nothing. I sink down onto the carpet with a groan, half grateful, half gut-punched that I have lost all recorded proof of Robert Holbeck's confession. The most important piece of advice Deonte gave to me, to copy the recording, and somehow I managed to fuck it up with my stupid bloated pregnant fingers.

"You okay, honey?" Edward asks, crouching down in front of me. "I don't want to be that guy, but you probably shouldn't be running around at this point, you know? At least probably not in heels," he adds carefully. "Was there something important on the tape?" he asks when I don't respond.

I straighten up and let out a sigh that could pass for many things. "No. No, it's fine. It was just research," I say, rubbing my face as if somehow I could rub the truth of my words into existence.

He leans in and kisses my forehead. "Ah, annoying. Sorry, honey. That sucks. Still, at least it was just research, right? Love this retro tech, though. Very analog, very nineties. Dad would love it. Heck, *I* love it," he chuckles, reaching back to the chair to grab it. "Is this for the book research too?"

A shiver runs up my spine at the meta nature of the conversation we are now having.

"Er, yeah," I answer. "It's a split timeline. The next book. Present day and the nineties. Lots of fun period stuff in there." I smile, gently taking the Olympus recorder back from him. "I just need to get the edits back and have a reshuffle before I start talking about it."

As I look down at the cassette window of the recorder in my hands, I suddenly realize that all might not be lost. Only one side will be wiped. While Side A is lost, Side B should be untouched.

"Sounds great. Can't wait to read it," he tells me, getting to his feet and offering me a hand up. I rise like a hobbled Bambi.

I watch Edward's back as he leads me through to the kitchen, and our champagne, then I steal another fleeting look down at the Olympus in my hands. A question reemerges. Why was Edward in my office in the first place? And a doubt slowly forms. Did I accidentally wipe the tape, or did he?

When I look back up, he's looking directly at me.

35

Road Trip

FRIDAY, DECEMBER 23

Bags packed and ready to go in the trunk of the car beneath Mount Sinai Hospital, we wait on the bleach-scented ward for our names to be called.

I try to think only one step ahead, of seeing the face of my baby, of finding out if I have a daughter or a son. My due date is July 7 next year. Hard to process that I have been pregnant for three months already without anyone but us knowing. I try not to speculate on what will come after that. I do not want the baby to feel my fear.

Edward looks up from his phone as a couple exits the scanning room. I watch his profile and wonder how long he was alone with that tape player in my office. Ten minutes? Fifteen? Twenty? I sat paralyzed by rumination in our bedroom for long enough.

I checked the recording I tried to make on my iPhone later that night, and it turns out it was my fault; I did accidentally wipe one side of the tape. There was an hour-long recording of an empty office on my iPhone with only five minutes of Edward and I talking at the end.

But I can't prize my thoughts from the image of the microcassette out of the player and in Edward's hand. He had enough time to turn it and listen to what was on the other side. There's no way I can be sure he didn't hear his father's voice.

A nurse rounds the corner and gives us a smile that asks if we're ready.

Moments later in the darkness of the sonography room, we are asked if we want to know the sex of our child from my blood results, and as the nurse tells us, something beautiful bursts open inside me.

The drive to The Hydes is long. After two hours of freeway and an hour of forest-flanked highway, we stop at a local gas station. It's the only sign of civilization we've seen for miles and it looks unstaffed. Edward jumps out to fill us up and I catch sight of an attendant in the cramped kiosk across the forecourt.

The GPS says we have another forty-five minutes before we arrive at The Hydes, and I still haven't had a chance to listen to the rest of the tape. I plunge a hand into my bag in the footwell and make sure it's still there, the dry foam of the headphones brushing reassuringly against my wrist. The tape is stored in a separate zip pocket. I feel safer with the two apart. The rest of Side B is waiting for me, and the sooner I can listen the better. I haven't had a second away from Edward since last night, though.

I look out at the gas station hoping for signs of a restroom. I could listen to it now, lock myself away in a grotty toilet for as long as I need and refuse to come out. But even as I imagine it, I know it's a terrible idea. What would Edward think? I watch as he ambles back to the car and slips in beside me, blissfully unaware of the thoughts and fears racing through me. He's certainly not acting as if he heard anything on the tape. He would have said something, surely, and we certainly wouldn't be on our way to his childhood home to meet his family if he'd heard what was on it.

He restarts the engine, handing me a chilled bottle of water and a gas station snack with a smile. "This'll keep you going," he says, and I think how great a husband he's going to be; a great father, if we ever get that far.

We roll out of the station and I let my gaze skim the landscape rushing past, mile after mile of thickly packed forest still standing between us and them.

As we drive, Edward tells me more about The Hydes and I try to picture it.

"John Livingston Holbeck bought the land back in 1886, but the house wasn't there then. He demolished the original building, razed it to the ground and rebuilt something bigger, grander. Something with more history."

"He built something with more *history*? What the hell does that mean? How would a new building have more history?" I interject, my European sensibilities ruffled.

"Because it wasn't a new building. He bought a stone mansion from somewhere in the hills outside Budapest. A castle. He had it taken apart and shipped over here to the US. They rebuilt it, stone by stone, and it became The Hydes. Alma, John's wife, had remarked on it from a carriage on their honeymoon. The building had fallen into disrepair, so the story goes, and it had made her sad."

"It made her sad so he rescued it, brought it home to America? Like a dog at the pound?"

Edward chuckles. "Yeah, I guess. But you have to remember, J.L. basically owned logistics back then, so it was nothing to him to move things. To build. If you wanted to get anything in the US from A to B, you had to pay John Livingston Holbeck's companies to do it for you. So he could cover a lot of ground on a whim."

I nod, conceding the point. He had a monopoly, or close to one. Back then you had no choice but to make J. L. Holbeck richer.

"So," Edward continues, "he shipped the house over, bricks and all, and had it reconstructed here. It was an enormous project, took them two years to finish. He brought over Hungarian stonemasons, landscapers, set up a kind of village of workers. He wanted it to be perfect for Alma."

"Romantic," I mutter under my breath, because if I'm honest I have to wonder whether Alma really did want a giant stone house erected in the middle of nowhere, miles from anyone she knew. Then again, perhaps she did, and maybe I'm being unfair.

"I can't wait for you to see the place," he says, his eyes on the road. "You know, you can get used to things, having things, and it's only when you show other people that you see them again. With fresh eyes."

The blue arrow on the satnav glides on, unstoppable; we're nearly there. Nerves flutter inside me like something trapped.

The trees on one side of us begin to recede from the road and are suddenly overtaken by a high and ominous wall. The perimeter of the vast Holbeck property, its stone topped with razor wire, like a federal complex, a fortress. So much wealth within its walls, I imagine it probably warrants such fortifications.

Edward clicks on the car's hazard lights, even though we are the only car on the road, and we begin to slow.

We idle in front of an enormous set of wrought-iron gates, their Hieronymus Bosch tangle of vines and creatures shuddering open to reveal a long evergreen-lined driveway beyond. Edward's hand slips into mine and squeezes.

"It's okay to be nervous," he tells me. "I'm nervous too." We begin our steady crawl up the winding drive and I watch in the rearview as the twelve-foot-high gates swing firmly shut behind us.

As we proceed along the winding driveway, the sheer size of the estate becomes apparent. The house is still nowhere to be seen but the road spools on with no sign of ending. After a while the trees flanking us loosen to reveal the rolling parkland beyond.

I pick out the slow-moving forms of deer, their tawny hides coming into view as they raise their heads from the grass.

Then I catch sight of it, in the distance, rising from the landscape. The size of it is breathtaking.

Immaculate ornamental gardens rise up to meet its wide stone steps and there, the hulk of the building crouches, like a creature lying in wait. Four floors, glinting window upon window all the way up to the spire-like crenellations that top each of its four wings. It is monstrous and overwhelming in its scope.

Another tunnel of trees swallows us and my view is blocked once more as I feel our speed creep up. When we break through into the open again, I catch sight of a massive maze, growing in the center of the lawns that lead up to the house. Beyond it a long ornamental fountain flows right up to the stairs leading up to the house.

I marvel at the money it must have cost J. L. Holbeck to create this place—the extent of it, the vision required to even conceive of the idea, as if somehow with enough money reality can become malleable.

"Jesus," I say with a sharp intake of breath, and I feel Edward's eyes on me, concern tangibly pulsing from him. He's worried I don't like it, that it's too much, but I cannot pull my eyes from the building as we glide toward it. Pale, weatherworn marble statues stand sentinel on the edges of the lawn running all the way up to The Hydes, their plinths staggered at intervals, their bodies arranged in classical poses like so many frozen people. And above them the quiet darkness of the building rises up to a castellated summit, its darkly balustraded peaks popping starkly against the cloudy winter sky.

"It's so big," is all I manage as the car bends around to the front of the building, the flutter inside me morphing into dread. Robert is in there; they all are.

The Hydes is a foxhole and I am a rabbit. A stupid, pregnant rabbit.

Edward cuts the engine and turns in his seat to look at me.

"You okay? You look a little . . ."

I decide to be as honest as I can. "I'm fucking terrified, Ed," I huff out.

He gives my hand a quick kiss.

"You are amazing and I love you. They love you. Look at me. This will be fun; Christmas will be fun." I must look unconvinced because he chases it up with more. "We can go home. Right now. If that's what you want?"

I take in his concern. The idea alone is more than I dare to allow myself to indulge in. I can leave this place, but I can't stop what's going to happen from happening.

"No, it's fine. I'm just—"

"You don't need to impress anyone. Everyone likes you. Matilda, Mom, Ollie, everyone. Even Dad, and he's a tough nut. And you don't need to worry about what they'll think of the pregnancy. They'll love it, trust me. They will *love* it."

"That's kind of what I'm worried about, Ed. I'm not sure I want them to be too into it. I'm not sure I want them to be too into *anything*."

He nods, taking in my words. "I see. Yeah. Stealing the first-born. Hexes, et cetera. Could be an issue, for sure." He grins; he's joking. Nothing seems quite so bad when Edward shines his warm light of rationality on it.

He tucks a stray strand of hair behind my ear and I feel my heart rate beginning to settle. He gives me a supportive nod, then briskly unfastens his seatbelt and pops the car door.

"Okay, let's do this," he says, getting out, his energy propelling me out into the crisp December air too.

36

The Hydes

FRIDAY, DECEMBER 23

"Why is it called The Hydes?" I ask as Edward carries our bags to the front door. I've meant to ask the question so many times before, but it's only standing here on the doorstep that I realize I still don't have an answer.

"This was all forest once," Edward says, gesturing out at the parkland. "When J.L. bought it, he leveled the building the previous landowner had erected and rebuilt. It was just wild North American forest before us, before them. Hunting ground," he says, leaning past me to rap the door's heavy knocker, the slow reverb of metal-on-metal echoing within. After a few moments in the cold, he shakes his head, leans around the doorway to a nearby window, and bellows into the glass of the house, "Someone, let us in!"

I raise an eyebrow and he shrugs innocently. "They know we're here. They opened the damn gates."

I feel a smile creep across my face at the normalcy of what he just did. After everything, it's a relief to see evidence that the Holbecks are just another family, with all that that entails.

Edward sighs as he tries to recapture his train of thought. "Hunting ground, yeah. It was all forest, all hunting land. White-tailed deer, wild turkeys, waterfowl, black bears. Mitzi had a thing for bears," he says with a shake of the head. "When the house fell to her and Alfred, she filled it with Black Forest crafts. Carvings, art. Black bears, the forest. There's hardly any of it left now—Mother is a minimalist at heart—but there's the odd relic. Anyway, New York State still has some of the best hunting in the country, thousands of acres of game. So the name, The Hydes, kind of came from that, but there was a mistake. No, wait, what's it called—a . . . an orthographical error? You're a writer, you must have heard of those. Someone, somewhere, at some point, mishearing, misunderstanding a name, writing it down wrong. An auditory error. Or a conceptual error." He catches my perplexed expression and explains further. "The name was written down wrong in the deeds. It was meant to say The Hides. Like hiding. With an *i*. Because of the old hunting hides that used to pepper the property. But someone wrote it down as The Hydes, with a *y*. Like the family name. I guess they thought the family that bought the land were called Hyde."

"Like Jekyll and Hyde?"

"Ha," he scoffed. "Yeah."

"Wait, there are hunting hides here?" I interject. "Like hidden lookouts?"

"Yeah, hidden shelters in the forest, in the undergrowth, up high. Hunters would set up in them and wait to pick off game below. Like snipers."

"Are they still there?" I ask cautiously, the idea of them nestling in the forest strangely unsettling.

"What, the snipers?" he teases.

"No. The hides."

"Yeah, I guess," Edward says with a chuckle, unsure why the idea has hooked me so much. "We used to play in them as kids. They wouldn't be in great condition now, but they'd still be there."

I look to the edges of the dense woodland across the lawns. I let my thoughts slip between the gaps in the tall trees and fly up to those unseen structures deep within.

The sun breaks through the winter clouds, forcing me to look away. "So the house's name is spelled wrong," I say, returning to his story. "Couldn't J.L. have fixed that? With all the money in the world, couldn't he just have corrected the deeds?"

"No way. He loved it," Edward tells me with a grin. "The Holbecks have a weird sense of humor. J.L. had one for sure. He liked it as an origin story. He liked the reminder that no matter what you do, how much work you put in, it will always be misunderstood. There's something in there about the inadequacy of the human condition—I don't know. The human element in any enterprise will always be its sticking point. My family loves myth creation. They managed to turn a simple spelling mistake into some kind of life lesson. Hence The Hydes."

As if on cue, the front door's bolts are drawn back, its oak façade creaking open to reveal Matilda, her pale face beaming in the dim hallway.

"Well, hello, strangers. It's about time. What kept you?"

Unimpressed by the wait, Edward bends to pick up our baggage as I follow Matilda into the warm darkness of the house.

Our bags left in the hall, Matilda leads us briskly through the vast carved stone hallway. "Everyone's waiting in the sunroom," she says as I absorb the house flowing past me. The hallway opens out to an enormous stairwell, and on its opposite wall gapes a monstrous fireplace carved directly into the Hungarian stone of the building. From the staircase walls, portraits rise and disappear around the bending flights.

"The whole mob's been scratching around for tea for the past half hour," Matilda explains, turning back to us with a smile. "It fell to me to beat them off with a stick. You see, we only have two staff over the holidays, Harry."

I can't keep the ghost of a smirk from flickering across my features. "Only two? Wow," I say innocently as we turn another corridor.

"Uh-huh, so I always end up doing more than my fair share of the grunt work over the holidays. Point is, I was holding everyone off for you lovebirds. I sent tea back to keep it warm. I've told them to bring up some more now, fresh." She suddenly stops dead in her tracks in front of a door and I narrowly avoid bumping straight into her.

"They're in here," she sighs, clearly already too full of Christmas spirit. The dread I'd been managing to push down until now crests inside me at the thought of them all in there. "Tea in the sunroom," she trills as she swings the door open.

Walking into the light of the sunroom after the dimness of the halls is blinding as warm winter sun floods through the vast orangery windows. The room is high-ceilinged and airy, giving an immense sense of space. My eyes struggle to adjust as I try to make out their faces in the blazing light, one face in particular more important than the rest. In front of the massive glare of the windows a table is laid with a brilliant white tablecloth, silverware flaring in the light, glasses refracting, the shape and blur of stacked tiers of cakes, savory fare, petits fours.

"Welcome to The Hydes," Matilda adds with self-aware grandiosity.

The figures at the table rise, in silhouette, as we enter, their shapes beginning to make sense. "Harriet, Edward," comes a voice I recognize as Eleanor's. I shield my eyes and she comes into focus. "We thought you'd slipped off the face of the earth," she quips with a light shake of her chic gray bob. "We were expecting you this morning."

"We had a little appointment this morning," Edward answers, just holding back, and I realize we have to tell them imminently.

Over Eleanor's shoulder I notice the view beyond the colossal sunroom windows, and it snatches my breath clean away. Beyond the twinkling glass, the full panorama of the Holbecks' palatial gardens stretches out in all directions; the epic sprawl of it, a god's-eye view. The ornamental gardens spill with bright bursts of color set against tight evergreen borders, winter blooms in full flower pouring over crisp paths. Out toward the splashing fountain, a long shallow pool of rippling water carries on deep into the lawns. The fountain itself is an elaborate sculpture, water pouring from mouths, claws, eyes, and hands, creatures twisting as the sunlight catches and refracts in the water.

Past it, the green carpet of lawn rolls out to the edge of the dark forest.

Eleanor follows my gaze. "Ah, the grounds. Yes, they're quite lovely this time of year, aren't they?" she says with a modest smile. "Tea?"

Edward pulls out my chair and I sit, letting out an audible sigh when I realize Robert is not here.

"Yes, I'd love some," I say, the dread inside me loosened. I watch the rest of the family as they slip back into conversation. Two uniformed maids enter, unacknowledged, with steaming tea in silver pots.

I take in everything, this family in its natural environment, the warm scent of lemon cake, buttery scones, the bubble of conversation, dust particles sparkling in the air, and the delicate roll of heat off the tops of teacups.

I let my eyes flicker over the Holbecks: Matilda and Eleanor, Stuart and Lila, Oliver and Fiona, Edward and me.

The children aren't present, and neither is Nunu. Which brings me back full circle to Robert.

"Is, ah—" I begin, but my voice catches as eyes find me. I clear my throat. "Is Robert joining us?"

I feel Edward's gaze on me now too, surprised by the question.

Eleanor dabs her mouth with a napkin. "Mm, sorry, yes, I should have said. Robert is just tying up a few loose ends," she answers, then chuckles, giving her children a solicitous look.

"Though Robert missing our pre-holiday tea is as much an annual tradition as the tea itself."

A surge of relief buffets through me. He's not coming. I might not see him until tonight. Which means I will have time to listen to the rest of the tape.

Edward's hand slips onto my thigh, making me jolt slightly. His look is inquiring: *Why are you asking about my father? Is everything okay?*

I shake my head lightly, chasing his question away with a quick smile. But he holds my gaze and I suddenly realize I have misunderstood him. He thinks I want Robert here so that we can tell everyone about the pregnancy together.

He's asking if I want to tell them now.

"Oh, okay," I say, hearing the surprise in my own voice.

He gives a decisive nod then takes my hand in his and places both down on the white linen tablecloth pointedly.

Eleanor raises an eyebrow at our clasped hands. "I have a feeling something's coming, Ed," she says softly. "What's coming?"

Silence descends around the table, teacups caught halfway to mouths, chewing paused.

I flush as Edward speaks beside me, his words somehow muffled as I feel a flutter in my chest. Palpitations. The obstetrician told me the hormones might do this. No stress, he warned me— no stress and plenty of fluids. I down the cool glass of water in front of me.

Smiling eyes flit between Edward and me.

". . . And this morning we found out that we are having a baby girl," Edward finishes, beaming.

Eleanor's hand flies to her mouth. "Oh, Edward, a little girl," she gasps with genuine joy.

Words of congratulations cascade around us. Oliver nods his, but beside him I note Fiona's blank expression. She looks concerned—for me perhaps? for our child?—and for the first time I wonder how much she really knows about this family. My focus is pulled by Lila squeezing me into a tight hug, her eyes twinkling with excitement.

"A girl," Stuart intones wryly. "Dad's going to love that. He's always said we could do with more female energy in the place. Right?"

Matilda smirks. "I think he just says that to you, Stu."

"Do you have a name yet?" Eleanor asks.

"Her name is Iris," I say.

Iris: a beautiful flower. Or the sharp aperture of a human eye—a jewel-toned, star-speckled universe in miniature.

"Iris," Eleanor repeats, savoring the word. "Beautiful."

37

A Moment's Peace

FRIDAY, DECEMBER 23

After tea, the family peels off, promising to reconvene for supper at seven. For a moment I think I might get the opportunity I've been waiting for to slip away and listen to Robert's tape, but Eleanor intercedes.

"I'll show you around, Harriet, if you're not too tired from the journey?"

I think of making an excuse but realize I don't even know what room I'm staying in yet, so I have nowhere to escape to anyway.

Eleanor ferries me and Edward through the property, creaking open door after door to opulent rooms filled with beautiful objects, the house a curated marvel of fine textiles and artwork.

However, when we reach the farthest wing, the aesthetic changes.

"This is the new wing," Eleanor informs me as underfoot the floor switches abruptly from antique parquet to polished concrete. Ahead of us through a glass corridor the walls are lime-washed and minimalist. We stop, our way on blocked by a state-of-the-art glass security door with a keypad entry system.

Beside me Edward's phone bursts to life. He attempts to ignore it for a few rings before Eleanor gives him a look that says she will go no farther until it is silenced.

"I'll leave you two to it, then?" he says, pulling the phone out. "I should probably take this." He plants a kiss on my cheek. "I'll catch you back in the room before dinner."

"Sure," I say, nodding.

"Blue room, Mom?"

Eleanor nods. "Yes, your bags should be up there already. Don't work too hard, Eddie. It's Christmas, remember? And you have a very special guest to look after."

"Forty-five minutes max," he calls back as we watch him disappear around the corridor.

I do not see the numbers Eleanor keys into the system, but once we are inside I realize the new wing is actually the most impressive part of the house.

Glass doors puff open into beautiful rooms constructed with glass, concrete, pale wood, and rough quartz. The lighting is ambient, the temperature climate-controlled, and everything in this wing has a beautifully designed function. It must have cost millions.

"The old wing burned down back when the children still lived here. Absolutely terrifying, as you can imagine, but everyone survived. Robert's old study was lost, though. The whole wing was rubble and ash. I blame the cigars. But the new wing can withstand anything. The insurance otherwise"—she rolls her eyes—"you wouldn't believe."

"Do you like it?" I ask Eleanor, her sharp gray bob swishing as she turns to me.

"The new wing? I do," she answers after a moment's consideration. "Truth be told I like it a lot more than the rest of the house. I like knowing what everything is for and that everything works. I've never been a fan of the needlessly complex. Of collections. You?"

I don't get the chance to answer as the sound of a voice raised in anger and the smashing of glass reaches us from the room at the end of the corridor. It is Robert's, and he's arguing with someone. I can't make out his words but the tone is clear.

Eleanor gives me an apologetic, indulgent look. She shakes her head.

"I swear to you, Harriet. Every Christmas, without fail. He won't let things go. Work, work, work. And that Holbeck temper. Every year he winds himself up into a filthy mood." She looks at her watch. "Don't worry, he'll boil over by six and be as soft as a kitten for suppertime."

That Holbeck temper. As she says it, I realize I'm not sure I've ever witnessed it. Edward is the calmest man I know; compared with previous boyfriends he's a positive saint. And Oliver and Stuart seem more tired than angry, from my experience. But then I know what is on Robert's tape. Perhaps temper can be measured in different ways.

I listen once more but the new wing is silent.

Ten minutes later, pregnancy excuses made, I am lying on a duck-egg-blue bed in a duck-egg-blue room, surrounded by duck-egg-blue curtains and cobalt objets d'art. On the bedside table beside me a cool glass of water sits next to a small vase of freshly picked hothouse cornflowers.

Once I have heard Eleanor's footsteps tap back down the wide stone steps of the main staircase, I scramble over to my bag, lock the bedroom door, and slip on the headphones.

38

The Tape

PART 4

I am under no illusions that you have not done your homework.
You will have looked into the names I have given you.

The thing about us orphans is that we find it incredibly hard
to relinquish control, don't we? If we want a thing done, then we
do it ourselves. I would not expect you to take my word on anything, least of all the veracity of what I am telling you. Just as I
would never take you at your word, my dear Harriet, at least not
yet. We both have much to prove to each other. Perhaps we will
get there. Perhaps we will not. Time will tell.

But again, I digress.

As I'm sure you have gleaned, it is wise to be wary of my
whole family at this stage. I know your past; I will continue to
keep an eye on who and what comes in and out of your life. But
I am not the only one who may have taken this precaution. Other

members of my family will always have their own concerns and access to similar resources, and perhaps they will not hold you in quite the same esteem as I.

You will be invited, if you haven't been already, to an event at my son Oliver's house. A family tradition, Germanic as so many of ours are. It's a child's game but not so childish if the rules are not known. That is how we play it. You will not know what is real and what is not; it only works on the imagination this way. But whatever you fear, do not fear exposure from me; do not fear the things you have heard on this tape. If you have listened to this tape in its entirety before Krampusnacht, then do not discuss it with me at that house. There are no private places there; everything is seen. Play the game as well as I know you can, because everyone will be watching.

Wait and I will bring you to me. I will bring you to The Hydes. It is there that we will speak and I will ask my favor of you.

People have died, Harriet—not because of bloodlust; I think you know that. Necessity is often the only real motive anyone can hold in their head and act on.

You have done things out of necessity—as have I.

You will receive an invitation to The Hydes. Do not be scared; accept it and have faith in the knowledge that I keep those of value close to me.

Here is what I need you to do.

We play a game on Christmas Eve, another tradition from the old country. I'm sure you're surprised that a family like ours plays so many childish games, but, Harriet, that is the common misconception about the nature of games. Games take us as close as is acceptable to the strategies we use in life. Games reveal our most base instinct: the instinct to survive. Under the mask of enjoyment, we reveal ourselves, we reveal how we play at life, our methods, how we navigate others' strengths and weaknesses.

A game is only a game if you do not fully understand it. We play as we live. And I want you to play a game with me, Harriet. The stakes will be high but there is everything to play for.

The game begins at eight P.M. on Christmas Eve, and it is a

treasure hunt. Edward will want you to sit it out, or to play with him. He will try to shelter you from us, but you must play and play alone. We all play alone.

Each player will have a present waiting for them at the end of their hunt, and clues that will lead them there. Follow your clues, watch your back, and when you find what I hope you will find, all will be revealed. I have no doubt that everything will come together in your mind before you reach the end.

If you have listened to this recording by the time we meet at The Hydes, I would ask you to show me a sign. There will be flowers in your room. Wear one to supper and we will understand each other. Until then: good luck, Harriet.

Oh, and a point of interest: my children no longer sleep in their childhood bedrooms. Those old rooms are kept just as they were. Eleanor wanted to have them cleared, but I like the memories. It might be worth taking a look if you're interested. You can tell a lot about a person from the mess they leave behind.

39

The First Night

FRIDAY, DECEMBER 23

The tape clicks off. I fast-forward, hoping for more—more explanation, more anything—but there's only the crackle of virgin tape. Robert is gone. That is all I get.

It's clear I should have listened to the entire tape long ago. Before Krampusnacht, and well before I arrived here. Robert must have assumed I'd listen to it the day after he gave it to me. I would have had so much more time to try to decode it if I had, but life got in the way.

I rewind the tape and press PLAY again, carefully recording Robert's list of names onto my phone. I may have lost the whole first half of the cassette, but I still have the list of dead girls. It might just be enough to save me. Once the recording is finished, I email it to myself. It should be waiting on my laptop back at home. If anything was to happen to me out here, the trail is laid and it will lead straight back to Robert Holbeck.

Edward doesn't get back to the room until after the tape player is finished and packed away, my work done.

He's finalizing things with Hong Kong, signing off on the little details still remaining. And he had a beer with Oliver. I smell the sweet hops on his breath.

"What have you been up to?" he asks.

I give him the same pregnancy excuse I gave his mother and his hand flies to my head solicitously to check my temperature.

"I'm fine, Ed. It's just been a long day."

He holds my gaze as if to test the truth of my statement and, seemingly satisfied, removes his hand. "Luckily, we're skipping the family dinner tonight. Dad's in the middle of something."

I stop breathing, my eyes trained on Edward. "No family dinner?"

"Well, we'll eat, just not together. God knows what he's in the middle of. But we'll see everyone at dinner tomorrow anyway. He can't avoid Christmas entirely."

"You think he's avoiding us?" I ask before I can stop myself.

Edward seems surprised at the question. "No, of course not. Turn of phrase. But who knows? Who knows what goes on in his mind? He'd certainly never deign to tell us. But we'll see him tomorrow for sure. We play a game on Christmas Eve. Family tradition. There are clues; you find presents. He wouldn't miss that. But don't worry, after what happened at Fiona and Oliver's, no one's going to expect you to take part in any of that."

"How come you didn't tell me about it before?"

"Because there's no way I'm letting you do it, not after Krampus."

"Letting me?" I inquire archly, though the sentiment is oddly comforting given everything going on right now. "Is it similar to the Krampus Race?" I ask, fully aware that I need to take part in the game willingly or this will never work. "I did okay in that, right?"

Edward looks amused. "Um, yeah, you did amazing, but, I mean, you hated it, right? No offense, honey, but I really don't think this one is a good idea. I'll be honest with you, it's a really weird game. And sure, there's no monster chasing you in this one, but there is my family. Besides, no one is expecting you to do this. You're pregnant. You can definitely sit it out."

"No way am I sitting it out," I say with as much enthusiasm as I can muster. A look of confusion passes over his features and I quickly continue. "I might have overreacted about the whole Krampus thing. It was fun, in retrospect. I just should have known a bit more about it before it started. But the rules of this game aren't a secret too, are they?"

His expression lifts. "No, it's just clues. A treasure hunt. You're racing the other players but no one's going to be chasing you."

That's what you think, I reply in my mind.

While eating a dinner in our room later that evening, I decide to broach a question that's been niggling me since I first listened to Robert's tape. I can't get the idea out of my head that in some way Edward, and the rest of the family, must have an inkling of what their father is really capable of.

I know it's a risk bringing this up, but I need to know the answer and there will never be a good time to ask.

"Edward, why didn't you tell me the truth about Bobby? That he jumped?"

He looks up at me, startled.

"He didn't die from the drug interaction," I continue gently. "Well, I suppose in a way he did, but why didn't you tell me he committed suicide?"

I watch him flinch at my choice of words and immediately I regret them. "Because I was ashamed. For him. Of him. He wasn't like that, you see. I don't want him remembered like that. He was strong, and suicide seems so—"

"I feel like you should have told me, Ed," I say, not harshly, but I can't deny I am starting to feel a little alone on a limb. "I had to hear it from Lila," I lie.

He gives a slow nod, a question answered.

"I'm not good at talking about my emotions," he tells me, and I feel his vulnerability for the first time in a long time. "Stuart is better at it. Heck, they all are. Being the eldest has been hard. If I don't mention it then it didn't happen and if it didn't happen then it can't happen to me. I don't know . . ." He trails off, embarrassed, like he has said too much.

There I was thinking the man I found was too perfect, but it turns out he's just under more pressure to hide his fears than the regular guy. "It's okay. I understand. And you don't have to worry about that happening to you, Ed, because I am here with you. Every step of the way. Nothing ever has to be that hard again. I promise you." As I say it, I know I mean it even though it's not true. Because I don't even know if I'm going to make it through the next two days let alone be with him for a lifetime. But my words seem to salve his worries.

"I'm trying, Harry, I can't tell you how hard, to be open with you. I'm glad you can be with me. This is the closest I have ever gotten to—" He stops himself with a gentle shake of his head. "I just love you. I'm glad we're here, together. I'm glad you came."

Beyond the bedroom window, thick flakes of snow are beginning to drift. We watch it swirl and settle, dusting the moonlit gardens as far as the eye can see. A winter wonderland in the making. I try to imagine the view through Edward's eyes, try to imagine the feeling of owning all of this, owning the grass, the snow, the walls, the windows, the moon bone white in the sky. But the idea, like quicksilver, is too mercurial to hold in my mind.

We sit in our moonlit rectangle of light, one hand grasping the other's, and finish our meal as virgin snow blankets The Hydes.

40

The Players and the Game

SATURDAY, DECEMBER 24

When we wake, the snow has settled and continues to fall. The Hydes has been blanketed in white and the branches of the forest hang laden.

From the bedroom window I take it in and that age-old Christmas feeling flexes itself awake inside me, in spite of everything.

My thoughts are interrupted by a knock on the door and Sylvia, the maid who brought up our dinner the night before, enters with a heavy breakfast tray.

"It's a beautiful morning," she says, singsong, as she lays out freshly brewed coffee and a selection of pastries.

"What's everyone up to this morning?" Edward asks from the bathroom doorway. He's shirtless, with a towel about his waist.

She blushes noticeably as she lays the cutlery and plates, pouring us two steaming cups of coffee. "Mr. Robert is in his office.

Mrs. Eleanor is in the orangery. Your brothers are planning on fishing this morning. Jimmy is preparing the kit in the boot room." She looks up at Edward. "Shall I ask him to prepare your things too?"

"No, thank you, Sylvia. I think I'll show Harriet around today. Maybe we'll take lunch in the snug? Is it free?"

"It is, sir."

"Say one-thirty?"

"Perfect." She smiles. "And, er, I don't know if you've been told, but the children are staying in the keeper's cottage with Nunu tonight. Something about staying up for Santa," she adds with a knowing smile.

"God, Nunu is a saint," Edward remarks, causing a sharp flirtatious giggle to erupt from Sylvia. Sometimes I forget how attractive Edward is until I see him in action and it's like a kick in the head.

"Oh, and Ms. Erikson is swimming," Sylvia adds, seemingly without judgment. Edward's gaze snaps up.

"What, in the lake?" Edward asks, clearly taken aback.

Sylvia nods slowly. "She's Scandinavian," she offers, by way of explanation, then shrugs, leaving it at that. We grunt our understanding. Swimming in freezing water in the snow makes a little more sense in that context.

The breakfast served and the whereabouts of the entire Holbeck clan accounted for, Sylvia takes her leave.

After breakfast, Edward and I trek out into the garden bundled up in layers, our breath fogging in the cold air. Edward leads us out across the crunchy snow toward the bulk of the maze.

"There's a trick to the maze," Edward says with a smile as we approach its entrance. "Want to hear it, or prefer to try your luck first?"

From the driveway it looked fun, but standing right in front of it, its size really hits home and I find myself wondering what would actually happen if you got stuck inside it. The densely packed hedges making up its walls must be over fifteen feet high. It's unlikely you could climb it or crawl through it if you had to break the rules.

"I don't know. Be honest: how hard is it?" I ask.

He raises an eyebrow. *"Hard."*

"Well, then, I think I'm going to need the trick. It's going to be a long day otherwise."

Edward lets out a laugh. "Yeah, maybe a maze, my family, *and* a treasure hunt is a bit much for your first Christmas."

In front of the maze's opening, I notice a small wooden sign at knee height with the words ENTER HERE hand-etched onto it.

"Creepy," I say.

"Yep," he says with a sigh. "Now imagine being seven and having to celebrate Krampusnacht here."

"Bloody hell."

"Exactly," he says. "So the trick with mazes is . . ." He lifts his right hand in demonstration. "You know this one, right?" he says, checking.

I shake my head and then he places his right hand on the maze wall. "In that case, this works on most mazes. It certainly does on this one. Keep your right hand on the maze wall from start to finish. No matter what happens, you keep that hand on. Dead end? You keep your hand on the wall and walk around. All the walls are connected, you see, so if you follow one wall all the way through, you'll get there in the end. It's a much longer route, but it's a route."

He starts walking, his gloved hand brushing loose snow from the hedging as we disappear into the towering green maze. "FYI, this method is particularly useful if you're running away from something terrifying and it's pitch-black. At least, it was when we were kids," he adds with a self-deprecating laugh.

He's talking about Krampuses long passed, but I can't help but feel the very real possibility of this advice becoming necessary at some point during my stay.

"And you're certain this method works?" I ask, casting my eyes up to the high edges of the maze walls.

"Yeah, it'll get you in and out. But it only works on a simple maze," he says.

"Wait, this is a *simple* maze?" I say, pulling him up.

"*Simple maze* is a term. It doesn't mean it's easy; it's a technical description of the structure. A simple maze is a maze with one connected wall. A complex maze has bridges, unconnected walls. To get out of one of those you'd need to use Trémaux's algorithm."

I look up at Edward, suddenly getting a glimpse of what his childhood must have really been like.

"Trémaux's algorithm? Bloody hell, Ed. How many you been stuck in?"

"Enough," he says with good humor. "I won't bore you with Trémaux. Unless we go to the place in Rouen, it won't become relevant."

As we turn the next corner, I bump directly into a sweaty, red-faced Lila.

"Jesus Christ," she yelps, grabbing her throat. Wet hair pokes out beneath her thick bobble hat, her cheeks flushed with cold and exertion. "Oh my God. Thank God—people," she gasps, letting out a convulsive giggle. "How the hell do you get out of this fucking hedge? I was on a call with Milo's dad and I wandered in here. Thought the distraction might calm me down. It did not," she declares, shivering deeply. She must be absolutely freezing after her swim.

"It's fine. We'll walk you out," I tell her.

"Yes. Yes, please," she says, a sigh juddering from her. "I need to get back and sort Milo out."

"I thought Milo was staying at his dad's until Boxing Day?" I ask as we lead her efficiently back the way we came.

"Yeah, it's not going well. Milo won't leave his room. Just screaming for me to come pick him up. They can't do anything with him. I feel guilty but then, you know, I also don't. The new girlfriend is a real number—"

Lila clocks my apparently not-so-masked surprise at the judgment.

"I would never say it around Milo, of course," she adds, horrified at the thought. "Anyway, they want me to come pick Milo up. Now. And they want me to arrange therapy for Milo for next year." She shakes her head.

"Jesus," Edward intones. "I wish there was something we could do. Do you want to talk to Mother about it? She knows some people in the city."

Lila looks up, suddenly a little lost. "Um, yeah. God, maybe they're right, maybe the whole thing hit him harder than I thought." She sighs.

"I'll get Mother to pass some names on to Stu for you," Edward says gently. Lila cracks a weak smile before nodding.

"Great. Only thing is now I've got a five-hour drive. Stuart should definitely stay here; I do not need him meeting my ex on top of everything else. I'll pick Milo up, stay overnight at a hotel, and we'll make it back here for Christmas morning."

"I'm so sorry this is happening on Christmas Eve. That you can't stay and relax," I say with sympathy for her, but the truth is I feel like I'm losing an ally here at The Hydes.

"No, God. I'd cross the country ten times over for my child. Besides, it'll be fun. Road trip. I just wish I didn't have to drag him through this kind of thing every holiday. Every birthday. This back-and-forth bullshit." She grimaces as she turns from us to head back inside. "Sorry, I'm cold and cranky. Thank you for listening."

Edward and I spend the rest of the morning exploring the grounds before feeding and grooming the horses at the stables. I make peace with not being able to ride, given the pregnancy, and offer up a few handfuls of oats to a gorgeous dun mare instead while Edward fills me in on Matilda's teenage equestrian glories.

The estate is a positive menagerie; we cuddle goats, feed chickens, peek into deer shelters, pass hay over paddocks to llamas, and all the while I try to piece together the childhood Edward must have had.

Our tour moves on to outbuildings, the majestic glass orangery filled with thick palms and a cozy reading corner. We pass groundskeeper workshops where men who I presume work for the Holbecks potter away with wood and metal. Matilda gave the impression that only two people were working at the house over the holidays, but now I see she must have meant *inside* the house.

As we head into an overgrown patch of land, Edward directs my gaze into the undergrowth, where I can just about make out a well. "The house isn't connected to a main water source; all our water comes from wells. That one's ornamental, but you get the idea."

The low stone well is a perfect circle, moss visible beneath the thin layer of snow. It's pretty.

I peer over the edge into the dripping darkness beyond and a thought occurs to me. "Why wouldn't you be connected to the water mains?"

"The wells mean we don't need to be. Besides, we're too far from the nearest pipelines anyway. The water companies would need to run new lines out here to reach us," he explains.

"How far are we from the nearest town?" I ask as I watch flecks of snow sail down and disappear into the murky depths.

"From town? Twenty minutes in the car. Ten, fifteen miles. Why?"

"Just curious," I say, pulling back from the well's edge. Ten miles is a long run—over an hour and a half without a break.

He pulls me close, oblivious to my fears, and plants a kiss on my forehead. "Shall we head back and get some lunch?" he asks.

"Sure," I say. "Can you just show me one last thing? Is that okay?" I pitch my voice sugar-sweet. "Can you show me the hides?"

The nearest town is ten miles away. If worse comes to worst, I won't be able to run; I'll have to *hide*.

The structure hangs in the air above us, moss-greened and hidden. Its sheer height throws my stomach through loops.

"Is it safe?" I ask as Edward wraps his arms tight around me and cranes his neck up, taking in its off-kilter angle.

"Who knows now," he says with a grin. "We used to go up all the time as kids, and it was fine. But that was a long time ago and we were a lot smaller." He gives me a squeeze, then an idea seems to excite him. "Why don't I test it out?" He takes in my concerned expression then adds, "Probably best you stay here—"

I watch him apply pressure to the first few rungs, then, with a hopeful glance back at me, he slowly begins to climb.

I watch, heart in throat, as he rises one moss-slimed rung after another, checking each foothold firmly before trusting it with his weight. At the top he uses a free hand to give the platform above a solid shake. Surprisingly, it doesn't budge.

"Seems okay," he calls down. He must be at least thirty feet above the forest floor. He lets out a half laugh, half grunt as he hauls his weight onto the platform.

"Careful," I call up as the whole structure shifts visibly. Everything in me is clenched. Edward, unfazed, calmly shifts his weight into a better position, settling on the platform, hands tightly gripping a low branch as he takes in the view across the forest and finally dropping his eyes to me.

"You look so small down there," he says with a chuckle, and for the first time today I feel the cold.

41

We Play Alone

SATURDAY, DECEMBER 24

At around seven o'clock, Christmas music begins to fill every room of the house, a soft jingle with an almost recognizable melody I can't quite put my finger on. It's unclear where it's coming from, but it fills the building like the scent of oranges, wine, and roasted meats coming through from the kitchen.

It's nearly time for dinner.

Up in the blue room, I slip into the dress Edward bought me and examine myself in the full-length mirror. Behind me, Edward shrugs on a crisp suit. I watch his reflection as he fixes his cuff links, take in his dark, tousled hair, his strong features, so similar to his father's but so different. He grins as he catches me looking and I feel desire stretch awake inside me.

"You look good," I tell him.

He slips an arm around my waist as he holds my gaze in the

mirror, his lips traveling to kiss my bare neck as far down as my dress allows. I try to push my fears about tonight from my mind. I try to be present, with Edward, but I cannot stop my thoughts. Robert is waiting for me downstairs. The only man in the world who knows what I truly am and the only one who can destroy everything. I let my eyes bat closed as Edward's hand slips into the opening of my dress and over my breast. I lean back into him, giving myself over to my animal need for him. I let my mouth find his, warm and wet, as the distinctions between father and son blur once more.

Matilda and Stuart are seated by the fire when we make it down to the drawing room. Eleanor, elegant in a white rollneck complimenting her sharp gray bob, turns from the candles she is lighting as we enter.

"There we are," she coos, gesturing for us to settle wherever. I take a seat on the sofa opposite Stuart and Matilda. Matilda's wearing green cigarette pants, an emerald necklace popping against her red hair. Edward perches on the sofa edge beside me, protective.

"We were just talking about how Stuart always scares women off." Matilda grins, nudging Stuart. "Lila's cut and run already."

Edward splutters out a laugh as Fiona and Oliver walk in.

"What's so funny?" Oliver asks, slipping into an armchair.

"Stuart," Matilda says simply.

"Dinner in ten, everyone," Eleanor declares as she hands around drinks. "We're just waiting for your father to come down."

Fiona sinks into the sofa beside me with a sigh. She pushes her brunette waves to one side, revealing the thin red spaghetti straps of her figure-skimming dress. She leans back heavily into the sofa cushions.

"The kids are with Nunu for the night. In the lodge." She exhales with a shake of the head. "God, I love coming here for Christmas." I take in her outfit, her incredible figure. Up until now I had no idea she even *had* a figure hidden under her casual everyday clothing.

She looks at me conspiratorially, an oddly different person now that her children are elsewhere.

"You look amazing," I tell her beneath the hubbub of conversation.

"You too," she says, smiling, then leans in to whisper, "I guess you got the dress code memo."

"Edward bought it for me," I say, looking down at my dress.

"Oh, and cute flower."

I follow her gaze to my lapel and the bright pop of blue there. The flower Robert told me to wear if I understood his instructions. My secret admission of knowledge visible for all to see.

I sip my sparkling water, wishing it were something stronger as the conversation ebbs and flows around me, one eye constantly locked on the doorway.

He must have used another entrance, however, because I hear his voice behind me before I see him.

"Well, here we all are," he says, cold and warm all at the same time.

"Drink, Robert?" Eleanor asks, handing him a glass of scotch with a peck on the cheek as he enters my field of vision.

I look away.

And when I look back, Robert is looking straight at me. "Harriet Reed, I hear congratulations are in order. You're with child." He raises his glass to us both and Edward responds in kind, the air between them crackling.

Robert's gaze dips to the blue flower on my breast, his expression unfaltering. "Not that we didn't take you seriously before, Harriet," he says carefully. "But this certainly changes things. Wouldn't you say, Edward?"

As we file out of the drawing room for dinner, Edward is plucked from beside me by Eleanor.

"You don't mind if I steal him away, Harriet, dear?" she asks. "There's one more clue to arrange before this evening. And I need someone tall." She pats her son on the shoulder.

"Of course," I demure, aware that if I'm unchaperoned I am open to Robert.

Edward plants a quick kiss on my cheek and mother and son slip back into the drawing room while I follow the rest of the Holbecks to dinner.

Robert's hand finds my elbow on the threshold of the candlelit dining room, strong but gentle, tender almost. "A word?" His voice goes straight through me, hitting all my sweet spots.

I look up at him as the rest of the family find their seats, too busy juggling drinks and conversations to notice. We're as alone as we could be.

"Yes," I say carefully.

"Good." His gaze falls on the flower on my lapel. "Thank you for following my instructions. The color suits you," he says with a smile that undercuts everything, and I feel a giddiness for which I hate myself.

I cannot take my eyes off him, and I do not want to, partly because I fear what he would do if I did, and partly because I do not want to break this spell. It's like he's devouring me and I, in turn, him.

"You listened to it," he says simply. "And you're here. That's a good start. I had a feeling you would be capable of engaging with this."

"I'm here because I have to be," I answer, and hope my meaning is clear. I am here to end whatever this is so I can live my life. My life with Edward.

"Aren't we all, Harriet? Aren't we all? We can speak more after the game tonight. I think you should have a better understanding of things by then." He rips his gaze from me, eyeing his seated family. "Remember, whatever happens, you must play alone tonight. Do you understand?"

I nod.

"Of course you do," he says with finality.

42

The Rules

At the gleaming, opulently laid Christmas table, I find my seat next to Matilda's.

Conversation bubbles on, crystal glasses sparkle, eyes crease with laughter. Down the middle of the table candles flicker in a braided evergreen centerpiece, the whole scene reminiscent of a Dickens illustration; a cornucopia.

Stuart is holding court on the Lila situation. Updating those who do not know on why she is absent.

I keep silent. I watch Robert in the flickering light; I watch them all. This odd family who are now my family, my future. I remember Robert's warning about them, how any one of them could know about me. That they, like him, are not to be trusted. I wish I were Lila; I wish I were not here; I wish I were free. But then I would not get Edward, and that is all I want.

When he and Eleanor finally rejoin us, he slips into the seat beside his father's with barely a look to the place card. I wonder if he knew he would be sitting there, beside his father, or if he's just covering well.

"So you're, what, twelve weeks now?" Matilda asks, snapping me back to reality. "When does that make you due?"

I rip my eyes away from father and son to answer her.

"Oh, so a summer baby," she trills. Robert looks over and holds my gaze.

Sylvia and the other maid, Anya, flit silently in and out of the room with the first course. I watch the others delicately fork food into their mouths and force myself to do the same. It's going to be a long night and I will need my strength.

The courses flow into one another. Voices rise and fall, peaking and troughing with the flow of conversation, and I watch the evening swirl around us. There are two murderers at this table, and I have no idea how many of them know that.

Coffee is served back by the fire in the drawing room. The family's eyes are glazed with festive cheer and alcohol as the clock in the hall sounds ten.

The first chime silences the room; the second summons knowing smiles and a sharp giggle from Fiona. Robert places his coffee down and stands.

"I should probably say a few words before we start this year. Unfortunately, Lila could not attend tonight, but Harriet is here. So for those who do not know, or possibly for those that need reminding, here are the rules," Robert says gently as I watch Matilda shove Stuart hard in the ribs.

"There will be only one present on Christmas Eve. If you find your present, then you get to keep it; if you do not find it, then you do not. Most of you here know the rhyme well, but for Harriet's benefit I'll say it again:

"Nothing in this life is free
we work for what we have and see

if you cannot in the time you're given
then harder harder you should have striven."

The last phrase is said with such singsong cadence, it is clear that the words are ingrained in Holbeck family history. In my mind's eye I picture Mitzi Holbeck, decked in 1930s evening wear, German accent thick, as she recites the rhyme Robert just intoned.

The sentiment of the poem is extremely questionable given the extraordinary wealth these people inherited before any of them lifted a finger, but perhaps that is the point of the rhyme.

"Players, your first clues are on the cards marked with your names," Robert continues, and all eyes fly to the green baize table beside the fire. On it I see one of Mitzi's carved Black Forest bears standing, paws aloft, behind eight cream envelopes. He holds a silver dice cup in his claws. "No conferring, no hints, no help," Robert continues.

Edward shifts uncomfortably beside me. "Wait, I'm not sure it's appropriate that Harriet play. Given everything," he says lightly. He takes my hand in his, giving it a supportive squeeze, though I know what's coming before Robert even opens his mouth.

"Well, hold on for a moment now, Edward," Robert says with almost theatrical caution. "Perhaps we should ask Harriet herself if she wants to play. After all, if memory serves me correctly, she's a very capable young woman. She won the last game she played in record time, didn't she?"

All eyes turn to me, expectant.

"Are you happy to play, Harriet? Or would you like to sit this one out? Lila has been removed from the game. It's perfectly possible for you to be as well." There's something in the way he mentions Lila that makes me suddenly worry for her safety.

"Yes, I'll play," I say conclusively, as if I ever really had a choice. The rest of the gathered faces fizz with a new kind of excitement.

"Now we're talking." Oliver grins.

"Then it's decided," Robert says, clearing his throat, a glimmer of triumph in his tone. "Harriet plays, like everyone else. In which case, you should hear a bit more about the game you'll be playing, Harriet. Your first card will be a riddle, and it will lead you to the next. There are three clue cards in total, with the third location holding your Christmas gift. It is a traditional treasure hunt in that respect. You may have played similar games before, but this version is slightly different. In our game, the prizes are tailored specifically to the needs of each player. Would anyone care to explain, by example?" The room around me goes silent, smiles fading with discomfort.

"No, I didn't think so," Robert continues. "You see, Harriet, the gifts involved are extremely personal, and always very timely. They are things that the receiver may need badly but may be unable to achieve unaided. Sometimes they might not even know they need them, or that anybody else is aware of their need." I tense at his words; the thought occurs that somehow my secret will be involved in this game.

Robert elaborates, his focus now entirely directed at me. "To save the blushes of those in this room, I will use Great-Uncle Nelson as an example of how the game works."

Stuart snorts out a laugh, which Eleanor quickly shushes.

"Great-Uncle Nelson," Robert continues, my discomfort rising, "had something of a gambling addiction. Perhaps Stuart finds my choice of example amusing given its simplicity, but I think it sums up the game's core drive. In 1969 Nelson Holbeck's Christmas Eve gift was the complete erasure of his debt, professional and personal. Nelson had accrued over three-quarters of a million in backroom poker debt as well as significant losses through bad investment. If he had won the game that year, he would have had all his debts paid off in full by the family, his balance sheet balanced."

Robert falls silent.

"But what? He didn't play?" I ask, eyes surveying the silent Holbecks. "Or he couldn't solve the clues and find the present?"

"Oh no. Nelson played," Robert answers. "He played his heart out. But he lost. You see, someone else won that year, and there is only one winner. We play against one another. It's a family game. Whoever gets to their present first wins and the game stops." He pauses, waiting for his words to sink in. "One winner; one gift. No one else receives theirs, and the winner is told what the other players' gifts were—what each other player needed more than anything in the world."

"But how could you possibly know what people need?" I ask with a lightness I realize we are long past.

"There are ways to find these things out. I think you might have an inkling how. We do our research—all in the service of picking the perfect gift, you understand?"

I look at the benevolent faces around me and realize this game, its cruelty and its indulgence, is normal to these people. Even to Edward.

"Okay, I buy it," I reply grudgingly, after a pause. "But what then?"

"The winner can use their newfound information in any way they see fit. Whoever won in 1969 could have helped old Uncle Nelson, or at the very least they could have kept his embarrassment to a minimum, but they chose otherwise. If you win, Harriet, you win what you need most *and* the knowledge of what everyone else needed. But if you lose, you lose what you need most as well as the secret of that. I think you'll agree, the stakes are high. So we all play to win here, because we know everyone else will do the same."

I look at the other players then back to Robert before choosing my words carefully. "You think you know what I need?"

"You'll have to play to find out, won't you?" he replies, with a degree of kindness.

Edward puts a hand on my leg in reassurance.

"You don't have to play," he reiterates. And I suddenly wonder what on earth Edward could have to gain from playing this game.

I turn to the rest of the family. "But, I mean, why would any of you want to play this? How is it even a game? I mean, it's meant to be Christmas, for God's sake! Isn't it all a bit . . ." I struggle for a word to describe what *this* is.

Edward leans in now, taking charge. "Okay, why doesn't Harry just sit it out this year? Considering everything," he says lightly, gesturing in the direction of my stomach, "it might be worth taking the stress out of her first Christmas with the family. She can play next year—if she wants."

Robert looks across at me expectantly. "Would you like to skip this year, Harriet?"

It's not a question.

"No, I would not," I answer by rote. "I'll *do* it. I just, I don't get how it's a *Christmas* game, that's all. I mean, where's the Christmas spirit?"

Robert sips his scotch and perches on the arm of a sofa with an amused smile. "What could be more in the spirit of Christmas than offering everyone in the family a chance to *do the right thing*? Whoever wins has the opportunity to act with kindness as much as greed, you see? You choose. The game gives us a chance to rebalance the scales, once a year, to rectify the power balance in the family. It reminds us that we must be good to one another all year long or risk the consequences if the tables are turned." He breaks off, Eleanor topping up his glass. "But as Edward rightly says, it is just a game. No one gets hurt here; by the end there are just bruised egos, some damaged pride, and it has always meant a lot to those who play it. The only reason you might have to fear the game is if you have something to hide. Do you have something to hide?"

"Nothing you wouldn't already know," I answer.

"Then you'll play," Robert concludes.

"Of course," I say with a smile that I hope presents as authentic. "After all, it's not the winning that counts, right?" I ask hopefully. "It's just the taking part. That's what they say, right?"

"Ha, I bet they do," Stuart mutters, a sharp look from Oliver quickly shutting him down.

"Well, then. I think we're decided. If we're ready," Eleanor suggests as she lifts the silver dice cup from the black bear's wooden claws and jostles it. Inside, dice rattle. "Highest number starts the game," she instructs, offering up the cup to the group. "Who wants to roll first?"

43

One Clue. Two Clue.

SATURDAY, DECEMBER 24

Standing in front of the card table, the fire roaring, I pull my card from its envelope. Two players have already gone before me.

I can feel the family's eyes on me, but having watched both Fiona and Stuart take their turns, I know not to give anything away as I read my card.

> Up the wooden hill to Bed-ford-shire,
> Heading for the land of dreams.
> When I look back to those happy childhood days,
> <u>Nothing is quite what it seems.</u>

I look up at the faces staring back at me.
"Who writes these?" I ask.

All eyes swivel to Robert, answering the question for me. "And who writes yours?" I ask.

"I do," Eleanor answers, then gestures to my card. "Does everything there make sense?" she asks with generosity.

I look down at it again.

"I think so, yes," I reply.

Like the players before me, I drop my card into the roaring fire, carefully watching as it burns to nothing.

"Wonderful." Eleanor beams. "Then good luck, Harriet, and happy hunting."

I feel Edward's eyes on me but I do not engage with him, or anyone else, for fear that somehow the truth will pour out of me, out of my face, my eyes. Instead, head high, I make my way straight past the remaining players and directly out of the room.

I need to go up the wooden hill—the stairs—to find a bedroom, that much is clear. A *childhood* bedroom. I'm reminded of the ones Robert mentioned in his tape, his children's childhood rooms. There I will find my next clue, and hopefully the trail Robert is leaving me will start to make sense.

My heels tap a sharp rhythm across the parquet hallway and muffle as I take the carpeted stairs up two at a time. Time is against me. The previous players have a decent head start already. I listen ahead for the sound of Fiona or Stuart, but the low hum of Christmas music is all that greets me.

At the top of the stairs, I catch my breath and take in the landing, its four wings branching off in different directions. To my right are the guest bedrooms we have been staying in, to my left the wing where Robert and Eleanor sleep; which leaves the two wings behind me as possibilities.

I turn and face them, the right-hand corridor dimly lit and matching the style of the rest of the house, the left-hand corridor bright and new, part of the new wing protected by a glass security door. The childhood bedrooms certainly won't be in the new wing.

I grab the banister and propel myself around the landing toward the old wing, unsteady in my heels.

I pull up short. I can't spend the rest of the evening like this. I listen for movement from downstairs, checking if I can hear the next player beginning, but the hall is silent. Taking my opportunity, I squat down, unstrap my heels, and abandon them in the hallway as I race back to the blue room and grab my trainers. After shoving them on, I bolt back in the direction of the old wing.

I dash around the staircase, following the bend of the corridor away from the main building, and as the hallway doors appear, I throw one open after another looking for anything that resembles a childhood bedroom.

I don't know why, but Bobby's name springs to mind as I go. My clue mentions nothing being "quite what it seems," and nobody knew how ill Bobby was before he died, so perhaps I need to find Bobby's old room.

The first childhood room I stumble across is all in pink. Matilda's, I surmise, and quickly move on. The next room is green and filled with sports trophies, wrestling, football, boxing. A photo of a young man padded up for a football game—broad, muscular, his helmet raised in triumph. Oliver's room.

The next is red, on its walls jet fighters twisting in the air, miniature supercars lining the shelves, a faded 1997 Pirelli calendar hanging dog-eared by the window. Stuart's room. I fly on down the corridor.

The next room is blue. I pause, instinct telling me to. This room is harder to read. It's eerily impersonal. A computer, a 1990s beige plastic box, dominates the sparseness of the space. Pictures line the walls; a young man sailing, rowing, swimming. Again, trophies. Bobby rowed, but so did Edward. It's impossible to tell from the doorway whose room this was, but the computer edges me toward it being Edward's.

A door slamming somewhere deep in the house forces my gaze back down the corridor in the direction I have just come, but of course there is no one there.

I check the time on my mobile phone in the pocket of my blazer dress. I have been going for sixteen minutes already. Time is ticking, and I'm pretty sure I know what will happen if I lose this game.

I walk into the blue room and head for the nearest photo. It's of Edward—younger, his face fuller, with an expression I do not recognize. There is something different in his eyes. I scan the room for another photo and find a framed one on the dresser; Edward sits beside Eleanor and someone else at a garden table, flowers in bloom around them. I gasp. The boy in the photo isn't Edward, because Edward, much younger, is sitting right beside him.

The boy is Bobby. This is Bobby's room. They looked so alike as children, and I realize that up until now I haven't seen a photograph of them together when they were young. The uncanny thing is that young Bobby looks incredibly similar to Edward as he is now, as an adult. And now that I think about it, this whole room, its aesthetic, had felt like Edward's room when I entered it. The computer, the color, the tidiness, the simplicity. Which makes me wonder: were they always so similar, or did Edward become more like his brother after the accident?

I leave Bobby's door ajar and head to the next room.

Edward's bedroom door swings open and I feel my brow pucker with confusion. This last room is incredibly busy, the walls lined with lithographs of historical architecture, intricate blueprints of elaborate and complex buildings. Columns and cornicing depicted in forensic detail, cross sections, elevations. I step into the room, uncertain; I must have mixed the rooms up somehow, because nothing about this room is Edward. I let my eyes sweep the surfaces for anything that reminds me of him but there isn't even a computer in here. Just books; books on books: Roman history, the Greeks, the American Civil War, the world wars. History.

I take a photo from the bedside table. It is the whole family, except him; Edward must have taken it himself. I replace it carefully, my eye drawn to another photo hanging back by the door, Edward flanked by his mother and father. Eleanor is beaming, while father and son are serious; the usual spark behind Edward's eyes is not present.

I try to shake off the odd feeling swelling inside me that I do not recognize the man I love from this photo, from this room. Bobby's death must have changed him more than I ever considered, I think. But then my parents' death made me who I am. The hairs on the back of my neck prickle; this must be what Robert wanted me to see. That Edward changed, after Bobby's death. That Edward was not always as he is today. My Edward seems to fit the childhood bedroom of Bobby more than his own, but then he had to fill Bobby's shoes, didn't he?

The sound of a clock chiming somewhere in the house shakes me from my reverie. I need to keep moving. I need to find the next clue.

A childhood bed, not what it seems, I puzzle, paraphrasing the first clue.

On an impulse, I head toward Edward's bed and slip a hand under his pillow. My fingers come into contact with the stiff card of another envelope.

Another clue.

> You know me well, but not well enough.
> Come look harder, though you scramble and scuff.
> Peer into my darkness, it's cold and deep,
> <u>But to win you must find the secrets I keep.</u>

My hand goes to my mouth as I realize this clue leads me outside. I need to scramble and scuff in the cold and dark.

I try to shake off the dread of what I don't quite understand yet. I carefully reread my clue.

"*You know me well, but not well enough,*" I repeat out loud, and just like that the words jump into focus. "You know me *well,* but not *well* enough." I will find the next clue out by the well.

The well that Edward showed me earlier today—the well that used to supply the property with water.

You must find the secrets I keep.

There's something in the well. I have to get in it. *Scramble and scuff.* I think of the inky blackness I stared down into this morning. The damp hole spiraling down into darkness. Whether I want to do this or not, whether it is safe or not, I have to go.

I gave up my right to an easy life when I did what I did twenty years ago. My secret must be kept, because there is no excusing it.

You can say I didn't know what I was doing back then, but I did. I wanted him to hurt like I did; I wanted him to pay. And this is the price *I* now have to pay.

This game might be my shot at wiping the slate clean. Robert hinted that my prize might just be that: my secret safe.

I shove the new clue in my pocket and leave Edward's childhood behind me. After all, we all used to be different people, didn't we?

And with that thought, my walk breaks into a run.

44

Stiff Competition

SATURDAY, DECEMBER 24

I emerge back onto the central landing and dart across to the blue room to grab what I need. Safely inside, I scramble through the pile of clothes gathered on the chair beside my suitcase and shrug on my warm puffy coat over my dress. Then, dropping back down to my suitcase, I forage for something else, and in among the shoes, hair tongs, and straighteners, I come into contact with its hard solid form. The paperweight. I slip it from the sock and hold it in one hand. I might not need it, but better to have it; who knows what I'll find out there in the darkness. I slide its smooth glass into my coat pocket and fumble for the cold metal of my torch. I had a feeling it might come in handy at some point during this trip, and I was right.

I flick it on in the dim lamplight of the blue room and its bright beam fires out, flaring against the dark glass of the sash windows.

Shit. I quickly turn it off as its light tunnels out into the dark night air beyond the glass. The last thing I want is someone seeing the light and following my next move. I now know this game is competitive, but I don't know to what extent. I'm guessing slowing other players down might be strategically worthwhile for some players, however, so best to avoid all contact with Holbecks until the game is over. If Robert is leading me to something that he wants only me to see, the last thing I need is an audience.

I zip up my coat, slip my phone into the other pocket, and head out of the blue room as stealthily as I can.

The house is quiet as I steal through it, silent save for the ghostly piano music and the soft crackle of the hall fire. No people stir; there is no movement at all. At the back door I ease quietly out into the sharp chill outside.

The white-sprinkled gardens sparkle in the moonlight. Around me the air is full of snowflakes tumbling down in slow fluffy clusters. Deep snow is setting in, and as I look down I realize what this means for me: footprints.

But there's little I can do about that. If the snow continues to fall they should disappear before too long anyway. I can only hope no one stumbles across them before then.

Outside the main house, I head quickly toward the maze, casting a look back at the house, its insides lit up, warm and cozy, a toy house hinged open for all to see.

On the second floor I catch sight of Eleanor searching through a bookcase, illuminated in her endeavor. Below her, at the corner of the building, I see Oliver in the flicker of candlelight through the giant windows of the sunroom, intent on unearthing something from the fireplace. But I don't have time for spying. I turn and break into a run but only make it a few yards before someone rounds the corner of the maze and propels straight into me, knocking me to the ground.

I look up and the figure towering over me is Fiona, her floor-length red silk dress hitched up over rubber wellies and partially covered with a waxed jacket. Her expression is as confrontational as the shovel grasped tightly in her hand.

"Of course. It's you," she says, rubbing her shoulder. She offers an unapologetic hand to pull me up. Her usually soft, open demeanor is gone to such an extent that I have to wonder if I imagined it in the first place. It's funny how wrong I could have been about the type of person Oliver's wife was. I guess I made the mistake of assuming all stay-at-home mums are cut from the same cloth. Fiona's cloth is not quite as forgiving as I had supposed.

I give her my hand and she yanks me up to standing.

"Have you seen any of the others?" she asks with a directness that tells me we are not playing as a team.

"I saw Oliver and Eleanor through the windows. The others I don't know."

She nods, looking back toward the house, then seems to decide something. "Yeah, I think I saw Edward or Stuart a minute ago," she says, absentmindedly casting her gaze toward the driveway. Then she looks me up and down. "And where are you going?"

"I'm not going to tell you that, Fiona."

She laughs humorlessly. "Whatever. I'll find out anyway." I try not to focus too much on the shovel in her hands, or on the fact that she will be able to track my footprints in the snow and doesn't seem like a very forgiving winner who might keep my secret. Something in my demeanor amuses her.

"Oh my God. You're terrified, aren't you?" she registers with a chuckle. "That's hilarious. What have they got on you? What's Robert got on you? God, it must be good."

"I don't know what you're talking about, Fiona," I say, walking away.

"Wait," she shouts after me, pulling me up short, her tone aggressive. "Whatever it is, I don't care. I'll make you a deal. Your secret, if Oliver or I win, we'll make it go away."

Her eyes gleam in the moonlight, snowflakes catching in her tumbling brown hair.

"And what would I have to do in return?" I ask tentatively. "You want me to keep your secrets if *I* win?"

Fiona lets out a bright burst of laughter. "Oh my God, you're

not going to win, Harry! That's so sweet. Did you really think—"
She gives me a cartoonish expression of mock-sympathy. "That
is so cute. You really don't know who you're playing against
here, do you?" she says with a shake of her head, before adding
seriously, "No, the deal is: if Oliver or I win, then you and Ed
don't have kids."

"What?" I snort out a laugh. "I'm already pregnant. How the
hell does that work?"

She frowns at my stupidity. "Have a think about it, Harry,
you'll get there in the end."

What she's suggesting suddenly hits me square in the chest.
"Jesus Christ. You want me to get an abortion? For a game?
Jesus Christ, Fiona."

"This is not a game—we both know that. I want you to have
an abortion and not to have any children with him, at all. That is
the deal. They have something on you, and believe me I'll find out
what it is. You've done something bad, I can tell. It must be fucking awful, because there's no way you'd have agreed to play tonight if it weren't. You had to play, didn't you? You might be able
to fool Edward, but I see you."

I pull myself up to full height. This is taking too long; I need
this to end.

"Fiona, get a fucking grip. I am not aborting my child for you,
so fuck off. Is this about inheritance or some bullshit? Because I
don't want their money, or need it. We've got more than enough.
How much does anyone need anyway?"

Fiona hardens. "Right now, my children are the only grand-
children, do you understand that? If you have that child, if you
have *Edward's* child, you are taking from my sons. And I am
their mother. Does that make sense to you? If you want to keep
whatever dirty little secret you've managed to keep hidden from
Ed, then you'll do exactly what I tell you to do. Do you understand me?"

"Ed and I aren't even married. My child won't even be a Holbeck. They wouldn't be able to inherit anything, so they'll take
nothing from your kids. What is the problem here?"

"God, you're a stupid little bitch, aren't you?" she snarls, casting her eyes back to the house in disbelief. "I guess this is why he fell for you. Because you're easy. You don't know anything about this family, do you? You haven't looked into the entailment, have you? Holbeck inheritance runs by *blood*."

"What? What does that—"

"Edward is the firstborn. If he has a child with anyone—married, not married, whatever—then that child inherits everything. It doesn't matter about you, if you're married to him; you mean nothing. Only blood counts. Only our children count. Even their gender is irrelevant. Blood counts. Children count. We are nothing."

"We're nothing?" I repeat, turning the idea of that over in my mind. "Okay," I say finally, her eyes boring into me. "Well, in that case, I guess you're completely fucked, then, aren't you, Fiona? Because I'm having this baby and *I* don't give a shit what happens to you either. If you win tonight, which I highly doubt, I'm still having this baby, and this family will have no choice but to accept my child no matter what I did or didn't do—according to you. So the question is, really, do *you* understand? Because it sounds to me like you probably should have done a bit more research yourself, shouldn't you? Before you got knocked up by the wrong fucking brother, you stupid cunt."

Fiona's mouth drops open in a satisfying gawp. There it is. I guess she must have read me wrong too.

I turn with a hot ember of triumph glowing inside me and crunch on at a jog through the swirling snow.

Once I've passed the maze, I slip behind some bushes and let out the tension I've been holding in my body. A quick look back toward the house confirms that she isn't following me, and I'm relieved to see she's gone.

I shove my burning-cold hands into my pockets and continue on, replaying Fiona's words. My baby, the creature growing inside me, will inherit everything. Everything here, everything in New York and London and France and Italy and LA and Switzerland. All of it. Everywhere. Everything. The whole Holbeck empire.

The idea is beyond real understanding. The weight of all that shouldn't rest on one person. You only have to look at history, at the lives of all those who have inherited, at *Bobby,* to know what a mixed blessing inherited wealth can be.

I don't want that much weight for my unborn child. I want a new world for her. A fresh world for her to find her own happiness in.

But Fiona's words throw new light on my situation and on Robert's interest in me. The fact that I am still here is perhaps more due to the life growing inside me than I ever realized. He must have known. Somehow, before we met that Thanksgiving evening. And suddenly I remember Dr. Leyman. We visited him the morning before Thanksgiving dinner. A simple phone call between old friends could have told him everything. Given what I know of the Holbecks I doubt doctor/patient confidentiality has ever stood in their way.

Finally I reach the lip of the well, and with one hand resting on the icy stone I lean over to shine my torch into the darkness. The hole's dripping walls disappear down into a void, and I fumble in the snow-covered dirt beside the well for something to drop down into it to gauge its depth, but as I do my hand comes into contact with something and I quickly pull away. It felt like human hair. I yelp, jumping back, my heart thumping erratically in my chest. There I was expecting to find horrors down the well, but here they are right on the surface.

Every fiber of my body tells me to run, to forget the game, to forget Robert and Edward and even the life growing inside me. The sudden possibility that I might die here tonight finally hits me with its cold, hard reality. A pure animal instinct for survival overtakes everything but I do not move, because if I run now, how long will I last out in the world with enemies like the Holbecks? If I make an enemy of Robert, I'm as good as dead.

I suck in a lungful of frozen air and force myself to pull it together. I've seen dead bodies before; I have seen those I love still and quiet; I am certainly strong enough to bear the death of a stranger.

I dip my hand back into the snow, keeping the beam of my torch on my hand as I tunnel into the gap. My fingertips find it again: a thick tendril of matted hair, coarse and frozen by the cold. I carefully brush the snow away and see I am wrong. It is not hair. It is not a body. Held in my hand instead is a frayed length of hemp rope. I pull at it and the snow all around the well shifts as the rungs of a rope ladder emerge from beneath. I rise to standing, dragging it up and out of the snowy scrub. At one end of it is a large double-claw hook.

I guess I will have to go down the well after all.

45

The Point of No Return

SATURDAY, DECEMBER 24

There are times in your life when you really do question where it all went wrong; and if scrambling into a pitch-black well at night, in a snow flurry, wearing a Balmain blazer dress, just shy of three months' pregnant, with a torch rammed in your mouth isn't one of those times then I don't know what is.

The rope creaks but it does not give. It held my weight when I tested it on the outside of the well wall but now, looking down into the darkness, doubts surface regarding its reliability.

I know there's water down there—a dropped stone proved that—so if I do fall, at least I'll hit water, even if it is freezing. The question is, how would I get out if I fell?

I pat my pocket for my iPhone and feel its reassuring bulk. It can survive being fully submerged in water, or so popular advertising would have me believe. If worse comes to worst, I can call someone. Edward. He can get me out. I might lose this game; I might have to tell him everything, but at least I wouldn't die of hypothermia. Granted, I may lose him in the process, but I'd have to call him if it came to it.

The opening of the well recedes above me, the midnight sky visible in blue through the breaks in the clouds as white flakes land delicate and cool on my upturned face.

I'd estimate the ladder to be approximately fifty feet long, and watching the shimmer of water far below, fifty feet seems about right.

The smell hits me a few more feet down. It is so overwhelming that I have to stop, take the torch from my mouth, and bury my face in my elbow crease to keep from retching. It's the unmistakable smell of rot, of something dead. I force my mind to picture a rat, a fox, a coyote—anything but the dead thing I fear is actually waiting down there for me.

Peer into my darkness, it's cold and deep,
<u>But to win you must find the secrets I keep.</u>

For the first time this evening, I wonder if I'm really playing the same game as the rest of the family. There's a chance my clues lead me only down here and nowhere else. For all I know, I might have crawled into my own grave.

My gaze shoots up to the opening of the well, fully expecting to see a figure above me—a figure who will send me splashing down into the darkness, unable to find a way out. But there is no one there.

Another terrifying thought occurs and I fish the iPhone from my pocket, careful to hold it with the firmest grip as my eyes fly to the signal bar. I let out an audible sigh of relief because I do not live in a horror movie; even down here in this well, there is a signal. If I fall, I can still call for help.

Robert is no fool; if he'd planned to kill me down here, he'd have damn well made sure I didn't have a phone on me.

I secure my phone back in its zipped pocket and pull out an

old tissue. I rip it in two with one hand and my teeth, dampen each section with saliva, and force them up my nostrils to block out the vomit-inducing stench.

Below me, the ladder meets the water and the well opens out into a small cavern, its walls no longer man-made but craggy rock.

I shine the flashlight into the water beneath me. It's clouded, so impossible to gauge its depth. I swing the torch beam around the cave walls, their wet slime glimmering and flaring in the roaming light. Then something catches my attention and I swing back. The pop of a bright envelope. My next clue. The third clue. I could still win this. I just need to get that envelope.

I hover above the water, the envelope still a good six feet away from me, positioned high on a jutting section of rock. I'll need to get in the freezing water if I want to reach it. I shine the torch into the murk beneath once more.

I plunge a trainer in and let the cold seep through and fill it. My breath catches; it's freezing. I tell myself I can do this; people swim in cold water every day. Lila did this morning. As long as I'm in and out quickly, as long as I can get dry, I'll be fine.

I push the smell from my mind as I gently ease my body into the water. I take in a sharp breath as it seeps through my clothes and reaches my skin, the cold somehow burning hot, but I sink no deeper. The cave floor is solid underfoot, and the water only reaches to my waist.

I wade to the ledge and haul myself up from the waterline, grabbing the card from the rock shelf. I rip it open and read.

> You've come so far, you're almost there.
> The next clue is something she would wear.
> You can sense her, she's right here,
> Reach out and check,
> <u>Your present is **under** what's around her neck.</u>

There is someone here. Oh my God. I swing my torch back over the milky water. One of the women from Robert's list is here. It could be Melissa, Aliza, any of them. Though the smell suggests one of the more recent women on the list.

The cold is inside me now, my whole body quaking. I need to get out. I need to find this body and get out of here.

I stuff my clue card into a pocket above the waterline and shine my torch across the dark pool. I know what I need to do. I don't want to do it, but that's irrelevant. Someone's in here and I need to see whatever is around her neck.

I wade through the foul water, my arms searching for something solid in the soup.

It touches my bare right leg first, and in spite of knowing it's coming, I leap back, causing stinking water to splash up as far as my hair. I quickly wipe putrid water from my eyes using my dry shoulder, then I shine my torch into the water above the submerged object. It's funny, there's knowing something, and then there's experiencing it. I have experienced dead bodies, I have felt them, the strange weight they suddenly have, the cooling and hardening of once soft skin, the difference life makes to flesh, to bone, to hair.

I know and yet, inches from this person, I am scared. An animal instinct, a reflexive fear of death overriding my system. It's strange, because the dead are really the only things in the world who can't hurt us anymore.

I push away thoughts of who this girl might be, of how she ended up down here. All I need to focus on is what is around her neck.

Do not look at her face, I remind myself. *If you do see it, you will never forget it. Do not look at her face.*

I thrust my hands deep into the brown water. They make contact as expected with cold slippery flesh and tangled-up clothing. She is hard and soft at the same time, like rotten fruit. I slip one arm under her and cradle her body up toward the surface.

Do not think, I remind myself, *just do.*

She breaches the surface white and bloated, the stench overwhelming. I gasp in spite of myself. A bare shoulder comes into view but I keep my gaze elliptic, skimming over the edges of what

I see as I handle it. Mousy brown hair tangled into wet swirls curled against the gray-white flesh. It's Melissa. Aliza had jet-black hair. Melissa is wearing a red blouse, rotten and water-logged. Khaki slacks, a belt. Each image I let in is an image I know will haunt me. I've played this game before. I know how it goes. Then I locate it: a silver necklace around her bruised throat.

I focus only on that, my torch gritted between my teeth. I catch the edges of her chin, a bottom lip thick and purpled. Her hair is so close to my face; the smell, too much.

The silver of her chain twinkles, and as her head tilts back into the water I use my free hand to turn her necklace. The charm on it glistens into view, winking in the torchlight. It's a star. A sparkling diamond star.

That is all I need.

I let her sink back into the water and she disappears, the pool eddying around her until it is still once more. I do not have time to mourn. I think of Melissa's family, her friends perhaps unaware she is even gone yet, and my heart is full of sadness.

I am shuddering enough to ripple the water around me now. I need to get warm or risk hypothermia. I need to get out.

I scramble across to the ladder and haul my soaking body out, cold hands raw against the rope.

My Christmas Eve present, and whatever fresh hell that might entail, is hidden under a star. And I know exactly where I might find one of those.

46

Something Clicks

SUNDAY, DECEMBER 25

I barrel back across the lawn toward the house. There's a chance I could still win this, if everyone else has been going through the same awful things I have.

I push from my mind what might happen after this game ends. My desire to call the police and confess everything just so I can drag the whole Holbeck family kicking and screaming to justice is pretty heady, though I know I'd only go down with them.

Right now, I tell myself, I just need to finish this game. I need to win—and when I know every single thing each of these people has done, I will decide what I should do with that knowledge. I'm going to beat them at their own fucked-up game and then I'm going to beat them for real.

I scramble past the maze and on to the ornamental garden, my trainers slipping in the snow, my muscles erratic and juddering from the cold. Ahead, the lights of the house are warm and inviting and so close.

Something catches my trainer and sends me sprawling forward into the snow, knocking the air from me.

I roll over, arms up to protect myself, but there is nobody there. I rise on my elbows and look at what tripped me. There's a half-buried wellie jutting from the snow.

Immediately I know whose boot it is; she was standing here with me in them spewing bile less than an hour ago. Dread rises inside me as I clamber to my feet.

"Fiona," I call softly, but there is no one there.

I scan the ground for footprints, and in the beam of my torch her tracks appear heading back toward the maze. Judging by her gait, and the fact that she didn't stop to retrieve her boot, she must have been running. Something must have scared her so much that losing a boot seemed irrelevant. Something tells me to ignore this diversion and carry on with my own game, but if something happened to her, even though I don't like the woman, I'm not sure I could live with that.

At the maze's entrance, I notice a torn piece of red silk flapping, snagged on a low branch.

Oh God. Not in the maze, seriously?

If I'm going in there, I need something with a bit more heft than the paperweight in my pocket. I look around the maze's entrance for something, anything, I can use as a weapon. I really only have one option. I squat over the wooden maze arrow sign and heave it from the frozen ground. It pops out of the earth after a few wiggles and I fall back, a sharp wooden stake in hand.

At the maze's entrance, I raise my right hand to the wall and start to run, branches whipping across my open right palm as I go.

"Fiona," I call ahead, doubting a response but eager to interrupt whatever might be going on ahead of me. Then I recall that when I was talking to Fiona earlier, she was carrying a shovel.

It's only now that I wonder why.

It crosses my mind that she might be waiting for me in here. She has a weapon; this could all be a trick of some kind. And just as I'm thinking how unlikely it is that Fiona might want to hurt me, I remember what the baby inside me stands to inherit. Everything she would get would be taken from Fiona's children. People have killed for much, much less.

I round the next corner and pull up short. There is a spray of blood in the snow, the ground disturbed, like in the aftermath of a struggle. Beyond the patch of scrambled mud and meltwater, I see another set of footprints in the snow. Someone was waiting in here for her. She must have run straight into them. The new set of footprints is the only one that continues on into the maze, but the red drip continues with it, a red dotted line in the whiteness.

Something about the trail of blood up ahead makes me steel myself. I finally release my right hand from the maze wall and raise my weapon in both hands. I pause again before the next corner as I take a steadying breath before propelling myself around it.

A monstrous stone fountain looms over me and I stumble back, surprised to find myself at the heart of the maze. My gaze darts around the center of it, searching for a person, but there is no one here. I shuffle hesitantly around the fountain to make sure. Snow fills the fountain's tiers; no water is flowing from the gaping mouths of fish and sea creatures, which instead seem to scream silently up into the moonlight. I shiver. Lila was right; it is a creepy fountain.

Carefully I continue to make my way around the center of the fountain, following the line of blood, and as I do the shovel Fiona was carrying comes into sight. The soil beneath it has recently been turned. It is a mound; there is something buried beneath. A shallow grave.

In the silence the soil gently moves and I fly back from it, letting out an animal noise as I do. Whatever is under there is still alive. I edge closer to it once more.

"Fiona," I whisper gently, and from my tone it's clear I don't really want an answer.

The mound remains still and I step closer. It suddenly shifts and I leap back again, hand to heart, as its soil crumbs tumble and settle.

I dive to the ground and use my numb hands to scrape the soil away from her. A hand, an arm, a nose, lips, and, for a second, I really think she might be okay. But when I clear the soil from her face I see the wide set of her mouth and the dirt filling it. I continue to uncover her, scooping her onto her side, into the recovery position, but as I turn her, I feel a warmth spread across my own stomach, across my arms. I look down and see the thick blood pouring from her, congealed and soupy brown. I release her back onto the dirt and see the wound in her abdomen: deep and wet and dark. I gently place a hand on her chest; she's warm, but not warm enough. I hold for a heartbeat but there is none.

One of her legs kicks out again, reflexively, and I realize what is going on. Cadaveric muscle spasms. You can learn a lot of things researching novels. Bodies can move even after death: muscles contract, mouths open, faces twitch. I pull back from her, my arms and coat thick with her blood, the skin of my arms and thighs drenched in it. Fiona is dead.

I jerk up to standing, my breath coming in sharp snatches.

The game, already terrifying, just kicked up a gear into something else entirely.

Robert is picking off members of the family. It suddenly occurs to me why I might be here: my USP. I have a history of violence, and now Fiona's blood is all over me. I was also one of the last people to see her.

I realize how easily her death could be pinned on me. Anyone's death could be pinned on me. Robert has literally invited me here to get away with murder. He's sent me on a wild goose chase around the property in order to give himself time. I will take the blame for this if I don't end up dead myself. I need to stop him.

I rise, remove my phone from my blood-soaked puffer coat, and pull it off, wiping as much of Fiona's blood from me as I can before discarding the coat entirely.

I abandon the paperweight, grabbing the shovel instead, and

head out of the maze. Fiona said she'd seen either Stuart or Edward outside too, and with a jolt of terror I wonder if I am too late to warn him.

I dial Edward's number on my phone. The game has changed; none of us are safe.

Edward answers after one ring. "Where are you?" he huffs, his breath short, his concern knocking the emotion clean out of me. Wherever he is, he knows what's happening too. Floodgates open inside me.

"Ed, something awful is happening," I say to him, my voice quivering with cold and fear. I look down at my trembling body in a blazer dress and trainers, my arms filthy with mud and blood and God knows what else.

His voice is a whisper when it comes; he must be hiding inside the house. "I know. Same here. Listen, listen to me, Harry. Are you safe where you are?"

I look around at the moonlit garden. "Um, I think so," I tell him.

"Great, where are you, exactly?" he asks, and there's an urgency in his voice. "Tell me and I'll come get you."

"Is everyone okay there, Ed? Is everyone in the house okay?"

Silence and then, "No. No. I don't think so. No."

"Oh my God," I hear myself say. But the truth is, this is my fault; I thought I could fix this by myself. I selfishly tried to protect my secret by not going to the police and now Edward is in danger.

"Where are you, Harry?" Edward repeats, trying to focus me.

"I'm outside. It's so cold. I need to come in. I can't stay out here. Where are you? I'll come find you."

He is silent for a moment. "Okay, yeah, come find me," he says, but I can tell it's not what he wants. And now there's something strange in his tone. "I'll meet you in our room," he continues. "But listen, be careful, coming in the house. Don't talk to anyone. Don't stop for anyone until you find me. Don't let anyone see you. Do you understand? You need to make sure you get up to me without talking to anyone, okay?"

"Yeah. Yes, I can do that," I say, though every bone in my body is telling me there's something not right about this. Edward sounds different.

Robert could have Edward already; he could be forcing him to say this to draw me in. But my Edward wouldn't do that; he wouldn't lure me anywhere, even at gunpoint. Besides, Edward wanted to come to me; it was my idea to go back inside.

And just like that, Samantha Belson, the Holbecks' nanny, comes back to me. I thought *she* was the blonde at 7 East 88th the day Bobby jumped, but she was here, at The Hydes, with the children. But who were the children? *Bobby was a twenty-year-old man,* she'd said. *He certainly didn't need a nanny.*

It occurs to me now that Edward was eighteen years old when Bobby died. He certainly didn't need a nanny either. And with terrifying ease, a series of thoughts slot themselves into place and a question forms in my mind.

"Edward?" I ask.

"Yes."

"Where were you the day Bobby died?"

The line is silent for long enough for my creeping dread to blossom into something worse. "I was upstairs," he says after a moment.

Inside me, something yawns wide open with panic.

"Okay," I say as neutrally as I can, buying myself a precious moment to order my mind.

"But I love you, Harry," he says simply, and I feel my tears come. Edward was there the day his brother died. Something triggered Bobby to jump, and Lucy knew exactly what. Edward was with Bobby when he committed suicide.

The silence between us is thick, and I feel his sadness down the line.

"I know what you are too," he tells me cautiously. "But I still love you."

His words hit me viscerally, knocking the last remaining doubt from my unwilling mind. Edward had a hand in Bobby's death. He killed Lucy, and then Alison and Gianna, Aliza and Melissa.

And now Fiona and who knows who else. As the facts come together, I feel the Edward I know disintegrate.

I've had the wrong end of the stick this whole time. Robert's tape is real, but it's not Robert's confession. He fed me the truth, but in the only way I would be able to hear it. If he'd told me outright, I would have thought he was lying, trying to scare me off his son. I would have told Edward. All this time, I've been condemning the wrong Holbeck, terrified Edward might find out my own awful secret. But he knows. He knew all along; in me, he found someone as broken as he was.

And suddenly I get an inkling of what the favor Robert Holbeck requires from me might be. He wants me to know who his son really is, to know whose child I am having and what that might mean. Robert wants me to stop Edward.

I squeeze my eyes tight shut to block out what is happening, but I am instantly barraged by flickering images of the bloated body in the well. Images of Lucy's hair caught in the wind outside 7 East 88th, of Gianna dancing on that New Year's Eve, of Alison's family alone and still waiting after twenty years. These women did nothing to warrant their fates.

And suddenly, with a seismic shift, I feel myself break away from Edward.

I feel him being ripped from me, not by Robert, or by his controlling family, but by the real Edward.

My Edward—my good, kind, funny Edward—never really existed. I created him. Well, Edward Holbeck created him, a copy of the brother he killed.

I feel the loss of the man I knew with aching clarity as warm tears stream down my face. I will never see that man again; he will never hold me again. He was only ever the idea of a man, the ghost of one that I saw reflected in Edward Holbeck.

My eyes glide back to the house ahead, its lights warm and welcoming, but the man in there isn't who I thought he was. He's a killer, and not the kind of killer I am. That's why Edward chose me: my past. He thought perhaps he'd found a kindred spirit. That's why I've survived this long; that's why he asked me to marry him, why I'm carrying his child. He thinks we are the same.

Everything clicks into place, just as Robert told me it would, and I realize what Robert wants me to do. What his tape has been leading me toward.

I don't have a family of my own; I lost them long ago. But I do have something.

I gently place a hand on my abdomen and slow my breathing. Robert is offering me a chance at a new family. I have a little girl growing inside me, whose family needs me to keep them safe.

"I'm coming back now, Edward," I say into the receiver. "I'll see you soon."

47

The Whole Family

SUNDAY, DECEMBER 25

Light spills from the crack beneath the boot room door as I listen for voices. I don't know what has been happening in the house since I left, but it can't be good. After a moment I try the door handle, hands numb with cold.

The stark white corridor beyond must be one for staff, as it's unlike any other part of the building I've seen. I follow it along until I see a room ahead, shadows dancing within, and only once I'm sure it is silent do I peer inside.

A small television plays on mute, a Christmas movie. Beside it, a small table covered with well-leafed magazines, and at the end of the room a low gray sofa on which Sylvia and Anya slump, seemingly asleep.

"Hello," I try softly, but the two women do not stir. "Shit."

I approach carefully, kneeling before the unmoving pair. I

touch Sylvia's shoulder gently. She slips onto Anya. I raise my fingers to her nose; she's still breathing, just unconscious.

I let out a huff of relief. Both have drained coffee cups abandoned in their laps. Drugged but alive.

I leave them where they sit, carefully closing the door to their break room behind me.

Farther along the corridor, I find myself in a cavernous working kitchen. Leftovers from tonight's dinner are covered in wrap, ready to be stacked and refrigerated. Breakfast trays are laid out, ready to be filled for the morning. On the kitchen island, mince pies cool on wire. The smell of them mixes with the scent of rot coming off me, making me want to vomit.

There's another smell in the kitchen, though. I look across to my warped reflection in the copper pots hanging over the gas cooker. Then my eye catches something on the ground jutting out from the other side of the kitchen island. An ankle, a shoe, a foot. Tom Ford heels and green nail polish. It's Matilda.

I dash around the island unit where I find Eleanor and Matilda propped against the cupboards in front of the cooker, the doors of which are open. The soft hiss of gas fills the room. I grab a tea towel and thrust it over my face, leaning past their bodies to twist off the gas dials.

Then I drop to a crouch beside Matilda, checking her pulse. She stirs, sluggish, eyes fluttering open, drugged and dazed. I move to Eleanor; her pulse is slow and stable too, though she does not stir.

"Harry. Harriet," Matilda groans, her eyes glazed. "Careful. He's in a mood," she slurs.

"Who's in a mood, Matty?" I ask, though I know the answer.

"Little Eddy Teddy Bear." She giggles. "I feel mushy."

They've been drugged with whatever Sylvia and Anya got, I'm guessing.

"I know," I tell her. "Do you think you can stand up, Matty?"

She looks at her towering shoes with a frown and shakes her head. I dutifully remove them.

"How about now?"

She shifts forward slowly, making her way up onto all fours. "I think someone put something in my drink," she mumbles, more to herself than to me. "Not the first time," she giggles. Then, after a moment, she pulls herself up to a very wobbly stand using the kitchen island as leverage. "I'm up. I'm up."

"Okay, we need to keep it quiet, Matty, okay?"

Matilda lifts a finger to her lips and nods earnestly.

I take her hands in mine and hold her gaze, focusing her. "Matilda, it's very important you do what I say now, okay?" She nods, squinting at me with concentration. "I need you to take your mother somewhere and hide. Okay? Can you do that?"

Matilda suddenly seems to notice her mother for the first time down on the floor beside her, and she covers her mouth to stifle a giggle. "Oops. Her too. Oh, okay. I can, we can, do that. Safe. Yep." She nods for an extended period.

"Great. But you need to hide away from here. Do you understand? It's not safe in the house. Something is going on."

She nods and juts out her lower lip. "Yeah, Daddy and Eddy are fighting again. We can hide. I'm a good hider," she whispers, tapping the side of her nose.

"Do you know where the hunting hides are, Matty? The hide at the edge of the forest?"

She grins.

"Good, go there. If I don't come get you by the morning, you need to call the police, okay?"

She juts her lip out. "No phone."

Fuck.

There's no way around it. I fish my own phone from my pocket, remove my passcode settings, and hand it to her. "Do not lose this. And do not use it until the morning. I'm going to sort this out, but if I can't, you need to call the cops when it gets light."

Matilda looks baffled at the concept but gives an undaunted shrug. "Good for you, Harry," she says cheerfully, then claps me on the back and raises the phone. "No cops till daytime." She uses the phone to salute me then promptly turns to inspect her prone mother.

I watch her pocket the phone and when I'm certain she knows what she's doing, I pick up my discarded shovel and head out of the kitchen.

As I shift through the house, heart thumping light and fast in my chest, a plan begins to form. I know what I need to do. I need to find Robert. He set this game in motion; he must have a solution, a plan. I'm aware my plan is basically to find out what Robert's plan is, but I think it's fair to admit that he's had longer to think this through than I have. And it's definitely time we had our chat.

At the entrance to the new wing, I see Edward slumped against the glass on the other side of the security door. I only catch him from the back, his suit jacket crumpled and rucked on the transparent wall, his white shirt collar stained with the blood still dripping from his hairline. He's locked himself in there, his bloody fingerprints smeared across the control panel. Someone must have gotten to him before me.

I watch his shoulders gently rising and falling as I approach and, safe in the knowledge that glass door is locked, I sink to the ground behind him, my breath fogging as I crane to get a better look at his face.

Over his shoulder I can see his lap, his bloodstained hands, and the small pinkie ring on his little finger. It's not Edward; it's Stuart. Something inside me unclenches.

I tap delicately on the glass next to Stuart's head. He jolts up, shocked at my proximity, and as he turns, I can see that his movements are as slow and fuzzy as Matilda's. There must have been something in the drinks this evening, or the coffee. Stuart wouldn't have been drinking, so it must have been the latter.

His face is a mess, his right eye swollen, bruised shut, the wound to his right temple congealed, but there are bloodstains on his cheek and neck all the way to his collar. He must have just gotten away from Edward, crawled in here where he knew he'd be safe. Edward doesn't know the passcode to the new wing. I remember him trying to ignore his call the other day before Eleanor tapped in the keypad code. He wanted to see it, to get in here.

Stuart is saying something, but the glass is soundproof. I shake my head and he squeezes his eyes tight shut with annoyance. After a moment he regroups, and with great effort turns his body to face me fully, pointing past me, his eyes flaring. Suddenly certain Edward is directly behind me, I spin, grabbing my shovel, but the main hallway beyond is empty.

I wheel back to Stuart and he shakes his head slowly, trying to make me understand, a characteristic smirk blossoming beneath his injuries. *No,* he mouths carefully. He gestures past me again and I follow his gaze out into the hallway. When I look back at him, he jabs a finger left, indicating through the hall and left. *Edward,* he mouths, then, with finality, he slumps back against the glass wall, exhausted. Edward went that way. He closes his eyes and unseeingly raises a hand to wave me off.

I grab my shovel and leave Stuart behind, safe in the knowledge that he's protected by two inches of security glass.

So far only Fiona is dead. Stuart is safe; Matilda is safe; Eleanor is safe. The kids are safe down in the lodge with Nunu—now it seems to make more sense why Robert chose this year to allow that. Some of my new family is safe. Which leaves only Edward, Robert, and Oliver unaccounted for.

I creep into the main hallway, careful to watch where I place my trainers on the creaking parquet, my shovel raised and ready, and it suddenly occurs to me that I have no idea what happened to Oliver. Or where he went. He's the biggest and strongest Holbeck, the family's very own all-American linebacker. Why isn't *he* doing something about all this?

And at that exact moment, my vision flashes white as pain crests at the back of my skull, and everything goes black.

48

Merry Christmas, Harriet

SUNDAY, DECEMBER 25

And this is where we started.

I come to on the hall floor. I cannot tell how long I have been out, and I cannot lift my head. Around me the house twinkles on, Christmas music still jingling softly through the hallways.

I just need a second, I tell myself. I know this because it took time to move after our car rolled to a stop twenty years ago. I hung in the creaking cold for what seemed like an eternity that morning. But my body came back to life.

The smell of gasoline is thick on the floor around me, making my eyes water as the breeze from the open door wafts it into my face. I swivel my gaze across to the hall fireplace, its logs burning brightly. It could catch so easily, but I imagine that is someone's plan, when the time is right. Whether it is Robert's plan or Edward's or even Oliver's, I no longer know.

If I could stand, I could run. I could just leave them all, save myself, bolt and call the cops—but then I see the story being constructed around me and I understand what it is designed to look like.

The gasoline, the flames, the bodies. What is happening here is being carefully staged, and if this building goes up in flames, I have no doubt who will be held accountable. Whoever is doing this has enough on me to ensure that.

If I run, I don't get a say in how this ends.

I try to lift my face again. Straining every sinew, I manage to lift myself a few inches from the floor, just enough to turn my head in the other direction.

I gasp. Oliver's lifeless face rests inches from mine, his mouth open, his eyes glassy. I stifle a yelp. His hand is still pressed tight to the wet wound across his throat, though blood no longer pumps from it.

By the look of things, it's safe to say that Oliver is not the mastermind behind all of this. At least, if he ever was, he's not anymore.

On the floor beside him I see a wrought-iron fireplace poker; that must be what he hit me with. He must have thought I was responsible for all of this. Then the sound of a scuffle must have brought the real perpetrator straight to us, to him. I am still alive, though, which can only mean one thing: either Edward or Robert needs me to play my part in what happens next.

I become aware of the weight of Oliver's legs on mine, pinning me to the floor, and I slowly edge myself out from under him. From there I struggle up to all fours and then carefully onto unsteady feet. I wait for my dizziness to settle, then quietly stalk to the stairs, where I see my shovel kicked to the side.

As I creep, I hear the muffled noises of someone moving about in the sitting room. The sound of furniture being rearranged. I freeze, crouched beside the shovel. Something is happening in there. I could run, but I know what that will bring down on me. I will spend the rest of my life in jail, framed as the woman who burned down the Holbecks' mansion with the whole family inside. But they can't say that if I try to stop it—if I save everyone.

I carefully rise, lifting the shovel and hefting it in both hands.

The sitting room looks different when I enter: the log fire roars on, the Christmas tree lights twinkle in hazy halos, and beneath, brightly wrapped presents silently wait, but now all of the furniture has been moved to the edges of the room. All that remains in the center is a rug, wet with gasoline, and two armchairs facing each other.

In the armchair facing me sits an unconscious Robert Davison Holbeck, his head peacefully resting against the high back of the chair. Beside him stands his son Edward. If Edward did not have a shotgun pointed directly at Robert's head, the scene might easily resemble one of the family's historic oil paintings.

"Harry," Edward says, with an oddly welcoming tone, as he takes in my blood- and mud-smeared appearance. "It's been a long night, hasn't it? But you made it." His voice has a sardonic lilt to it that I do not recognize, which gives me the distinct impression that I'm meeting this man for the first time.

There are a million things I could say to him, that I want to ask him, but only one question really matters.

"How long did you know?" I ask, careful not to play the idiot. "What I was?" I'm pretty sure we both know what's going on here; I just need some of the gaps filled.

"Very early," he says gently. "I had you vetted the day after we met. A week later I had everything. But in a sense I knew from the beginning. I felt it. Your strength, your loyalty, your love. I loved you the night I saved you but by God did I love you more when I found out what you were capable of. How you responded under pressure. That man took from you, but you took straight back, without hesitation. What you could do for love, what you had done—" He breaks off with a shake of the head. "I spent a lifetime looking for you. Looking for someone I could be honest with, finally be myself with."

Robert stirs slightly in the seat beside him, but Edward's focus is on me. I don't know what his plan is, but I know I need to keep his attention.

"But you weren't honest," I nudge gently, careful to stay the right side of empathetic. "All this time you knew about me, but you said nothing. Why?" I ask, and in spite of everything I hear the rattle of emotion in my voice, because however twisted his thought process was or is, I loved him.

"I wanted *you* to tell *me* first. It might seem childish, but I wanted you to trust me enough to show me who you were," he answers. "Then I would know what I felt was real. But you never said a word, did you?"

A sickening wave of guilt hits me in spite of what he has done, and who I have found him to be, because he is right: I have never, in my life, trusted anyone with my truth. Least of all the people I have loved. I feel myself bristle at the accusation.

"I was scared you wouldn't love me. That I'd lose you if you knew," I tell him honestly. "Isn't that what you felt too? You didn't trust that *I* could love *you*. The real you. If I knew what you had done, that you had killed Bobby and Lucy, and Alison, and Gianna. And all the others."

He looks away fleetingly. "I didn't kill Bobby."

"You had something to do with it."

"Yes," he says, taking the hit with a strange, disarming honesty. "He wasn't taking Adderall. I was slipping it to him, in his meals back at the apartment. I found a way to make the drugs interact. He would never have taken a stupid drug like that. I think they all knew, afterward. Dad knew. He was pulling away from what Dad wanted. He would have taken the company, everything, in the wrong direction. I wanted to take him out of the game, that's all. I wanted to force him to step aside, for his health; I wanted to break him. But it went much further than I anticipated; he had a mind of his own and I lost control of things. I tried to stop him that day; I told him it was all in his head, what he was feeling wasn't real, but it was too late. He wasn't listening. It was my first time and I made mistakes. I didn't mean to kill my brother. He did that to himself."

"You wanted to be Bobby? To have the company? Why did you hand it all over to Oliver, then?"

He looks down at the man beside him. "We made a deal, Dad and I. He would keep it all quiet if I waited until he thought the time was right for me to take over. Oliver was only ever supposed to be there until Dad stepped down," he says. "And that hasn't happened yet. I thought it best to do my own thing until full control passed to me. But by God did they want me back in the fold, where they could keep an eye on me. I'm not the only one in this family with secrets, but I'm sure you know that."

Robert stirs once more in the seat beside him, his eyes flickering hazily open, disoriented.

"Why did you kill them, Ed?" I ask, desperate to buy more time for Robert to come around.

He studies me for a second before speaking. "Why did you kill him?"

I'm momentarily back-footed by a question no one has ever asked. I think about obfuscating, but there is little point, and part of me desperately longs for the release of unfettered honesty. "Because I wanted him to pay, to suffer, to understand what he did."

"And do you think he did?"

I consider the question for the first time in my life. "Yes, actually. Yes, I think he understood."

"So you got what you wanted?" he asks simply.

"In a way, but I have to live with that. That a momentary whim of mine cost an entire human life."

"His whim cost you two lives, though, didn't it?" he argues, and I see what he is doing.

"We aren't the same, Edward."

He tilts his head to one side. "No, we are not. You meant to kill your first; mine was a mistake."

The distinction smarts. "But the second wasn't, was it?"

"The second was necessary. Lucy was there the day he died; she heard everything. I had little choice."

"And Alison. She was your first real girlfriend, wasn't she? Did you have no choice then?"

He flinches at my words. "Yes, I had no choice. I thought I loved her, that she loved me. I tried to tell her everything, about Bobby, about Lucy; I tried to be honest. She ran from me. I don't know what I expected; she was young and good and it was naïve to think she'd forgive anything, but I had to try. You know that impulse, I'm sure, even if you've never followed through. I thought it would be safe to share my secrets, but it was not. I had no idea what she might do, who she might tell. And then Gianna. I pulled her close in the hope I might be able to uncover how much she knew or suspected. But she had a strange way about her. I could never be sure what Alison had told her; how much she knew. Is this what you want to hear?" he asks suddenly. "The why of everything?"

There's a pragmatism to the question that I suddenly realize means he is still hoping for the other shoe to drop with me. There's still a part of him certain that if he is honest enough, open enough, I will somehow understand and I will be able to continue loving him. But what if I don't?

"Are you going to kill me, Edward?" I ask.

He studies me silently. "I know what's been going on between you two," he says gently, looking to the slumped Robert in the chair beside him.

He knows about the tape. He must have heard Robert's voice that night I found him with it in his hands. He must have known what it was as soon as he heard that list of names. He knows I've lied to him for weeks.

"You heard him on the tape?"

Edward nods. "I expected it from him. But not from you. He tried to avoid me, to manipulate the situation. To gain your trust."

In my mind, I desperately rewind the events of the past few

days. I recall Edward getting a phone call and leaving me with Eleanor to see the new wing, then, moments later, Robert arguing and smashing something in his office. He was on the phone with Edward. It is possible Edward confronted him in that call, which resulted in dinner being canceled.

"I brought you here to force the point," he continues. "I hoped you might listen to the tape and tell me who you were of your own free will. I hoped maybe it could be good for us. Has it been good for us?"

In the chair beside Edward, Robert straightens slightly as he takes me in, a muted smile blooming on his face. "Harriet," he croaks, his voice hoarse. "You made it, just in time." He shifts in the seat with difficulty, nursing a wound on his side. "Did you find your final clue?" he asks hazily.

Edward watches intently for my reaction, clearly as invested in the answer as Robert. I try to recall what my final clue was—the game now a distant memory. Then I remember the well, the stench, the weight of Melissa's body in my arms.

"Harriet, I need you to tell me if this relationship is still what you want," Edward says with disarming simplicity.

Robert gives me a pointed look and I force my mind back to the final clue.

Your present is under what's around her neck.

My gift is under a star, I'm guessing a Christmas tree star. Though the house is full of them and unless my gift is another shotgun, I don't see what use it could possibly be to me now.

I nod to Robert. I understand the clue. His eyes flick behind me and suddenly I recall what lies there, in the corner of this very room.

A Christmas tree!

"What happens tonight if I say yes? If I say I still want this?" I ask Edward, with care.

He pauses before responding. "If you say yes, what happens here tonight is an accident. We walk away, we survive, everything becomes ours. Together, like Mitzi and Alfred."

I do not want what he is offering. I do not want that life. I do not want to be that person. It must only be a micro-reaction I give, but it is enough. He sees it, and I cannot pull it back. I watch the disappointment crest inside him as his last hope fades and a cold calm settles over him.

"Okay," he says after a moment. "I need you to sit in that chair, Harry." He tips the barrel of his gun toward the armchair opposite Robert's. "Can you do that for me?"

Robert is silent beside him but everything about this situation tells me not to do as Edward says. I think of the star, and it takes every ounce of willpower I have left not to spin around and look straight up at the star sparkling on top of the Holbeck tree behind me.

"I don't want to sit in the chair, Ed," I say, shifting the weight of my shovel. I know a shovel is useless against a shotgun, of course, but there is only one of Edward and two of us, and Edward can't point the gun at both of us. If Robert and I both move, one of us might survive.

"Just sit in the chair, Harry," Edward barks.

My present is right behind me under the tree. That's what Robert is telling me, and from the look on his face, it seems like it might really help our current situation.

I desperately play for time.

"Why kill Aliza? She wasn't even close to you. Or Melissa?" I ask, scrambling for a break in his concentration, or a sign from Robert.

"Aliza asked too many questions, about the past, about our family. Matilda is too trusting and Aliza got a little too close to the truth. But she had secrets as bad as yours. Worse, perhaps. I warned her, but she was dangerous, so—"

"I found Melissa, by the way," I say, for Robert's benefit. I want him to know I have worked out where my gift is and I am ready to get it.

Edward shrugs. "An assistant working above her pay grade," he says without further explanation. He lifts the gun directly at me. "Sit. Down."

Robert gives an almost imperceptible nod and I make a show of slowly lowering my weapon to the floor for Edward.

I place my shovel down gently on the edge of the rug. "I'll sit in the chair if you put the gun down."

Edward gives a surprised smile. "I'm not going to do that," he says.

Hands still gripping the shovel, I catch a glimpse of something in my periphery beneath the tree. It pops out, bright yellow against the reds of other wrapped presents, completely out of place. A palm-sized canister of Ronsonol lighter fluid decorated with a massive red bow.

That's my gift: a very dark joke. I look back at Robert in disbelief and he gives a barely perceptible lift of the brows.

I guess I know what the gift was meant to symbolize: a release from the past; evidence removed, lost, my slate wiped clean. But that is no help now. And then what Robert is trying to tell me clicks into place. I catch sight of the fire still raging in the hearth behind Edward and I understand Robert's thinking. I need that can.

I gently let go of my shovel and raise my hands to Edward in surrender, my eyes trained on him as I rise to stand. As far as Edward is concerned, I am unarmed; I am doing as he asked.

"Thank you, Harriet," Edward says, his tone gentle as he gestures for me to make my way to the chair.

In my peripheral vision Robert raises a finger a few inches above the armrest of his chair and my eyes flick to him, then back to Edward. Robert raises two more fingers above the armrest. A countdown.

"You're going to burn it all down?" I ask Edward. "You've already killed Fiona and Oliver. You're going to kill everyone else and frame me?" I add, keeping Edward distracted as I prepare to make my move.

"The facts will tell a story of their own," Edward answers wearily.

The first of Robert's three raised fingers taps down.

Three.

"And you? You'll be alone. No family, no wife, no daughter. Can you live with that? All the money in the world but no one to talk to."

"The human element in any enterprise will always be its sticking point. It's always best to keep things simple," Edward says, his tone resigned.

The second of Robert's fingers taps down.

Two.

"I think we've all done enough talking, Harry," Edward continues.

The last of Robert's raised fingers hits the fabric of the armrest and everything happens at once.

One.

Robert suddenly makes a grab for Edward's shotgun barrel, yanking it down and away toward the ground, giving me an opening. I spin and dive for the bright yellow of the can beneath the tree. My hands grasp it just as a shot reverberates behind me and my gaze snaps back to the pair just in time to see Edward wrest back control of the weapon and whip the rifle butt into his father's face. Robert crumples down to the floor, blood oozing from his thigh. Edward spins, pointing the gun back at me.

He holds me in his sights for a second and then we both seem to realize the same thing at once. Edward's gun is a single-barrel shotgun; he needs to reload.

We both move at exactly the same time. He cracks open the gun, plunging a hand into his pocket for a cartridge, as I snap and twist the cap from the lighter fuel and run straight for him.

With terrifying efficiency, he slips a fresh cartridge into the weapon and snaps it shut before raising the weapon. But I am on him; I plow straight into him at full tilt, knocking him back as hard as I can. He bowls backward, losing his footing, having to grab the mantelpiece to stop himself from falling into the fire, the gun flailing now in his one free hand. And that is when I do it.

I squeeze the lighter fuel canister as hard as I can and a tight pressurized stream dances across Edward's clothes and face as he struggles to regain his balance. The acrid smell of butane fills the air and without stopping to think, I let the canister's stream hit the roaring fire behind Edward's back.

The flames flare white and engulf him, the gun clattering to the floor as his hands desperately fly to his face.

I do not stop to think. I advance on him even though I see his pain, his newfound terror. I see his openmouthed screams but I can barely hear them over the throb of blood in my own ears, the pounding of my heart, because I know I cannot stop until this is over. *He* will not stop until this is over.

I empty more and more of the fuel canister onto him as he lunges and swings madly toward me. The pain must become too much because suddenly he throws himself down to the rug to tamp out his flames. But he does not think it through; the gasoline-soaked rug beneath him leaps to life, flashing even brighter as fresh flames engulf him and creep out toward the rest of the room.

I look to Robert's prone form. We don't have much time before this fire is completely out of control. Robert and I need to leave.

I know what I need to do. I circle around Edward and pick up the discarded shotgun, its handle hot from the flame-engulfed floor, and raise it toward Edward's shuddering figure.

I get him in my sights, flames from the rug now lapping at my own bare legs, sending white-hot pain through me as I try to steady the weapon. I exhale calmly and pull the trigger. There is a rip of sound and Edward stops moving before the flames swallow him whole.

I drop the weapon and run to Robert's side, tearing an antique wall hanging from the wall above him to muffle out the flames approaching him. I thrash them out and pull him, coughing, up to sitting.

"We need to get out," I tell him. "Keep pressure on the leg wound." He nods, and with my help stumbles up to his feet.

"The other children? Eleanor?" he croaks.

"They're safe," I tell him. It's a half-truth. Eleanor is safe. Matilda is safe. Stuart I'm not so sure about, and Oliver and Fiona are dead.

We stumble from the sitting room into the hall where I steer Robert clear of the sight of Oliver's body and out the open front door.

We burst out into the snow and take in lungfuls of clean winter air. Robert is safe, but Stuart is still inside the building, and I am not like Edward. I cannot be responsible for any more death.

"Can you make it out to the woods?" I ask Robert as we stumble clear of the house. "Eleanor and Matilda are in the hide at the edge of the forest."

"Yes," he tells me, then grasps my wrist protectively. "Wait. Where are you going?"

"Stuart is still inside."

Robert shakes his head, grasping my wrist harder. "No. Don't go back in, Harriet. Think about your child."

I remember the life inside me, half Edward, half me, and I hesitate. Then I carefully remove his grip from my arm. "I am thinking of her," I say delicately. "She needs me to be a person who goes back in. *I* need me to be a person who goes back in."

The heat is hard to bear when I reenter the building, and the snow-drenched strip of fabric I thought might protect my lungs does not stop the hot burn in my throat. I dash back through the heat of the flaming hallway, my eyes stinging.

When I reach the new wing, Stuart is no longer behind the glass. He must have made it out another way.

I turn to leave again, but with a sudden jolt remember Sylvia and Anya propped up beside each other in their break room. I turn and sprint toward the staff quarters, through smoke-clogged corridors that lead back to the gas-filled kitchen.

I know nothing I can do will change the past; nothing can change what I did, or who I am in consequence. But the past can stop here. I can change. I can be better. A fresh start, a new me— a more honest me.

After all, isn't that what I want for my child? For my daughter? We all make mistakes and live with them, but we can make a virtue of that fact. We can turn one bad day into a hundred good ones. One bad choice into a lifetime of good choices.

Ahead of me I hear the sound of flames hitting gas and exploding as the force blows the kitchen door clean off its hinges, the backdraft knocking me off my feet. My hands fly to my buzzing ears as I choke on the cloud of smoke.

I stumble up to my feet and dart forward into the kitchen, dodging the flames lapping cabinets and bursting along the fabric of the half-rolled blinds.

I bolt into the white corridor beyond and then I see her. Anya freezes mid-step, the weight of a barely conscious Sylvia leaning against her, her expression terrified as she tries to work out if I am here to help or hurt.

But there is no time to explain. Wordlessly I slip an arm under Sylvia's other shoulder and take half her weight.

The three of us burst out into the frozen white of the garden and spill onto the snow gasping in clean air.

After a moment, Anya catches her breath and speaks. "The phone lines don't work. We need to call the fire department, the police. Do you have a phone? We aren't allowed our own phones in the house."

Of course they aren't.

"Matilda has my phone," I answer honestly.

Anya suddenly seems to remember the rest of the Holbeck family. "Oh God, where are they? I completely—" Her hand flies to her mouth. "Are they okay? I didn't think— There was only time to save Sylvia," she gabbles, emotion taking hold of her.

"Everyone else is okay," I lie. "Everyone is gathered down by the forest, away from the fire. We can walk down to meet them— call for help there."

Anya looks between me and her barely conscious friend and seems to come to the conclusion that I am, at least, the devil she knows.

"Okay," she says, "let's go."

49

Iris

MONDAY, JULY 10

Iris. Apple of my eye.

You stir in the clear bassinet beside my hospital bed as I shift into a more comfortable position.

Beyond the windows of Mount Sinai, the sky is blue. You are a summer baby; you arrived a little later than everyone expected, but you survived that night in the snow seven months ago. We both did.

We stood in the cold, the remaining Holbecks and I, and we watched The Hydes burn to the ground. The new wing would be all that would remain. A wing rising from the ashes. They say the rebuild will be completed by next spring, to Eleanor's minimalist specifications.

In the hospital corridors beyond my private room the ward buzzes with life, but you sleep on peacefully after the storm of hours before. I watch your tiny chest rise and fall—the life inside me now outside.

The last Christmas I spent with your father will always be burned into my memories and into my skin: the flesh of my hands, my calves, warped forever; my lungs scarred. I'll never run a marathon, but I was strong enough to keep us both alive.

They cut you from my abdomen in the early hours of this morning. Not because there was a problem, but because there wasn't. You just didn't want to leave; you were happy, *too* content nestled safe inside me.

But the world was waiting to see you. So they shucked me open, like an oyster, and popped you out, my pearl. My little Iris.

Granddad Robert paid for this room. He paid for everything, and he always will. He chose Mummy, you see, for a very important task: he saw something in me, a strength or a usefulness—whichever you prefer. Granddad knew one day we would do something amazing, you and I, that we would save him, that we would save the whole family. You won't hear it from me, but you will from them. You see, Mummy won a game—an old Christmas game. But we don't play that game anymore.

That last year we played, everyone got their presents—Mummy insisted. Auntie Fiona got a trust for her boys; Uncle Oliver got a company stake for them; Uncle Stuart got to take over Oliver's position in the company; and Mummy got a new family. And lest we forget, Granny and Granddad got you.

They found a gas leak at The Hydes; it could have killed us all. And while the insurance company would not pay out, the lawyers and investigators found enough evidence to close the case. An unforeseeable accident. Of course, we wish there was someone to blame for the deaths of three dearly loved people, but life takes as often as it gives. The temperatures reached in the main building meant only DNA could be recovered. Uncle Oliver, Auntie Fiona, and your father, all lost.

Sam, Tristan, and Billy became orphans that night, like Mummy. But you still have me.

I will not tell you how they moved their parents, how the scene was set, how the men that came in the early hours made everything go away. Your grandfather set wheels in motion. Money, power, leverage make the world go around. Sometimes knowing the *right people* for the job means knowing the *wrong people*.

But my hope is you never have to find that out.

Though, know this, if you ever need me to, my love, I will move the world for you. But no more than once. I have seen how chasing one mistake with another can become a habit.

They stayed up late, you see, after the rest of us went to bed. They must have fallen asleep in front of the fire, the rug caught and wooden doors warped with the heat. The smoke would have gotten them while they slept, and the fire did the rest. If it hadn't been for you, keeping me awake at night, I might not have noticed the heat, the smoke. I might not have been able to save those that I did.

I want you to know, Iris, my love, that Mummy tried to save Daddy. I mean that in the truest and the realest sense, but it was too late. And though he is no longer here, the man I met that one magical night, the man I fell in love with—he will live on in you. You are the best of him and he would have loved you so much. And while Daddy might be gone, you will have so many people who love you.

And when you are older, I will tell you the story of the family I lost, and the family I gained. The favor Granddad asked of me and the price he paid for it. The son he lost and the daughter he gained. My story might not be a perfect rendition of the facts, but sometimes it's easier to understand the truth of our lives through stories. Sometimes stories cut to the heart of things straighter, truer.

I know a mystery surrounds us, but the global interest in us, in my latest book, will be long gone by the time you are old enough to understand. They say the book is too close to life for comfort. That to write a thriller based on a real-life tragedy is distasteful in the extreme, but we all cope with what life throws at us in different ways. And people love a mystery.

Better fictional horror than the real sort, as your granddad would say.

Years from now you will inherit it all. The Holbeck fortune, the empire, the history, because you are the firstborn's first child. You take your father's mantle. Granddad and Uncle Stuart will hold down the fort until you are ready—if you want to be ready.

The family name is a heavy crown to bear if you overthink it. But I promise you, things will be different for you, my love. I will be here for you every step of the way—if you need me to be. You can choose the life you want to live, because you are not a Holbeck, not really. You're a Reed, and us Reeds—we have no history to live up to at all.

We only have our future.

Acknowledgments

Thank you to my wonderful editors: Kara Cesare at Penguin Random House in the United States and Bethan Jones at Simon & Schuster in the United Kingdom, who both added so many layers to this story with their invaluable thoughts, questions, and nudges. Huge thanks for making the editing process on this, and on every book, so creatively engaging and fun! I'm incredibly lucky to have you.

Massive thanks to the rest of the team at Penguin Random House and everyone who helped to get this book safely into your hands: Jesse Shuman, Allyson Lord, Allison Schuster, Yewon Son, Jennifer Hershey, Kim Hovey, Kara Welsh, Kelly Chian, Carlos Beltrán, Elizabeth A. D. Eno, and many more. Thank you for your hard work, enthusiasm, and creativity.

Special thanks go, as always, to my brilliant agent, Camilla Bolton at Darley Anderson, the best advocate an author could hope for—thank you for your continued support, dynamism, and knowledge of the industry.

Thank you, also, to the booksellers, reviewers, podcasters, and libraries for getting my books out there onto shelves and into people's hands.

And, of course, unending thanks to my husband, Ross, and my two daughters for everything else under the sun.

About the Author

CATHERINE STEADMAN is an actress and author based in London. She has appeared in leading roles on British and American television as well as onstage in the West End, where she has been nominated for a Laurence Olivier Award. She grew up in the New Forest, Hampshire, and now lives in North London with her husband and daughters. Catherine's first novel, *Something in the Water*, was a *New York Times* bestseller with rights sold in over thirty territories. She is the author of *Mr. Nobody* and *The Disappearing Act*.

Twitter: CatSteadman
Instagram: @catsteadman

About the Type

This book was set in Sabon, a typeface designed by the well-known German typographer Jan Tschichold (1902–74). Sabon's design is based upon the original letter forms of sixteenth-century French type designer Claude Garamond and was created specifically to be used for three sources: foundry type for hand composition, Linotype, and Monotype. Tschichold named his typeface for the famous Frankfurt typefounder Jacques Sabon (c. 1520–80).